Novels by Lee Swanson

The Calling of Alex Tate
No Man's Chattel (**No Man is Her Master** Book 1)
Her Perilous Game (**No Man is Her Master** Book 2)
Her Dangerous Journey Home (**No Man is Her Master** Book 3)

Coming Soon
She Serves the Realm (**No Man is Her Master** Book 4)

I0670331

Her

Perilous

Game

LEE SWANSON

Her Perilous Game
Book 2 in the No Man is Her Master series
Merchant's Largesse Books

copyright 2020 by Lee Swanson

Cover design by Tamian Wood,
www.Beyond Design Books.com

Second Edition
ISBN-13: 978-1-736-2436-0-2 (paperback edition)
ISBN-10: 1-736-2436-0-8

Books>Historical Fiction>Medieval

For Joan McCammon,
with appreciation for our conversations on matters historical

Canonical Hours

Throughout *Her Perilous Game*, the canonical hours established by the medieval Christian Church are used to tell time. Time variations are affected by seasonal differences in the rising and setting of the sun.

Matins:	Between 2:00 and 3:00 in the morning
Lauds:	Between 5:00 and 6:00 in the morning
Prime:	Around 7:00 AM or just prior to daybreak
Terce:	Around 9:00 in the morning
Sext	Noon or when the sun is at its zenith
Nones:	Between 2:00 and 3:00 in the afternoon
Vespers:	Between 4:00 and 6:00 in the afternoon
Compline:	Between 7:00 and 9:00 in the evening

Chapter 1

A Stormy Crossing
The English Channel, January, 1310

The flimsy pinewood door to her small cabin burst open and Christina half slid, half fell inside. Gallons of frigid sea water accompanied her as well as pelting sheets of driving rain and the maniacally shrieking wind. Just as she managed to get to her knees, *der Greif* lurched forward in the heavily rolling seas and she was thrown back toward the yawning entryway. The very real possibility of being puked back out onto the deck and over the side of the cog ship loomed in her mind as she scrambled frantically to force the door shut before it happened. As she tumbled backward, she thrust out her right leg and just managed to hook the edge of the door with her foot. A wave of acute pain coursed through her head as it thumped soundly against the now blocked portal an instant before the remainder of her body followed. She was bruised, bloody, and battered but, for the time being, she was safe.

The tiny room was enveloped in inky darkness.

I can't risk lighting a lanthorn, even if I could somehow strike a spark, she cautioned herself. *Besides, you know where everything is in this cabin, just think, Christina, damn you!*

Despite her wooziness, she forced herself to concentrate. She shuffled through the inch or so of cold seawater covering the floor, away from the door and to her left. Extending her hand, Christina found the leg of the small table that was firmly affixed to the decking. Using this to orientate herself, she blindly reached past, toward the bunk she knew would only be two feet beyond.

There she found it.

The heavy oaken bucket had not moved, despite the wild cavorting of the ship, lodged as it was between the two pieces of furniture. This was obviously an intentional resting place for it as, even in moderately rough seas, a spill would be inevitable if it were allowed to slide about the cabin floor.

Her stomach suddenly lurched and she felt as though she would have to use her makeshift chamber pot for a different purpose than the one she had originally intended.

Did I empty it this morning?

She tried hard to remember what the contents might be before she committed to putting the pail to use.

Whether it was the blow to her temple, the ship's violent motions, the odor that confirmed she had indeed neglected to attend to that particular chore, or combinations thereof; she felt her stomach's contents rush up her gullet. Ignoring the smell, she thrust her head inside, opened her mouth wide, and let the sour flow spew inside the bucket.

After a few minutes, the contractions of her guts subsided.

Damn my weak stomach.

She wiped her fouled mouth with the sleeve of her tunic.

Holding the side of the table for support, she rose shakily to her feet.

Now, finally.

Christina lifted her tunic and gathered it about her waist, holding it firmly in place with her elbows against her body. Next, she undid the cord securing her braies and, with an audible sigh of relief, slid them and her hose down around her ankles. She sat down on her chamber pot and voided her bladder forcefully.

Why did God play such a cruel joke on womankind? While a man pisses standing up; a woman squats on her haunches like a dog. How unfair it is!

Turning the image over in her mind, she guessed it had something to do with the Church's belief in man's role as the protector of his weaker counterpart.

What bullshit!

Christina snorted derisively.

She arose and, after securing her clothing back in place, turned and placed the steaming pail back within its customary resting place. Putting the ill-fitting wooden lid back atop her slops, she made herself a promise to be sure to throw the obscene contents over the side of the ship as soon as the storm subsided.

Having completed her essential task, she turned toward the door, then hesitated. She worried her bottom lip betwixt her small, white teeth until she tasted the metallic saltiness of her blood. Christina's brow furrowed as she sought to identify what was causing her muscles to balk. Then she realized: it was fear.

Christina had complete faith in the experience and skill of Matthias, the ship's master. Similarly, she recognized the crew were stalwart lads all, who knew their tasks well and would perform them courageously. *Der Greif* was a sound ship, well designed and in excellent repair.

So, why am I so terrified?

The answer was obvious. The ship tilted backwards as if it were a spirited stallion, rearing upwards to rid itself of the puny humans who sought to control it. Then, it dropped violently, threatening to break its own back in its vicious death throes. Even though the cog's prow was quite tall, as with all such vessels, the heavy waves were crashing over it as if they were a giant fist intent on pounding the ship under the frothing surface of the frigid water of the English Channel.

She cowered in the cabin, irrational thoughts racing through her mind.

I am only a woman; I would be useless among the men working on deck. Surely, they would want me to stay below out of their way; doubly so if they knew the truth about me.

The idea of using her true sex as an excuse for her cowardice suddenly filled her with self-loathing.

Bullshit! My place is on the deck, doing everything I can to save my ship, my crew, and my cargo. You've chosen your path in life, Christina, you can't just fucking give up when it gets difficult!

Resolutely, she forced one foot in front of the other and made her way toward the door of the cabin. Timing the rhythm of the ship's movements as best she could, she turned the latch and the door swept open of its own volition.

She stepped out into a hellish scene. Immense, rolling waves surrounded *der Greif* in all directions. The deck was awash with foam blown from the whitecaps, making the footing even more treacherous. She fought her way over to a massive shape hauling mightily on a thick rope that extended upwards until it disappeared almost magically into the darkened skies.

"Do you need some help, Wig?" she yelled as loudly as she could to make her voice heard over the shrieking wind.

Reiniken turned his head back at her in surprise. His mouth split into a gap-toothed grin despite the rain pelting his broad face.

God's great cock, Yur Worship, what the holy fuck are ya doin' out in this miserable shit? Yur skinny ass'll get blown off the side if yur not careful!"

"I want to help!" she repeated, somewhat startled to see his nostrils and mouth were encrusted with white rings of salt.

Reiniken nodded. He was a man who gave respect sparingly, and then only when it was well earned.

"Yur a tough little bastard, ya are! Go help Matthias keep this feckin' barge runnin' with the wind. Keepin' the tiller steady in this weather must be like wrestlin' a Spanish whore!"

She returned the man's grin and headed back toward the ship's stern. She had initially been shocked by Reiniken's vulgarity to the point of anger. Now, she realized he meant no offense by his coarse speech.

Even more importantly, he is hard-working, brave, and as strong as any two other men; that's good enough for me!

As she approached the ship's tiller, she realized Matthias was indeed having trouble maintaining the ship's heading toward the east. *Der Greif's* master was on one knee, his left leg thrust out behind him, wedged against the capstan used to hoist both the sails and cargo into the hold. Beside him lay a length of cordage, the parted end of which had once clearly been tied about the tiller post. The fury of the sea had snapped it like a thread. Now, should the ship unexpectedly roll to starboard, the tiller would pivot in the opposite direction, dragging Matthias after it. This would surely turn the ship broadside into the wind. A capsize would be inevitable, with the deaths of the crewmembers just as certain as that of their unfortunate vessel.

Christina ran to assist the struggling helmsman, all caution now disregarded. She threw her weight against the sturdy steering plank opposite Matthias, stabilizing it while he regained his feet. Although consuming every iota of their combined strength, together they held it true. Around them, crewmen scampered about, each intent on performing his singular task which, if left untended, might doom them all. They labored on with no sense of the passing hours, time measured only by the need to respond to the next looming crisis. At last, the storm's fury noticeably began to diminish. The crew began to exchange wild looks, amazed they had somehow weathered the storm intact.

Christina realized she was drenched to the bone, a creature that would seemingly be more at home in the water than on land. Her entire body ached, accentuated by various areas where a sharper pain was felt. She was nearly frozen and felt as if it had been days since she had eaten or taken a drink. She relinquished the tiller to Matthias' firm hand and looked into his slate gray eyes. He said nothing, as no words needed to be spoken. He only nodded but, with that slight gesture, communicated his appreciation for the crucial role she had played in saving the ship. A lump began to form in her throat and she turned away quickly before the tears she knew were sure to follow betrayed her acute need for emotional release.

She ran swiftly to her cabin and slammed the door shut behind her. Ragged sobs wracked her body as she leaned against the table to keep from collapsing in a heap on the floor. Random memories leapt within her mind, like the lightning bolts of the storm that had just passed. The image of her deceased father was followed by that of her brother, Frederick, smiling just as he had when last she had seen him, hours before the pirates had claimed his life as well.

But, no one even mourns you, do they Brother? Except for me, the only one who knows the truth. Everyone else believes it was me, Christina, who died in the attack, and Frederick is alive and well. Only that is a lie, one I myself have perpetuated. Christina lives now as Frederick, I as you. God forgive me!

She swiped angrily at her eyes with the sopping sleeve of her woolen tunic, hanging like a shapeless rag from her shoulders.

Regret won't bring them back and, even if I had not assumed Frederick's identity, he would still be just as dead. Pull yourself together, Christina, and get out on deck. You have work to do!

She walked from the cabin out into blinding sunlight. It seemed as if, as the skies had lightened, so too had the mood of the ship's crew. They gathered in small knots of three or four men, laughing and talking excitedly. Suddenly, she felt a solid whack across her back that almost knocked her to her knees. This was accompanied by a loud laugh that immediately stifled the anger quickly rising within her.

". . . and I hears, 'Do yas need some help? Sos I'm thinkin it's a fairy or maybe a big-titted mermaid's got washed up on the deck. Then, I look down and who do I spy? His Worship there, that's who, and I think, 'damn, I thought he'd gone over the side!' I'd already figured how many whores his share of the cargo was gonna buy me and, I tell ya boys, it was gonna keep me busy for a month! But there he stood, harder to get rid of than a fuckin' tick, that one is!" Reiniken farted wetly for emphasis.

Christina joined in the general laughter and said, "You're not getting rid of me that easily, Wig. Now, you'll just have to woo your whores with your good looks and gentlemanly charm."

As the men hooted, she clapped Reiniken on his back, although she was uncertain whether he even felt it.

She left the gaggle of sailors and continued moving forward, attempting to gauge what damage the ship had incurred in the storm. To her untrained eye, it appeared *der Greif* had weathered the tempest well. The sail miraculously appeared intact and, although some of the deck fixtures had been broken or displaced by the weight of the crashing waves, the harm to the ship appeared minor.

That really means little. What really matters is how the ship has fared below the water.

She hurried to find the ship's master, who she located on the forecastle of *der Greif*, his head and shoulders lowered over the side while one of the sailors held his legs firmly to keep him from falling into the water.

As she went up the steps, she saw Matthias' head appear. He righted himself and, gaining his feet, dismissing the crewman with a few terse words. Christina stepped aside to let him pass. She noticed the sailor was very tight-lipped as he walked toward her, with no sign of the levity shown by his mates further aft. With a growing sense of dread, she approached Matthias.

"Is there a problem?" she saw no need to preface her question with pleasantries.

"Aye," he responded with even a greater economy of words.

Christina stared at him expectantly; her gaze demanding he elaborate.

"Well," he began, rubbing his jaw in a gesture she had come to associate with the man's habitual reluctance to share negative information.

"Get on with it, man, for the love of Christ!" she demanded, patience never having been one of her virtues.

"The storm has badly cracked the stem post," he said simply. "It's holding together for the time being but, if it should break, the lapstrakes will separate and water will come rushing into the ship every time the prow dips below the water. We will do our best to strengthen it temporarily, of course, but we will need to shorten the sail considerably to avoid putting undue stress on our repairs. There's no permanent fix possible until we make port."

Christina nodded, understanding fully how closely they had come to complete disaster. If the stern post had broken during the storm, the ship would have foundered within minutes. She voiced a silent prayer of thanks to God for not allowing that to happen.

"I'm afraid that is not the worst of the telling," he began again.

Christina looked at him, this time saying nothing.

"We have also lost two of our crew during the storm, Dietmar and Ernestus."

Involuntarily, her head turned to look out over the port beam, knowing the chance that either of them had survived the night's ordeal was nil. She searched her brain, seeking to place the men.

Ah yes, Dietmar was a bit older than most of the crew and not very tall, but he made up in breath for what he lacked in height.

She couldn't recall whether they had ever spoken, but did remember he seemed to have a quiet assurance about him and was well respected by the other members of the ship's complement. He would certainly be missed.

On the other hand, she had no recollection of the other sailor. This bothered her greatly, as she felt she should at least be able to picture the man who had given his life in her service and, now, floated alone and unloved somewhere in the sea's mighty depths.

She made the sign of the cross and murmured, "I'm very sorry," for she knew that, unlike herself, Matthias had ensured he knew each man well and felt their loss sorely.

"Aye, they were both good lads," he responded, "but God takes each man in his turn."

He turned away; Christina did not know whether it was to set about his next task or to conceal a hint of emotion that might reveal itself on his ancient, rugged face. She had one more query, however, which she feared to ask but knew she must.

"Have you been below?" she questioned the ship's master in a soft voice.

Matthias looked at her quizzically, as if to wonder why she would ask such an absurd question.

"Yes, of course. Do you think I would be standing here gabbing with you if I had not? Could I have gauged *der Greif's* seaworthiness by checking what is above the water while ignoring what is below?"

His look of puzzlement disappeared as the reason for her enquiry finally dawned on him.

"I'm sorry, Master Frederick," Matthias said, "I was only thinking in terms of the ship and not her cargo. We have taken on a bit of water, of course. No ship is completely watertight, especially in a storm such as we have just endured. Overall, I think the damage to your cargo will be small."

Christina thought about the nearly five hundred large sacks of wool that were stacked in the ship's hold as a look of relief spread across her face. She was aware even a small amount of salt water could cause harm, diminishing the wool's value or even rendering it completely unsaleable. Even though she respected Matthias' opinion, she knew she must inspect the cargo herself to gauge the true extent of the storm's damage.

Before she left, she asked, "Do you know how long it will be until we are in Bruges?"

"It's hard to say," Matthias replied. "Before the storm, I would have said a day. Now, who knows? My best guess would be we were blown several leagues to the north. We will not truly know how far until we sight land, and only then if we can spy a familiar landmark. When that happens, we will follow the coastline southward. If we eventually make landfall and hear the people speaking Castillian, you'll know I made a mistake." Matthias smiled again, more broadly this time.

Christina fixed the man with a stern look and replied, "I certainly hope not. Trying to sell wool to the Spaniards would be like trying to sell squirrel pelts in Novgorod!"

The man's look of surprise at her grave words was more than Christina could endure. She burst out into sudden laughter which, unexpectedly, was joined into by the ship's master. Realizing they both had tasks to which they must attend, she left Matthias to his own work and walked to the hatch leading into the ship's cavernous hold.

She undid the latches that dogged the cover. She felt a sharp pain along her ribs as she pushed the cover open.

Why didn't I take the time to put on dry clothing when I had a chance?

She realized the long length of cloth she wrapped about her chest to conceal the swell of her breasts was just as wet as her outer garments and was now chafing irritatingly against her skin with every movement.

It will have to wait; I need to find out to what extent the cargo has been harmed. After all, wool is quite unlike other goods.

When the crew of *der Greif* had finished loading the woolsacks into the ship's hold ten days prior, the woolmonger Paul Butiler had casually asked whether she had ever transported wool aboard a ship before. Since Christina had never previously been responsible for any cargoes, she had asked Butiler to wait while she went to query Matthias. She had naively assumed a ship's master as experienced as he would know about all such things but, when she had asked, he had admitted he had never carried a cargo consisting entirely of fleeces. She returned to face the elderly merchant, somewhat chagrined she had staked much of her available capital on a cargo the transportation of which neither she nor her ship's master knew very much about.

Butiler's rheumy eyes crinkled with amusement. With his white beard and portly build, he bore a strong resemblance to her mother's father.

He raised his hand and slowly shook his finger in front of Christina's face, then he said in an admonishing tone, "That's what I was afraid of, Master Frederick. Will you accept a few words of advice from an old man?"

Christina nodded her head eagerly; she was always ready to learn new things.

"I have seen many merchants ruined who have undertaken the transport of wool, despite being very experienced with other cargoes. Much of their troubles arose from buying dirty or greasy wool at a bargain price, a problem you do not have as the quality of your purchase from me is uniformly good."

Again, she nodded, listening carefully.

"Problems may arise with even the finest of wool, however. Shipboard vermin and insects such as moths can cause considerable harm if they have access to the fleeces over a long period of time. The greatest danger, however, is posed by exposure to moisture, either from fresh or salt water. Did you notice the woolsacks were not tightly packed? Did you think this is because I am trying to cheat you?"

Christina's mouth began to form a reply assuring the merchant this was not the case.

Butiler again raised his hand, his gesture this time clearly an effort to still her response.

He then continued, "A certain amount of moisture is naturally absorbed from the air. In a damp environment such as a ship's hold, however, the wool may become turgid and increase in weight anywhere up to about eighteen percent. If it is packed too tightly, there will be no room for expansion in the sack. If this happens the damp wool will begin to heat, soon becoming warm to the touch. Within a day or two it will become yellow, in a few days more it will begin to blacken, rendering it worthless."

"I understand," Christina said, "If the wool gets wet, I need to dry it as soon as possible."

"Yes and no," he responded.

Christina's brow creased at his cryptic answer.

"It depends on whether the source of the moisture is sea water or fresh. Wool sacks contaminated by sea water must be opened and the contents scoured with fresh water. Unless this is done, it will not dry properly and the fiber will always be more prone to absorb moisture from the air. Regardless, the wool must ultimately be dried as soon as possible to minimize the damage."

Christina had thanked Butiler profusely for sharing his knowledge with her, information that would now prove invaluable if she discovered what she dreaded to find in the hold. She hoped she would not.

As she descended into the dark space, she stopped and sniffed the air speculatively, waiting for her eyes to adjust to the dim light. She was greatly reassured when she failed to discern the unmistakably cloying scent of mold. Instead, she was greeted with the same musty smell that had permeated the hold since soon after the loading of the woolsacks had been completed.

Christina stepped onto the rough decking and squinted downwards toward her feet. A small rivulet of water an inch or two deep flowed back and forth aligned with the motions of the ship making way.

Not too much though. At least not deep enough to do more than splash onto the raised planking upon which the cargo is stacked.

She said a prayer of gratitude for the ship's builder who had had the foresight to include this feature into the ship's design.

As she moved forward, she discovered her cargo had not escaped unscathed. She counted eight sacks with at least some evidence of water damage, another three badly so.

It could have been so much worse. Now, I need to discuss with Matthias how many men he can spare to drag the wet sacks from the hold, wash the contents, and then set them out to dry.

She hoped the good weather would hold long enough to complete these necessary tasks.

After talking to Matthias and agreeing on a course of action concerning the cargo, she went to her cabin and locked the door.

Not that anyone would intentionally intrude, but men accustomed to living together so intimately could very easily forget the meaning of a closed door and barge right inside. No way I can chance that.

She at last stripped off her wet clothing. Looking down, she was somewhat amused her feet and toes were white and wrinkly, as if they were parts of fish rather than a person. She became more sober, however, when she realized she had seen similar appendages previously, on a corpse that had been hauled from the sea after he had drowned.

Finally removing the cloth wrapped about her chest, her somber mood continued as she assessed the angry red welts that now encircled her body.

That's going to hurt like hell. I will need to ask Matthias for some grease to put on it. I really wish I had one of Mother's herbal salves to dress this properly.

She hung her sodden clothes on hooks strategically placed on the side wall of the small cabin and stood naked and shivering.

I would trade my entire cargo for a hot bath right now.

She imagined the sensual luxury of immersing herself in warm, scented water.

At least half of it anyway.

Christina smiled, admitting to herself her initial offer had left no room for further negotiations.

Well, I can't just stand here dreaming of the impossible until I turn into a block of ice, can I?

She considered crawling beneath the thick, heavy furs that covered the sleeping pallet and drifting off to sleep as her trapped body heat created a warm and cozy nest.

I am tired, she admitted to herself, having had no sleep the previous night as the ship fought the storm. *But so is everyone else. I can't expect the men to labor on while I laze away the day in here, can I?*

She opened the small trunk that held the few possessions Trudi had hurriedly gathered for her from their lodging at The Tabard in London. She couldn't help but smile at the thought of her trusted maid and companion.

How I miss you, my dear, sweet Trudi. If you were here, I know I couldn't resist getting into bed, cuddling next to your warm body would feel delicious.

Trudi had always been in her life, it seemed. First as childhood companions, sneaking cakes from the kitchen until they were shooed away by Trudi's mother, the Kohl family's housekeeper. Later, Christina had pulled Trudi away from her cleaning tasks so they could share secrets about the boys they fancied. They had both been overjoyed when they had manipulated Christina's mother into letting her accompany Christina on her voyage to London instead of Trudi's older sister, Anna. Her absence left Christina feeling sad.

Yes, and I even miss him now too.

The "him" she was referring to was Kurt Ziesolf. Although they often disagreed, Christina owed everything about her new life to the old knight. It was he who came up with the mad plan for her to impersonate her brother after the battle that claimed the lives of Frederick and her father. It was he who had trained her mercilessly, until she was now the match of any man with blade or fist. It was also he who had saved her life repeatedly.

I would love to have you both by my side right now, but there were important tasks that needed to be accomplished in London and I couldn't very well be in two places at once, could I?

Consequently, in Greenwich she had ordered both of her boon companions to return to the city, leaving her to voyage on to Bruges without them. Although their absence made her heartsick, she knew she had made the right decision.

The red tunic with the green embroidery is decidedly too fancy to be wearing at sea.

Christina examined the garment critically before putting it on; she had hoped to save it until she was in Bruges.

It would have been nice to have had a clean garment to wear in my negotiations with the mercers at the Cloth Hall instead of coming in stinking like the inside of a wet wool sack.

Having only a choice between wet and dry, she simply shrugged pragmatically and, raising her hands above her head, let the fine tunic slide down over her body. Clothed once more, she strode back out onto the main deck.

No more than three hours later, Christina was surprised to hear one of the sailors working on the forecastle excitedly shout, "Land! Off the starboard beam! Land!"

She turned her head in the direction the man had indicated but could discern nothing more than a slight haze seemingly hovering over the water in the distance, far ahead of the ship. Christina unconsciously shifted her weight as she felt the ship ponderously heel to starboard. From his position at the ship's tiller, Matthias called three men by their names and barked terse instructions to adjust the massive square sail now flapping noisily overhead, no longer filled by the wind. The men obeyed instantly and soon *der Greif* was moving forward cautiously on a leeward tack.

Christina walked swiftly towards the ship's master.

"Is it land? Where are we?" she asked as soon as she was within earshot of the man.

"Yes. Look now."

She turned to gaze over the port side of the ship. Straining her eyes, she could just make out the gentle swell of a bank of low sand dunes in the distance. Tiny shapes of seabirds hovered above the shoreline; they seemed so far away she didn't know whether the faint cries she heard were real or imagined.

"How long until we reach Bruges?" she queried Matthias anew.

"I'm not really sure," he admitted to her, then shouted to another man to go forward with a lead and line to sound the depth of the water. "As you can see, there are no landmarks and one sand dune appears very similar to the one next to it."

She knew it was pointless to ask him any other questions, as he had answered her truthfully. About her, it seemed the men working on the deck had noticeably quickened their pace, motivated by the promise of impending landfall.

Before long, the sailor at the bow yelled, "A quarter less seven!"

Observing the confusion on her face, Matthias explained, "That's about forty feet of water below us, Master Frederick. Seven fathoms at six feet each, minus a quarter of one as well. Laden as we are, we're drawing about thirteen feet, giving us a safe margin of about twenty-seven feet before we drag bottom. Of course, you can be certain we're not going to get near enough to shore to chance that."

Christina nodded, categorizing this information in her mind as very useful for the future.

Soon, Matthias set the ship on a starboard tack and it slowed perceptively as it began to sail closer to the wind. This pattern of course changes continued throughout the afternoon until, just as the skies began to darken in impending nightfall, he ordered the sail to be raised and the anchors to be dropped. Although she fully understood the sailing master's caution, Christina nonetheless was exasperated their arrival in Bruges was to be delayed once more.

Chapter 2

A Lesson, a Sale, and Promises Kept
Bruges, January, 1310

Christina awoke early the next morning feeling immensely refreshed after a sound night's sleep. She pushed back the furs which covered her bed and sat up. She immediately felt the cold that permeated the air in the cabin and went about her morning ablutions at a quickened pace. Once dressed, she grabbed a small loaf from the oiled sack that contained the foodstuffs Trudi had thoughtfully packed for her. She gnawed the now stale bread voraciously, following every few mouthfuls with a swig from a jug of watered ale.

God, I can hardly wait to eat real food again, she mused, daydreaming about the taste of mutton, goose, and a large spread of her favorite sweetmeats. *That will have to wait,* she chided, but promising herself her first meal in Bruges would be a memorable one. *First, a more loathsome task waits to be performed.*

Standing, she brushed the crumbs from the front of her clean tunic and exited the cabin, chamber pot in hand.

She climbed the steps to the stern castle and, holding her breath, removed the lid from the bucket. She heaved her slops over the ship's side. Then, tying a length of cord to one of the bucket's round eyes, she dropped it into the sea below. She allowed it to drift a few feet astern, then hauled it back on deck. Satisfied with the results of her efforts, she returned the bucket to its rightful place and went out onto the main deck.

Christina was pleased to note she was one of the first to rise. Usually, the entire crew were already about their tasks when she awoke. She knew she had not preceded Matthias, however. *Der Greif* had been underway since she had awakened and the ship's master would never allow the ship to sail in unfamiliar coastal waters unless under his direct supervision.

She smiled with happiness, realizing the value of the man. She looked back toward the tiller, expecting to see Matthias at his customary station. Instead, she was surprised to see the bulky figure of Gotz, one of the two sailors the sailing master entrusted with steering the ship. Scanning the deck, she located Matthias on the forecastle, leaning forward as if the ship were a horse to which he was applying the spurs to hasten it on.

Christina hurried forward with curiosity, moving to align herself beside the sailing master. Before she could, she was shocked to see a rise of miniscule buildings appear in the distance. She watched as they grew until they were clearly defined against the cloudless azure sky.

"What is this place?" she asked.

"That, Master Frederick, is our destination," Matthias answered with evident satisfaction.

"It seems rather small," Christina said, trying to keep the disappointment from her voice.

She had imagined Bruges to be a wonderous city, as huge and exciting as London. Instead, it appeared smaller even than her hometown of Lübeck.

"Oh, I'm sorry," Matthias remarked with a laugh. "I thought you knew. The town over there is Sluys, not Bruges. This is where we must anchor as the channel to Bruges is too silted to accommodate even a ship of *der Greif's* shallow draught. Once you have arranged a buyer for your wool, it will be transshipped on small, flat-bottomed skiffs into the city. Each of these should be capable of safely carrying about fifteen woolsacks, I figure, so it will take some time to shift the entire cargo. The same process will happen with the goods you purchase, only in reverse. A bit of extra bother and cost, of course, but the system works quite efficiently."

In less than two hours, *der Greif* was gently pulling alongside the quay in Sluys. Although the town was indeed small, the port area was extensive and abuzz with activity. Men scurried about their tasks like crabs on the ebb tide, unloading cargoes from some of the ships while moving a wide array of merchandise into others. As Christina jumped from the wooden walkway onto the stone flagstones, she was extremely impressed by such a scene of systematic efficiency.

As she gawked at the activity unfolding about her, Matthias approached one of the lightermen and, after a brief conversation and an exchange of coins, returned to Christina's side.

"He," Matthias gestured toward the boatman, "will transport you and half the men up the Oude Zwin to the city. I would advise finding lodging before you do anything else as the inns tend to fill up as the day progresses and more people arrive."

"But what about you?" she queried.

"I must attend to the repair of *der Greif*, of course. You do want her seaworthy when we are ready to depart, don't you?" he asked rhetorically, pursing his lips in annoyance that she would even pose such a silly question.

"Of course," she responded; a bit embarrassed.

She knew Matthias' first duty was always to the ship and he had no time to chaperone her about Bruges. She turned away and walked toward the gangly young man waiting by the lighter.

She grew a bit more apprehensive as she approached.

What if he doesn't understand German, or English, or even Latin

She had never been on her own before in a strange city.

When I arrived in London, I had Ziesolf to guide me around until I found my bearings. Besides, I knew the language pretty well. Here, I don't know a damned word of Flemish other than ones that are the same as in German and there's not nearly enough of those!"

The youth looked at her and said, "*Hey*," flashing a smile from his ruddy, angular face.

Seeing a confused look spreading across her face, he repeated his greeting with words she immediately recognized.

"Hello, my name is Tammo. So, you and your men want me take you to Bruges, yes?"

"Um, yes! Thank you!"

Christina was overjoyed.

"So, you speak German?" she asked, stating the obvious.

"Yes, of course. English, French, and some Italian and Spanish also. If I is to do well in Bruges, I must be able to speak language you understands, yes?"

She nodded, feeling as if a weight had been lifted from her shoulders. Hearing a bustling behind her, Christina turned and saw seven of *der Greif's* crewmen sauntering in her direction. Led by Reiniken, they laughed, swore, and poked each other like a group of boys afoot on their first outing. The group bore faint resemblance to the grim-faced men who had fought for their lives in the raging storm little more than a day before.

The group tumbled into the boat and Reiniken roared, "What ur ya waitin' fur, Yur Worship, an invite?"

Christina lithely hopped over the side of the spacious boat and settled at its bow. She then turned to Reiniken and retorted, "What's your hurry, Wig? They have ample cellars in Bruges, I've heard. Enough even for the thirstiest bastards to drink their fill and have plenty left for the next day."

The huge sailor looked at her with a look of feigned surprise.

"Drinkin'? Why, Master Frederick, yur cruel words wound my pure heart. We've been on the ship so long that we smell like festering shit. Right boys?" he asked his shipmates, who all looked at Christina solemnly, nodding their agreement.

She knew she was somehow being made the butt of a joke, but she had no idea where Reiniken was going with his jest.

I'm sure I'll find out soon enough.

She waited silently for the man to make himself clear.

As expected, Reiniken continued almost immediately.

"Why, we're all goin' to the baths, that's what we're doin'. Clean body and a clean soul, they say," he held his hands together in prayer and lifted his eyes virtuously toward heaven.

A couple of the other men sniggered and nudged each other, obviously taking pleasure at Christina's obvious puzzlement.

Christina's ire began to rise when she noticed the young man, Tammo, was grinning from ear to ear.

It's bad enough the men of my own crew are laughing at me, I'll be damned if I'm going to let this upstart be amused at my expense as well.

She fixed Tammo with an angry glare but, before she could say anything, he chose to speak himself.

"The public baths are very, very good. People in huge tubs of hot water, sometimes many people in one tub together. They rub themselves with sprigs of sage plant, both for its good smell and its healing. Some baths just men, some only women, others men and women. You want to meet prostitutes? Very best in the city at the baths. They will make you very, very happy, or at least I am told so," he added with a slight shrug of his shoulders.

"What? Whores - in the bath tubs! Why I never heard of such a thing!" exclaimed Reiniken, attempting to keep a straight face.

Suddenly, he could contain himself no longer. His hooting laughter echoed across the water, amplified further as the rest of *der Greif's* sailors joined in. After a few seconds, Christina's own voice was added to the discordant chorus of their merriment.

Suddenly, Reiniken pointed a sausage-like finger at Christina and proclaimed, "Yur comin' with us as well, ain't he boys?"

The crewmen voiced their unanimous agreement.

Christina immediately panicked. Clearly, there was no way she could get naked and jump into a tub of water with *der Greif's* crew. She said the first thing that came to her mind.

"Not fucking likely, you lot! While you're off enjoying yourselves, somebody has to make the money to pay for your pleasure, and the repairs to the ship, and the cost of a new cargo, and all the other things about which you haven't a care in the world. Now, you all go have a good time but, me, I've got work to do!"

It made Christina sad to see the crestfallen looks on her crewmen's faces.

Well, I should take it as a compliment, I guess. The fact they wanted to include me in their fun shows they accept me as one of their own. Besides, it would have been wonderful to soak for an hour in a tub of hot, sweet-smelling water. I wonder if I can risk going after the men return to the ship? To the ones set aside for women, of course.

Although she was sorely tempted, she realized she simply could not take the chance of meeting someone in the baths as Christina whom she would later encounter in her guise as Frederick. She put the idea from her head, for the time being at least.

As they neared their destination in the city center, Christina was astounded by a massive structure that began to materialize once they rounded a slight bend in the waterway. It was a huge crane, obviously used to lift heavy goods from the lighters and place them onto the cobblestoned quay. She had seen crane mechanisms before of course, both in Lübeck and in London, but they were absolutely dwarfed by the monster that loomed before her now. Besides the wooden gantry structure that rose what must have been thirty feet in the air, there was a large circular cage in which four men walked forward, causing it to rotate. She was completely enthralled as she saw a large tun of wine lifted effortlessly into the air via a rope and pulley system attached to the cage. The crane then swung about and the barrel descended gently to the ground. She looked at the sailors and saw they too stared at the wonderous machine slack-jawed.

Tammo said enthusiastically, "You are surprised, yes? The Great Crane is the biggest in the world. It is very, very good, yes?"

He guided the boat to the side of the quay and one of the other oarsmen jumped over the side and secured a rope around a cleat secured to the pavers. Furtively avoiding eye contact with her, the men waited deferentially for Christina to disembark first. The men then clambered off the small vessel and looked about, uncertain as to which way to go.

Christina cleared her throat to get the men's attention and stated dryly, "It would not be right for the best crew in Bruges to be able to afford only the old and ugly among the city's whores."

She reached into the leather pouch she wore at her side and drew out several silver pennies.

"Here's for some who are young and pretty!" she said, passing the coins to Reiniken.

The men grinned at each other and murmured words of thanks.

Reiniken said, "Thank ye, Yur Worship! I'll let ya smell my cock when we get back since ya don't have time to enjoy a fuck for yourself!"

Christina chuckled and shook her head slowly from side to side. The man was totally incorrigible.

As she watched her crew disappear down one of the side streets, she heard a voice behind her say, "That was good, is important for master to look after his men if he wants them look after him."

She turned to acknowledge Tammo's words with a solemn nod of her head, then asked, "Do you happen to know of a reputable tavern where I might be able to find lodging, and a good meal?" she added, acutely aware of the rumbling sounds emanating from her stomach.

"Sure," he answered, "We have the best here. The Monpellier is near, only a few hundred yards to the east of the market square on *Philipstockstraat*. The Mint is very good, the same distance to the west on *Geldmuntstraat*. Both have clean room and very good food. You want I take you?"

Provided with detailed instructions to both establishments by Tammo, she thanked him for his offer, but felt she could find them on her own. After he left, she stood for a few seconds while she sorted out her bearings. She then strode off purposefully, having decided to take Matthias' advice and procure her lodging prior to seeing to her business.

She had only walked a couple of minutes when the street opened onto the Great Market. Once again, she stood gawking about herself in amazement. To her front was the imposing structure she knew was the Old Hall, clearly identified by the massive belfry that rose from its center. The building also served as the seat of the city's administration. Within its confines were also halls dedicated to a number of the trades, such as the Spice Hall, the Glovemaker's Hall and, most importantly, the Cloth Hall. It was to this area where Christina would travel to conduct the sale of her wool and, hopefully, the purchase of Flemish cloth as cargo for *der Greif's* return voyage to London town.

The thought of the tasks before her brought Christina's sightseeing to a halt. She turned west and, leaving the square, easily found *Geldmuntstraat* and the inn appropriately named The Mint. Christina went inside the sturdily-constructed brick building and, without any trouble at all, procured a private room for herself on the third floor. As the skies were beginning to darken, she decided to forego returning to the Cloth Hall until the morning.

Instead, she ordered a large tankard of dark beer and a steaming plate of hearty beef casserole with a thick gravy that was simply perfect for sopping up with the fresh, crusty bread that accompanied the dish. She finished her meal off with a fluffy almond pastry the girl who brought her food referred to as a *mattentaart*. Full to bursting, Christina went up the stairs to her room and retired for the night.

She awoke the next morning with a determined sense of purpose. She felt guilty she had not visited the Cloth Hall the previous day, deciding instead to place her personal comfort before the conduct of business.

Father would have certainly never chosen to do so.

Vowing to now commit herself solely to her essential tasks, Christina left the inn and soon found herself before the imposing entrance to the mercantile center of the city, the Cloth Hall. Taking a deep breath to steady her nerves, she went inside.

It was nearly dark when she returned to The Mint. She was exceptionally pleased with the day's proceedings. Christina had negotiated a very good price for her wool, even allowing for the reduction in value of the sacks she had honestly disclosed as having been dampened by seawater. Master Pauwels, the mercer who, contingent upon later inspection, agreed to purchase her cargo, had reluctantly admitted there was a dearth of good English wool in Bruges at the time. Although the winter weather was prohibitively dangerous for its transport across the English Channel, the cloth weavers' demand had continued unabated. Consequently, the supply that had been amassed in the summer months of good sailing had all but been exhausted.

Which means it's unquestionably a seller's market. The interminable weeks it had taken the wagons of wool to get from Ludlow to London had seemed like such a setback at the time. Who would have known the delay would have substantially increased my profits from its sale in Bruges?

Her potential good fortune might even extend beyond the sale of her current cargo.

She vowed to visit the Church of the Holy Blood on the morrow to offer a prayer of thankfulness for her good fortune. She had also overheard two men talking in The Mint the previous evening about rumors the pope would soon issue a papal bull granting indulgences to those who visit the chapel to view the relic.

In light of my actions over the past few months, it might be prudent to have my sins absolved.

Her musings were more serious than she would have admitted.

The next few days passed quickly as she attended to the myriad of details essential for the sale of a foreign commodity in the city of Bruges and the purchase of a new cargo for export. Accompanied by Master Pauwels, she returned to *der Greif* on the early morning ebb tide, where his experienced eye made a quick assessment of the quality of the cargo of wool.

"The fibers of that lot are a bit more damaged than you described, young sir," he looked at her plaintively, then cast his eyes downward in pained disappointment.

"I respectfully beg to differ," she replied.

She reached down and plucked one of the fleeces he had been examining from the deck. She then roughed one area between her fingers. "See the fineness of the fibers here, Master Mercer? Very strong too, I might add. The staple is long and has a good crimp throughout the fleece. No signs of discoloration either."

Pauwels raised his eyes and met Christina's steady gaze. He nodded his head, though whether it was in agreement with her assessment or as a token of grudging respect for the slight youth who stood before him, she was not sure. After a wait of a few pregnant seconds, he spoke again.

"The price we agreed upon, fifty-six marks for each unblemished sarplar of good fleeces is fair, as is forty-eight for those of middling quality. I would value those that suffered water damage at no more than thirty-two."

Christina's brow furrowed and she opened her mouth to speak. Pauwels raised his hand slightly and began again before she could utter a word.

"However," he began slowly and deliberately, "However, I respect the way you conduct your business, Master Frederick. I have dealt with many young men who, when their opinion is challenged, become angry and say or do things they might later regret. Instead, you countered my arguments calmly and persuasively. I believe we can do much business in the future that will be profitable to us both. Thirty-eight for those that were wet."

Christina worried her lip between her teeth.

I had hoped for at least forty-two, but I can't take a chance on offending this man for the sake of a few more coins. The opportunity to develop a standing agreement with him is too valuable.

Swallowing her pride, she nodded her head slightly to the mercer and said, "Agreed."

With their immediate negotiations concluded, Master Pauwels informed Christina he would arrange transportation for the transfer of goods for two days hence. He also asked if she would meet him at the Cloth Hall an hour before sunset to seal the documents of sale.

Trying hard to conceal her glee, Christina readily agreed.

As she watched the portly mercer's figure slowly disappear into the crowd moving along the quay, Christina allowed a broad smile to break out upon her face.

Another successful transaction, she thought, pleased with herself to no end. *Providing there is no last-minute misfortune, that is,* cautioning herself to not salt the fish until it is off the hook.

She was too exhilarated to remain on *der Greif* until the appointed time of her meeting with Pauwels. Instead, she returned to the city center.

Firstly, I have a promise to keep.

She returned to the Great Market, resisting the urge to look about her once again in awe at the panorama of architectural mastery. She turned instead to the relatively modest Romanesque structure tucked almost unobtrusively into the corner of the market square. Although the chapel had been dedicated to Saint Basil the Great, it was commonly referred to by its most precious relic, a vial of the holy blood of Jesus Christ.

Christina entered the chapel and made her way down the central nave. She gazed to her right, beholding a magnificent wooden carving of the Madonna and Child. Halting a few feet before the altar, she descended to her knees. She thanked God for her good fortune, then prayed for the souls of those she had lost as well as for the safety of the men and women who relied on her to keep them safe. Tears then filled her eyes as the image of her mother appeared in her mind.

Please Lord, keep her close to your bosom most of all.

She ended her supplications by asking for forgiveness for her many sins and transgressions. Arising, Christina walked to exit the chapel just as quietly as she had entered.

She paused and turned her head to observe a priest appeared from a side chapel. He cast his eyes about the deserted nave in apparent puzzlement.

Moving into the dim shadows adjacent to the door, Christina watched as he spied a small cloth bag on the floor in front of the altar. Obviously curious, he walked forward and picked it up, surprised at its hefty weight. The priest looked inside and was astounded by the large number of gold and silver coins within. Looking to the entrance door, and then to the altar, he offered a prayer of thankfulness to the chapel's mysterious benefactor, regardless of whether he or she was of worldly or divine origin.

Exiting into the square, Christina pondered what to do next. Guiltily, her thoughts pulled her once more to visit the baths.

I feel my skin is absolutely encrusted! Between the accumulated sweat, sea salt, and general filth, a quick wash with a rag has accomplished naught. If I cannot take a lengthy soak, I will need to scrape my skin with a knife to cleanse it.

There was another allure that drew her to the baths, one she rather ashamedly sought to ignore. In her idleness, remembrances of her passionate night with Sybille, the prostitute at the Nag's Head tavern in Southwark, were increasingly dominating her thoughts. The feel of her practiced fingers and tongue exploring her body had instilled a heat within her she had not previously felt.

But could another woman's touch so easily substitute for that of Sybille, even one who is similarly skilled? It was not merely the pleasures I experienced, some of which I had already attained through my own secretive explorations of my body. It was instead the sharing of it all, two souls melded for an instant of time as one. To imagine another could fulfill this purpose is to cheapen it, turning our love making into something tawdry and mean. That I cannot do.

With regret, she decided once more the risk of visiting the baths was too great. Vowing to return to her lodging early to devote an extended time to thoroughly cleanse herself, she began a detailed exploration of the city. She walked for hours through the city streets, eventually returning to her lodging happily exhausted. After another hearty repast, she retired to her chamber where she fulfilled her promise to herself before indulging in a well-deserved night of dreamless slumber.

Two days later, Christina waited with growing impatience for Master Pauwels to make his arrival quayside. Under the watchful eye of Matthias, the crew of *der Greif* were busying themselves on the ship, manhandling the heavy woolsacks from the hold, onto the deck, and then onto the wharf.

Damn his eyes if he doesn't show. All this work will be for naught if we wind up having to load it all back aboard. I'm certainly not going to leave my cargo exposed to the elements overnight.

Involuntarily, she cast an eye toward the sky, but it remained the same caerulean blue that had greeted her when she first stepped onto the deck that morning. She nodded slightly as if to confirm her decision to begin the unloading.

Besides, the men might as well do a bit of work to earn the money I've been paying them the entire time they'd been in port.

Although she rued the fact she had been doing little more than subsidizing their drinking and whoring, maintaining a crew she knew and trusted was much better than the alternative. She might have been able to save a few pennies if she had discharged the men upon their arrival in Bruges, but experienced seamen were always in high demand, especially in such a cosmopolitan port. Soon, they would have been added to other ships' companies, leaving Matthias to try to pull together a crew from the dockyard leftovers.

There was more, however.

These men have fought alongside me. Some have saved my life, even at the risk of their own. How could I repay their loyalty by just casting them aside?

A few anxious hours later, several large lighters appeared on the canal. Christina was relieved to see Master Pauwels seated in the prow of the lead craft. As they moored along the quayside, Christina walked briskly to greet the mercer.

Before she could speak, Master Pauwels said, "Forgive me, Master Frederick, for my tardy arrival. I trust you were not too seriously inconvenienced?"

Christina gritted her teeth, but replied in a pleasant enough voice, "No, good master, of course not. You see, I have already taken the liberty to begin shifting my woolsacks onto the quay."

Pauwels nodded judiciously, then said, "I will do likewise. Then, we can conduct the final inspection of our respective purchases before we begin loading them."

The exasperated look on her face must have been obvious.

Is he making one last attempt to quibble? We have already sealed the agreement and settled the tax payment. Is there never an end to these merchants' infatuation with haggling?

Seeing her reaction to his previous statement, Pauwels's face grew more serious, then he continued, "Please do not take offense, Master Frederick. In no way was I attempting to challenge your honor as a merchant; however, sometimes honest mistakes can be made. A woolsack might appear unblemished on the top; yet, it could be black with mold below. It is far better to examine each article carefully now than to find problems later. Besides, if we are to continue our relationship, is it not better to go into future negotiations with no past grudges in our hearts?"

Although somewhat chagrined by the merchant's mild rebuke, Christina lips formed what she hoped passed as a friendly smile.

"Of course; I agree with your reasoning completely, Master Pauwels. Shall we begin then?"

As the mercer's men systematically began turning the woolsacks this way and that, exposing each side in turn to their master's expert scrutiny, Christina paid them no mind, as her attention became focused on the several bales of cloth they had just finished stacking neatly on the opposite side of the quay.

Obviously, Christina's tasks had not ended with the sale of the wool contained within *der Greif's* spacious hold. Although the thought of returning to London with nothing more than sacks of gold groschens had guiltily crossed her mind, she knew it would be absurd to make the journey back without a new cargo aboard, one that could be parlayed into even greater profits.

After all, that's what a merchant does, is it not? If I am destined to play this game, I will play to win!

She beckoned to Matthias who moved quickly to her side. She explained what she wanted in a few words. He, in turn, called two of the ship's most burly crewmen over to where they stood; Reiniken, of course, and Alwin, a young giant of a man with flowing blond locks of hair far past his shoulders matched by a braided mustache that extended equally as far.

The two men made short work of placing each bale on the wooden decking of the quay and untying the cordage that held it together. While they went about their task, Christina walked briskly to her cabin aboard *der Greif*, returning in a few minutes with her ledger and a short wooden staff. They then stood aside as Christina, assisted by Matthias, began her close inspection of the contents.

She had taken considerable care selecting her purchases. Most were lengths of finely woven broadcloth from thirty to forty-five ells long, by two to three ells wide; although there were also a few exquisite brocades as well. The lengths were in a variety of colors, brown, perse, murrey, and sanguine to name only a few. Prized above all others, however, were the three lengths of very fine scarlet woolens colored from the vivid red dyestuff known as kermes. This dye was extracted at enormous cost from the bodies of small Mediterranean insects, but produced a cloth that valued as highly as the finest silks from the Holy Land. She knew she could realize tremendous profits from the sale of this fabric to the London drapers who counted the highest of the English nobility among their clientele; yet, she guiltily coveted a garment made from the fine material for herself. She knew she would need to be cautious, however. The last thing she needed was more trouble with the chief alderman by running afoul of the strict English sumptuary laws.

Christina examined each length of cloth painstakingly, checking the quality of the weave as well as whether it had been blemished by damp, discoloration, or damage from pests, such as moths or mice. She used the small staff, or ell-wand, to confirm the measurements of the cloth had not been reduced in size by surreptitious cutting from what she had recorded in her ledger. As she completed her scrupulous inspection of each bale, she moved on to the next while the two crewmembers retied the bale, stacking it with the others Christina had finished. It was a smooth process; yet, it took most of the afternoon to examine them all.

As she stood erect, she arched her back to dissipate the ache caused from the many hours spent bending over. After a few seconds of stretching, Christina turned and walked over to where the mercer waited patiently, sprawling comfortably on a woolsack.

He arose from his makeshift pallet and asked pleasantly, "I trust you found everything in order?"

"Yes, for the most part at least," she replied. "There were a few minor flaws, but of not enough importance to note."

She did not add that, since her current examination had been much more meticulous than the first, she had the niggling suspicious she had not noted the discrepancies previously.

I was very fortunate this man did not have it in his heart to cheat me. If he had, who knows how much valuation I would have squandered in my haste. In the future, I will take the time to ensure I know exactly what it is I am paying for.

He nodded and said, "And I the same, Master Frederick. Please forgive me if I depart with some haste. I must secure my newly-acquired goods in my warehouse before they take on the night's damp. Farewell, my friend, and I hope you see fit to bring such a cargo to my doorstep again in the near future!"

Bidding Pauwels adieu, Christina briskly set the crew of *der Greif* to stowing the bales of cloth aboard the ship for the same reason. By the time the skies began to darken for the evening, Pauwels' lighters were disappearing up the canal and the cog's new cargo was safely aboard.

Before Christina could congratulate herself for a job well done, Matthias approached with a worried look on his face. Clearly, all was not well.

Chapter 3

An Opportunity and a Challenge
Bruges, February, 1310

"What is it, Matthias?" Christina asked, not look forward to what the ship's master had to say.

"The weight of the finished cloth we now have in the hold is only a fraction of that of our previous cargo," he stated simply.

"Yes, and . . .?"

Her voice was edged with a growing hint of irritation.

I have no interest in playing guessing games right now, man! Speak plainly! she thought to herself, although sensibly refraining from chiding Matthias aloud.

Christina's head was beginning to ache.

"The ship is too lightly loaded to safely sail in the open water. We can easily take on more ballast, but that gains nothing other than extra work and expense. Alternatively, additional cargo can serve the same purpose."

He ceased speaking and looked at her impassively.

"Of course, Matthias," she replied, chagrined she had not thought of something so obvious herself. "What you are suggesting makes perfect sense. I will return to the city on the morrow and procure enough goods to fill our hold to the brim. Perhaps a few hundred sacks of goose down would be sufficient?"

Now it was her turn to fix him with an innocent stare.

Matthias seemed puzzled by her response but, after a few seconds, the cloud upon his weathered face lifted and a guttural laugh issued from deep within his throat.

"Or perhaps not, Frederick. Try to acquire something with a bit more weight to it, please."

Christina grinned at the sailing master, clapped him cheerily on the back, and together they walked back to *der Greif*.

It's been a full day, she admitted to herself as she entered her small cabin. *Some bread and cheese for supper and then to bed.*

She hoped she would be able to conclude her additional business quickly, perhaps in only a few days. The unseasonably clear weather they now enjoyed would not last forever. She could only pray it would hold until they had returned to England.

Only a fool would risk another stormy sea crossing in the middle of winter, and there's a limit to even my foolhardiness.

She awoke early the next morning in high spirits, greeted by the dawning of another beautiful day. Although there was a faint chilly breeze wafting in from landward, the temperature was moderated by the sharp intensity of the bright sunlight. Only a few wispy clouds blemished the sky, joined by massive pirouetting flocks of squawking seabirds.

This is a day in which one feels good to be alive.

She quickly found passage on one of the canal boats and departed Sluys on the short journey into Bruges.

Hopefully, I will feel the same when I return.

Three days later, Christina stood naked in her cabin on *der Greif*, having just removed the fine garments she had worn during her brief stay in the city of Bruges. She smiled at the goosebumps that covered her skin, stark evidence the weather had turned much colder. The wind, that had previously blown from the southeast, had now switched to a much more northerly course. The majority of her good luck had held as the skies remained substantially clear, promising a swift and hopefully calm return to England.

That was not the full extent of her good fortune. She had spent her first day making polite inquiries among the city's wine merchants concerning making a bulk purchase. She had arisen the following morning with a head thick from imprudent sampling.

I should have brought Reiniken to do that, except the only standards that matter to him is whether the wine is alcoholic and if it is wet.

Believing she had the measure of the going price structure, Christina returned to the dimly lit trade room of the de Groods and began negotiations in earnest. Without too much haggling she had soon procured two hundred hogshead casks of a vintage she particularly favored.

Yes, and which will be arriving any time, she scolded herself for her idle woolgathering. *So, unless you intend to load four hundred-pound barrels with your bare ass waving in the wind, you had better get some clothes on. Now, move girl!*

She quickly responded to her self-admonishment. In a matter of a few minutes, she was fully dressed in suitable work clothes and on the deck, just in time to see a now-familiar formation of lighters make their way to the moorage closest to *der Greif.* Around her, the ship's company began to stir, ready to be tasked. Matthias set the men to their duties, well aware of how to make the best use of each man's abilities.

She was surprised to see two unfamiliar faces among the crew. Clearly, these were men Matthias had added to the ship's compliment to replace the poor unfortunate souls who had been lost overboard during the storm. There was nothing about them that particularly set the men apart from others who had moved up and down the quay over the past few weeks. They were both clearly in their mid-twenties to thirties, muscular, ill-kept, and rough looking.

I don't give a damn how they look, just as long as they're willing to do an honest day's work for a fair wage.

She knew she had no need to fret about that; she was certain Matthias had made his expectations abundantly clear to the men before signing them on.

Der Greif's master was already in consultation with one of the workers from the lighters, whom she assumed to be their foreman. The man then turned and barked a few commands to his fellows. As each cask was set down on the wooden deck of the quay, Matthias checked it meticulously to ensure the wood was undamaged; there was no sign of leakage, odor of spoilage, and the bung had not been loosened or displaced. Once completely satisfied, he motioned for a pair of *der Greif's* crewmen to roll it carefully to the ship. Soon, a line of barrels began to wend its way toward the cargo hatch.

Like beads on a rosary.

Suddenly, a heavy blow to her back sent Christina sprawling to the deck, barely catching herself in time to avoid hitting her face on the hold cover.

Behind her, she heard a deep voice say, "Get yur feckin' ass out of the way, boy! There's man's work to be done here. Next time, you'll get a bath in the water!"

Christina twisted about to see one of the new men staring down at her. A wide grin split his face, revealing a few discolored teeth randomly populating his mouth. She felt a surge of white-hot rage extend over her body as she scrambled back to her feet.

Before she was fully erect, the man suddenly moved forward and, extending his arms into her chest, pushed her back down again, only this time onto her butt.

He laughed harshly, then said, "Stay down, pup, before you do somethin' ya might really regret!"

Ignoring the man's remarks, she again regained her feet, albeit this time much more cautiously; backing away and placing her body well outside of the man's immediate reach. She was furious, her breath coming in ragged gulps as she fought to resist her immediate urge to charge the man like a maddened bull and pummel his sneering face into a pulp.

In the few seconds it took to somewhat calm herself, Christina considered her options.

This is my ship; he has no rights or privileges here. Why do I not just order the crewmen to throw him off the ship?

This was certainly her prerogative and she was sure the sailors would do as they were told. She hesitated, however, from issuing this command.

She slowly passed her gaze over the faces of the sailors who had almost unconsciously formed into a ring around the two potential combatants. Faces she knew so well were almost unrecognizable, now appearing almost animalistic as they jostled among themselves, excited by the possibility of the brutality of a no-holds-barred fight.

Christina knew she needed the respect of these men, a quality that could not be earned merely through the power of a few silver coins. She had freely chosen to enter their world, one in which you earned your place by your ability to physically defend it.

Yes, they may obey me if I tell them to protect me, but I perhaps will have lost their respect forever if I do.

*God damned me*n! she thought in exasperation as she shifted her weight forward onto the balls of her feet. *Giving them the power in the world was the sweet Lord's ultimate punishment!*

"What are ya thinkin', boy? I'll not be playin' with ya." The man said slowly and deliberately, then spat a large yellow gob on the deck for emphasis.

Christina said nothing, only began to slowly circle to her left in order to close the distance between herself and her assailant. For his part, he simply stood his ground, the infuriating sneer still frozen upon his bewhiskered face.

She knew she should be patient and let the man force the issue, but she could withhold her anger no more. She moved forward with blinding speed, landing a quick, heavy, jab to the man's right eye. Just as quickly she stepped back but, instead of withdrawing, she spun around and delivered a hard backhand to the same side of the man's face. She moved cautiously backwards, out of the reach of a possible counter-attack, before once again circling to her left.

Her opponent seemed stunned by the sudden violence of her attack. He shook his head vigorously from side to side to clear the cobwebs from his brain. Once again, he spat on the deck, only this time it was blood red rather than yellow. The left side of his face had turned a bright pink and the skin about his right eye appeared somewhat puffy. Appraising the damage, Christina was quite satisfied by her initial handiwork.

"So, a dancer ya are, eh? Mighty fancy, I must say. Too bad ya hit like a feckin' little girl!" the man seemed to have regained his wits about him.

His heckling jarred Christina.

Has he uncovered that I am indeed a woman?

A sudden wave of panic coursed through her body.

No, she realized with relief, he's only trying to goad me with an insult that would seemingly offend any man. Well, let's see if I can change his mind about how hard a girl can hit!

Her opponent now joined her in circling the deck space inside the makeshift ring of animated crewmen. He feinted charging toward her, an action she had somewhat expected, instead quickly cutting off her lateral movement and pinning her against the mass of bystanders.

Christina threw another jab at his face, followed immediately with a powerful punch to the man's stomach. He used his arms to block these blows, which consequently had little effect. A small whooshing sound escaped his lips as his meaty right hand dug into her lower ribcage. He followed it up with a left into her own midsection. The pain was overpowering, the worst she had ever experienced. She felt like she was going to immediately be sick to her stomach.

She knew she had no time to allow her body to react, however. Another blow or two like those he had just thrown and she would have no chance, she would be totally incapacitated from the pain. She had to get out of the range of the man's punches; yet, she was trapped between the bulk of his body and those of the sailors.

She ducked under his left fist that hooked toward the side of her head. She then fell toward the deck, summersaulting away to regain some distance. She regained her feet again only, this time, with much greater difficulty. The tremendously excruciating pain in her side made breathing difficult. It was all she could do to refrain from calling on the ring of sailors for assistance.

"An acrobat as well? Ain't that lovely? Ya should be performin' on the street for pennies!"

Christina gritted her teeth and ignored his jibe, once more assumed a defensive posture.

I'll be damned if I'll give this bastard the satisfaction of beating me on my own ship, she thought with considerably more bravado than she really felt.

She realized she needed to be very careful. This was not a clumsy lout of a boy with abilities that were no match for her own. This man had the skill, power, and experience to hurt her and hurt her badly. For the first time, she felt actual fear of someone.

Again, they circled.

What if I am injured so badly my wounds need to be treated? I would be exposed for who I truly am. What would become of me then?

Christina knew she must ignore these additional anxieties if she was ever to have a chance against this man.

He moved closer, seeking to trap her against the side of the ship this time. She pirouetted away more quickly this time, denying him the opportunity to take advantage of his greater weight and power. Now, as he lunged to catch her, she reached forward and grabbed his arm, falling backwards and using the combined force of their two bodies to pull him after her.

Christina landed on her bottom and continued to roll onto her back. Simultaneously, she lifted her legs and tucked them close to her body. Like a spring, she thrust them upward, using their power to flip her opponent over her head. He fell in a crumpled heap against the ship's mast. She was rewarded by the audible thud made by the man's landing.

Her feeling of satisfaction was short-lived, as her adversary scrambled angrily to his feet. His expression was no longer one of belligerent amusement. Nor did he make any comment this time. Instead, he slowly reached downward and pulled a wicked-looking knife from his boot. Unexpectedly, he moved his hand swiftly upward, flipping his hold neatly so he now held it by its blade.

Oh my God, he's going to throw it at me!

She had no time to move, hardly any time to react. She involuntarily thrust her hand in front of her face, despite knowing this would probably do little good.

A second passed and still she had not felt the sharp pain of the blade cutting into her body. She moved her hand and was amazed to see Reiniken now holding her assailant's wrist as if in a vise. He squeezed harder and the man dropped the blade. One of the other sailors stooped to pick it up.

Reiniken then released his grip on the man, commenting, "Let's keep it friendly, eh, Arnst?"

Christina was amazed she at last knew the name of the man pummeling her. It mattered little, as she now realized their scrap had become deadly serious. The fact Arnst had drawn his knife had escalated the fight. It would now only end when one of them was incapacitated at the least, lifeless at the worst.

Arnst shrugged away from Reiniken's grasp; his attention focused solely now on the still prone body of Christina, who had pushed herself upright so she could lift her head and gauge his measured approach. He saw the look of apparent fear on her face, but it made no difference to him. He had been embarrassed by this upstart, had been stung by the laughter of his fellow sailors when he had been struck. This would not be the first man he had killed, and it certainly would not be the last.

Arnst began to reach down, intent on pulling Christina to her feet. This placed most of his weight onto his right leg, a movement she had anticipated. Rather than continuing to back away, she now used her hands to thrust her body forward, toward Arnst. She hooked the toe of her left boot around the heal of his forward leg then, with all the strength she could muster, kicked out with her right leg until it met his right shin. The snap of the bone made a sharp crack like the breaking of kindling for a winter fire.

Screaming from the sudden intense pain of his injury, Arnst hobbled backwards, steadying himself against the bulwark of the ship as he tried to balance on his good leg.

Christina arose deliberately, trying hard not to disclose the degree of pain she was still experiencing from her injured ribs. She looked about the faces that ringed the deck, all of whom seemed uncertain as to what she was about to do next.

She gazed across the approximately eight feet of deck that separated her from Arnst. What she beheld was a face deeply etched by the pain he was experiencing; yet, dominated more by a powerful sense of hatred toward her. Without thinking, she ran forward and pushed Arnst over the side of the ship and into the frigid water below.

The sailors seemed surprised by her sudden action.

Young Dietmar asked, "But what if he can't swim? Especially with his leg and all."

Christina spoke savagely. "Well, that's his problem and not mine, isn't it?"

She refrained from looking into the water to see if, in fact, he was foundering.

I'll be damned if I'll lend him a hand if he is, or let anyone else aboard help him either!"

Despite her vow, she felt relieved when Dietmar said, "Look! There he is! A couple of lads are helping him onto the wharf!"

She was suddenly beset with anger that her crew would be more concerned with the welfare of a man they had only known a day or two at most than they were by her own.

As she began to painfully shuffle toward the entrance to her cabin, she was surprised to hear a loud cheer issue from the throats of the men behind her. She turned and saw Reiniken ambling toward her.

"You're a dangerous little bastard, ya are, Yur Worship!"

Despite the usual irreverence in his voice, Christina wondered whether she was imagining what seemed like a new sense of respect from the man. He circled his bear-like arm about her shoulder and gave her a massive hug. She was unable to stifle the sharp whimper of acute pain that issued forth from her lips as a result. He released Christina and looked down at her in surprise.

"Hurt ya, did he? Must have been the one to the ribs, right? Hell of a nasty blow. Ya think he broke one?" Reiniken said with obvious concern in his voice.

"I'm not sure," she replied, hoping her voice sounded less weepy to the sailor than it did to her.

"Well, let me have a look. We should probably wrap it."

Some of the other sailors nodded their heads in assent to the sense of Reiniken's observation.

"No!" Christina mustered all the venom she could into her voice. "We've wasted enough time here. Do you lot think I'm paying you to stand about and be entertained all day? Maybe we should break open one of these casks of wine and have a proper piss-about? Get your asses to work and if all these barrels aren't properly stowed by sunset, I'll beat it out of all of you, one by one!"

The crewmen fell to their duties with a newfound sense of immediacy. Even Reiniken didn't stop to make a sarcastic remark, instead moving swiftly back down onto the wharf and rolling one of the heavy hogsheads up the ramp by himself.

Christina turned and took a guarded look back onto the quay. She was somewhat thankful to see no sign of Arnst. In spite of herself, she wished the man no ill will. He had probably been a bully all his life. They were all the same, even the ones she had known as a child in Lübeck. Men who took advantage of those who were weaker, who always needed a new victim to make themselves feel strong.

What will he do now? she wondered.

She knew it was a nasty break of his legbone, one that would take many months to heal, if it did so at all. Even at best, she was sure he would probably always walk with a limp for the remainder of his life.

He probably won't be as eager to start a fight in the future either. Such men often become cowards when bested.

Her thoughts turned away from concern for Arnst and her cargo and toward her own well-being. The pain in her side was no longer as sharp, now it had receded into a dull, powerful ache. She shuffled to her cabin, hoping to make it there before she collapsed.

Christina sat down heavily on her bunk. She began to remove her clothing with extreme care, trying hard not to cause the throbbing ache in her side flare into the intense pain she had experienced previously. At this task she failed miserably. Her flesh glided over the heavily bruised ribs along her left side as she gingerly raised her arm to remove her tunic. She stifled a scream between clenched teeth, emitting a guttural gasp in its stead.

She then removed the pin that held the linen fabric wrapped about her upper torso. She looked down at her injured side. A large purplish discoloration was swelling up where he had hit her. She lightly ran her fingers across the skin, pleased there was no evidence of any fragments of bone protruding upwards.

How I wish Trudi were here. I would give the entire contents of the hold to feel her passing a warm sponge over my body.

Her maid, however, was many miles away; across a sea that possibly was being wracked with violent storms this very moment.

I have only myself to rely on now.

Using her right hand, she dipped an unbleached linen cloth in water left over from an earlier wash she had forgotten to empty. She scrubbed the sweat and dirt from her face and body as best she could. She even worked her hand under her left armpit without causing too much pain.

It was nothing near as satisfying as a hot bath, but it will have to do for now. Now, how in the hell am I going to get this back around me?

She considered the length of cloth that had been wound about her chest. Normally, binding herself was a simple task that only took a minute – and two arms. Now she only had one that was completely usable.

The wrapping must be tighter as well, as now it is not only useful as part of my deception but also to help support my injured ribs.

After a few seconds of thought, she believed she had found an answer. She fixed one end of the cloth to a hook in the wall she used to hang clothes upon. She then walked the opposite end of the fabric across to the other side of the cabin.

"Christ's nails!" she exclaimed under her breath, exasperated that she had run out of cabin before she had run out of cloth.

She walked back to the hook, now fastening the wrap in the approximate middle of the length. Christina returned to the opposite end of the cabin and, holding the fabric tightly against her skin, pulled it taunt.

She laboriously began the task of wrapping the cloth about her. She slowly turned her body around and around, leaning backwards a bit to keep the fabric taut. Soon, she was affixing the pin again, well satisfied with the quality of her self-aid.

Although she would have liked nothing more than surrendering herself to the almost overwhelming urge to rest, she knew she could not do so yet. Clumsily, she pulled her tunic back over her head, this time bracing herself for what she knew would be the inevitable associated pain. She then walked out the door, needing to make sure every wine cask was properly stowed so they could finally begin their journey back to England.

Back home.

Christina's good fortune ebbed and flowed like the tides on the journey across the English sea. The next day after leaving port, a sudden switch in the wind forced them back into the harbor. This time, however, they anchored offshore.

No need to pay port duties, she decided. *Or to risk any more trouble ashore,* she added as a judicious afterthought.

In a few days, however, Matthias decided their sail could catch enough wind to begin their journey once more. It was a laborious process, tacking first southward, then back to the north, sometimes gaining only a mile west for ten miles sailing. Fortunately, although the surface of the sea was rough, with foam-flecked waves roiling as far as the eye could see, they were not so tempestuous that they posed an overt danger to *der Greif* or her crew. Despite the obstacles, both great and small, that had impeded their voyage, they entered the Thames estuary on the auspicious day of Ash Wednesday.

How difficult to believe we have only been away less than two full months; so much has happened. Yet, I only know half the story. What has transpired here in London while I have been away? Are Trudi and Ziesolf safe and healthy? Has there been any word from Lübeck?

These and hundreds more questions filled her head to bursting, preventing her from sleeping as the ship rode at anchor, awaiting the morning's tide to begin to wend its way upriver.

At least it's no longer the pain in my ribs that's keeping me awake.

She had at last decided that none had been broken.

For the greater part of the time since they departed Bruges, sleeping had been a vexing problem for her. Laying on either of her sides had been impossible. Even being on her back was no good for, as soon as she drifted off to sleep, she would invariably move slightly, awakening herself with a new shock of pain coursing through her body. Sleeping upright in a chair, her head on her arm lain across the small table in front of her, had provided her only respite. Even with this technique, what rest she had achieved had been fitful and in small measures. When she discovered the ache in her ribs was finally subsiding, she had slept for what seemed an eternity, spending the entire day in her cabin. This was so unlike her that Matthias had knocked at the door, querying whether she was alright.

I am now, she thought, smiling to herself.

Chapter 4

New Knowledge and an Old Vow
London, March, 1310

By mid-afternoon, *der Greif* was approaching its customary moorage at Billingsgate. Christina, as well as many of the younger crewmen, were very surprised when the ship continued past without stopping. A few minutes later, Matthias angled the vessel toward a moorage unfamiliar to her. A few of the sailors leapt over the side with heavy hawsers to secure the ship wharf-side.

"Why are we stopping here, Matthias?" she asked the master with curiosity.

"This is Garlickhithe Wharf," he explained, "one of the two moorages designated for the import of wine into the kingdom, the other being Queenhithe. They are the closest docks to the great hall of the Vintner's Guild, the members of which who will have great interest in the casks below. It is the law for ships carrying wine to be imported through London moor here, awaiting the arrival of the King's chamberlain and his sheriffs, before proceeding elsewhere."

"But the king has granted we Hanseatic merchants a special privilege, exempting us from the customary taxation on our goods," she protested.

"Yes, I know," he responded with a wry smile, "on all cargoes, that is, except for wine. King Edward's father, Longshanks, maintained his right to prisage."

Before Christina could question Matthias further, their attention was drawn to a small officious procession working its way toward the ship. In the forefront was a young man who, judging by his attire, was clearly a member of the nobility, followed by another whom she assumed was a sheriff. Six men in distinctive livery completed the composition of the party.

Matthias barked an order and two of the ship's sailors hoisted the heavy plank walkway over *der Greif's* side, fixing one end securely in its grooved place on the ship while the other rested on the wharf. Without further invitation, the two men Christina assumed were the chamberlain and the sheriff strode aboard. She and Matthias walked to meet them as they came aboard, both of them bowing in deference to the representative of the royal court.

Christina wisely let Matthias do the talking as she had no idea about what was to happen. After the exchange of a few formalities, he led the two men below deck and into the hold. She was shocked to see Matthias prying open the bung of the first hogshead. Before she could voice a protest, however, he fixed her with a severe expression of warning that left little doubt in her mind she should refrain from speaking.

Wordlessly, she looked on in annoyance as the chamberlain drew a sample from the contents of the cask; working the wine about in his mouth, before spitting it out into a small bucket Matthias had produced for the purpose. He then leaned over and whispered something to the sheriff, who then used a bit of chalk to make a mark upon the barrel. The nobleman then nodded to Matthias, who reinserted the bung, securing it firmly with a small tap from a wooden mallet Christina had not before noticed him picking up.

Well, at least this is over.

Instead of returning to the deck, however, Christina was amazed to see the men proceed to the next hogshead. Soon, they had repeated the tasting of the second cask and moved to the third. This sequence continued as they methodically worked their way the entire length of the ship. A few times, she saw the heavy black eyebrows of the chamberlain lift appreciatively, once even bringing a broad smile to his lips. Conversely, she counted eleven times when he unceremoniously spat the sample upon the deck of the hold rather than into the bucket, apparently indicative of his disgust at its taste. Christina had so many pressing questions for Matthias she could barely contain herself.

Having apparently completed their task, the two men climbed back onto the main deck, strode down the gangway, and disappeared into the distance as enigmatically as they had come. As soon as it became clear their inspection of the ship's cargo was complete, Christina turned to Matthias and questions began to tumble in an avalanche from her mouth.

"As I said previously," he began answering patiently, "Longshanks withheld the right of prisage on all wine coming into England. This law allows the king to take one tun of wine from every ship importing from ten to twenty tuns and two tuns from every ship importing twenty or more. Consequently, the chamberlain has made his selection of those casks that will constitute the king's share."

Two full tuns appropriated by the king! Why, that's eight hogsheads for which I will see no profits. Except for the pleasure of knowing they are gracing the royal table.

Realizing she had no recourse in the matter, Christina asked, "So what do we do now? Are we free to go?"

"Yes," replied Matthias. "I would suggest though you proceed to the vintner's guild hall without tarrying any further. Hopefully, you can find someone interested in making a purchase even at this late hour."

Christina agreed with the ship's master completely.

The sooner we are rid of this portion of our cargo the better I will like it. It is truthfully beginning to leave a bitter taste in my mouth.

She couldn't keep her lips from pursing into a cynical smile at her unintended jest.

She was indeed fortunate enough to find a potential buyer in the guild's great hall. He agreed to visit *der Greif* at first light to inspect the hogsheads of wine and, if pleased with what he found, make her an offer.

Realizing there was little more she could do, she began to retrace her steps back to the wharf, observing business among the vintners must be booming, considering the richness and opulence of the furnishings in their hall. Most striking of all had been the superbly carved golden-brown hardwoods highlighted with gold leaf that decorated the tall columns that supported the high ceiling. It hurt her head to try to calculate how many tuns of wine had been sold to afford to purchase such casual extravagance.

Well, they're not going to get richer at my expense, she vowed, still bristling at what she considered the excessive degree of the king's share. *I'll drink the whole damn lot of it myself before I let them take advantage of me!*

As she walked the short distance back to *der Greif,* she was torn as to what she should do next. It would certainly be easiest to spend the night on board, then be ready to meet with Master

Baynard in the morning. Although that course of action would certainly make the most sense, her heart drew her strongly in another direction.

The journey to Bruges and back had separated her from Trudi for nearly two months. In all her life, they had never been apart for more than a couple of days. The young woman was her best friend, now perhaps her only friend, as others she had met in London still seemed no more than mere acquaintances.

But there is also Ziesolf; is he a friend? Perhaps, but our relationship is certainly more complicated than that. He is my teacher, my advisor, and often my biggest pain in the ass. I have no doubt he cares about me, however, and would gladly risk his own life to defend mine. Yes, certainly more than just a friend; he is my family now.

Strong emotion caused her throat to tighten.

Knowing the two awaited her return, she felt compelled to speed to them without delay. Of course, they would be overjoyed to see her and, after the initial delight subsided, she would entertain them far into the night with tales of her exploits. She realized they would have things to tell her as well, particularly Ziesolf, who had been left in charge of her affairs in London.

Am I eager to be beset by a new set of worries, even before I have attended to those before me now? Undoubtedly, problems would have presented themselves while I was gone. Just as certainly Ziesolf would feel the need to appraise me as soon as possible, asking me to make immediate decisions even before I have my boots off.

Finally, she decided to delay their reunion, but by only a day. Looking up, she was surprised to see she had arrived back at Garlickhithe Wharf. Walking back aboard *der Greif*, she found Matthias and apprised him as to what was expected to transpire the next morning.

Christina stirred from her bed early and walked out onto a deck awash in fog so dense she could barely discern the mast of the ship. Already beginning to feel the sharp bite of the frigid air, she stepped back inside the cabin to fetch her heavy fur-lined cloak. She now regretted her decision to remain onboard the previous night rather than to enjoy the toasty-warm comfort of the manor house she had been bequeathed by her aunt.

At least I have the pleasure in knowing that was the final night I'll spend here for the foreseeable future.

As he had promised, Master Baynard appeared just as an almost imperceptible brightening of the atmosphere indicated the day was finally dawning. The sequence followed by the vintner closely mirrored that used by the chamberlain the day before. Christina, however, was determined to query Baynard as to what he was doing rather than remain mute as she had felt obliged to do during the visit by the royal representative.

"What do those symbols mean?" Christina asked, pointing to the cryptic hieroglyphics Baynard had just chalked onto the barrel.

She was curious, as those the chamberlain had made were completely different.

Baynard smiled and said, "Each of us possesses his own vintner's marks. Appraising the quality of a cask of wine is a very subjective process, you see. The note I make indicates the cask's value to me, not to others."

"And the 'X?' on this cask, and on those ones over there?" Both the chamberlain and Baynard had scrawled identical marks on those barrels

"Alas, Master Frederick, that has a universal meaning, not one that you want to hear, I am afraid. The wine in those hogsheads has soured, it is little more than vinegar."

Is this a bargaining ploy?

She wondered if the vintner was attempting to talk down the value of her cargo.

"May I?" she asked.

Readily, Baynard handed Christina the small ladle he had been using to sample the casks. She dipped it down through the bunghole and scooped a small measure of the barrel's contents, then bought it up to her lips. The taste was so terrible she spat it out involuntarily.

Baynard chuckled at what must have been the look of disgust on her face. She handed the ladle back to him, exchanging it for his bit of chalk. Solemnly, she added her 'X' to the other two already upon the cask.

Once the vintner had finished his inspection, Christina asked the question that had increasingly troubled her mind.

"How many are spoiled?"

She could have figured it out herself, of course, but she considered it bad form to return to the beginning and start counting the barrels marked with 'X'.

"Twelve are corrupted," Baynard answered readily, "And there are ten more that have suffered leakage, diminishing their value to varying degrees, of course."

Christina was completely crestfallen.

The eight best barrels had been confiscated by the king's chamberlain, Now, twelve others are virtually worthless and ten others almost so. Is there no end to the bad news today? In Bruges, I trusted Master de Grood too much and he has betrayed me. How could I have been so naïve?

Seeing the look of despair on Christina's face, Baynard placed a hand upon Christina's shoulder and gently told her, "Do not be so hard on yourself. This is your first cargo of wine, yes?

Christina nodded, somewhat ashamed her emotions were so readily on display.

"Your disappointment is a normal reaction for those coming newly to the trade of wine. Most believe that, if you purchase a hundred casks at the market on the Continent, then you should be able to sell one hundred casks here, realizing a tidy profit on each as well."

She listened intently.

I know there is always some damage or spoilage to any cargo transported over the oceans, but it is difficult to accept there has been so much to this one.

She decided to allow the wine merchant to finish before voicing her concerns.

"Believe it or not, your losses are actually very low. We have calculated approximately fifteen percent of cargoes of wine arriving in London is spoiled. Add to this another ten to twelve percent of the casks have lost value, both in quality and quantity, due to leakage. Taxation, most from which you Germans are exempt, absorbs about eight percent of what profit remains."

Her eyes grew larger as Baynard recited the figures.

"So," he continued patiently, "A merchant might routinely expect to profit from about two-thirds of his ship's cargo, minus of course the losses he incurred purchasing the other third for which he paid full price. You, on the other hand, have a full eighty-five percent of your cargo of hogsheads intact. The wine itself in these casks varies in quality from middling to quite flavorsome so, of course, each deserves its own valuation. Would you prefer I make an offer on each individually, probably ranging from three to seven pence per gallon, or a single amount for the lot?"

Christina's mouth worked to form a response, probably resembling the gasping maw of a pike her brother had once pulled from the Trave in Lübeck. She was so astounded by the vintner's sudden transformation from teacher to merchant that words did not come readily to her mouth.

She realized now she had been foolhardy in the extreme in taking on a cargo of wine, a commodity she knew little more about then what she had enjoyed from the brim of a cup. She had been fortunate indeed that Master de Grood had been an honest man, however, she knew she had still overpaid him for the wine, just not embarrassingly so.

I believe Master Baynard to be an honorable man as well. It seems better to deal with him, rather than risk being taken advantage of by someone else with far less scruples. The sooner I have rid myself of this cargo, the better I will feel!

Christina asked the vintner if he would be so good as to calculate his offer based upon the cargo of casks in their entirety. He said he would do so, returning in an hour or so to complete their negotiations. She readily agreed, chafing at yet another delay; yet, having no alternative but to do so.

As promised, Baynard returned and, after a bit of bargaining that seemed mostly a formality, they agreed on a purchase price. As was Christina's preference in all monetary transactions, they then traveled together to the London home of the Bardi family on Lombard Street in order to transfer the funds into her accounts held by the Florentine bankers. This business completed, she returned to *der Greif*.

She was somewhat surprised to see the casks already being unloaded, her crew members assisted by the vintner's stout laborers, all grunting and heaving to move the heavy barrels from the ship's hold. Christina observed that, while Matthias supervised the men's activities while on the ship, another man she did not know organized the efficient separation of the casks into diverse groupings wharf-side.

A practical division of labor.

While some of the casks were being loaded directly onto sturdy wagons hitched to large, placid dray horses, others were being repaired by a gang of coopers. She watched with interest as the men rolled the barrels to expose what must be the leaking staves. They then used an awl to make a hole, into which they tapped a conical piece of wood. She surmised the plug would be made from soft wood, one that would expand on contact with the liquid inside the cask, sealing the leak nicely.

Her interest in the coopers' work was distracted by the sudden appearance of two armed men in royal livery striding purposefully across the wharf and toward *der Greif's* mooring. Christina grew increasingly alarmed as the men came on deck and moved to confront Matthias. After a few words, the ship's master turned and pointed toward her.

She gulped involuntarily as the men approached, recalling it had only been a few months prior that she had been arrested and dragged through the streets to Newgate prison. She had absolutely no desire to reenact that scene now.

What do they want?

She wracked her brain to recall any new transgression she may have committed. She could not, and now they stood before her.

One asked directly through a mouthful of ruined teeth, "You be Frederick Kohl?"

"Aye," she replied, gazing evenly into the man's eyes as she voiced her response.

Her outward calmness belied the growing fear that nestled in her belly liked a coiled snake.

"You'd be comin' with us, if ya please, young master."

The man's terse words were direct and to the point.

I'll be damned if I'm going to let this saucy bastard order me about like a scullery dog!

"Where is it that we will be going? And did your master expressly instruct you to address me with such bold insolence?"

Christina's eyes were filled with growing fire as they continued to lock on those of the man who had spoken to her so rudely.

The man's face flushed with sudden alarm.

"Beggin' your pardon, young sir. I meant you no offense. I was told to fetch you to the Tower by his Grace, the Earl of Cornwall."

Christina's feelings of relief were palpable. She had first met Gaveston soon after arriving in London, when he rescued her from a band of varlets who had attacked her at the Nag's Head tavern. He had also given her a fair price for *der Greif's* entire cargo, something no London merchant had been prepared to do.

I owe much to this man.

"I will go," she said simply.

She walked over to Matthias to tell him to where she was traveling. Preoccupied with the final stages of the cargo transfer, he nodded but said nothing. Turning back, she followed the two liverymen as they began the journey to Tower Castle.

As she kept up with the men's brisk pace, she recalled the last time she had seen Gaveston, blind drunk and apparently fearing for his very life. He was convinced the other barons of the land were banding against him, jealous of the sway he held over the king. The earl had felt his arrest might be likely, a blade between the ribs even more so.

Soon they arrived at their destination. They passed over the sturdy oaken drawbridge spanning the broad wet moat and through the colossal stone curtain wall without being challenged by the soldiers guarding the entrance.

Once inside the castle complex, she was somewhat relieved to see the men were leading her toward the Lanthorn Tower, a structure she knew contained Gaveston's apartments.

At least he's not imprisoned in the dungeon. If he has experienced a fall from Edward's grace, at least it has not been too far.

Uncertain about the degree of warmth she would experience in Gaveston's reception, she climbed the stairs of the tower a touch hesitantly. The liveryman she had previously rebuked turned from the head of the stairs and motioned for her to hurry, clearly eager to complete the task he had been assigned and rid himself of this arrogant foreigner. She quickened her step and soon found herself facing the ornately carved door leading into the earl's apartments.

Suddenly, the door swung open and Gaveston stood before her. Any doubts she might have had concerning the earl's feelings toward her were quickly dispelled as he grabbed her firmly by the shoulders, pulled her toward him, and kissed her firmly on the lips. After a second or two, he pulled his head away, but a lingering taste of cinnamon continued to tantalizingly saturate her mouth. She smiled broadly at him; genuinely happy she had not fallen into his disfavor.

Gaveston extended his arm across her shoulders and guided Christina toward an intricately carved cherrywood divan set against the outer wall. She unconsciously noted it as a new addition to the room's opulent décor as they settled down upon the thick, blue upholstered cushions that padded its top. At last, Gaveston began to speak.

"My dear, dear Frederick. How pleased I am to see you once more! When I encountered Edmund, the king's chamberlain, at the keep, he told me of a German ship that had arrived with a hold bursting with Rhenish wine. I assumed the only merchant bold enough to choose to test the Channel waters in the dead of winter was Frederick Kohl. So, I chanced sending men to fetch this intrepid sailor and here you are!"

Gaveston vaguely motioned to his man servant who had been hovering inconspicuously in the corner of the room. Clearly familiar with the meaning of the earl's gesture, he quickly and efficiently poured two bowls of wine, handed them to Gaveston and Christina, and departed the room. He closed the door firmly behind him with an audible thud.

"But I am even more happy to see you again, Christina!'

Her mind momentarily turned to the last time she had been in this room. An overabundance of wine had prompted her to succumb to Gaveston's amorous advances, only to find he had thought he was seducing a boy rather than what he discovered was a maiden in disguise. Surprisingly, he had been greatly amused by her deception rather than angry. Besides Ziesolf and Trudi, he was the only person who held her most precious secret.

"And I you, your Grace, . . . I mean Piers!" she corrected herself immediately, remembering the man's insistence on informal address.

He laughed heartily, took a deep draught of his wine, and sprang to his feet.

"I have so much to tell you, my friend! Although Warwick and Lancaster tried to overthrow my influence at court, the King's friendship remains true and immutable. Their schemes came to naught, Christina!"

"That is very good news indeed," she agreed, although not as strongly as she might have.

Having enemies at one's back, retaining the ability to practice mischief, is still a worrisome concern.

"Yes! Yes, wonderful news. Why, the depth of the King's confidence in me is such that he even agreed to reform the royal household, if only I was to be allowed to return to his side! Oh, how he loves me, Christina!"

Gaveston now appeared to be almost beside himself with glee, literally prancing about the room and punctuating his words with emphatic gestures.

He then returned to sit closely beside her, his voice descending into a conspiratorial whisper.

"Do you want to know what else, my friend? While these other earls, these so-called "Ordainers," busy themselves haggling endlessly over the exact number of eyes needed to examine the king's stools each day, what will I be doing? I will be by the side of his beloved Majesty Edward, campaigning against the Scots in the North. No words for me, Christina, but instead actions to prove my value to England!"

Christina was taken aback to learn in such an offhand manner England was planning to attack its neighboring country to the north. She readily realized a major conflict would have a significant impact on both shipping and trade, not just with the vying nations, but others in the region as well. Consequently, she pressed Gaveston for additional information, and not just to satisfy her own innate curiosity.

"It is wonderful to see you in such a merry mood, friend Piers! When will you and the king move his army northward?" she queried, not so innocently.

Gaveston's beaming face took on a more thoughtful countenance as he gazed deeply into Christina's eyes, as if to judge whether he had already said too much. Then his smile returned and he raised the carefully manicured index finger of his right hand and waggled it a few inches in front of her nose.

"You are a sly one, Christina, I'll give you that. What merchant wouldn't want to know such information?"

She smiled in return and spread her hands in front of her in mock supplication. Gaveston laughed aloud once more, then took another heavy gulp of wine. He rose to his feet and walked away from her. He then stopped and hesitated for a few seconds before turning back in her direction.

"September, Christina. We will move the army northward in September."

Christina was confused a bit by the substance of the earl's disclosure.

It should take the King's forces at least a month or two to arrive on the border with Scotland. I thought armies were reluctant to fight in the winter?

She posed the question to Gaveston, who raised his bowl of wine in salute.

"God's teeth, Mistress Christina, you are an exceptional lass! Who would expect a woman to query of such things? No offense meant to your sex, of course."

She was rather perturbed by the man's dismissive slight, whether he meant it or not.

Does he not believe women have brains, and that most know how to use them better than their male counterparts?

Before she could voice her irritation, Gaveston continued.

"We know it to be a risk, but we plan on moving into winter quarters upon our arrival. With sufficient provisions on hand to sustain our hearty forces, we will be well set to counter the damnable Scots' raids on our territory as well as threaten them with those of our own. Then, with the arrival of spring, we will thrust our army northward to victory."

Christina nodded thoughtfully.

It seems like a sound plan, but hinges on many things going well and very few things going wrong.

She kept any further comments to herself, realizing the movement and deployment of vast armies was something of which she had no experience beyond the temper of common sense.

"Please forgive my rudeness. Enough talk of me, Christina! Allow me to pour us another bowl, then tell me of your own adventures since last we met!"

She had to stop and gather herself for a moment. It seemed she had lived a lifetime since she had last encountered Gaveston at the Nag's Head tavern, drunk, morose, and fearful for his life.

Christina began her tale with her uncle's murder, then on to his apprentice Richard's accusation against her as the perpetrator. Her arrest, her trial, her defeat of Richard in the wager by combat; she left few details out save for those that began as an attempt to evade her pursuers but ended as a night-long tryst with the young prostitute Sybille in the upstairs room of the Nag's Head.

That is a memory too private to share, even with a friend.

Gaveston did not pose any questions; instead, he seemed enthralled by Christina's account.

The man's eyes grew wide as she related the ordeal of the storm at sea and wider still as she described her fight in Sluys with the sailor, Arnst. Gaveston nodded thoughtfully as she told how she had pushed her opponent into the frigid sea waters afterwards.

"A fitting end for him, friend Christina. I hope he lets the icy remembrance of his meeting with you cool the heat of his temper the next time he seeks a fight."

She ended her account with a concise summary of *der Greif's* uneventful return to England.

For a few moments, the earl said nothing; then he remarked in a soft voice, "God's holy bones, Christina. You are the most formidable woman I have ever had the pleasure to meet!"

She blushed, gratified at what she knew was substantial praise.

"If one of the Kingdom's most adventuresome noblemen had told me such a tale, I would have still challenged the veracity of his recollection. Yet, you, a mere slip of a girl, relate it in such a matter-of-fact manner that I cannot help but believe it is true. Are you truly a reincarnation of Arthur Pendragon himself?"

Christina blushed again, imagining the earl was rendering her another compliment; yet, having no idea of the identity of the man to which she was being compared.

They talked on, comfortable in each other's company, until a servant brought in a lamp to assuage the late afternoon's gloom that had crept unbidden into the room.

This prompted Gaveston to exclaim, "I have stolen enough time from you for this day, Christina. I know you must be eager to return to your home and the bosom of your friends before dark."

She nodded in accord, knowing she had perhaps tarried too long here.

He rose and offered her his hand. Without thinking, she accepted it, rising to where she looked him steadily in his eyes.

He drew her into a close embrace, one which he held for some seconds. She responded in kind, drawing emotional sustenance from this man she knew so little; yet, understood so well.

He released her and stepped back.

"Know ye well you have another friend here in London town, one who holds you in great esteem. When I asked you to maintain your ship in London, I realized I was putting you at great risk, both financially and personally. But I had nowhere else to turn. I placed my life into the hands of a young woman, but one I sensed I could trust without question . . ."

A feeling of guilt and regret threatened to overwhelm her as mist clouded the corners of her eyes.

I swear to the Holy Virgin I will never again desert a friend in need, regardless of the consequences to myself.

". . . I pledge to you," he continued, "Upon my honor as a knight and a nobleman, I will be as a brother to you as long as I shall live."

For once ignoring the vast difference in their rank, it was now Christina's turn to catch Gaveston in a fierce embrace. Involuntarily, her thoughts turned to Frederick, the brother she had lost only months prior. Tears prompted by both her own repressed grief and Gaveston's chivalrous declaration rolled down her cheeks unimpeded by caution or embarrassment.

"And . . . and I a sister to you, dear Piers," she replied clumsily, uncertain if it was improper to address an earl with such familiarity.

"Now, go," he said, his beaming smile more than enough to destroy her doubts. "If not, we will spend the rest of the afternoon declaring our undying affection for each other.

He paused.

"An emotion that, for my part at least, needs no further verbalization, as I hope it's certainty is forever etched in your heart."

Christina felt weepy all over again. Not trusting her voice, she merely nodded and bid him adieu.

She departed the Tower grounds with a tremendous feeling of elation, immeasurably pleased Gaveston was safe, in the King's favor once again, and that he held her in such high esteem. She trod without thinking, like a birch leaf adrift on the water, buoyed by her inner happiness.

Eventually, she looked around to gather her bearings, finding her feet were carrying her to Bokerel House, the manor that was now her home.

Chapter 5

A Homecoming
London, March, 1310

As the sun disappeared behind the tall structures that bracketed Langburnestrate, her cheerfulness was dampened somewhat by the increasing chill in the air. Soon, enormous, intricately-formed snowflakes began to waft down from the sky. Although they were beautiful to behold, their fall upon her face added further to her discomfort. Christina was just beginning to shiver from the cold as she turned onto Bucklersbury Street. Within a couple of minutes, she perceived the outline of the stone archway that defined the entrance to her aunt's manor house.

My house.

She corrected herself absentmindedly as she hastened her step.

Approaching, she was surprised to find the wooden gates wide open and the yard filled with a flurry of activity. Two young men whom she did not know were hard at work repairing the door into one of the massive storerooms. Three others were busily unloading a two-wheeled car of what appeared to be foodstuffs into a smaller one. Christina began to salivate as she saw one of the men throw a large haunch of raw beef over his shoulder and carry it inside the dark entryway.

Sweet Jesus, have I really had nothing to eat since early this morn?

Never one to miss meals, the excitements of the day had uncharacteristically pushed the thought of food from her mind. Now, her empty stomach was growling for attention.

Her thoughts of a hearty supper were challenged, however, by a brooding sense of unease.

Who are these men?

The thought occurred to her that some legal calamity may have transpired and she could no longer claim the manor as her own.

Has my aunt reconsidered transferring the property to me? Have I inadvertently run afoul of the law once more?

Her misgivings disappeared in an instant when she heard a familiar voice behind her mutter, "Have you now grown so sure of yourself that you take no heed of someone approaching from behind you?"

She spun about and saw the weathered face of Kurt Ziesolf staring at her severely from his one good eye.

"Do you have no recollection of what I have taught you? Were the many hours I spent training you just a waste of my time? I would have kicked you squarely in the arse, had I not been so damned glad to see you!"

With that he uncharacteristically rushed forward and caught her in a tight embrace. She gave as good as she got, overwhelmingly happy to see the old knight healthy and in good spirits.

Ziesolf relinquished his hold and stepped back. He turned about and saw most of the workmen were staring at him and Christina. Although he said nothing, the men returned to their tasks hastily, obviously not wanted to risk arousing his ire.

Noticing Christina following his gaze, Ziesolf stated, "A good lot, all of them. I'll introduce you to 'em on the morrow. But now, let's get you out of this damnable night air before you come down with the croup. There's someone inside who might like to learn you're back."

Christina and Ziesolf strode purposefully up the steps and through the heavy oaken door of the manor house. Passing through the screened entrance passageway, she was amazed to find a bevy of young women energetically going about diverse tasks in the house's main hall. Christina looked about at the girls scrubbing the wooden trestle tables, polishing pewter tankards, and laying fresh rushes on the floor. Her eyes soon fell on two young women deep in conversation in the upper corner of the room. One was tall and thin, gazing toward one of the green-tinged glass windows that peaked overhead. The other's gaze was also toward the window glass, but the index finger of her right hand pointed upward as well. Clearly, she was providing detailed instructions of some kind.

Her message communicated, the smaller of the two girls turned about, noticing Christina's presence for the first time. A wide smile appeared on her face and she ran forward at a pace that belied her sturdy frame. Immediately, Christina was engulfed in another embrace, one even stronger than those she had endured from either of the two men earlier.

"Oh, Christina, it's so good to have you back!" Trudi whispered, before separating herself slightly and rendering a short, demure courtesy.

"Forgive me please, Master Frederick, but I was overcome with pleasure at your return. It is so good to see you back among us, safe and sound!"

All work in the room had ceased as the women now gawked at Christina as if she were a fish with two heads.

Trudi clapped her hands loudly, then said, "All right, you lot, back to work. We don't want Master Fredrick thinkin' he's paying you for doin' nothing, do we now?"

Having temporarily forgotten Ziesolf was still there in her joy at reuniting with her best friend, Christina was surprised to hear him say, "I know you are busy setting tasks for the morrow, Mistress Trudi, so we will not hold you up any longer. We will be in the solar; so join us, if you please, when you can get away."

Following Ziesolf from the hall to the more intimate room, Christina fixed the back of the man with a quizzical look. Somehow, while she had been away, the dynamic between the nobleman and the young servant girl had changed. She made a mental note to pursue the subject further, but at a later time.

For now, Christina's only desire was to luxuriate in the pleasant warmth of the room. She removed her heavy traveling cloak and tossed it in a heap upon a small table, then moved closely beside the brazier whose small yellow flames leapt merrily, radiating heat throughout the room. She rubbed her hands together briskly then held them palms downward above the fire, forcing the cold from her fingertips.

Meanwhile, Ziesolf had pulled a large chair with a light green cushion intricately embroidered with an image of a peafowl closer to the fire and motioned for her to sit. As she made herself comfortable, she realized guiltily she had undoubtedly appropriated her late uncle's seat in the room.

Ziesolf cleared his throat but, before he could speak, Trudi bustled into the room. Although Christina could not imagine a happier sight than to see her dear friend, she was nearly as pleased by the arrival of a waiflike young woman who followed in her wake, carrying a large tray of food and drink in her hands.

"Sit that down on the table here, Mary," Trudi directed the girl as she moved a small table to the side of Christina's chair. "Careful now, the idea is to have her eat it, not wear it."

Mary smiled at Christina as she deftly did as she was told.

"Now begone with you, girl. There's still baking aplenty to be finished before your chores are over."

"Yes, Mistress," she replied.

She took a quick glance at Christina before she exited the room, a quick smile ghosting across her thin lips.

"That one's a bit too clever for her own good," Trudi remarked dryly before taking a seat herself. "She's just fifteen, but she's a hard worker and gets along well with Bess, the cook. Sweet Jesus, Christina, was I that saucy when I was her age?"

Christina giggled and said around a large mouthful of heavily buttered bread, "I'm sure she can't hold a candle to your antics, Trudi. Remember the time you organized the kissing contest? You told the boys they had to choose which of us was the better kisser, a task to which they eagerly agreed. So, you had them stand up and blindfolded the lot of them. Then you took Otto by the hand, moved him in front of Heinrich, and pushed his head forward. Oh, my God, Trudi! Heinrich kissed him and then stuck his tongue into Otto's mouth! Well, Otto liked it so much that he moved his hand to the back of Heinrich's head to draw him closer. It was only then he discovered he had been made such a fool!"

Even Ziesolf grinned at the tale, saying, "Do I dare ask what happened next?"

Picking up the telling, Trudi remarked, "Well, when we saw the shocked look on their faces after they tore the blindfolds off, all we could do was roll around on the ground, so overwhelmed by laughter that we nearly pissed ourselves. Then we got up and ran for our lives into the house. We didn't go outside for a week after that 'cause we were certain they'd murder us."

At that, Trudi arose and said to Christina, "Now, eat; you must be famished. I'll go and get the girls to heat water for a nice hot bath for you. I can't imagine you've washed in a while because, frankly my dear sweet sister, you stink like a bear! We'll have time enough later to hear of your journey."

After she had left the room, Christina queried Ziesolf.

"It may just be my imagination, but is there something different about Trudi?"

Ziesolf looked at Christina intently with his good eye and asked, "Different? In what way?"

"Well, it's hard to put my finger on it really. She just seems so ... so ... so self-assured."

"Do you mean she is not the childish girl who was terrified to leave your side in Greenwich only a couple of months ago? Yes, I believe you are correct."

Christina stammered, "But what ... how?"

Ziesolf leaned back on the stool on which he was sitting and said, "When we returned to London, your aunt was preparing to depart. Before she did, however, she spoke confidentially with Trudi for a long while. I paid them little mind as I had tasks of my own that needed attention, but I did see Trudi paying close heed to Frau Kohl's words."

Christina nodded, urging the man to continue.

"After your aunt left, Trudi came to see me. She asked what were my intentions as to the running of the household. I was taken aback as, truthfully, I had not given thought to such matters. When I told her this, she asked if she might be allowed to take on these duties. I hesitated, thinking she lacked the good sense and maturity needed for the position, but she persisted. I finally relented, partly through the force of her arguments, but also because of the complications inherent to, how should I say, your unique needs?"

There was utter silence in the room, save for the slight crackling coming from the brazier. Christina waited impatiently for Ziesolf to continue.

"Since that day, Trudi has been the mistress of the house. When I provided her with what I believed was an adequate sum for necessary expenditures, she looked at me sourly and told me in no uncertain terms that what I offered was not nearly enough to pay half the staff that was required to maintain such an enormous dwelling. I countered by stating that, in Lübeck, your mother had made do with a kitchen staff of three and but two maids, one of whom was quite young and basically useless. Trudi did not rise to the jibe, however. Instead, she said there are nearly four times the number of rooms here, plus the enormous size of the great hall itself. She ticked her fingers as she named a variety of maids; chamber, scullery, kitchen, laundry, and more, who were needed to efficiently attend to the required tasks. I relented, firstly because I myself had no experience in such matters and secondly, because it was clear to me, she did. Since that time, your house has been Trudi's domain and, I am pleased to report, she has justified my trust. I have been in many noble houses throughout the continent and none exceeds yours in the quality of its table or the cleanliness of its spaces."

"When Matthias arrived this morning to inform us you had arrived, she immediately dispatched the cook and two of the yard men to the market to purchase fresh meats. Then she set her maids about their tasks with a vengeance. Not one dares to shirk her tasks, lest she would run afoul of their mistress' keen eye and even sharper tongue. One might almost imagine it was your mother's maid Anna who ruled this house and not her younger sister."

Christina's mouth stood wide open, as amazed by Ziesolf's recounting of Trudi's achievements as if he had said her maid had sprouted wings and flew about the hall like a bird.

Former maid, that is. Trudi has no more need for that title as she is now my chamberlain, my housekeeper, and, yes, the mistress of my household. Most importantly of all though, she is still my most trusted friend. Hopefully, she does not take on too many of Anna's more annoying traits.

She grimaced, remembering ruefully how she had loathed the older sister nearly as much as she loved the younger.

Her reverie was broken by Trudi's return to the room.

"That's enough talk for now, Christina. Come, the bath water grows colder by the minute."

Christina obediently followed Trudi through the doorway leading out of the solar and up the broad passageway leading to the primary private apartments of the manor. She was surprised when Trudi did not slow as they passed the door on the right side of the hallway that was the entrance to the room that had been Christina's when her uncle had owned the house.

Instead, they passed further up the long hallway to its end. Before them was a large oaken door, intricately carved with cavorting forest creatures. A pair of sly conies, the heads of a majestic stag, a ferocious bear, and a narrow-faced boar all looked back at her through marvelously lifelike eyes. Christina was absolutely mesmerized by the skill of the craftsman who had created this masterpiece.

Trudi hugged her and said softly, "I knew you would like such a thing."

Christina nodded mutely.

Her friend swung the door open and Christina entered a spacious room dimly lit by several candles and well-tended flames that danced in a massive stone fireplace set in the wall before her. As her eyes adjusted to the light in the room, she noticed a large wooden bathing vessel set closely to the side of the fire with vapors of steam hovering above the surface of the enclosed water.

"Oh Trudi," Christina crooned, "You don't know how many times I would have given my soul for even a cloth and fresh water with which to clean myself. Now this!"

She was overjoyed.

"All right then," Trudi replied, "It feels even better than it looks. In you go!"

Between her eagerness and Trudi's practiced hands, it was not long before Christina had been stripped of all her clothes. Placing her right hand on her friend's shoulder, she lifted her left leg and stepped into the tub. She gasped with pleasure as the heat of the water permeated her flesh, almost but not quite too warm to bear. She shifted her weight, bringing her other leg in as well. She turned and slowly lowered her back down to rest on the bleached woolen toweling that lined the bath.

Christina felt her muscles turn to jelly as she surrendered to the sensuous pleasure of the steaming liquid. For the first time she noticed the intoxicating scent of rose oil in the water.

I could stay here for the next year and still be filled with regret when it came to an get out.

Trudi removed her own outer garments, then pushed up the sleeves of her chemise. Picking up a small ceramic bowl that had rested inconspicuously on a side table, she knelt beside the bathing vessel and placed the bowl beside her on the floor. She then began to slowly work out the tangles in Christina's hair. She dipped her right hand down into the bowl repeatedly, massaging the mixture of ash, myrtle berries, and egg whites into the unruly locks. Afterwards, she used the bowl to dip bathwater from the tub, pouring it over Christina's head in a thorough rinse.

Trudi's hand next appeared from over her shoulder holding a large sponge. She immersed it into the water before her then Christina felt it move back to her shoulder. The sponge moved upon her skin with a circular caress rather than a perfunctory scrubbing motion.

Christina surrendered herself totally to Trudi's touch as the woman passed the sponge down the length of her mistress' body. She felt her small rosy nipples harden as the sponge moved in circular motions over her breasts, then eventually downward.

"Ow!" Christina yelped in pain.

Trudi bolted upright, a look of concern transforming her face.

"Sorry," Christina muttered through clenched teeth, "Just don't touch my side there."

"Turn over," Trudi commanded.

Christina grumpily complied.

The other woman inhaled sharply, suddenly alarmed at the deep purple and yellow bruising that marred Christina's otherwise unblemished ivory white skin.

Before Trudi could ask, Christina said, "I got into a bit of a scrap as we were leaving Flanders. The man I was fighting fared far worse; mine will heal completely in time, his will not. Actually, it's much better now than it was."

She flashed a wan smile at her friend, hoping her concise explanation would belay the other woman's concerns. It did not.

"Christina! In case you've forgotten, you are a girl, and a hopelessly pigheaded and stupid one at that! What did Ziesolf tell you? That the most important thing you must remember is you must preserve your secret at all costs. Otherwise, your world comes tumbling down like an ill-stacked cord of wood! You can't just go around fighting every man you meet. Sooner or later, one will best you, even if it's by cheating or through dumb luck. Are you listening at all to what I'm saying?"

Trudi's face was flushed with emotion as she looked down at her friend.

Christina chewed at her lip as she looked upward into the young woman's face. She didn't know what to say in reply that would assuage her friend's fears. So, she just stuck out her tongue.

Trudi's face clouded then she erupted into laughter as she said, "You are such an incorrigible brat! Lay back down and let me finish your bath before the water grows cold. Or I decide to drown you, whichever comes first."

"Yes, Mother," Christina replied mockingly.

Trudi's scolding was soon forgotten as she resumed the task of bathing her friend. Christina relaxed and gave herself completely into her friend's care. Soon, her eyes grew heavy as the excitement of the long day finally caught up with her.

Without warning, the water began to cool.

What the hell?

The now icy water began to rise, over her chest, neck, and then threatening to engulf her mouth. She looked about frantically and saw she was in her cabin in *der Greif.*

Dear Lord, we must be sinking!

She struggled to rise, to escape, but she could not.

Something is holding me down!

To her horror, she saw the mocking eyes of Arnst, the man with whom she had fought in Sluys, staring down at her, his hands resisting her efforts to stand. Although his lips moved to form words, she could not hear them.

What is it he is trying to tell me?

She awoke with a start; suddenly aware she had been violently thrashing about in the water of the bath. She saw now it was Trudi holding her, but protectively to her breast rather than threateningly. Christina's breath came in ragged gasps as she gulped the air greedily, immensely relieved to find she had no water in her lungs to purge.

Trudi released Christina, arose, and moved away, a look of fearfulness in her eyes. Her thin linen smock was soaked, clearly revealing the features of her somewhat ample body underneath. She felt no embarrassment, however, only deep concern.

"Are you alright? You fell asleep and then you had such a terrible nightmare that I feared for your life! I tried to comfort you but you struggled to push me away, calling me by a strange name! Are you alright?" she repeated.

"Yes." Christina replied. "I am now at least." She flashed what she hoped Trudi would perceive as a reassuring smile.

She felt anything but relieved herself, however. She did not know whether the dream stemmed from her fears during the storm as well as her fight with Arnst, or if it was a portent of dangers to come. Either way, it had shaken her to her very bones.

Trudi looked as though she wanted to ask Christina about the dream, but decided instead to hold her tongue, for now at least.

"Well, it seems your bath has come to a rather abrupt end, since there is now more water on me and the floor than in the tub. Stand up and let's get you dried before you catch your death of the cold."

Christina obeyed without speaking, letting Trudi rub her vigorously with a large, thick woolen towel until her body grew rosy red from the friction. Christina then began to reach for the clothing she had taken off earlier. Moving more quickly, Trudi snatched the garments away, holding them closely to her, then quickly away at arms' length.

"Oh no you don't," she said in a warning voice, while simultaneously wrinkling her nose. "You're lucky if we'll ever be able to get these clean. We might have to burn 'em instead!"

"All right," Christina conceded.

Now that she was clean herself, she did perceive the putrid stench arising from the garments her friend held in her hands.

"Well then, will you please fetch me some clean ones from my room? Or do you expect me to prance down the hallway naked to get them myself?"

Trudi momentarily looked at her quizzically then said, "Your clothes are not down the hall, you silly goose, these are your apartments now."

Christina looked about the room in shock.

How can all of this be my room?

Her family had been one of the wealthiest in all of Lübeck ; yet, her father's chamber was not nearly so grand while her own had been tiny and mean compared to that in which she now stood.

Her astonishment grew as Trudi led her through another doorway beside the fireplace and into the adjacent bedchamber which, if anything, was even more ostentatious. Plush embroidered tapestries hung on the walls, rivaling even those in Gaveston's apartments in the Tower. The focal point of the room, however, was the massive wooden bed, possibly white poplar with a walnut veneer, that dominated the room. In the middle of the headboard was a marquetry swag of spindle wood, above which, a thickly posted canopy stretched upwards, intermittently carved with birds in flight that seemed almost lifelike. Gorgeous interlined drapes of blue silk were pushed back, revealing a magnificently embroidered hunting scene on a coverlet of what must be silk. Christina's mouth gaped at the opulent beauty of the room like that of a country bumpkin on his first trip to the city.

Trudi's voice shook her from her reverie.

"Might I suggest you forego dressing and simply slip into your bed? There will be time enough in the morn to tell Ziesolf and me the story of your journey, as well as for us to tell you what has happened here since you left. Although our tales may not be as exciting as yours, they should be of interest nonetheless."

Although Christina opened her mouth to protest, she closed it just as quickly.

What she says makes sense. I am exhausted, and there is nothing to be said that cannot wait until the morning.

Christina pulled back the coverlet and saw to her further amazement that the underside was lined with white rabbit fur. She then peeled back the cambric linen top-sheet and crawled underneath, discovering to her further delight she was nestled atop what must certainly be a thick mattress of goose down. She knew she must beg the Lord's forgiveness at her next confession for indulging so shamelessly in the pleasures of the flesh this bed so lavishly provided.

"Trudi, tell Ziesolf I have unexpectedly taken ill this night, for I vow to never leave this bed for the next three days!" she said only half-jokingly.

Trudi responded with a chuckle. "You say that now, but I know you will up early in the morning, foraging for bread and ale before the sun rises in the east." She bent and kissed Christina firmly on the lips. "Now sleep, my love. I must hurry away before one of the girls suspects something untoward between us. Their wagging tongues will have sport enough without giving them the proof of their own eyes upon which to base their tales upon. Besides, one of them might then be so bold as to try to sneak into your chamber of her own accord!"

Trudi's eye flashed a small conspiratorial wink, then she laughed. She kissed Christina once again, this time on the forehead. When she left the room, Christina's thoughts drifted back to when she was small and her mother had kissed her goodnight in much the same way.

Yes, Trudi is different, but certainly not in a displeasing way.

She burrowed deeper into the comforts of her bed, feeling happy, safe, and loved.

Chapter 6

New Friends and Old
London, March, 1310

It seems the wench know me better than I know myself.

Christina grumpily sat up in bed, the rumbling complaints of her stomach demanding she arise and break her fast.

She looked about her and, for the first time, beheld her bed chamber in the light. It was even more beautiful than what she had observed the night before. The sunrise streamed through the narrow, peaked windows to her right, the parti-colored glass of their oriel panes painting a delightful rainbow that danced across the wood inlayed floor.

Regretfully, she turned away from the light, pushed back her covers, and swung her legs over the side of the bed. She stood up and braced herself for the feel of the cold morning air on her naked skin. Surprisingly, the room instead felt comfortably warm. She looked to the fireplace in its casement of Flemish tiles and saw several small logs had already been reduced to glowing embers in the fire-dogs.

How in the world?

She was puzzled how someone had been able to steal into the room without causing her to awaken. The mystery was solved when she noted the fireplace was also open to the reception room in which she had bathed the previous evening. Nodding slowly, Christina admired the architect's foresight that had allowed for the fire to be tended without intruding on the bedchamber's slumbering inhabitant.

A cursory inspection of the room revealed no clothing, so she padded into the other in her bare feet. There, she discovered a set of clothing had been set out for her, as well as a hearty plate of food. She looked from one item to the other, undecided as to which she should address first. Grabbing a thick slice of manchet loaf, she swirled one end into a bowl of creamy, sweet butter. This went quickly into her mouth. Delighted at the taste and her hunger momentarily abated, she set about dressing herself.

Christina hesitated before beginning, wondering whether she should avail herself of the ewer and bowl set over in the corner for a quick wash. She decided against it, thinking Trudi's thorough scrubbing of her body the previous evening would have cleansed her sufficiently.

Instead, she picked up the linen braies that were placed atop the stack of clothing. She sat down on a nearby stool and pulled the garment up over her legs. Now standing, she raised them further, over her hips and to her waist. She then pulled the drawcord taunt and rolled it over several times to prevent it from cutting into her skin.

She took another bite of bread before taking on what was a necessary, but somewhat onerous, part of her daily dressing routine. Taking the long strip of unbleached linen from the pile, she began the tedious task of wrapping it about her chest. She wondered whether Trudi had placed the clothing in the room or if she had instead delegated the task to one of the maids.

Would someone as sharp as that girl Mary wonder as to the purpose of a long strip of linen among her master's clothing? Or perhaps Trudi had told her about the injury to my ribs as justification?

She reminded herself to remember to ask her later.

After pinning the material closed, she rewarded herself with a bite of the cold pork shoulder aspic. The savory taste nearly overwhelmed her taste buds, with cardamom, pepper, and coriander all vying for her attention. She had to fight down the urge to gobble the rest down right there and then.

With the thought of the remaining repast that awaited her, Christina finished dressing rapidly. She again sat down to pull woolen chausses over her legs, one of green and one of blue. She then tied these to the braies. Next, a white linen shirt, followed by a tunic of brilliant red, which fell almost to her knee. She was delighted to find one of her favorite garments, a grey squirrel fur-lined pelisson, was included in the stack. She donned this over her tunic. A dark green woolen hood completed her ensemble, save for the sturdy leather boots which she pulled on last.

After quickly dispensing with the remainder of her morning feast, Christina departed the room and stepped back out into the long hallway.

She halted for a moment as a thought suddenly occurred to her.

This house may now be mine; yet, I am familiar with no more than a handful of its rooms.

She grew excited at the possibility of exploring the house.

Should I ask Trudi to accompany me? she thought.

She decided to consider this option later, depending upon whether her friend had available time.

Christina passed through the house quickly, the warmth of her winter clothes already causing her to become somewhat overheated. She passed through the exterior door and into the yard, which already held several men going about their tasks.

She noticed Ziesolf gauging the men's labors from near the gates. She waved her hand to get his attention, a gesture he returned as he began to walk her way.

"Good morning, Frederick," he stated amiably, slipping nimbly into addressing her in her masculine guise.

"And to you, Herr Ziesolf."

She looked around and made a wide gesture encompassing the expanse of the yard.

"Are all of these men employed here?" she asked. When he nodded, she observed, "It seems they number almost as many as the crew of *der Greif.*"

"'Tis no more than what is needed. Today we will be fetching the cargo from your ship, as well as taking delivery of six cords of good birch firewood. I would not have scheduled both for the same day, had I known in advance of *der Greif's* arrival."

Christina nodded and asked, "Well, should the men not now be introduced to the one who pays their wages?"

Ziesolf grinned and gave out a call for the men to gather round.

The workers stepped away from their tasks and began to walk toward Ziesolf and the unknown young man who stood by his side. They formed into a rough semicircle about six feet in front of the two.

"Well lads," Ziesolf began, "I told you our employer would be arriving soon and here he is. This is Master Frederick Kohl and he has just returned from a trading voyage to Flanders."

The group eyed Christina with mild interest. She was somewhat disappointed they did not seem impressed by the fact she had undertaken such a voyage in the dead of winter. Then she remembered probably none of them had ever been more than a few miles from where they now stood and had no idea of the perils the journey could entail.

They probably would have been more impressed if he had told them I had made a trip to Shrewsbury and back.

Ziesolf continued. "Master Frederick, that man over on the left is our new smith. Although his given name is Petrus, everyone calls him as Black Peter instead."

Christina judged the man to be in his middle to late twenties. At first, she was surprised by the small stature of the smith, that was until she noted the massive forearms and bulging biceps that provided a strong indication he could well meet the physical demands of his profession. He had a pleasantly rounded face, with well-separated brown eyes that sparkled out from beneath a shock of raven hair. He said nothing, but bowed his head toward her in respectful acknowledgement.

"Those two burly fellows next to him are Osbert and Warin, two of our yard men."

Christina understood the title of yardman was a bit misleading. In addition to performing manual labor, these men were expected to serve as guards for the compound.

Clearly, the massive size of these two will serve as a ready deterrent to thieves and rogues alike.

Ziesolf next pointed toward a gangling youth of approximately her own age with an unruly shock of tufted red hair.

"This one here is Malcolm, our stableman. Don't hold the fact he's a semi-tamed Scotsman against him, he's a wonder with horses and knows his way around a smithy as well."

The lad's ruddy freckled face lit up with an infectious wide grin that lightened the rather formal mood of the morning.

"I ken also ply the harp and sing lak a burd, Yung Sur," the youth added.

This one's worth seems to far outweigh his appearance, Christina thought.

"Valuable skills all," Christina replied, "There's nothing so cheerful as a merry tune."

The boy beamed, nodded, and tugged his forelock in a gesture of deference.

Ziesolf introduced the remainder of the men and, stepping to the side, looked at Christina expectantly.

Christ's holy nails, does he expect me to make a speech?

She wracked her brain for inspiring words appropriate for the occasion; yet, none popped into her brain.

Well, I have to say something.

"Er, uh, men," she began hesitantly.

Well. that's certainly a piss-poor beginning!

"I place complete faith in Herr Ziesolf's ability to judge men. He selected each of you, so I am as confident in you as if I had chosen you myself. Therefore, do not betray our trust. Work hard and be loyal, I cannot ask for more. For my part, you will be paid both well and on time, as well as being looked after as members of my household. Does any man among you have something to ask?"

Christina gazed evenly at the men who stood before her. Many of them were shifting their weight from foot to foot like a herd of restless cattle, embarrassed to be the focus of her attention.

Unexpectantly, Ziesolf interjected, "All right then, back to work, you lot. Did you think you'd just be left standing there until one of you addle-brains figured out something to say?"

The men turned and walked away, seemingly relieved to be returning to the duties they knew. Christina was happy to notice it seemed they were in a good mood, murmuring to each other in low voices as they went about their labors.

I certainly hope it's not disparaging comments made at my expense.

She feared she had made a fool of herself.

As if sensing her self-doubt, Ziesolf said, "Well put, Master Frederick. The men appreciated those words coming from you."

Christina exhaled deeply in relief.

He continued, "Now, we must let them get about their work. We will momentarily dispatch our cart to the wharf to begin loading *der Greif's* cargo and bringing it back here. We have cleaned out yonder storeroom for it."

With a nod of his head, he indicated one of the larger doors on the left side of the yard.

She walked forward, opened the door, and stepped inside. Although the floor appeared dry, there was a familiar musty smell in the room. Christina returned to the yard and picked up a small ladder she had noticed outside the woodshop. She returned to the storeroom and, placing the top of the ladder against the outside wall, began to climb. Nearing the ceiling of the room, she leaned forward, running her hand along the outside beam.

She called down to Ziesolf, "As I feared, there is a bit of damp seeping through the wall here. Not enough to matter for the storage of most cargoes, but far too much for a shipment of fine Flemish cloth."

Ziesolf was clearly embarrassed he had not discovered the leak himself. He opened his mouth to voice what was obviously to be words of apology, but was cut off by Christina's own words before he could speak.

"When I was young, I heard my father cursing loudly in the gable storeroom of our home in Lübeck. He was normally a mild-mannered person and not given to voicing the terrible oaths I often heard from other men as a matter of course. Curious, I went up the stairs to investigate. Hiding behind a crate, I saw my father show two workmen where a tile in the roof had slipped, allowing moisture to seep into the room below. They hurried away to make the repair. My father, on the other hand, remained, uttering curses under his breath as he unrolled a bolt of spoiled cloth. I had not forgotten the distinct reek of damp mold I smelled on that day, one which I recalled when I entered this storeroom."

"This room is sufficient for the wine tuns, but set the men to making sure the wall is made watertight as soon as possible. As for the fabric, speak with Trudi to identify a suitable room in the house that is not in use. We will store the bales of cloth there."

Ziesolf nodded silently and walked rapidly away to carry out Christina's instructions.

Leaving the men to their labors, she returned to the hall of the house to find the maids' equally as busy inside as their male counterparts outdoors. Trudi called them from their duties and, as Ziesolf had done earlier, informed Christina as to their names and duties. She was relieved when Trudi shooed them briskly back to their tasks rather than expect her to address them.

With the men and women of the house's staff hard at work under the watchful eyes of Ziesolf and Trudi, Christina suddenly felt somewhat redundant. Having nothing else to fill her time, she decided to begin an exploration of her house.

Over three hours later she sat down on the dusty floor of yet another disused room.

I had no idea the house was so immense. Why in the world would someone build such a structure?

She licked her parched lips, already knowing the answer.

The larger and more impressive the home, the greater its residents' prestige. It seems a bit illogical though. If someone had a fleet of twenty ships and only three ever left port, I'd call them stupid, not impressive. How silly are the rich!

Christina had begun her inspection in the kitchens, where doors had led to a maze of larders, both wet and dry; two pantries; the buttery, the ewery, and a middling-sized counting house. An inconspicuous door led to a small garden to the rear of the house where the boiling house and wood store were located. As she entered back into the house proper, she noticed a small side portal leading into a most charming garden parlor, with a bank of windows looking out upon the now ill-attended botanical plot.

I must speak with Ziesolf about this. Perhaps one of the men has a hand for gardening. If not, I will see one is hired. The outdoor space is simply too lovely to allow to remain in such abject ruin. I can readily see myself spending lavish hours ensconced here in the summertime.

She left her new-found idyll and retraced her steps to the great hall, stopping for a swift draught of ale along the way. Then it was up the main stairway to the floor above. On the right side of her uncle's chambers she now occupied, there were three others that were vacant. On the opposite side of the passageway were those occupied by Ziesolf, Trudi, and the one in which she herself had stayed while a guest in the house All of these were arranged down the central hallway leading from the stairs.

Christina went back to the landing, turning down the hallway leading to the right. She explored eight more empty chambers as she worked deeper into the house, four complete with wardrobe rooms and the other two with smaller closets. As the passage made a bend to the left, a door stood before her. She opened it to find a small balcony surrounded by a finely carved stone balustrade overlooking the green space she had discovered below.

Another pleasant diversion for a sunny day.

Realizing she had already devoted more time to her exploration than she had originally intended, she went back inside and walked further down the gallery. At its end, a large doorway opened into perhaps her most astonishing discovery of the day: a small chapel. She descended a narrow wooden stairway to the floor, paved in a quatrefoil pattern with green and yellow Flemish tiles. Beneath the high, groin-vaulted ceiling, the plastered walls had octagonal pinnacles formed by narrow traceried panels at the upper corners, matching the traceried niches between the windows on the outer wall. At a raised dais at the front of the room stood a stone altar, upon which rested a small, simple cross crafted from silver. On a small table to the left were the remnants of several candles.

The floor, like the other rooms in this portion of the house, was covered in dust, although much more lightly so. Peering closely, Christina could just make out sets of footprints approaching the altar, then melding into a more indistinct shape where someone had obviously knelt to pray.

It seems obvious this chapel served only as my Aunt Matilda's private sanctuary. Its condition seems to indicate a proper mass has not been said here for a long time. I can imagine her kneeling here, alone except for the reassuring presence of Christ. Thank you once again, dear aunt, for bequeathing me such a wonderous abode. This is another space I would like to see restored to its past grandeur.

She made the sign of the cross and departed the chapel, retracing her steps back the way she had come. Christina promised herself she would tour the upper floor, where the female staff were accommodated, at a later day. She also remembered she had not yet explored the cellars beneath the house, adding those to her future agenda as well.

I should probably also take the opportunity to descend the several sets of servants' stairs I passed to make my appraisal complete,

She realized she would need another full day for these tasks.

As she descended to the ground floor, she was distracted both by a clatter of horses' hooves on the flagstones of the yard and the enticing aroma of cooking emanating from the kitchen. She walked toward the great hall, resisting the urge to follow her nose instead. She was surprised to find not only many of the men to whom she had been introduced earlier in the day moving toward the tables and benches, which were being already laden with savory dishes, but the crew of *der Greif* as well.

Spotting Christina, Reiniken waved and sauntered toward her.

"Christ's blessed bollocks, Yur Worship, what a toothsome gaggle of wenches yuv got yurself here," he said, admiring the young women scurrying about filling tankards and setting large platters of meat and other foodstuffs on the tables. "Tell me which one ya have yur eye set on. I'll be well satisfied with ma pick from the rest ya know."

He gave Christina a lecherous wink for emphasis.

"Sit your randy ass down at the table, Wig," she said laughingly, clapping him heartily on the back for emphasis. "Let's take care of one appetite before you start thinking about another, shall we?"

The colossal sailor readily did as he was told and soon joined his fellows in consuming what amounted to a substantial feast. Spit-roasted beef haunch, pork loins, and honey-baked chicken vied with meat-filled pies as the diners' favorites. All the bits of which were washed down with multiple tankards of ale.

Something seemed a little peculiar to Christina, however, although she had a hard time placing it. Eventually, she identified it to be the behavior of *der Greif's* crew. As she would have expected, Matthias ate sparingly and relatively quietly, every so often exchanging a word or two with another of the men. It was the behavior of the other sailors that amazed her, however.

Left to their ease as they were now, she would have expected them to break out in lustily obscene songs or to be pawing at the young women who were serving them.

I wouldn't even be surprised if Ziesolf would have had to break up a fight or two between the crewmen and the men of the manor over some imagined slight or offense.

She was somewhat befuddled that, instead, it seemed the crewmen were on their best behavior.

Perhaps they're daunted by the size of the hall; surely. it is probably the largest enclosed space in which they have ever been, save church. Or maybe they're doing it out of respect for me.

The thought came to her unbeckoned.

Surely not, she countered dismissively, recalling Reiniken's habitual irreverence toward her.

Yet, when one of his fellows belched loudly, Wig fixed the man with a murderous glare, causing him to beg everyone's forgiveness.

A lump formed in her throat from her sudden realization for the affection she felt for these men with whom she had faced such adversity. Then she looked around the room. Ziesolf, Trudi, and the other men and women who now staffed the manor all looked to her for their sustenance and protection as well.

Holy Mary . . .

She prayed silently to herself, suddenly overwhelmed by the sheer magnitude of her newly realized responsibilities.

Could it really be less than a year ago Mother was scolding me for leaving my shift lying about on the floor? Then, I was just a girl with few cares in the world. Now; a ship, a house, servants, a crew, and cargoes; the safety and security of each resting on the soundness of my decisions.

She suddenly felt small and alone.

The sound of a low, clear voice shook her from her meandering self-doubts. She looked up from her food and saw the stable boy she had met that morning standing to her left in the upper corner of the hall in what she realized was a small gallery. In his hands he held a small triangular shape. He deftly moved the fingers of his right hand and melodious musical notes seemed to fill the vast room, matching those of the song he was singing.

What was his name again?

She wracked her brain for an answer.

Malcolm! That was it!

She gave no further mind to her thoughts or worries, now completely enraptured by his music.

Christina could not comprehend all of the words of Malcolm's song; she was certain some were unique to the land of his birth while others probably only seemed strange because of his thick accent. Regardless, she was able to understand the gist of the song. Malcolm sang of a young man who leaves his young wife to go to war. When he returns, he finds she had died. Having no reason to stay in his village, he now wanders the earth, a lost soul even while still living.

Tears flowed freely down her cheeks as the haunting melody came to a close. She gazed around the now silent room to find many others had been as profoundly affected by the music as she. Her attention returned to Malcolm as he began to play once more on the instrument. Now, however, his hand fairly skimmed the strings in a blur. As his voice joined in, a tune as merry as the last had been sad echoed about the hall. Some people began to clap along to the beat while others pounded the tables before them. By the time the song ended, a happy mood had been restored throughout the room.

Not long afterward, Christina was surprised to notice the sailors begin to rise from their benches and make ready to depart.

She walked over to Reiniken and said, "What? Are you leaving now, Wig? You're more than welcome to spend the night; there's ample room for you about the hall here. I might even be able to find a bit more ale for you," she added merrily.

The mountainous man looked at her and shook his head.

"Naw, the boys and me need to shove off, first night back in port and all, ya understand?"

Christina smiled and nodded, well aware of the sailors' assorted vices.

Suddenly, Reiniken's face grew solemn and he said, "We wants to thank ye and yur womenfolk for includin' us in yur homecoming. Not a one of us has ever had such a feast, nor et in such a fancy hall. Ya've done good fur yourself, Master Frederick, ya certainly have."

She was completely taken aback by the man's heartfelt sentiments. She could barely find the words to say, "Why you're most welcome, Wig."

She held out her hand and it disappeared into his bearlike paw. He released it and wiped clumsily at the corner of his eye before moving away.

He took a few steps before turning back to say, "Besides, I've got such a fart buildin' inside me that, if I don't get outside soon, I'll blow all them fancy winders ret outta thur casings!"

She laughed aloud at the man's profane humor. He gave her a wink and turned back to his fellows, whom he gathered and led out through the door of the hall. Reluctantly, the other men exited soon after to return to their duties in the yard as the women began to clear away the remnants of the feast,

Christina noticed Malcolm leaving and called him aside.

"Dear lord, man! Such a voice merits a place at the royal court! What on the earth are you doing here?"

Malcolm looked at her piercingly before slowly saying, "Freedom's a funny thing, ya see. Once ya gots it, yur fain to give it up. Besides, Ah likes horses!" His face lit up with a lopsided grin before turning away to continue out the door.

First Wig and now Malcolm, she thought shaking her head in amazement. *Are such men drawn to me or me to them?* she wondered. *Either way, I'm glad for it,* she decided.

For the remainder of the day Christina supervised the stowing of the goods that had been removed from *der Greif's* hold. Afterwards, she, Ziesolf, and Trudi retired to the solar with plentiful remnants from the midday feast. While they ate, Christina regaled the other two with the accounts of her voyages to Flanders and the return to London. She held little back, save for Gaveston's covert disclosure of the impending hostilities against England's neighboring country to the north.

It was then the turn of her two companions to bring her up-to-date with what had transpired in London since she had been gone.

"There are rumors, Christina, the king plans to sally north to attack the Scots," Ziesolf mentioned. "It seems there is much discord among the barons of the land; yet, war against an ancient foe will often bring even the most defiant liegeman back into the fold. If Edward is victorious that is."

"And what are the king's chances of that?" Christina asked.

"It is hard to say," Ziesolf answered.

It is not like him to be indecisive.

They sat in an uncomfortable silence for a few seconds before the old knight began speaking once more.

"The King's father, Longshanks, was a renowned and fearsome warrior. Although he was given the sobriquet "Hammer of the Scots," he was never able to fully subjugate them. The son is a brave warrior, but clearly his father's inferior as a leader. Can he count on the support of England's nobility? Will he be able to adequately fund his expedition north? Will the Scots choose to face him in a pitched, decisive battle, or will they melt away into the moors and highlands until England's resources are exhausted? Who knows?"

Christina listened intently. Gaveston had seemed so assured of an English victory, but had his confidence stemmed from his honest appraisal of the military situation or from his euphoria in regaining his position as the king's favorite she did not know.

I hope it is the former and not simply the latter.

Chapter 7

Surprise Visitations
London, March, 1310

Christina awoke the following morning feeling hot, crampy, and in a wretchedly sour mood.

Oh, Sweet Mary, Mother of God, not now!

Although she had well succeeded in disciplining her mind to think like a man, her body refused to be so compliant.

She carefully arose from her bed and lifted her nightshirt gingerly. She was greatly relieved to find no trace of her monthly flow had leaked onto the pristine white linen. Looking down, she found the same could be said about the bedsheet.

That's fortunate.

She pulled the shift over her head and threw it to the floor.

It would certainly start tongues wagging if a pool of blood were found in the middle of the master's bed, but not as much as if it were discovered on the bottom of his shirt!

Christina walked naked into her sitting room. Rummaging about, she found a small bit of toweling. She took the large washbowl and placed it on the floor, pouring into it a few inches of water from the ewer. Squatting down, she cleaned herself as best she could, the water increasingly becoming a tell-tale red.

Rising, Christina was uncertain as to how to dispose of the bloody water. She obviously could not simply pour it into the chamber pot, leaving it for the maid who tended her room to carry away later. Neither could she risk simply heaving it out the window, not knowing who might observe its fall from below. In the end, she slowly emptied the bowl into the bottom of the fireplace, hoping the heat of the flames would eventually evaporate all traces.

She grabbed more of the linen toweling and folded it into a bulky pad. Stepping into her braies, she pushed the pad betwixt her legs and pulled the garment up as far as she was able, wedging it in place. She then cinched her belt as tightly as she could bear. It was as uncomfortable as hell, but the best she could do for the immediate time being. Christina finished dressing and left her room, intent on locating Trudi as expeditiously as possible.

Christina found her taking stock in the kitchen with Juliana, the pantry maid. After a maddingly long exchange of pleasantries, during which she furtively sought to catch Trudi's eye, she was finally able to convey the idea she needed to speak to her alone.

They walked down the short passage to the buttery; Trudi firmly closing the door behind them.

She took one perceptive look into Christina's exasperated face and asked, "Oh, no. You too?"

Christina simply nodded.

Trudi said, "I'm so sorry, I should have known. We've shared the time of Eve's visitation since we first began to bleed. Are you all right for now?"

"Yes . . . for the time being, at least," Christina replied.

"Good. Now return to your chamber and I will fetch a supply of blood moss for you. You can dispose of what you've used by burning it in the fire. Should your supply be discovered by any of the maids, I will say you are using it to treat a troublesome wound. No need to say it's your cleft that bleeds, right?"

She did as she was instructed and, before long, she was joined by Trudi with a small basket. Christina undid her clothing and gladly exchanged the linen wad she had made for a pad Trudi had artfully fashioned from the soft moss. Pulling her braies back into position she now felt much more comfortable.

"This too," Trudy said with a wry smile as she handed a small cloth pouch to her friend.

Christina grinned sheepishly and fastened the drawstrings of the bag to the ties of her braies. The pungent scent of lavender began to permeate the room.

"That will at least keep the dogs from following you all day."

"Thank you, Trudi. What would I ever do without you?"

"Probably leave a damned trail of blood all over my clean floors," she giggled in reply. "Now, are you planning on leaving the house today?"

"Yes, now that I am so well-tended at least," Christina replied.

"Well, let me help you dress more warmly then, the weather's turned terribly cold once more," Trudi advised.

In a short while, Christina was suitably bundled to face the day and began her journey Cheapside, to the guildhall of the wool merchants. As she strode toward her destination, she recalled her last meeting with Master Butiler. He had been more than happy to sell the remnants of the previous autumn's shearings at a favorably reduced price.

That was then, however, and this was now.

She held no allusions of a similar bargain being made for the man's spring fleeces. What she did hope was they could strike an agreement providing her with the earliest shearings, which could then be transported to Bruges before the market became flooded and prices began to drop.

The plan seems to make sense to me at least. I have no idea whether Master Butiler will find it in his best interests as well.

She realized her feet had carried her to her destination when she looked up to see the massive stone Eleanor Cross towering before her. Ziesolf had told her the King's father had erected this and eleven other remembrance crosses throughout the land to commemorate the funeral procession route of his beloved queen, Eleanor. As Christina passed the pedestal, she read the Latin phrase *Orate pro anima* engraved on the side.

Pray for her soul . . . I would hope someone loves me as deeply at some time in my life.

In a short while she turned onto Basinghall Street and soon arrived at the hall of the wool merchants. Stepping inside, she was happy to see a familiar face busy at work copying a document.

"Peace be with you, Gilbert. How fare you on this cold and wintry day?"

The sound of Christina's voice startled the clerk, who had been diligently concentrating on his task. He set his quill down precisely, turned to her, and smiled.

"And may God set his favor on you, Master Frederick. It is so good to see you alive and well. Master Butiler and I have spoken quite often of you, wondering how you had fared on your journey to Bruges. All went well, I hope?"

"Aye, thank you. As well as could be expected at least," she replied, resisting the urge to elaborate on the perils she had faced.

She was also hesitant to reveal the extent of her gains to the intelligent young man who served as the chief clerk to the merchants of the guild.

A loose word here would soon be communicated to his master, who would have no qualms in citing my past profit margin as leverage in future negotiations . . . Better to change the subject.

"Would Master Butiler be present today? I have need to speak with him concerning making another purchase."

"Nay, sir, I regret to say. He is away in the Welsh Marches, visiting those who tend his flocks. I would not expect him to return to the city for another fortnight."

Christina was not pleased by the news, but knew there was nothing she could do other than to return two weeks hence. She hated the thought she had wasted her time, however.

On an outside chance she asked hopefully, "Might it be that I could discuss my business with you, in Master Butiler's absence, of course?"

The clerk gave a self-deprecating smile and shook his head.

"I am sorry, Master Frederick, but I have neither knowledge nor authority in the practical aspects of the woolmonger's trade. I but maintain the accounts, draw up contracts, and carry out correspondence for the masters of the guild. It is a rather boring and limited capacity, I know, but it suits my meager talents well."

Christina felt the clerk was being overly modest, but respected him for being so.

Too often, men's deeds are far surpassed by the ability of their words. This Gilbert, on the other hand, appears quite the opposite.

I like him.

Having no further business for the time being, she bid the clerk adieu after asking, should Butiler return early, to send her word of his arrival. Gilbert readily agreed to her request. As she closed the door to the guildhall behind her, she saw the young man had already set himself back to the task upon which he had been working when she entered.

Over the next week, Christina's days fell into a steady routine. She would arise and break her fast early. Afterwards, she would sometimes have conversations with Ziesolf, Trudi, or even pass a few words with one of the men or women in her employ as she got to know them better. At other times she would venture out into the city, particularly with the purpose of making the acquaintance of the drapers and mercers who might have an interest in purchasing from her store of fine cloth. Her afternoons were often spent hosting these same merchants who, for the most part, showed a keen interest in her stock. Several small sales were negotiated but, by the end of the week, Christina was disappointed that much of her inventory remained unsold.

Perhaps I've been spoiled that my previous cargo was held in such high esteem that it sold both immediately and enmasse.

She gazed upon an open bale of fabric before picking up the short length of murrey-colored broadcloth that lay on its top, worrying it between her fingers to gauge the fine weave. Truth be told, she had been made an offer for the whole lot by one of the drapers, but had found it to be almost insultingly low, an average of just a little over four silver marks per ell. Consequently, she had chosen instead to negotiate her sales piecemeal.

It's time-consuming, but I have little else to do until Butiler returns.

The sound of quick, light steps hurrying up the stairs drew her attention toward the passageway. Within a second or two, the slight figure of the young maid Mary appeared, scampering purposefully toward her.

"What is it, child?" Christina asked, slightly irritated she was being interrupted.

Then, she almost burst out laughing at the thought she had addressed the maid as "child," when she was probably no more than one or two years younger than she, if that.

"Begging your pardon, Master Frederick," her words were accompanied with an almost ridiculously deep curtsey that was flawlessly executed, "Mistress Trudi sent me to fetch you. There's a young man downstairs wishing to see you."

Christina's heartbeat quickened.

I am not expecting any visitors today, especially this early in the morning. Could it be Gilbert, the clerk from the Wool Guild? That could only mean Master Butiler has returned from the Marches a week early!

Her breath quickened with excitement.

All hope for an expedited meeting with the wool merchant was dashed as Mary leaned forward and said in a hushed voice, "I think he's German."

Christina now stood perplexed.

A German? If the caller had been one of der Greif's crew, certainly Trudi would have said so, wouldn't she? But who else could it be? There are obviously others from German lands in the city, both merchants whose ships lay temporarily anchored at the wharves and those who have settled permanently. Oh, sweet Jesus on the cross! Might it be a messenger from Herr Revele? Hopefully not!

Since departing London to journey to Bruges, Christina had given little thought to the chief alderman of the German community in London. Although his actions had probably saved her neck from the hangman's rope, she realized it had been done out of his sense of responsibility in his capacity as alderman rather than through any fondness for her.

She licked her lips unconsciously as they suddenly felt dry.

If the visitor is an emissary from Revele, it could only be a portent of bad things to come.

Mary still stood expectantly in front of her.

Christina realized she was waiting to be dismissed. Because of their long years of service, the servants in her home in Lübeck had almost seemed a part of the family, especially to a young girl who recalled them being about the house for as long as she could remember. They went about their work with no need for formality. On the other hand, this young girl had only been in service at the manor for a few short months.

Much better to be too cautious than to overstep her place.

Christina nodded her head approvingly.

"Thank you, Mary. Tell your mistress I shall come forthwith."

The girl beamed at the fact her master had remembered her name. She gave another demure curtesy and flew back up the hallway as quickly as she had come.

Christina finished measuring the length of the *Dickedinnen* broadcloth remnant, recording the figure in her ledger. She folded it carefully and sat it down before leaving the room to find out who it was that sought to disturb her day.

She entered the hall and saw a boy who must have been slightly younger than her standing just inside the entrance door. He fidgeted uneasily, shifting his weight from foot to foot. As she approached him, a tentative smile brightened his broad face.

"God be with you, sir. Be ye Herr Frederick Kohl?"

She immediately associated his accent with the Baltic coastal region near her hometown.

"Aye," she replied cautiously, although it seemed the boy posed no immediate threat.

"Um, well . . ." he seemed flustered by Christina's curt response. "I, well, you see I don't know where to begin."

Christina's patience was beginning to wear thin but, before she could vent her tongue, he reached into the capacious soft deerskin pouch he wore attached to the right side of his belt and drew out a small page of tightly rolled vellum sealed with a liberal dollop of red wax. He held this out toward her and she took it from him, silently composing a venomous remark to chide him for his vexing behavior. She said nothing, however, instead staring dumbstruck at what she held in her hand. She looked once more at the wax, hesitant to believe her eyes.

"It's my father's seal!" she exclaimed in a soft voice, caring not whether the messenger heard her or not.

Clutching the vellum tightly in her hand, she bade the young man to have a seat at one of the tables. She then hurried into the kitchen, finding one of the scullery maids, one whose name she could not recall, hard at work scrubbing an iron pot.

"There is a man seated in the rear of the hall. Take him food and drink, anything he wants, and be quick about it please. See to any other needs he has as well. Tell him I will return shortly. Do you understand?"

Aye, Master, I'll fetch it right away."

No curtsying from this one.

Christina observed absentmindedly as the girl ran immediately to the larder to piece together an impromptu repast as instructed.

Feeling she had now satisfied the obligation for hospitality; Christina now strode rapidly to the solar. She hesitated slightly, then continued on to her chambers.

I cannot bear an interruption.

She clasped the small scroll tightly to her bosom.

. . . Not even from Trudi or Ziesolf.

Once inside, she closed the door and ran to the chair that sat before the windows. She held the wax seal of the rolled vellum closely before her eyes, then brought it to her lips and kissed it lightly. Christina pulled her eating knife from its scabbard on her belt and deftly bisected the semi-pliable wax with one quick slice.

She unrolled the parchment slowly. Suddenly she caught her breath as a lump formed in her throat.

Mother's hand! I'd know it anywhere!

With rapidly misting eyes, she began to read.

My Precious Frederick,

I hope this missive finds you in good health and safely under the blessings of our dear Lord.

It was with great sadness that I learned of the death of your father and most beloved sister, Christina, may their places in Heaven be forever at God's side. I have bequeathed six silver marks to the priests of the *Marienkirche* for a requiem mass to be said for the salvation of their souls. I am nearly overcome with grief at the numerous tragedies that have befallen our beloved family in such a few short months, but I am greatly heartened in the knowledge that at least you have survived.

I have so much to tell you, but find it very difficult to do so. I wish with all my heart you were here, at our home in Lübeck. I would make you a fine meal of roast lampreys, your favorite you know, and we would talk late into the night about what must be done to preserve your father's trade. Alas though, you are not here, so I will try to provide you with what information and advice I may, so you can decide what best to do. I am but a mere woman; yet, I have faith you believe women too can give wise counsel.

First, know God continues to bestow good health upon me and I want for nothing, other than to see you again. Anna's friend, Beatrice, has joined our household, which continues to function efficiently. I could tell you much more, of marriages, births, and deaths in our dear Lübeck, but must leave that until later as we have matters of much more import to discuss.

My most fervent prayer is that you have had the good fortune to have claimed your father's ledger. It will provide you with much information concerning his holdings, transactions, and profits and losses therefrom. If not, do not worry. He was exacting in recording his contracts at the *Rathaus*, so there is always a record here if someone should voice a dispute.

As to our business, the *winterfahrer* will soon be returning from faraway Novgorod. Your father holds a claim to one half of the cargo of Gherwen Strateken, as well as a third each of those of Hermann Claessoen and Peter Nirmheim. As these are men well experienced in trade with the 'Rus, I would anticipate sweet profits to be shared by all.

Now, to the problem. As you may be aware, the code of Lübeck provides specific rights to its citizens. One of these is that the widow of a merchant in good standing may continue to trade in his name until she remarries. This is very good, as I may legally lay claim to our family's share of these cargoes without dispute. I could also sell them here quite easily at a fair wholesale price, as your father's friends would be fain to dishonor themselves by attempting to cheat his widow.

Every merchant of the Hansa knows, however, that true profit is always to be gained by marketing these exotic goods in the great cities to the South. Many times, your father's returns were increased ten-fold by selling Novgorodian furs in Bruges and London. Perhaps you have been fortunate enough to find this true, if *der Greif's* cargo remained intact and you were fortunate enough to find a purchaser, but who knows?

So, why do I not just buy a ship and carry on trading as if your father were still alive and sitting here beside me, you may ask? The lot of women is never that simple, you see. No man wants to answer to a woman, especially one who does not share his bed. Nor can a man perceive of a woman as an equal, so he will never treat her as such. The intent of the law is clear; to allow the widow to tie up the loose ends of her husband's affairs, not to carry them on. The Hansa will never allow a woman to trade freely in her own right, be she widow or not.

As soon as you are able, send me word of what you wish to do with the winter furs. Better still, dispatch *der Greif* or another ship to Lübeck so the pelts may be sent to the markets of London, or elsewhere if you wish.

Although I will never think of you as such, you are now a man, my dear Frederick. Under your name, our business can continue to thrive, God willing. I know you are ill-prepared to assume these duties. Your youth, lack of a proper apprenticeship, and life in a foreign city without the comfort and support of your family must all conspire to cause you to doubt yourself. But do not despair my child! You have a quick wit and the support of Herr Ziesolf, who I trust will provide help and support in all your endeavors. Even Trudi must be a source of comfort and support, as I know she has a good heart that makes up for her other shortcomings.

Even with the support of these two, I know you must at times feel abandoned and alone. That is why I have sent the young man who carries this missive to you. He is the son of my brother Volkmar, who lives in Luneburg. I believe you may have met him once when you were very young. He is a clever boy but, more importantly, I believe him to be steadfast and honest. Teach him well and support him as he will one day support you.

I will bring my writing now to a close, as it has rambled on far too long already. Know always that I love you and hope, someday soon, to hold you closely to my bosom once again.

With praise to God and His Angels,

Your Mother

Christina arose and sat the parchment down gently on a nearby table, her mind awash in a cacophony of diverse feelings. One thought overshadowed all others, however:

She knows.

She had no doubt her mother knew her true identity; she had made it more than clear through clues she had left in her letter.

When he was twelve years old, Frederick had become deathly ill after eating a platter of roast eels. Since that day, Mother has never prepared them for a family meal. Much to my disappointment, as it had always been one of my favorite dishes.

The reference to never thinking of Frederick as a man was also a blatant hint.

Of course, she would not consider him a man, since she now knew him in reality to be her daughter!

She wondered little about what had first caused her mother to believe it was she who had survived rather than Frederick. The message she had dispatched had been inscribed in her own handwriting, a small and somewhat elegant script of which she was quite proud. On the other hand, Frederick's letters were almost scrawls, oversized and ill-formed. To the mother who had taught them both, the truth of the situation would be quite apparent at first glance.

Very clever, Mother. Your words also make it obvious you know much more about being a merchant than your stupid daughter! Clearly, I have not been thinking beyond the end of my nose.

It is all well and good to purchase wool to sell in Bruges, equally so to fill der Greif's hold with Flemish cloth to market in London. These transactions assuredly turn over a tidy profit, one which will support me and my growing household very comfortably. To continue to do so has been the extent of the plans I have made for the future so far.

But I am not just a young journeyman trader, struggling with a single ship to make a name for myself. My father was a master merchant, one of the most successful in Lübeck. I have not just inherited his wealth but also his status. Why have I not thought about the return of the winterfahrer from Novgorod? Because I am so stupid!

Christina felt like slapping herself.

I must send word to Mother to not sell our portions to the wholesalers. No. Better still, I will dispatch der Greif to Lübeck immediately, filled with as much cargo as I can muster of interest to the Novgorodian markets. Matthias is well known and respected there; Mother and I can both trust him to act as our agent. When he has completed his transactions with the winterfahrer merchants, he can return here, with der Greif's hold full of furs, honey, and wax. Meanwhile, I must find another ship to carry on with my plans here.

Christina realized her lackadaisical days were now at an end.

So many things to do!

Her mind raced in several directions all at once. Then, she remembered her cousin had undoubtedly finished his refreshments and awaited her return to the hall.

Damn! Taking some ignorant boy under my wing is the last thing I need right now. Why did you saddle me with this additional burden, Mother?

Realizing she had no other alternative; she strode back to the hall where she found Jost still totally immersed in voraciously consuming the foodstuffs laid before him. As Christina walked closer, he looked up in surprise and hastily rose to his feet, remnants of roast pork and cheese still clinging to the corners of his mouth.

"The purpose of eating is to get the food down the hole of your throat," Christina commented sarcastically.

Jost's face flushed a deep red and he wiped the sleeve of his begrimed tunic hastily across his mouth, dislodging most of the debris to fall across his garment or onto the floor.

"I . . . I beg your forgiveness," he stammered before adding, "I have never voyaged across the sea before and we were plagued by foul weather the entire trip. What food I was able to consume issued immediately back up the way it had come. Only in the final few hours of the passage has my stomach settled. I feel now as if my entire body is a vast void, one which I now must fill."

Christina couldn't help but feel empathetic, having experienced a similar effect on her voyage to Bruges.

She gave the lad what she hoped was an encouraging smile and said, "Please, enjoy my table until you have had your fill."

Taking Christina's words literally, Jost returned to his previous seat and began to eat feverishly once more.

Although a bit irritated at his seemingly unwitting rudeness, she sat down across the table from him and, forcing another smile, said, "I thank ye for carrying the message from my mother. Is there a name I might call you?"

With a look of surprised embarrassment once more spreading across his face, Jost hastily rose and said, "Again, I beg your pardon, Master Frederick. My name is Jost and I am your cousin from Luneburg."

She replied, "Well met, young Jost from Luneburg. May I ask what are your plans now that my mother's task for you has been completed?"

He again hesitated before speaking. It was obvious to her he had believed her mother's message had explained his proposed apprenticeship under Christina's supervision. Although it had, she felt it was the boy's responsibility to say so in his own words.

Searching to form the correct words, he finally said, "I believe I am to stay with you, Cousin, as your apprentice."

Finally! Getting information from him is like slogging across a muddy field in April!

"Oh really?" she asked in what she hoped was an innocent voice. "And who was it that told you this?"

"Why, first my father and then your mother," he replied, now seemingly beginning to panic. "Are their words not right? What am I supposed to do, if not stay with you?"

"Yes, yes, you may stay," she said reassuringly, then, "And what do you know about being an apprentice?"

"Well, just that I am supposed to learn from you. I mean, in Luneburg many boys are apprentices. But the bricklayer teaches his how to make a wall, and the cooper teaches his how to make a barrel. I understand that. But I don't actually even know what it is that you do," he confessed.

Oh, Sweet Jesus, give me patience.

She thought a moment, wracking her brain to figure out a starting point.

"Can you read and write?" she asked hopefully.

"Yes, Friar Noel from the monastery taught quite a few of us local boys."

Christina felt somewhat reassured that gobbling down food was not Jost's sole ability.

"And I can do sums as well. Friar Noel said I was the best of the lot at it!" Jost added a bit more assertively now.

Perhaps there are uses I can make of this boy after all.

"Well, Cousin, finish your meal and I will bid my housekeeper to arrange bedding for you. Once you are settled, I will introduce you to Herr Ziesolf, who will get you started on some tasks. How does that sound to you?"

"Great!" he exclaimed, now grinning from ear to ear. "I won't disappoint you, neither!"

Well, I'll be the judge of that.

She attempted to remain pragmatic, but actually felt well pleased by her cousin's enthusiasm.

Chapter 8

An Unexpected Request
London, March, 1310

A few days later, Christina stood in the room where the bales of cloth were stored, trying hard not to allow her mouth to gape open with amazement. She had set Jost the task of continuing to measure each length of fabric, then left him to the task for about two hours. She had hoped he would complete the accounting of the open bale before she returned. To her surprise, he had not only finished that. but had completed four others as well.

"A job well done!" she gushed.

Although hesitant to lavish praise too soon, she was so impressed by the boy's progress she was unable to restrain herself.

Before she could commend him further, she was interrupted by the arrival of Trudi, bustling hurriedly up the passageway.

"Pardon me, Master Fredrick," she managed to say despite being evidently out of breath.

"Yes, Mistress Trudi, what is it?" Christina replied evenly despite wondering if she was to always be interrupted every time she attempted to work in the room.

"There are three soldiers in the hall. They say you are to accompany them to the Tower forthwith."

Gaveston again.

Although not displeased by the opportunity to chat with her friend once more, she was somewhat vexed by the imperious tone of the summons.

Perhaps he himself does not fashion his request in the form of a command; rather, it is those who serve him who interpret his every whim as an imperative. I've never served a member of the nobility, so who knows for sure?

"Thank you. I will be along shortly. Please offer them some ale to stifle their impatience."

Trudi left the room and Christina turned back toward Jost, who seemed completely entranced by the sight of Trudi's departure.

"If I may have your attention for a few moments, I will give you your tasks for the afternoon. That is, if I might distract you from your admiration of our Mistress Trudi's fetching backside," she said dryly.

Flustered once more, Jost cast his eyes downward in mortification as the now familiar red flush slowly crept upward from his neck to his face. He slowly raised his head and was surprised to see Christina grinning ear to ear.

"It's alright, you randy whelp," she said, laughing in spite of herself at the boy's obvious discomfort. "You're not the first lad to be taken in by the swing of that one's hips."

Jost responded with a grin of his own, albeit much more shyly.

After providing her instructions to the apprentice, she too departed down the passageway, taking time only to grab her heavy cloak from her chamber before continuing to the hall. She joined the soldiers and, without speaking, they departed on the unpleasant trek to Tower Castle.

As they wound through the streets, the rain pelted them relentlessly, causing water to run from their hoods down onto their cloaks in steady rivulets. What few people she saw were sheltered closely to the sides of the buildings leaving the middle thoroughfare free for Christina and her escorts to pass uninterrupted. She pulled her cloak tightly about her body, happy she had had the foresight to grab it before leaving her house.

Her mood began to darken with each step of the thick leather soles of her boots on the cobblestones.

I would wager Gaveston has not set a foot out from the cheery warmth of his apartments all day.; yet, he has no qualms about dragging me halfway across London in a piss-down storm just to help him while away the hours. Bosom friend, indeed!

Although the downpour eased to an intermittent drizzle shortly before they arrived at the castle complex, the day remained dreary, cold, and damp. They trudged stoically across the courtyard before coming at last to the ground-level entrance of Lanthorn Tower. She was surprised to find two sentries in gleaming breastplates stationed outside the doorway, where none had been before. They stood sharply erect, each holding a well-polished halberd in his right hand. Silently, one turned and opened the door, motioning her to go inside.

Sweet Jesus, Piers. What trouble have you gotten yourself into now?

Her anxiety intensified as she mounted the stone steps to the floor above.

Strangely, she found the ornate outer door to the earl's apartments ajar. She hesitated before entering, not knowing whether this sufficed as an invitation to enter or if she should cautiously wait outside instead.

Should I call his name?

Even though their relationship had grown rather informal, she could not bring herself to summoning an earl of the realm as if he were a common day servant. After a few further seconds wait, however, she decided to venture inside.

The substantial door swung open soundlessly on its well-greased hinges. She stepped inside and was puzzled to find the room seemingly empty. Only a few tapers were lit which, combined with the heavily clouded sky outside, created a dim, somber ambiance. She scanned the room once more and was surprised to find she was not alone as she had first thought. A solitary figure stood motionlessly before the window, gazing outward through the thick panes of nearly transparent glass. She grew alarmed, as the man was obviously not Gaveston.

He had seemingly not noticed Christina's entrance into the room, or perhaps consciously chose not to acknowledge it. Although his back was turned to her, she could readily assess he was both tall and powerfully built beneath his very well-tailored garments. His auburn hair fell in manicured curls onto a collar of some type of whitish fur that adorned his particolored surcoat.

In a graceful motion the man turned about, seemingly noticing her presence in the room at last.

"God be with you on this dreary day, sir," he said quite amiably.

"And to you as well, your Grace," she fell back on her earlier plan to address anyone of unknown rank thusly, rather than to risk insulting someone by implying they were of lower standing by referring to them as such.

"You must be the inimitable Frederick, merchant of Lübeck, and adventurer extraordinaire. Piers has entertained me often with the tales of your exploits."

Christina was rather embarrassed by the knowledge Gaveston had shared information about her life with this unidentified man, then she became more alarmed.

To how much of my past is this man privy?

Her thoughts turned over fretfully before replying, "I am Frederick Kohl, yes."

"I am happy to finally make your acquaintance, Master Frederick," the stranger said, inclining his head slightly toward her as he did.

Christina was confused as to what to do next. She still had no idea as to the identity of the stranger, although it seemed obvious from the cut of his clothes and his informal reference to Earl Gaveston as "Piers," that he was also a nobleman of high standing.

Well, was I not directed by the earl to refer to him as "Piers," and I am not of noble birth?

He began walking toward her and the mystery of his identity soon became clear to her.

The purfelle of his surcoat is ermine! How could I have missed this?

Even at a distance, any Hanseatic fur merchant would immediately recognize the fluffy white pelts of the short-tailed stoat from that of other animals by the distinctive white tabs at the tip of the tails. Ermine was prized above all other furs and, as such, was restricted by English sumptuary law to be worn by only one class of society – royalty.

"I'm Edward," he said simply, with a slightly puzzled grin beginning to spread across his face.

"Your Majesty," Christina responded as she took a hasty knee.

"Oh, no need for all that, really. May I call you Frederick?"

What an absurd question for a king to ask! He can call me any fucking thing he wants!

"Of course, Sire. As you wish," she choked out a reply.

"Good then. Come have a seat, Frederick. I am certain Earl Piers regrets not being here to offer his hospitality himself, but he has already departed to attend to certain business of mine in the North, more of which we will speak of later. For now, you must consider me to be your humble host. Would you care for a bowl of wine? It is a fulsome Rhenish vintage, newly arrived from a Flemish port."

Christina felt her face grow hot.

Aye, aboard my damn ship!

Her ire dissipated as rapidly as it had arisen when she saw the merry look in his eyes; realizing only then the king had intended the comment as a jest.

"Yes, thank you, Your Majesty," Christina responded politely to the king's invitation, moving in measured steps toward the proffered bench to ensure the king sat before she did so herself.

She knew she must obviously treat the man with deference and respect; yet, his casual behavior toward her and the lack of attendants were making her nervous. She had not yet removed her dripping cloak and wished the king would either state his purpose in summoning her or bring their meeting to a swift close; the likelihood of either of which seemed forthcoming

He sat opposite her intended seat and took a moderate sip of wine, gesturing for her to help herself from the vessel. After she had, he sat his bowl on the table next to the chair in which he sat and, leaning forward toward her, began to speak once again.

"I was looking out the window earlier, mournful the weather had taken such an unkind turn today. I had hopes it would soon begin to warm and I could chance a swim in one of the nearby ponds. As one so traveled upon the sea, I would believe you swim yourself, Frederick?"

"Sadly, no Sire. It is a practice for which I have no talent," she answered, although knowing herself to be a strong swimmer.

Was it a sin to lie to an anointed sovereign?

Regardless, she could not risk take the chance of him asking her to join him at his sport.

"A pity. You must take great care not to fall into the ocean," he advised. "Or you will wind up feeding the fishes!" He laughed in a pleasingly deep baritone voice at his own feeble jest. His face grew serious and he pulled his chair closer to Christina, as if an unconscious signal the time for idle pleasantries had now ended.

"My dear friend Piers marks you as one with a quick and nimble brain; thus, I will consider you the same and speak plainly. I am sure you have heard rumors I plan to war against the Scots, have you not?"

"Aye, Sire," she answered, although refraining from adding it had been Gaveston who informed her so.

"My father spent most of his life fighting to unite this isle under his authority. The Welsh and even his own barons sought to best him; yet, he prevailed. Only in the North did his foes continue their resistance, a defiance that exists unto this day. It is my desire to succeed where my father failed, to bring the Scots under England's heel once and for all."

Christina listened to the young monarch without comment, still puzzled as to the purpose of his disclosure.

"In September, I will lead a mighty contingent of England's finest warriors northward, invading the Scottish borderlands. This force will be accompanied by an enormous supply train that will provide ample provisions for the winter months. Rested and well-fed, our solders will sally out with the advent of the spring thaw to force the Scottish rabble to battle, and their ultimate defeat."

This is much the same I heard from Gaveston. Why does he feel he has need to tell me this?

126

"By God's good graces, our victory is assured, but only if our plans are thorough and precisely executed. That is the purpose for which I have summoned you here today, Frederick."

Christina was now more confused than ever.

"Piers considers you to be his friend, as I now do as well. But this is not enough, young Frederick. You must now be England's comrade as well! Providing arms and provisions for a force of men thousands strong is a massive enterprise, one which may only be undertaken at great expense. I find the royal coffers do not hold the amount needed to assure this venture. That is why I ask you, Frederick Kohl, to help fund our noble cause with a loan of five thousand pounds sterling."

It was fortunate Christina had not been taking a gulp of wine as she most certainly would have involuntarily spat it back out, drenching the king. As it was, she could only stare at the man's earnest face with a look of stark disbelief etched upon her own.

By Christ's thorny crown! What does this man think, anointed king or not! I could buy two dozen cog-ships the size of der Greif with that amount of money! What's more, do I even possess such a sum?

She tried to mentally assess her ready assets, but her mind refused to function properly, overwhelmed as it was with the sheer boldness of King Edward's request.

The king still looked at Christina, his damnably encouraging smile seemingly frozen on his lips.

I know I must say something, but what? I can't merely agree to his request, handing over all of the profits I have made to leave myself near-penniless.

A moment of thought brought her to a sobering conclusion.

But can I refuse him? Is that even possible? And, if it is, will I incur his everlasting animosity? This man can kill with a word, a movement of his finger. I cannot afford such a powerful enemy, especially in a land not truly my own.

"I must think upon this, Your Majesty," she said choosing her words with extreme care. "I know not whether I even possess such a great sum."

"I do understand, but please consider our force's immediate need. May I assume an answer within one week's time?" he asked, although it seemed more like a demand than a question.

"Yes, Sire, seven days' time should be sufficient to take stock of my assets."

"Excellent," he said, clapping his hands together for emphasis.

Or is it a signal our conversation is concluded, now that he has made his true reason for meeting with me known?

His intent became obvious as he began to rise from his chair. She immediately followed his lead.

"I look forward to our next meeting, Frederick. I shall wait for you here, at this same hour, in seven days hence," he said, again slightly nodding his head in her direction.

"Certainly, as Your Majesty desires," she replied, scarcely remembering to execute a simultaneous bow in acknowledgement.

As she backed toward the entranceway, he returned to gazing out the window, his long-limbed frame once more merging with the growing shadows. She exited the room and made her way down the stairs and out into the cold twilight of the day. Christina walked only a few steps before doubling over, suddenly overcome by nausea. Although she did not vomit, she tasted the acidic residue of her stomach's contents rise into her throat. After a moment, her queasiness passed and she began to stride once more toward the exit from the castle grounds.

She soon left the royal enclave. Now that the rain had ceased, many more pedestrians crowded the city streets. She barely noticed, however, several times eliciting sharp elbows, angry words, and belligerent stares as she inadvertently bumped into people. These she barely registered, so preoccupied was she with her own thoughts.

What am I to do?

She asked this of herself repeatedly.

For once, she had no viable plan of action as the situation confronting her was completely beyond her own scope of experiences. By the time she arrived back home, she had come to only one conclusion.

I need advice.

But who can I ask about such things?

As with most matters, she knew the first person she should consult would be Ziesolf.

The old knight was not difficult to find. He stood at the stone archway leading into the courtyard, engaged in an animated discussion with the smith, Black Peter. Ziesolf was kneeling, picking with his fingers at the lowest wrought iron hinge-points on the left-hand gate while the other man slowly nodded his head in response. Ziesolf rose slowly as he finished giving instructions to the smith. Noticing Christina's approach, the two men stopped what they were doing and looked in her direction expectantly.

"Sorry to interrupt," her unusually clipped words drawing an immediate look of puzzlement from Ziesolf. "May I ask you to accompany me to the solar forthwith?" pointedly directing the question at the former member of the Teutonic knighthood.

Recognizing Christina's unusually grave demeanor, he replied simply, "Of course. Peter and I had just finished our discussion, had we not, Master Smith?"

Realizing he had been dismissed, the smith nodded and walked back toward his shop without comment.

"A good man, this one," Ziesolf commented as they mounted the stairway to the upper floor. "Knows well how to maintain the proper heat of a forge so the metal is neither brittle nor soft."

They entered the solar and he closed the door behind them.

As they settled into their customary seats in the room, he on a high-backed stool and her into a tawny beechwood chair with a gayly embroidered cushion, he asked, "So what is it, Christina, that troubles you so?"

Her summarized account of her meeting with the king elicited a rare response of astonishment from her companion. When she had finished, he looked downward while wiping his hand heavily across his forehead as if hoping to rub an answer from it. After a minute or two, he raised his head and spoke.

"Certainly, the masters of our order in the great castle *Marienburg* would have experience in dealing with such regal matters. I, however, was but a poor knight serving at a remote posting in Samogitia. I am sorry to say I have no counsel for you."

"Well, what the hell am I supposed to do?" she asked in frustration, seemingly ignoring his previous admission.

"Could you discuss this matter with one of the English merchants?" Ziesolf asked, looking intently into her eyes as he did.

"Perhaps Master Butiler, but he is still away in the midlands. Otherwise, I know of no one possessing the necessary resources to be of similar interest to the Crown."

"Perhaps someone who is not English then?" He seemingly posed the question innocently; yet, already knowing where Christina's nimble mind would lead her.

"Surely you jest, Kurt!" she cried, so astounded by his implication she referred to him by his given name, which she rarely did. "I hope to never see the man again, if I can help it!"

"It seems you are left with no alternative course of action. Herr Revele is the only person who assuredly has the knowledge of matters of which you speak."

Christina knew Ziesolf's words to be true.

As chief alderman of the Hansa merchants in London, it is Revele who negotiates the treaties, privileges, and agreements with the English government on behalf of we Germans. He will certainly have knowledge of the proper protocols to be used in financial transactions with the King.

"Sweet Jesus, why does it have to be him?" she moaned aloud.

She had affronted the man more than once; having refused to agree to a marriage to his daughter, the sale of her cargo of furs directly to Gaveston, and just her own general brazenness toward him to name but a few.

But would Revele risk a German merchant giving offense to the king just to satisfy a personal grudge?

The existing relationship between the Germans and the ruling monarchy of England had been amiable since the time of the reign of Henry II, but it was still a fragile thing. Revele would certainly not want a rift to grow simply because a Hansa member had offended the king.

If for no other motive, the desire to maintain good relations with the English will lead Revele to provide me with sage and useful counsel.

"Although I wish it were not so, I can't help but agree with your conclusion Herr Revele is the only person capable of providing me with the advice I need. Therefore, please travel to his house without delay and arrange an appointment betwixt us."

Ziesolf simply nodded his agreement and departed the room without delay.

On the other hand, Christina tarried, mentally composing a plan as to how to approach the myriad of tasks looming before her. After several minutes, she went to her chamber and fetched her ledger. Her relief was palpable as she confirmed the conclusion to which she had arrived on her return from the castle.

I have enough!

Cautiously, she rechecked her calculations and found them to be correct. The total of her deposits with the Italian bankers totaled 7,463 pounds sterling, 17 shillings, and 8 pence with roughly 240 pounds on hand. Even not counting the unsold merchandise she held in her storerooms, she had more than sufficient funds to meet the King's request.

The next question is whether I have enough money to purchase another ship as well. Spring is never the best time for this for, as the weather clears, vessels that have been laid-up over the winter readily begin to take aboard crews eager to ply their livelihood. Perhaps I am still early enough to strike a bargain with a ship-owner so desperate for money he is willing to part with his vessel rather than wait for fairer weather.

She hoped to purchase another cog; primarily because of her familiarity with the vessel type. Cogs were also highly maneuverable, seaworthy, and had a relatively shallow draft. She would certainly stay away from larger vessels, especially the massive hulks like those riding heavily at anchor at the quay at Queenhithe. More suited to the transport of bulk cargoes, such as grain and salt, they would prove quite uneconomical for conveying the high-end goods Christina favored. Another reason for her disinterest in purchasing this type of vessel was its price, which could be double that of the 300 pounds she had allotted for a cog.

Christina had turned her attention to determining the composition of the cargo she would dispatch aboard *der Greif* for the voyage to Lübeck when Ziesolf returned, informing her an audience with Revele had been granted for sunset two days hence.

She was overjoyed the alderman had seen fit to meet with her within the time allotted by the king to convey to him her decision.

Perhaps he has cause to view me more favorably.

At that point, Trudi came into the room, announcing the evening meal was ready. Instead of heading up the stairs to the solar, or back into the great hall, Trudi mysteriously led them down the rearward passageway and into the garden parlor Christina had discovered on her initial inspection of the house. Although it was but sparsely decorated as of yet, the room had been scrupulously cleaned. A substantial brazier stood in the far corner, radiating heat from the crackling fire burning within. The windows looked out onto a scene still desolate from the winter's deprivations; yet, Christina knew it would abound with living shoots and leaves once the days regained their warmth.

"Thank you, Trudi, for such a lovely surprise!" she gushed.

They enjoyed their mouthwatering repast greatly, interspacing their light conversation with longing looks into the outdoor space as they each imagined the long-awaited coming of springtime.

Chapter 9

———————

Encounters Both Good and Bad
London, March, 1310

Christina was awakened by the faint sound of one of the maids scurrying about in her antechamber.

As she turned over in bed, she reached down and examined the blood moss from between her legs; happily, it was unsullied.

It seems Eve's Blessing is no longer upon me.

She arose from her bed with a surge of renewed energy.

I have many important tasks before me; yet, none I can move forward to today. Perhaps this is a fortuitous time to renew one other acquaintance.

She used the water the maid had left to conduct her morning toilet. She scrubbed herself thoroughly with a coarse sponge and a cake of soap until her skin glowed red from her efforts. Christina next cleaned her teeth and gums with a small bit of linen dipped into a paste of powdered charcoal from the stems of the rosemary plant and wine. She followed this by washing her mouth with a mixture of wine and crushed cloves. Feeling more refreshed than she had for days, she ventured to the kitchen to have her morning meal and to commit a sin she was loathe to do: lie to Trudi.

As expected, Christina found her friend already bustling about the heart of the house, ensuring the cook and her helpers were busily preparing a hearty fare to feed the hungry men and women who would soon crowd into the hall to break their fast.

"Good morn to you, Mistress Trudi, how fare thee today?"

"Why, Master Frederick, I believed you had decided to sleep your life away!" Trudi retorted with a bit of playful sarcasm. "I am fine, as always when I know you are safely at home with us. This is a late rise for you is it not?"

"Aye, but not one of which I shall make a habit, I believe," Christina responded.

"And where is it you wish your meal to be served?"

"A place in the hall will suit my purposes fine. Is there a slice of that tasty shank of beef that still remains?" she asked hopefully.

Trudi nodded and relayed Christina's request to Sarah, the scullery maid. The girl scampered off, eager to please both Trudi and her master.

Before Trudi could speak, Christina said in what she hoped was a seemingly nonchalant manner, "Oh, by the way, I shall not be returning for the meal this evening. I have an appointment with a possible buyer which could run later into the evening."

Trudi looked at her inquisitively, her deep blue eyes staring into those of Christina piercingly. Christina met her gaze squarely, willing herself to appear as if her statement had been made in complete innocence. Trudi then smiled and nodded her head in assent, although whether it was because she believed what Christina had said or supposed her friend was entitled to her own secrets it was impossible to know.

Either way, I feel badly having been false to my closest friend; I will share everything with her later.

If I can.

She grimaced as she made her promise conditional.

Christina spent the remainder of the morning dallying with small tasks about the house; among them taking the time to doublecheck Jost's measurements of her fabrics. She found no more than an inch's variance between his calculations and those of her own; which she then meticulously recorded into what had been her father's account book, but that now she considered her own.

Having had her fill of enclosed spaces, she decided to take a breath of air in the rear garden. Opening the door, she was thrilled to find the day was sunny and pleasantly temperate. She walked around the perimeter of the garden, just inside the formidable boundary of the nearly ten-foot-high stone wall defining the space. Christina was further delighted to find two apple trees set in the southeast corner; she knew they would soon be budding delicate white blossoms.

A sure portent spring is finally coming to the land.

She felt contented, imagining nothing could be more pleasant than enjoying the sweet taste of a warm apple tart made from apples plucked freshly from one of her very own trees.

Although she knew she could tarry in this small paradise for the rest of the day, Christina realized she should delay no longer if she was to follow through on her earlier plan. With some reluctance, she departed the garden, knowing it was a place she was bound to often return.

Walking down the passageway and past the kitchen, Christina paused for a moment to consider whether she should linger to enjoy a bite to eat before proceeding onward. She decided against it, as her growing sense of anticipation caused her stomach to quiver with nervousness. She left the house and walked purposefully through the courtyard, taking no opportunity to speak with the men who labored on their diverse tasks there.

Turning into the street, Christina set a brisk pace for her destination. Soon, she crossed the great bridge to Southwark.

How I had been amazed the first time I walked here. I had been like a country bumpkin gazing about with my mouth widely open to catch any flies that buzzed past. Now, I hardly even notice when I pass over. Perhaps I am now a true Londoner?

Within about fifteen minutes, she arrived at the Nag's Head. It had been a few months since she had last beheld the tavern, but its appearance had not improved. If anything, it looked even more dilapidated and ill-kept than before. As she approached the entrance, the familiar smell of piss and stale ale assaulted her nose, causing her to halt for a moment and question her decision to return to this place. She then resolutely resumed her path forward, through the door and into the dimly-lit interior of the tavern. The odors within the common room replicated those without, only more intensely so within the confined space. She made a conscious effort to refrain from retching as she moved to the roughly hewn bar in the front corner of the room.

She ordered a tankard of ale from the same man who had served her on previous occasions. He gave no hint of recognition, only grunting something indistinguishable as he accepted Christina's coin. She felt the curious eyes of the few other patrons upon her as she accepted her tankard and turned to find a place to sit. She made no eye contact with anyone as they had already turned away.

This is not a place where you show too much interest in what is clearly not your own business. Men have perished here for less, nearly so myself!

Christina took a seat at a small table in the corner adjacent to where she had met with Gaveston during her first time at the inn. She consumed about half the contents of her tankard in deliberately slow, measured sips as a few of her fellow drinkers departed, to be replaced by a couple of others. The anxiety she felt in the pit of her stomach rebelled against the warm, somewhat sour ale. Finally, she could force no more down her throat. Mustering her courage somewhat, she stood and walked back over to the barman who gauged her approach with mild interest.

"Wha' kin I do fur ya, friend? Will ya be wantin' another?" he said gesturing back toward her still half-full tankard.

"No, not right yet," she answered before asking, "What I was wondering though is whether the girl named Sybille is here?"

He smirked at her question, then pointed at her with his index finger before saying, "I remember ya now. Had that little cat squallin' half the night away, ya did!"

She said nothing more, her expression fixed in an icy half-smile.

The barman seemed disappointed he received no response to his lewd comment.

"She's upstairs. You want I should fetch her?" he asked.

Christina simply nodded, not wishing to engage with the man any further than that.

He did not move; instead choosing to stare at her expectantly.

She tossed him a small coin and he disappeared up the stairs, returning in a few minutes to state, "She'll be right down," before returning to behind the bar.

Christina returned to her table and forced down a few more swallows of the ale to quench her suddenly dry throat. Her heartbeat quickened in anticipation. Finally, hearing light footsteps upon the creaky stairs, she turned to see the young woman she sought descending into the room.

Sybille's thick dark mane of hair was unadorned, falling well below her shoulders in bold ringlets. Her face was perfectly framed by these locks, the most striking feature being her well-spaced eyes set below plucked brows; large, even without the kohl which she had previously applied to accent them. Christina inhaled sharply; the woman was even more beautiful than the fond image she had recalled frequently over the past months.

Sybille walked delicately to her side and stooped to kiss her fully upon the mouth. Christina inhaled the minted sweetness of the woman's breath and felt her body grow strangely weak.

"Upstairs, no?" Sybille asked, already knowing the reply.

Sybille led her up the stairs and to the small room they had once shared for an evening. Going inside, Christina was somewhat surprised to see the chamber had now been decorated somewhat. A pretty lace-edged coverlet and a matching cushion now lay upon the bed. A table with two stools stood in a corner that had been empty at her last visit; a wooden carving of a small songbird sat next to the candleholder on its surface.

All in all, the room now has the appearance of a place where someone lives, and is doing good business.

"Do you like it?" Sybille hesitated coyly, before asking, "Do you like me?"

She put her arms around Christina's waist and pulled her close, nuzzling her lips lightly upon Christina's neck.

"Yes. Very much, yes," she answered, feeling a warm blissfulness overtake her body. She wanted nothing more than to collapse upon the bed.

"Do you have four pence for me, my love?" Sybille enquired sweetly, letting her hands descend to where they kneaded Christina's buttocks enticingly through her clothes.

"Yes, um . . . right here," she said, breaking away awkwardly to fumble in her pouch for the money.

"Thank you," the tiny woman murmured as she took the coins, casting them casually upon the table.

Sybille then demurely moved away from Christina as she began to loosen her clothing. She dropped her daffodil-yellow kirtle about her feet, leaving only her thin, translucent shift to cover her nakedness. She stood there nearly motionless for a moment, allowing Christina time to admire every aspect of her lovely figure. Then she began a subtle swaying of her hips as she drew her remaining garment slowly upward and over her head. Sybille threw it to the side as she turned to face Christina.

"Now, come to me, my love."

Christina obeyed like one entranced; stepping forward until their bodies were just inches apart. Christina stood, not daring to move further forward, her breath coming in ragged gasps as the other woman began to undress her. Soon, her body was bare as well. Her back arched involuntarily as she felt Sybille's lips caressing the nipple of her right breast. She reached down and angled the other woman's mouth toward hers. Christina's head lowered as she matched her lips to Sybille's. This kiss was long and deeply passionate. There was no urgency to their lovemaking as there had been before. Each had only one all-consuming desire; to satisfy the other completely.

Hours later, Christina lay on her side in the bed, a fine sheen of sweat covering her naked body. Her right arm encircled Sybille's toned abdomen, which rose and fell slightly in time with her gentle breathing. The scent of musk filled her nostrils, reminding her of their fervent passion.

Although Christina's body seemed relaxed and calm, her mind was working furiously.

"Sybille, my darling?" she finally persuaded herself to ask.

"Yes, what is it?" the other woman asked sleepily without stirring her body.

"I've been thinking," Christina began, "Why do you not leave this awful place and come to live with me? My house is massive; you could have a suite of rooms, if you wished. That way, we could be together any time we wished."

Sybille turned around, moving further upward in the bed until their faces were opposite from one another. She stared at Christina for a few seconds, a faint, quizzical smile on her lips and her forehead slightly furrowed. She craned her neck forward and lightly kissed Christina's lips.

"You are so sweet, my Christina," she said in a cooing voice. "Tell me, why do you continue this masquerade as a man? You have made considerable profits. Why do you not drop your silly disguise, move to another city, and marry a respectable man? Your husband would take care of you and you would have no worries beyond what clothes to wear each day. Why are you so set on remaining Master Frederick Kohl?"

Christina did not comprehend how this line of thought pertained to her own question, but answered truthfully.

"It is the freedom. I enjoy making my own decisions and being responsible only to myself. It is important to me to be thought of as a person and not just property. I believe this is only possible for me in the guise of a man."

"But yet you ask me to become a bird in a cage for you, to be available for your pleasure anytime your cleft begins to moisten. You would not even have to travel across the bridge to enjoy me! How convenient for you!"

"No, it is not like that at all! I was merely . . ." Christina hastily sought to clarify her meaning.

Yes, my love, it is exactly like that," Sybille's beautiful green eyes now grew sad. "Do you believe you are the first person who has offered to take me away from this life. to make an honest woman of me? You are not. I rejected them as I now refuse you."

Christina stared at the woman's elfin face in disbelief, stunned she would choose the life of a whore over one with her.

"I am here because this is where I want to be. I lay with whom I wish and refuse those with whom I do not. I pay the owner a portion of my earnings, but he owns the room, not me."

"But the men, they mistreat you. Surely you do not enjoy that?

"A hardship of the trade, I'm afraid. But you are a merchant, do you not endure storms at sea and violent disagreements ashore? What are these wounds, here, and here, and here?" Sybille used her forefinger to indicate scars on Christina's body. "Did you receive these sitting comfortably before your fire in your fine home? No, you did not."

Christina found no words to counter the woman's arguments. She could only look at her in supplication, her tearful eyes begging Sybille to reconsider.

She reached out her hand to gently stroke Christina's cheek before saying, "I am who and what I am, do not try to change me. I look forward to our times together with fondness. You smell sweet and do not need to cause me pain to achieve your own satisfaction. Please believe me when I tell you that, when I am with you, I have thoughts of no one else. My entire being exists solely to satisfy you and your desires. Your wish is to pleasure me as well, and that is a bonus. But then you are gone, and your thoughts turn to other matters, as do mine."

Sybille silently arose from the bed and began to dress.

Seeing no other recourse, Christina began to do the same.

She felt a great emptiness inside her.

They now stood across from each other, as they had before their lovemaking began. Sybille looked upward at the face of the taller woman.

"I have never said this to one with whom I have shared a bed before," Sybille began hesitantly, "I will not become your wife, nor your kept woman. But, if you will have me, I will be your friend."

Christina nodded her head slightly as she fought to control the accumulated feelings pent up inside her. She bit her quivering lower lip hard to refrain from commenting that friends don't usually need to pay to enjoy the other's company. Suddenly, the dam that had been restraining her emotions burst and she began to sob uncontrollably. She fell onto the bed and Sybille moved to silently console her, holding her close and running her fingers reassuringly through Christina's damp hair.

Time passed indeterminably. Eventually, through some unspoken agreement, they arose and shared a chaste goodbye kiss. Christina left; descending the stairs and exiting out into the cool night air. She had no idea how she returned home, her mind was completely numb and registered few details until she found herself standing before the door to her own room. She had never felt more alone, desolate in the reality of her shattered dreams of life with Sybille and how it had broken her heart. She undressed and slipped into bed. Laying very still, she could still faintly smell Sybille's scent on her body. The reminiscence of her touch and taste seemed almost tangible. She found the woman's lingering presence consoling somehow. Closing her eyes, she fought to retain a grasp on the memory as sleep overcame her.

Soon after she broke her fast the next morning, she was surprised by Trudi's announcement that Matthias was waiting in the hall. She hurried down to meet *der Greif's* master, hoping his news would somehow ease her from her feelings of melancholy.

"Good day to you, Matthias," she said evenly as she came into the room.

"God be with you, Master Frederick," he replied excitedly. "I may have welcome tidings for you."

Christina quickened her step and slipped lithely onto the bench across the table from where the man was sitting. The interested look on her face imploring him to continue.

"Yesterday, you asked me to stealthily inquire about the waterfront as to whether anyone may have a ship they might be willing to sell. Doing as you requested, I was surprised to learn Olbrecht Bromse's *Seelöwe* could be available. It is a good vessel of almost fifty lasts, from what I could discover. It seems he seeks a sale because of his desire to purchase a larger vessel to ply the Bergen codfish trade."

"This is wonderful news, Matthias!" Christina exclaimed, her mood lightening. "Will you please inquire as to when we can take a look at it?"

The corners of his mouth turned upward slightly in a faint semblance of a smile as he said, "I have taken the liberty to have done so already. The ship's master awaits us anon, at your pleasure of course."

"Done!" Christina said emphatically, happy for the distraction from her morose reflections. "Let us depart immediately!"

As they rose, Christina heard animated voices coming from the yard outside. Curious as to what could be the cause of such a ruckus, she rushed outside into the fresh morning air. She immediately spotting a gaggle of male figures grouped in an all too familiar semi-circle.

"For the love of God," she muttered through clenched teeth as she moved swiftly to where the animated figures of the men stood.

There's only one reason why men cluster themselves in such a manner!

Some of the men noticed her approach and, gaining the attention of their fellows, they parted, allowing her to view the source of their excitement. The stableman Malcolm was laying with his back on the ground, using his arms to fend off the wildly swinging fists of her new apprentice. Before she could speak, the situation reversed and Malcolm was the one raining down blows on Jost. Fortunately, they were no more effectual than those he himself had received.

"Cease your fucking brawling right now, you two, or you'll discover how a smack alongside your empty heads really feels!" Christina snarled loudly. "Now, get your asses out of the horseshit and explain to me how in the hell this row started or I'll have your bollocks for breakfast!"

"It was him!" Jost muttered as he stood up. "He was making crude remarks about Mistress Trudi!"

"Ah, fur Christ's sek, awl I sed wer she be a fine figur' of a gurl. Whet ar ya, a feckin' prist or somethin'? Malcolm responded, albeit not without a mischievous twinkle in his eyes.

"All you said?" Jost continued in a still heated voice. "How about how you'd like to feel her cleft?"

"Ah, now, boyo, thet be only wishful thinkin'!" he replied, a wide grin now spreading across his lips.

At that comment, Jost rushed toward the taller boy like a mad boar, throwing him once more onto the ground. Christina took three steps and swung her foot forward, landing a heavy kick squarely into Jost's arse. He rolled off the other boy in surprise, his hand involuntarily moving to clutch his injured buttock.

Christina then reached her hand down toward Malcolm and, taking him firmly by the ear, pulled him roughly to his feet.

"Now, you listen carefully to what I say," she spoke in a measured tone which she hoped he took as serious. "I want you to scrub this entire yard until its clean enough to eat off, which you might be doing, if you piss me off again. Do you understand me?"

Suitably chastised, he nodded silently, all mirth now wiped from his face.

Christina then turned to her cousin.

"And you," she began, "Get your ass to the scullery and tell Isabel you are to scrub all the pots until they shine. Now, off with you both!"

Neither boy waited to be asked a second time as they scrambled to begin their assigned tasks.

Turning around, she could already see the other men hastening to return to their duties so as not to incur the wrath of Christina's sharp tongue themselves. She was about to give them a scolding for good measure, then thought better of it. She returned to the entranceway to find Matthias standing there.

"They're more a danger to themselves than each other," he chuckled. "Those two will not soon forget this lesson, but neither did they suffer undue damage because of it."

She appreciated Matthias' comment, knowing her problem was small compared to his need to maintain discipline over his many crews of unruly sailors over the years. Still, she remained annoyed as to the root of the altercation. Although she loved Trudi with all of her heart, she knew her friend to be an accomplished flirt. She already pegged Jost to be smitten, but had not realized Malcolm too had succumbed to Trudi's wiles. Christina vowed to carefully watch for future strife between Malcolm and Jost, and to ask

Ziesolf to be vigilant as well. Although further fisticuffs were certainly to be discouraged, she could not permit the feud to escalate to more serious weapons where they might do actual damage to one another.

"So, should we continue forth?" she asked Matthias. "Hopefully, we will not bear witness to a full-blown battle upon our return."

As they moved through the city streets toward the river, another thought came into Christina's head.

Sweet Jesus, has neither of those two ever been in a fight before? I've seen ten-year-old boys scuffle with more skill than what I saw today. They'd have no chance against a bully like Richard, let alone someone like the sailor who attacked me in Sluys.

She recalled with disgust her uncle's treacherous apprentice against whom she had fought.

Christina made a mental note to ask Ziesolf to provide some rudimentary training to the two young men so they could at least defend themselves. It occurred to her that, perhaps, she too should work with them.

When was the last time I trained?

She knew it had been a month or two at least.

A bit of exercise could certainly do me good.

They arrived at the Thames and, turning upriver, walked along the embankment until they arrived at the *Seelöwe's* moorage. Both Christina and Matthias stepped back away from the ship so they could better observe its lines.

The vessel was slightly longer than *der Greif*, but not significantly so. The typical lapstrake planking of the hull overlapped evenly, with regular placement of the heads of the double-clenched iron nails that secured them. The mast appeared straight with no evidence of having been spliced or significantly repaired. The stern castle was spacious, extending slightly outward from the main hull of the ship. In addition, there was an enclosed cabin space at the forecastle, a feature *der Greif* did not share.

Certainly, this is a handsome craft from all outward appearance, but looks can be deceiving.

Christina cautioned herself against being swayed too soon.

They walked to the side of the ship and were invited aboard by a man named Thorsten, the apparent master of the vessel. He was probably only in his mid-twenties; yet, appeared much older because of the thick, dark beard that encompassed his entire lower face. Matthias took the lead in examining the condition of every interior detail of *Seelöwe*. For her part, Christina remained a silent, but keenly interested, observer.

Returning to the main deck from the capacious hold, Matthias asked Thorsten, "She appears fit, but how does she sail?"

"She knifes through the water like a dolphin, she does." Thorsten's boast was stated so matter-of-factly it seemed as if he were voicing an inarguable fact.

Christina found it impossible to conceive of a speed comparison between an ungainly cog ship and the agile ocean creature, however.

"When can we take the ship out upon the water?" was Matthias' following question.

"I can piece together a crew in three days' time. Be here early in the morning and we'll put her through her paces for you."

With their next meeting time agreed, Christina and Matthias left Thorsten on board and began walking back the way they had come. They had barely passed beyond the earshot of the *Seelöwe's* master when Christina could no longer contain her excitement.

"What do you think, Matthias?"

"She is a fine vessel, of sound construction and well looked after. A master would be proud to have such a ship under his feet. If she sails as well as she looks, she will be a sound investment."

They parted ways soon after, Matthias returning to *der Greif,* and Christina back to Bokerel House.

Her mood was buoyant as she entered her courtyard. She even felt a twinge of guilt when she saw Malcolm on his hands and knees, scrubbing one of the flagstones. She went swiftly into the house before she became tempted to alleviate his punishment.

Chapter 10

___

Price of Advice is Most Dear
London, March, 1310

Christina changed her workaday clothes for ones more presentable and passed the afternoon alternating pleasant thoughts of her possible acquisition of *Seelöwe* with fretting about her impending audience with the chief alderman. At last, she could stand her idleness no more.

The sun is surely beginning its descent in the sky; if I walk slowly, I will arrive at Revele's house at nearly the appointed time.

Sooner than expected Christina stood in the street outside the house of the chief alderman. She could not help but gaze once more in appreciation at the beauty of the imposing façade, with its uniform rows of arched windows. Despite being aware she could while away an hour admiring the architectural exquisiteness of the building, she decided to announce her arrival instead. Stepping forward, she pulled the rope that hung at the side of the handsomely crafted wrought iron gate.

Somewhere inside the large compound a bell must have rung, announcing the presence of a visitor. In less than a minute, the same liveried servant who had greeted her on her first visit opened the sally inset in the gate and beckoned her through.

"Good day to you, young master," the man greeted her in a formal manner.

Christina did not immediately respond, her attention consumed as her eyes swept the breath of the courtyard.

Could it have only been a few months ago I was last here?

She was shaken from her reverie by the sound of Revele's servant loudly clearing his throat. She looked in his direction to see him staring belligerently at her. She locked eyes with him, no longer as tolerant of the impudence of her social inferiors as she had once been. He turned away, leading her into the manor house.

They passed through the lavishly decorated hall, ascending the stairways that led to the alderman's solar. She was surprised to find the room rather dimly lit considering the late hour of the day. Without uttering a word, the servant left her alone in the chamber, bringing the door firmly to a close behind him. Despite her anxiety, Christina visually explored the room and its contents with substantial interest. She counted twenty-seven pieces of English glass in the large dormer window to her right, including two large ones that bore armorial crests. The other three walls were covered in intricately carved wainscot paneling of honey oak. Overall, the room seemed warm and cheery; yet, left the visitor with no doubts as to the affluence of its owner.

Her further musings were interrupted by the sound of the inner door to the room opening. She began to silently rehearse what it was she intended to say to the alderman before, unexpectedly, her mind went blank with shock. The diminutive figure entering the room was not that of Revele; rather, it was the person of his daughter, Katharine.

The young woman walked to the large, cushioned chair that seemingly was the favorite of her father and sat down primly.

Without any trace of affected modesty, she looked boldly into Christina's brown eyes with her own of sea-green. Katharine adjusted her position on the chair slightly, smoothed her green velvet gown, and folded her hands comfortably in her lap before beginning to speak.

"Why Frederick Kohl, how well pleased I am to once more make your acquaintance!"

The words from her rose-tinted lips were issued in a lilting, almost musical, voice.

"I am happy to see you as well," replied Christina politely despite knowing this was very far from the truth. "But my business is with your father. I have matters important to both of us I wish to discuss, hoping to obtain his sage advice so it might guide me in making prudent decisions."

"Ah, I see. Regrettably, my father is indisposed, suffering greatly from a mysterious malady that may imperil his very life. Even now, he is being attended by learned healers who ply their craft, seeking to restore him to his previous good health."

"I am sorry to learn of his illness. And your brother?" Christina asked, remembering the sad eyed, pale young man she had met on her first audience with Revele.

"Why do you ask of him? Is it that I make you nervous?"

She stared peevishly at Christina.

"If you must know, Father has dispatched him to Lübeck, to serve as an apprentice to one of his trade partners. I pity the man, to be burdened with such a whimpering sprat as my brother."

"Then I must say I beg your forgiveness as one who has troubled you unnecessarily," Christina said, despite her irritation that this audience had been a complete waste of time. "I will pray fervently for your father's complete recovery."

152

Christina made as if to depart the room.

"Have you no manners, Herr Kohl? "Katharine's voice suddenly became tinged with iron. "I have not given you leave to go, sir."

Christ's Nails! What game is this wench playing at now?

"My apologies, mi 'lady," Christina muttered, "but my business is with the chief alderman. If he is incapacitated, I must seek out one of his fellows. Now, may I have your permission to go?

"In fact, your man requested a meeting betwixt you and Herr Revele, not one with the chief alderman. Although I have no authority to speak as a representative of the Hansa, I certainly do as my father's daughter."

"A simple mistake, one for which I also beg your forgiveness. Please realize the advice which I seek concerns matters of trade which I am sure are of little interest to you. Now . . ." Christina began before being abruptly interrupted.

"Do not take me lightly!" the young woman's harsh tone belayed her youth and the beauty of her countenance. "Just because you are a man you believe I, a mere woman, am your inferior, lacking any sort of intelligence or common sense. How wrong you are! My father has been the chief alderman of London Hanseatic community for over a decade, more than half the years I have been on earth! Throughout this time, I have listened and learned, sometimes in this very room and others while outside with my ear to the door."

Katharine arose and paced angrily about the room.

"Do you think I do not have knowledge of my father's dealings; the clandestine alliances, the secret compacts made, the cunning betrayals? Yet, instead you seek to run to one of the other aldermen for advice, simply because they are men who hold a position to which I am forbidden to aspire. Do you believe one's brain increases with age, like a tree grow a ring larger with each passing year? Go then, Frederick Kohl, go and be damned!"

Christina was stunned.

Have I dismissed this woman solely because of her sex, just as I rued being so underestimated myself?

"King Edward has asked to borrow from me the sum of 5,000 pounds sterling and I know not what to do," Christina stated forthrightly, deciding in an instant to disregard the abject distrust she had of this woman.

"What?" Katharine's anger seemingly dissipated in an instant, replaced by an acute interest in Christina's disclosure. She returned purposefully to her seat and, with her composure regained, asked Christina to explain how this request had come about.

"The king summoned me to meet with him at the Tower. He then asked for a loan of 5,000 pounds," Christina repeated, cautiously fearing she may have already shared too much. She steadfastly decided to withhold elaborating on her complicated relationship with Gaveston.

"God's Teeth," Katharine mused aloud. "Do you have such a sum?"

"Aye, I do," Christina replied, still believing brevity was in her best interests.

"And what is it that you would seek in return, for the loan of this amount?"

"Return?"

"Surety. Surely you did not envision showing up with bags of silver pennies and strewing them about the king's feet? Rumor has it he is already indebted to the Frescobaldi bankers for over 20,000 pounds; will his first commitment be to repay them or you?"

Katharine remarked sarcastically then, seeing the crestfallen look upon Christina's face, said, "Please say you didn't agree to the King's request without arranging a guarantee for the loan."

Embarrassed at her own naivety, Christina protested, "I did not think it proper to haggle with an anointed king as if he were a common tradesman."

"Oh, you didn't, did you?" the young woman's giggle was more stinging than her words. "You must protect your money from a king just as readily as you do from a baker whose loaves are too light. Kings are well known to have short memories when it comes time to repay the money they borrow. If he chooses to ignore his debt, to whom can you appeal other than God, who seldom becomes involved in matters of finance."

Christina said nothing, somewhat cowed by the overt reproach of the young woman's words.

"So, in the case of loaning to royalty, you contract for something the monarch values as surety until he repays his loan. This could be as tangible as his jewels or his regalia. There is a story that a prior king named Henry did not wear his royal crown for six years because it was being held as surety in the home of a Jew in Herefordshire. Another possibility is the King allows the lender to collect certain taxes or duties that he is owed until such time as the debt is repaid."

Christina's interest suddenly perked up.

A steady source of income is clearly preferable to being responsible for maintaining the King's crown.

"What form might these taxes take?"

"Well, the principal of these is on wool, although others are assessed on leather, lead, tin, cheese, and diverse other commodities to a lesser degree." Katharine replied.

"And the king agrees to this?" Christina could still not bring herself to trust Revele's daughter completely.

"What choice does he have? If he has desperate need of immediate capital, he will gladly barter away future profits to procure it."

The response of the alderman's daughter was confident and assured. Then, a sly smile formed on her childlike countenance.

Is it possible the king seeks these monies to finance a possible war? One that is rumored to be impending, perhaps against the Scots? You can tell me, Frederick. Am I not worthy of your trust?"

"The King did not confide in me the purpose of his request, only that his need was great."

The lie slipped easily off her tongue, as she had no desire to be the source of a disclosure of Edward's confidential plans, especially not to this woman. Katharine raised her sculpted eyebrows, a gesture Christina interpreted as a sign of disbelief. As if to belie her mistrust of the veracity of Christina's statement, the woman's smile widened, displaying the unblemished whiteness of her evenly spaced teeth. She arose and walked slowly toward Christina, stopping a mere three feet away. Although Christina towered over the elfin creature by several inches, she felt as if she were at a distinct disadvantage.

Katharine's glittering eyes slowly slithered upward to meet those of Christina.

"Did you know I am to be married?" she stated evenly. "No? Well, it is true. I am to wed Herr Volker, the senior alderman after my father."

Christina searched her memories to place the man, as the name seemed somehow familiar to her. She suddenly remembered him, recalling he had sat as one of the judges at her trial.

This cannot be!

Christina sensibilities were shocked by the woman's disclosure.

That man must have been sixty years old if he was a day! Surely, she must mean his son, or even his grandson!

"Ah, I can tell by the look of revulsion on your face you know of my darling betrothed."

"But . . . but how could your father have misused you so? To promise one so young as you to a man of Herr Volker's age is unjustly cruel!" Christina cried, outraged by the apparent injustice of the act.

"Cruel? My father? Oh yes, Frederick, in ways you will never understand. But not in this case. You see, it was I who convinced father to contract me to Herr Volker."

In disbelief, Christina blurted out, "But why, for the love of God, would you do such a thing?"

The alderman's daughter heard the disgust in Christina's question and responded in an even and emotionless voice.

"Why? A good question, Frederick, an excellent one even. Why would a young girl seek to wed a shriveled ancient over thrice her age? The Hansa is no different than society in general; governance is held by a few old men who have risen to command not through their competence and audacity, but because of their longevity and caution. But old men can be very foolish, you see. What can they deny to the young, sweet mouth that gladly encompasses their wizened member?"

Christina brain could form no intelligible response to the woman's crude question.

"Nothing," with no reply from Christina, Katharine answered her own question. "They can deny nothing. Should my father die, Volker will become the new chief alderman for the London entrepot. In turn, I will govern my lord husband with a firm hand and a clever tongue. In fact, leaving me as the true chief alderman, don't you think?"

Christina remained speechless, struck dumb by the unmitigated ambition of the woman.

"Please do not fear for me, dear Frederick. There are other ways in which you may help assuage the frustrations of my loveless match. So many interesting, pleasant things you may do to compensate for my husband's feeble impotence."

The tip of her tongue now began exploring the incising edges of her teeth. Without warning, she turned away and, burying her face into the seat of her father's chair, reached behind and in one smooth motion hiked her skirts up over her hips. She spread her legs widely, boldly exposing her sex.

"Come, Frederick, let us play! Who knows, in the future my husband may even find sport in watching our games!"

The young woman's voice was guttural, as she surrendered to the violence of her unfulfilled passions.

Christina gasped and said, "No! I cannot deflower a woman promised to another man!"

She realized her response sounded comically prudish; yet, it was the only thing she could think to say on the spur of the moment.

Katharine pivoted toward her with surprising speed, her skirts still in disarray. She reached out and grabbed the front of Christina's braies and jerked the larger woman violently towards her. Her desires were now uncontrollable, like a wild beast at the heights of its heat.

"For the love of God, are you a man, or no?" Her voice had been reduced to a breathless whisper as she clumsily struggled to untie Christina's braies.

"Stop! Get back from me, you sluttish bitch!" Christina cried, roughly pushing the other woman backwards until she fell, to lie in a heap upon the floor.

Stiffly, Katharine stood erect, letting her gown fall back to the fullness of its length.

With her cheeks flaming from indignation and frustration, she turned back toward Christina and said in a mocking voice now devoid of all warmth, "Deflower? You stupid, vain fool! Are you so naive as to believe this furrow has not already been set to plow, that I have guarded my virgin cleft against all others, only to surrender it gladly to you? Some have not been as hesitant to enjoy my proffered pleasures as yourself. Perhaps they realize it is better to number me as a friend than as an enemy?"

How can I extricate myself from this cesspit?

Christina felt her stomach lurch with revulsion.

"I truly do want you to consider me a friend, Mistress Revele," she hoped she was choosing her words with adequate care. "I thank you earnestly for your sage advice, and . . ."

Katharine interrupted her, scalding contempt permeating her every word.

"A pox on your thanks! They hold no value to me, much as you do yourself. Beware my reach, young Kohl, beware my reach!"

The woman stormed from the room, slamming the door after her. Christina was left alone, certain only that she desired to depart this house immediately. She descended the stairs quickly, taking no time to admire feature or fixture. For her, the loveliness of the house would forevermore be despoiled by the wickedness of the depraved young woman who dwelt within.

She inhaled deeply as she stepped out into the clean, night air.

I must step more carefully than ever.

Where the father's malevolence was held back by his sense of duty to his position, the daughter's ire knew no such restraint.

I must truly be careful, she repeated to herself, knowing her very life depended on it.

She returned home, sharing as few words as possible with Trudi and Ziesolf in the solar. She would discuss her meeting with Katharine Revele with each of them, but only at a later time when she felt more ready to talk. After a brief supper, she went directly to her chamber, hoping the morrow would hold the same promise as that which had begun this day and none of the problems with which it had ended.

The next day thankfully passed uneventfully, marred by no reoccurrence of brawls, threats, or unpleasant disclosures. Christina spoke with Ziesolf concerning the practical aspects of her meeting with Revele's daughter, editing out the more intimate details. These she did share with Trudi, whose eyes widened as she learned of Katharine's audaciously frank sexuality.

"But did not her wantonness excite you?" Trudi asked.

"Aye," Christina grudgingly admitted, "But what was I to do? I could not reveal myself to her; she would hold power over me the remainder of my life."

They talked and laughed, Christina's good humor returning in the relaxed atmosphere of their conversation. Afterwards, she even cast a smile toward Jost; although she was unsure whether he marked it. Seeing her, he turned and fled like a threatened hart rather than chancing her wrath once again. She vowed to speak to him, to reassure him her anger had long since cooled.

Must I always put the wrong foot forward?

She promised herself to be more circumspect in word and deed in the future.

Chapter 11

A Purchase, a Loan, and a Disclosure
London, March, 1310

Christina walked rapidly toward the river, as much to warm her body against the chilled early morning air as from her excitement. Arriving, she waved to Matthias who was waiting patiently, sitting on a hefty wooden bollard. She continued walking toward *Seelöwe*, while Matthias rose and set a course to intercept hers. For the last hundred feet, they approached the ship together, each quietly assessing the flurry of activity amongst the men who moved about her deck.

Soon after Christina and Matthias boarded the ship, two of Thorsten's crewmen released the heavy hawsers binding *Seelöwe* to its moorings, then nimbly scrambled back aboard. At the same time, eight other sailors began to heave heavily on the thick halyard lines, lifting the massive square-rigged sail into place. Immediately after it dropped into position, the sturdy linen sheet began to fill.

Mattias put his mouth to Christina's ear and said, "Do you see how narrow the individual cloths are? That's very good, in my mind. Less likely for the sail to stretch. "

Christina's eye traveled to the sail, confirming the sailing master's experienced observation. She placed her hand on one of the wooden blocks maintaining tension on the shrouds to steady herself as the cog slowly nosed into the river course. Matthias moved to the stern and Thorsten relinquished the rudder post to him. Soon, they were heading downriver at the slow but steady pace of about three knots per hour.

Seelöwe more resembles her namesake than a dolphin.

Christina was not dissatisfied by the fact. The vessel rode easily upon the water, although this was hardly a test of its seaworthiness.

I hope I am equally as pleased when under sail in a North Sea gale with a full hold of cargo.

The day was just beginning to darken when *Seelöwe* returned to her mooring. A cold rain now fell in a steady drizzle, blending the sky and the water of the river to the point where each grew indistinguishable from the other in the distance. Christina and Matthias departed the vessel and hurried through the crowded streets toward her home. They at last arrived, walking hurriedly through the courtyard and into the hall. They shed their sopping cloaks and hoods near the door, then moved briskly toward the blazing fireplace. They stood as close as they dared to the crackling flames, allowing the intense heat to seep into their chilled bodies. They sat down after a few moments, intent on discussing the merits of the ship on which they had spent most of the day.

The maidservant Mary entered the room, executing a perfect curtsy despite carrying a tray with two steaming bowls of mulled wine. Christina idly wondered whether she had decided to do so of her own initiative, or if she had been so instructed by Trudi. Leaving the room as swiftly as she had entered and bracketed by another curtsy, she flashed a smile at Christina as she departed.

"By the one true Cross, could I have ever been so young? That one has a hankering for you, I think," remarked Matthias.

"Nay, Master Matthias, I believe she has an eye for you!"

The old man's weathered face smiled, but he said nothing more on the subject, preferring instead to begin their discussion of the merits of *Seelöwe*. They wasted little time before agreeing the ship was a sturdy, seaworthy vessel that would serve Christina's intended purpose very well. After sharing another round of the steaming, sweet wine, Matthias bid Christina farewell, promising to carry her offer of 280 silver marks to Thorsten on the morrow, so he might then convey it to the ship's owner.

After that, it is in God's hands, and those of Olbrecht Bromse.

Christina knew she would think of little else until she had received an answer.

Except for how to explain to a king I place such little faith in his word that he must provide me with a surety before I lend him the money he seeks. I did not think to ask Katharine Revele whether it is I who should propose the nature of the guarantee or if it is the prerogative of the King to make an offer. It is certainly too late now to seek her counsel once again.

A few days later, Christina departed from her audience with King Edward in a daze, amazed at what had just transpired. This meeting had been much less personal than the first, as the site had been changed to the voluminous audience chamber at the royal palace at Westminster. There were also several court functionaries in attendance, each fawning about King Edward most outrageously. Christina's attention was drawn, however, to focus on the one person in the room who seemed strangely detached from the courtly panorama. Sitting next to the king was a slender, pale-skinned beauty of a young woman, whom Christina recognized as Edward's French queen, Isabella. Although she remained silent throughout the proceedings, her severe expression radiated her sense of displeasure quite plainly. Christina was taken aback that some of the woman's most poisonous glances were reserved for her.

What have I done to incur the ire of this woman? Having made a foe of Katharine Revele is enough. I surely need not count the queen among my enemies as well.

The negotiation had seemed rather anticlimactic. Edward had sparse regard for detail, his singular focus seemingly only on the ready funds Christina's loan would provide him. He readily agreed to Christina's request for a third of the staple customs on wool exported through the port of London, a sum of two shillings and two and a half pence on each woolsack. He ordered a man whom she assumed to be his chancellor to have a contract drawn to that effect. The chancellor then asked for Christina to return three days hence to sign the contract and to provide him with the bill of transfer for 5,000 pounds sterling, if she could compile the funds within that short amount of time. She agreed and left forthwith, happy to escape the wrathful scrutiny of Queen Isabella.

Over the next few days, Christina's life seemed to be a whirlwind of activity. She began negotiations in earnest with Olbrecht Bromse over the purchase of *Seelöwe*. The merchant countered her offer with a demand for a price of 340 pounds. Eventually, they settled on 308; more than she had originally budgeted, but still very reasonable for a ship of *Seelöwe's* quality.

Since she was now assured of a second vessel, Christina set about purchasing cargo to fill *der Greif's* hold for its journey to Lübeck. She augmented her stock of Flemish fabric with a large purchase of less desirable English cloth. Having learned during her voyage to Bruges about the need to stabilize a ship with either additional ballast or weightier goods, she also purchased hundreds of ingots of tin from the royal stannary in Ashburton, Devon.

Once these are delivered, Der Greif's cargo will be complete, Matthias may then leave for Lübeck immediately.

She unconsciously nodded her head slightly in approval.

Christina also took time to craft a response to her mother's letter. In carefully chosen words, she explained her strategy for maintaining the axis of trade her father had worked so hard to establish. She also thanked her mother for sending her cousin to assist her, although she diplomatically omitted his most recent martial exploits from mention. Finished, she carefully folded the sheet of vellum.

Taking the small taper she had used for illumination in one hand, she used her other to bring a stick of sealing wax directly above where the flaps of the parchment met. She brought the flame near the wax, ensuring it remained at a forty-five-degree angle so as not to infuse the seal with black wavy lines of carbon. Within a few seconds several drops of wax had melted onto the vellum, forming a neat two-inch diameter circle across the fold.

She now took her seal in her right hand and pressed it firmly down into the warm wax. Holding the paper down with her left hand, she lifted the seal directly upward. She was pleased to find no distortion marring the imprint, leaving the image of the cog ship and two wool sacks sharply defined. She was proud of her new seal, having designed it herself. She hoped her mother would like it as well. Completing this, Christina entrusted the document to Matthias for delivery.

On the appointed day, she returned to Westminster Palace to complete her transaction with the king. She was surprised Edward was not present at this meeting, he being represented by his chamberlain in his place. Instead of the audience chamber, the meeting occurred in a small antechamber with only two other men in attendance. The chamberlain read the document aloud while Christina followed along on a duplicate. Afterwards, the documents were quickly signed and sealed and the chamberlain presented Christina with her copy. Relieved by the relative ease by which the proceedings were concluded, Christina prepared to depart. Suddenly, the two clerics ceased their whispered conversation and looked nervously to the chamberlain, whose face turned ashen as he executed a clumsy bow in the direction of the entrance portal.

The sound of delicate, but purposeful, steps approaching prompted Christina to turn her head toward the doorway as well. Her guts began to tighten deeply within the pit of her stomach as she beheld the English queen fast approaching. She bowed low, hoping to escape Isabella's notice.

"You," the queen's girlish voice was clearly commanding, "Leave us now."

Christina had hoped the "us" was intended to indicate the chamberlain; however, he and the two clerics immediately scampered from the room, leaving her alone with the queen.

Christina started to stand erect.

"I did not give you permission to rise in my presence, Hansard!" Isabella said in an imperious voice.

"My apologies, . . ." Christina began before she was cut off.

"Nor to speak," continued the queen.

Christina said nothing more, realizing her most sensible course of action was to remain motionless until directed to do otherwise.

"My lord husband is well pleased by you, Frederick Kohl. With your loan, his plan to make war on the Scots moves closer to fruition. Soon, he will depart for the north, rejoining his beloved Gaveston at last. Perhaps you will be there as well?"

Christina was unsure whether the queen desired a response to the question, or if it was posed rhetorically. She chose to say nothing, waiting instead for the other woman to continue.

"I know not if you are another player in their blasphemous charade, one which offends me both as a woman and a wife to my very core."

How may I make her understand I am not only innocent of what she implies, but also incapable?

Christina's mind was rife with indecision.

I cannot very well disclose my true nature to her, can I?

"Despite my low regard for you, I do thank you for your generosity in providing sorely needed funds at this precarious time. I fear greatly my Edward lacks the support of many of his barons, some of whom will most likely employ his absence to foment treacheries against him. A great triumph in Scotland, however, will surely buoy his popularity and go far to secure our reign against their insurrection. You have proven useful, Hansard, but that makes you no more palatable to me."

Isabella turned and departed the room without further comment. Christina waited until she could no longer hear her footsteps, then regained her feet. She stretched the cramps that had formed in her back and legs from remaining in her awkward, bowing position too long. Clutching her copy of the agreement in her hand, she swiftly exited the palace grounds, unconsciously refraining from drawing a full breath until the fortress was far behind her.

Over the next few days, Christina's apprehension concerning her ill-fated encounter with Queen Isabella gradually faded. The tin shipment from Ashburton arrived and was loaded into *der Greif's* hold. With nothing more to delay the ship's departure, the bales of cloth both Flemish and English were finally brought aboard, having minimized their risk of damage from the elements by waiting until the last moment.

As Christina stood on the wharf early the next morning, bidding farewell to Matthias and the other crewmen, she was surprised to see Reiniken separate himself from those sailors who were now boarding the ship.

"Where are you off to, Wig?" she asked in curiosity.

"Ah ain't goin'," he stated simply with a gap-toothed grin. "Ya see, ah lak it here in this London town and there's still a lot of whores ah gots left to tup!"

The news the mammoth man was leaving her employ was unexpected and disappointing. She had initially encountered him when boarding *Der Greif* for the first time, her negative first impressions had gradually evolved into genuine warmth and fondness as she got to know him better. She had neither met such a purveyor of profanity or lover of lewd behavior in her life, nor had she known a more stalwart companion.

He will be sorely missed.

"Besides, Yur Worship, I mite haves udder prospects in mind," he added with a conspiratorial wink in her direction before sauntering downriver along the quay.

In less than an hour's time, *der Greif* was fading into the distance, embarking on its weeks long journey to Lübeck. Christina remained on the wharf for a goodly time after the ship had disappeared completely, unbidden anxieties filling her mind. She at last departed, knowing the only help she could provide the ship and its crew now would be through the power of her prayers.

She returned to Bokerel House and, stepping into the hall, found Ziesolf warming himself near the fire. She pulled up a stool and sat down beside him. The two remained there for several minutes before Ziesolf broke the comfortable silence.

"They're off then?" he asked.

"Aye. There's a fair wind that should speed them safely to the mouth of the river by midday. Then it's the long pull north," she replied.

"Safe journey to 'em," he said in a quiet voice.

"Yes, safe journey," Christina echoed, suddenly feeling morose once more.

"With the storerooms now all but emptied, I'll have the lads at work sweeping them out till the floors shine. Maybe we'll even whitewash the insides, who knows? Better to keep the lot of them busy than allowing them to fill their time with mischief," Ziesolf's brisk tones broke her morose reverie.

"Perhaps there is another task we could set them to," she posited.

He looked at her expectantly, waiting for her to verbalize her thoughts.

"If the men have spare time, might we engage them in a bit of training? They seem a goodly lot but, if the scrap between the two lads was any indication, they would not be worth a piss in a barfight, let alone if there arose a situation where we needed them to stand beside us."

At this suggestion, Ziesolf's craggy face broke into a semblance of a smile while his good eye brightened.

"A goodly plan, Christina, a goodly plan. I have seen the results of towns and villages being attacked; it is never a pretty sight. Although the men fought hard to protect their homes and families, they stood no chance against a determined enemy, one that knew how to use their weapons. Although we might think London is more civilized, it does not take much prompting for men to turn to savagery. You are correct, we should be prepared."

It is not just men that I fear.

A cold shiver having nothing to do with the temperature of the room ran down her back as she remembered the two influential women whose animosity she seemingly had incurred.

Ziesolf arose slowly and remarked, "Well, I'd best be off. It seems we now have more to fill our day than previously imagined."

Giving Christina a hearty pat on her shoulder as he passed, Ziesolf exited out to the courtyard and she was once more alone with her thoughts.

Sweet Jesus, how old is he?

Christina stared after her departed mentor.

Is it my imagination or does he linger ever longer by the fire each day?

She remembered Ziesolf had originally resisted the offer of a room, first from her uncle, then from Christina herself at The Tabard inn, choosing instead to sleep in the damp aboard *der Greif.* He had only relented when he decided his presence was needed to protect her and Trudi from what had then been an unknown assassin. She was happy he now enjoyed a well-heated chamber just down the hallway from her own apartments.

The heavens smiled on England over the next few weeks as temperatures rose unseasonably and what rainfall there was fell in a gentle caress upon the verdant land. These conditions favored Christina greatly as, if continued, they would herald an early shearing season. She had met with Butiler and, after the customary haggling, agreed upon a price they both could stomach without feeling undue hardship.

With any luck, I can take delivery by mid-June. If I sail immediately, Seelöwe should be able to return by some time in August.

170

She spent at least an hour each morning assisting Ziesolf in training the men of her household to fight. A few demonstrated a surprising aptitude, while the remainder were hardly capable of mastering even the most basic techniques.

"Christ's holy nails, Warin, will you never learn you must keep your balance!" Christina said in frustration, having tripped the man once more to fall headfirst on the unyielding cobblestones.

He struggled to regain his feet.

"I nearly had you that time, Master Frederick!" he replied in a good-natured voice.

"Once more, then," she said resolutely, though resigned to the fact the results would undoubtedly remain the same.

Christina heard a loud "woof" behind her. She turned to see Malcolm lying on his back with his breath knocked from him, a grinning Jost hovering above. Suddenly, she felt herself lifted off the ground in a bear-like hug, Warin's thickly muscled arms tightening about her like a vice. Without thinking, she kicked the heel of her left boot sharply backwards, connecting with the man's shinbone. He yelped in pain and released his grip immediately. As he bent down to rub his injured lower leg, Christina pivoted to face him and delivered a sharp uppercut blow to his chin with her right fist. Dazed, he began to wobble backward, but Christina caught the front of his tunic to steady him. She moved her face as closely as she could bear to the onion-stenched breath emanating from the man's mouth.

Lifting her gaze to look him directly in the eye, she said in a measured tone, "This is not sport, I would have no desire to waste my time with you if it were. I pay you good money to work as a watchman here, protecting me and those in my employ from any and all dangers that threaten us. Yet, I do not believe you could defend yourself from an angry milkmaid sporting a butter knife, let alone a determined foe intent on doing us evil. Mark me well. Take this training seriously and learn from it; otherwise, you will soon find yourself out on the street!"

Christina loosened her grip on the man's garment and he backed away a few steps. His face had no trace of its previous mirthfulness. He stared at her blankly; she felt as if she could see gears slowly grinding within his head as he considered the weight of her warning.

"Aye, you're right. It's just no one ever took the time to teach me anythin' before, not even my pa. Thank ye, Master Frederick. I'll never be as good as you, but it won't be from lack of trying."

She moved forward and clapped the man on his shoulder. She then turned back to the two boys who had distracted her attention previously. Malcolm had regained his feet and was cautiously turning to keep his face toward his circling opponent. Jost suddenly darted forward. As Malcolm began to hastily retreat, Jost lunged and caught the back of his leg. Off balance, Malcolm again tumbled onto his backside.

"A quick one, he is," said Ziesolf, drawing up alongside her. "Reminds me of someone else I know, although he's not so pigheaded. He actually listens to what he is told."

Christina turned toward the old knight, who was certainly referring to her own obstinate nature, and scrunched her face up. He laughed heartily and moved over to take her place with Warin.

She was indeed encouraged by Jost's progress, both as a fighter and in his apprentice's duties. He had accompanied her during her meetings with the wool merchant Butiler and had readily absorbed much knowledge concerning the trade. She now felt it was a good time to unveil the surprise she had for him.

"Malcolm, might I borrow Jost from you for a few minutes?"

"Aye, tek 'im an 'is sly ways," he muttered, struggling to his feet once more.

Jost walked to face Christina, a look of curiosity on his face.

"It seems you're progressing well here. Did Herr Ziesolf teach you to do that?" she asked, referring to his tripping of Malcolm.

"No. It just seemed like a good thing to do," he replied.

"Nicely done," she said, pausing a moment before adding, "I am well pleased with you as my apprentice as well. So much so I have spoken to Master Butiler and he has agreed to let you accompany him to Ludlow when he travels there for the shearing. I have no firsthand knowledge of this process myself. Having someone within our business who fully understands how the wool is shorn, graded, prepared, and stored will, I believe, be greatly to our advantage."

Christina was surprised to see disappointment suddenly cloud Jost's eyes, rather than the eager excitement she had anticipated.

"Are you not pleased?" she asked, more than a little affronted by the boy's tepid reaction. "I would have thought this to be both an opportunity to learn as well as a bit of adventure for you."

Jost looked downward as he began to move his right foot around in small circles on the ground.

"It is," he replied slowly," and I thank you, it's just . . ."

"Just what?" she was beginning to lose her patience now.

"Just . . . Mistress Trudi, you see . . . "

"Oh, for the love of sweet Jesus!" she exclaimed, now completely exasperated.

The silly little git is completely besotted with Trudi! He's afraid if he goes to Ludlow for a few weeks, Malcolm will have free rein with her. He'll learn nothing if all his mind can manage is fretful thoughts about the advances his rival is making in his absence. What can I do about this?

Once again, she was uncertain as to what action to take.

"Go back to what you were doing," she commanded.

"I'm sorry, Master Frederick . . ." he began.

"Do as you've been told, damn you!" Christina barked, immediately regretting her outburst of emotion as a sudden silence fell over the yard.

A wounded expression swept across Jost's face as he walked back toward Malcolm, who at least had the good sense to remain expressionless this time.

Christina turned and strode swiftly into the manor. She realized she could no longer put off speaking with Trudi to ascertain her feelings toward each of the two young men. With this knowledge in her head, she hoped she could find a way to circumvent any further disruption in her household.

She found Trudi already in the solar. Christina sat down and decided it was best to get directly to the point without preamble.

"Did you know two of our young men are totally in love with you?"

"Really?" Trudi's eyes grew large in mock surprise, "Are you sure it is only two?"

Her giggly response was cut short when she noted the seriousness of Christina's demeanor.

"Who is it of whom you speak?" Trudi asked, now in a more thoughtful tone.

"Jost and Malcolm."

"Christina, I do have affection for both of them, as each one is pleasing in his own way; yet, I have done nothing beyond a smile and a kind word to encourage either."

What would I have done if she had declared herself for either boy?

Christina was quite relieved by Trudi's reassurances.

"I have been meaning to talk to you though," Trudi said, uncharacteristically shyly, "but you have been so busily occupied I thought not to bother you with my trifles."

"Oh, don't be so silly. You know I always have time for you! You are as close to me as if you were a sister!" Christina responded in a hurt voice.

"Well," Trudi's voice lowered into a conspiratorial tone, "You see, I have set my eye on someone."

In a shocked voice, Christina blurted out, "Who?"

"It's Peter, the smith,"

"Black Peter?" Christina asked, surprise evident in her voice.

How have I noticed nothing?

Christina chided herself, frantically searching her memory for a clue she had missed.

"Yes! He is a sweet and serious man, who professes his deep affections for me. He makes me so happy! Oh, Christina, are you angry with me?"

"Angry? Oh, God no! I am delighted beyond words!"

Christina sprang from her seat and showered Trudi's beaming face with kisses. She feared her heart would rend in two, unable to hold the immense joy she felt for her friend's happiness. After a short while, she left the solar to return to the yard. She walked with a lightness of step that reflected her buoyant mood. She knew she still faced the difficult task of telling Jost Trudi's love had been pledged to another. Even this did not dampen her spirits, as she suspected his young heart would, in the end, prove to be resilient.

Chapter 12

Encounters Both Good and Bad
London, April, 1310

A little over two weeks later, Christina bid farewell to Jost as he departed with Master Butiler on their way to Shropshire. The boy had taken the news that his amorous interest in Trudi was unrequited reasonably well, although he had moped about for a few days, eating little and speaking less. Eventually though, he returned to his old self, displaying increasing excitement at the prospect of traveling north. As she watched Jost and the merchant's entourage begin their journey, she felt a pang of loss, realizing she had become quite fond of her cousin.

"Godspeed, young apprentice, and fare thee well," she said under her breath. "Return to us safely and in good health."

Over the following weeks, Christina began to notice a growing number of small hints of the growing fondness between Trudi and her smith. Although they both continued to scrupulously attend to their duties, she often discovered them together when they were not. Heads bent in close conversation, looks of rapt enjoyment in the pleasure of each other's company, and entwined hands all provided unmistakable evidence of the seriousness of their romance. Christina suspected it was only a matter of time before the two could no longer bear to exist except as husband and wife. Despite times when her bittersweet memories of Sybille unexpectedly surfaced to haunt her, she felt no jealousy against Trudi's happiness, taking pleasure in the fact that at least one of them seemed to have found someone with whom to share her life.

As joyful as she felt about the relationship budding under her own roof, Christina's heart was sickened when Ziesolf informed her the first day of the banns had been called, announcing the impending wedding of Katharine Revele and the alderman, Herr Volker. Apparently, her father's health had rallied slightly and the ceremony would be held as soon as the additional two pronouncements had been made. Sadly, Christina knew the only love involved in this marriage would be Katharine's love of power. She felt little sympathy for Volker, however.

What depravity drives a man of such ancient years to satisfy his lusts on a girl who has barely reached womanhood?

Her righteous disgust was immediately tempered by a sober recollection that troubled her deeply.

Yet, did I not have my own fears Father was preparing to barter me off in the same way? Does that not mark him as wicked as well?

To take her mind off such disconcerting matters, she decided to pay a visit to *Seelöwe*. She had been delighted when Thorsten, the former master of the ship, had surprisingly appeared at her gate one day, asking if she might engage him to be so once again. She had agreed immediately as Matthias, whose judgement in such matters she trusted completely, had marked the man as one capable of handling both the ship and its men.

She had instructed Thorsten to assemble a crew and ready the ship for a mid-June departure for Bruges. As the day was fair and balmy and she had no other tasks pressing upon her, she decided this was a favorable time to assess his progress. As soon as she came in sight of the ship at its moorage, she heard a voice calling her name from behind her.

She turned to find Malcolm, the stableboy, running toward her. Reaching her side, he bent over at the waist, taking a few seconds to inhale vast draughts of air into his lungs before speaking.

Somewhat recovered, he managed to say, "Mester Frederick, Mistress Trudi sez cum beck naw!"

Although the individual words of the boy were, as always, difficult to understand, the substance of the meaning of his message was not.

The ship will have to wait.

Turning about, she strode swiftly back the way she had come.

I've never known Trudi to be so imperative.

She soon found herself running as her fear of the nature of the calamity she would find upon her return increased with every step.

Uncharacteristically, Trudi was awaiting her return in the courtyard, hovering nervously near the entrance gates. As Christina came into sight, she rushed to meet her in the street outside the neighboring property.

Trudi pulled her aside and in a hushed voice said, "Oh, Christina! I didn't know what to do!"

"What is it, Trudi?" she asked, her anxiety somewhat assuaged although her curiosity was not.

"He refused to leave until he had spoken with you!" she blurted then, seeing the confusion on Christina's face, clarified her statement by adding, "Goodman Roger, Herr Revele's servant."

Christina uttered several blasphemous words under her breath. She knew any communications from the Revele household could only be a portent of ill tidings to come.

"He would not state the nature of his business, only that it was for your ears alone. I know their family brings you great unease, so I believed it best to notify you straight away."

"Yes, thank you, Trudi," Christina said before continuing in what she hoped was a reassuring tone, "Well, let us discover what news the Reveles bring to our door today."

They walked to the hall and entered, Trudi continuing on into the kitchen and Christina halting before the Revele's servant.

He stood and in his customary tone of borderline insolence he said, "God be with you, young Kohl. I apologize if my arrival has somehow inconvenienced you. I have come to you on the most urgent business of my master, the chief alderman."

Revele; at least it is not at the insistence of his damnable daughter.

"He asks that I convey to you, a fellow Hansard, his request for the pleasure of your company at the wedding feast of his daughter, Katharine, and her betrothed, Adolphus Volker, to be held two days hence."

Surely this is a jest!

Christina was dumbfounded by what she had heard.

Revele holds no liking for me, and his daughter even less. I would rather cut off my toe than grace that house again voluntarily!

Once her initial shock passed, however, she recalled the formal manner in which the invitation had been worded.

Could it be Revele feels bound, as the chief alderman of the Hanseatic merchants residing in London, to invite each of those under his governance?

It made sense, as did what she now felt obliged to say in return.

"Please thank your master for his gracious invitation and tell him I am most happy to accept."

Roger gave a small bow of his head in acknowledgement then departed without so much as a "by your leave." Christina took no pains to admonish the man's ill manners, choosing instead to sit down heavily on a nearby bench.

Sweet Jesus on the Cross, why do the Reveles continue to plague me like a troublesome rash? Have they nothing better to do than involve me in their tedious plots and schemes?

The two days passed swiftly and Christina soon found herself on her way once more to the Revele residence; only this time dressed in her finest garments, a tunic of green velvet worn under a cotehardie of vermillion garnished with embroidered birds. In her hands she carried her gift to the wedding couple; a matched pair of silver cups.

Having no interest in impressing Katharine and her husband with the munificence of her wedding present, Christina sought only to ensure she did not offend them with one of too paltry worth. A day before, she had rifled through her own possessions, in time finding what it was for which she searched: a finely-crafted pair of silver drinking cups with gilded ropework delicately encircling their foot and lip. They had been a wedding gift from the patriarch of one of the leading families of Lübeck, but to Marguerite, her dead sister, and not to her. She had always been loath to put them to use, irrationally reasoning to do so would somehow be a slight to the memory of a sister who had not really been her friend.

Better to pass them along and be done with them. If Marguerite is to unleash ill-will from beyond her grave, far better it falls on Katharine Revele and not me.

Entering the massive hall, a wave of heat threatened to overwhelm her. Several braziers had been placed about the room, adding both warmth and light. At least two hundred people clustered about the room, almost all of whom must have been of

Hanseatic origin judging from the snippets of various Germanic dialects she overheard in their conversations.

Looking about the hall, Christina felt that, although the garments of the attendees were rich of fabric and adornment, they were also rather old-fashioned; straight-seamed and voluminous, rather than the more form-fitting cut favored by the English. As she was making this appraisal, her eyes chanced to glance on a curious sight. A pallet had been installed unobtrusively to the side of the high table at the head of the room. Before she could give it further thought, a horn call was sounded and the guests went to their seats.

Soon after, those of the high table moved to their places, led by Herr Volker and his new bride, Katharine.

Am I the only one to notice?

Christina looked about aghast.

Katharine had chosen to wear a beautiful silken surcoat, heavily embroidered with silver thread. But it was not the richness of her garment that had shocked Christina, it was the color. The bride's garment, as well as the gown she wore beneath, were of contrasting shades of blue.

Blue, the color of virtue and purity. Most women would see fit to modestly add a collar or sleeves of the hue to allude to their innocence, but not this one! She revels in the irony of proclaiming her virginity; all the while wallowing in the knowledge of her own sexual depravity.

Christina shuddered and crossed herself involuntarily.

The minstrels struck up merry tunes as scrumptious course after course were delivered to the tables. Surprisingly, Christina ate with sparse appetite, merely picking at her food as, several times throughout the feast, she looked up to find Katharine's eyes staring in her direction. She would glance away quickly, but still it felt as if the new bride's gaze was fixed upon her, but for what reason she knew not why.

So, Christina spent most of the meal with her eyes downward. On the contrary, her ears worked actively, learning oddments of useful information from those around her.

". . . not much longer to live. That is why the wedding was so hastily held, so it would not be delayed by the prescribed period of mourning," a man two seats from Christina was telling the woman sitting across the table.

Sweet Mary, that must be Revele himself!

Christina's eyes involuntarily turned toward the pallet.

As if in reply, she saw a gaunt hand rise a few inches, then fall quickly back down. A young man rushed to the figure's side and bent down low over what most certainly must have been the ailing man's mouth.

I have no love for this man; yet, I will pray for his health to return to him, though whether it is on his behalf or to stem his daughter's ascending influence I know not which.

Unbidden, her thoughts returned to the last wedding feast she had attended, that of Marguerite.

How happy and carefree I had been then! It seems like it was a lifetime ago; could it have only been a half year? I am not even the same person now.

Mercifully, the feast appeared to be at last coming to an end, signaled by a flourish of delicate sweetmeats. Despite herself, Christina could not resist some of her favorites, including the small marzipan cakes and *krapfen*. She was just reaching for another of the deep-fried pastries when she noticed Roger, the Revele's chamberlain, had irritatingly appeared once more at her elbow.

"Master Frederick, Alderman Volker has chosen you to attend him in the bedding."

"What? You must be mistaken. The alderman does not even know me," Christina retorted sharply, immediately feeling beads of sweat form on her forehead.

"On the contrary, he asked specifically for you to be included."

To what lengths will that harlot go to bedevil me? It could only be her sly tongue that planted this thought into the old man's head.

Roger did not even wait for her response, obviously believing agreement was irrefutable.

"I shall gather the others and we will proceed to the dressing chamber forthwith," he said, walking away before she could form a protest.

Although she had an incomplete knowledge of what actually occurred during a bedding ceremony, Christina was aware its purpose was to assist in the preparations of the bride and groom for their first night together. For a woman, she expected the practicalities to include the braiding of hair, the application of rouge and lip stain, and the provision of comforting reassurances. As to fulfilling the needs of the man, however, she could not even venture a guess.

Before long, Christina, in the company of half a dozen men all probably at least twice her age, were waiting in the chamber for the appearance of the ancient groom. His eventual entrance was met by a chorus of ribald remarks and lewd hoots, eliciting a wide grin from his near toothless mouth. After sharing hearty draughts of Catalonian wine directly from the bottle, the company set about what she supposed were their prescribed duties.

Two of the men assisting in taking off the old man's clothing, a clumsy process as the groom was well down the road to inebriation. While stepping from his braies, Volker managed to muster a massive fart, mighty both in scent and sound. This caused another round of laughter among the gathering, although Christina could not imagine the reason why, as the stench was revolting.

For her part, Christina was happy to gather the groom's garments as they were removed, rationalizing this assistance to be much preferable to others which she had imagined. Soon, Volker was naked, the first adult male she had ever seen to be so.

And the last, I hope, if this is a typical specimen.

Tufts of wispy hair scarcely covered a portion of his mottled scalp, as opposed to the lush growth that emanated from his ears and nostrils. His neck was thin, with folds of skin creating deep vertical channels like newly ploughed pastureland after a cloudburst. Coarse grey hair covered his sunken chest, disappearing until it resumed its path directly below his navel. Mercifully, she saw no evidence of his shrunken cock, which was obscured from her view by his protruding belly and the thick gray thatch below. A pair of bird-like legs ending in discolored feet with long, talon-like nails completed her assessment.

Does she fully realize she has chosen this living carcass as a bedmate?

She could not believe even Katharine Volker could be so single-minded in her pursuit of influence.

The men next pulled a finely stitched linen gown over Volker's head, the front of which he immediately dampened with a drizzle of spittle that fell unnoticed from a corner of his lips.

Unsteadily, Volker tottered onto his feet, requiring his dressers to prop him up. This resulted in another round of crude jests as well as the emptying of another bottle. With their duties fulfilled, the group now brought their charge down the passageway and to the marital bed chamber.

After a few unsuccessful attempts. One man finally opened the door and the entire party spilled into the room. Discovering the area to the left side of the bed occupied by the bride's attendants, they gathered to the right. One of their number turned down the sheets while another moved Volker forward. After a further bit of assistance, the old man was finally abed.

As one of the male attendants pulled the sheets up over the old man's chest, Christina beheld the young figure on the distaff side of the bed. Katharine was lying on her side, her head propped up on her hand as she gazed over the figure of her husband and upon the drunken group of male onlookers arrayed beside him. Her eyes found those of Christina and her mouth opened, revealing the movements of her tongue as it slowly glided over the backs of her teeth. Katharine's tiny body began to wriggle lasciviously, her hand beginning to move downward under the covers and toward her sex, like the course of a viper stealing toward its lair. The men scarcely breathed, transfixed by the lewd spectacle.

I can stand this no more!

Christina moved forward quickly and pulled the curtains of the bed closely together, obstructing further view. The men regained their senses, some looking toward Christina with resentment, while others looked away with embarrassment. The women must have drawn the curtains shut on their side of the bed as well, as they began to move as a group toward the door. Seizing upon her chance for escape, Christina followed closely behind. She did not wait to see whether the men would follow suit, caring nothing whether they did or not.

Christina's rapid steps took her down the stairs. She did not stop there, surreptitiously exiting the house as well. She was well down the street before she took time to catch her breath. She was sickened by Katharine's outrageous behavior, feeling even a small pang of sympathy for the inevitably cuckolded husband who lay unsuspecting beside his new bride while she lewdly performed for the group of onlookers.

Or was her overt sexuality directed toward me alone?

Christina considered this thought carefully. She was certain it had been Katharine who had dispatched Roger with the invitation, her father's grave illness logically preventing him from playing any part in the planning. Certainly, it had also been her who had arranged for Christina to be a part of the bedding party.

But for what purpose?

It could only be that, in Katharine's warped mind, having me there was some sort of warped revenge scheme. Mayhaps, she believed it would be hurtful to me to witness her bedded with another man; to regret that I had refused what she had so freely offered. Will this be enough now? Does she believe my pride has been injured sufficiently to cause her to consider no further reprisals?

Although Christina hoped fervently this would be the end of Katharine's devilment, she feared it might just be the beginning.

Over time, Christina's memories of Katharine Revele's wedding faded just as surely as those of the cold and winter past.

On the 18th of June, she was overjoyed by the arrival of a message from Gilbert, Master Butiler's clerk, that the train of wool carts was no more than three days from London. The next few days became frenetic, as *Seelöwe* was readied to receive its first cargo under Christina's ownership. She planned to leave immediately after the heavy sarplars of wool were stowed, as she believed the first merchants arriving in Bruges would reap the best price.

The punctual arrival of her wool three days later was not the only cause for gladness in her heart. Jost greeted her heartily, seeming to possess a newfound air of self-assurance. His darkly tanned face and forearms evidenced he had spent considerable time in the sheepfolds while he had been away.

Is it my imagination, or has he also grown taller during his absence?

She dismissed her thoughts as overly sentimental. Regardless, she was happy to have her apprentice with her once more.

Christina had another reason to be thankful to be departing soon. King Edward's plan to wage war against the Scots was by necessity no longer a confidential one. His levies had been summoned and soon they would be massing outside the city. Already, a vast quantity of provisions was being gathered, both to meet the immediate needs of the king's army and to prepare for their sustenance over the winter. Among the shipowners and sailing masters of the city, rumors abounded of Edward's possible intention to impound a number of vessels and impress their crews, using them to convey much of his supplies north by sea. Lightened of much of its additional burden, the army would be able to proceed much more expeditiously, reducing the chances of encountering inclement weather while still on the march. Christina didn't know whether her financial assistance to the King's cause would exempt her ship being levied as a supply transport, but was certain she had no reason to worry if it was already safely at sea.

Chapter 13

Heartening News and Dangerous Tidings
London, August, 1310

It was nearing the end of August when *Seelöwe* once again returned to the safety of the Thames estuary. Standing upon the forecastle, Christina held onto the braided hemp shrouds tightly to keep her balance as the warm, prevailing breeze rocked the ship gently. She was well satisfied with ship, master, and crew; all of which had worked flawlessly to convey her safely and efficiently to the Flemish coast without mishap. A strong, vexing headwind had delayed their departure from Sluys, extending the date of their return by nearly two weeks. Shielding her eyes from the sun with her now bronze-tanned hand, she gazed over the shimmering, undulating water toward the distant shore.

Finally, we will soon be home. I only wish I knew what news awaits me upon my return.

It did not take long after her arrival to discern there was a change of atmosphere in London. As she walked the familiar route to Bokerel House, the normally vibrant crowds of people going about their business on the streets seemed more subdued, furtive even. Many gathered in small clusters of no more than three or four, glancing about with mistrustful eyes as they carried on hushed, but heated conversations. She could not shake the unsettling feeling she was being watched; she quickened her step.

Finally arriving at Bokerel House, Christina turned the handle on the inset gate and was surprised to find it was locked.

It's only early afternoon. Where could everyone be?

She pulled the slender bell rope and was soon gratified by the sound of the gate bar being lifted. The gate opened and Osbert, one of her watchmen, stood before her with a sudden, happy expression overwhelming his face.

"Master Frederick, what an excellent surprise! We had received no word *Seelöwe* had returned!"

He moved aside, allowing her to step into the deserted yard.

"I'm glad to be back, Osbert," replied Christina distractedly as her eyes scanned the workshops and storerooms that lined the yard. There was no sign of life, even the telltale white smoke from the blacksmith's forge was absent.

"Where is everyone?" she asked finally, unable to come up with a plausible answer to the mystery on her own.

"Why, did you not know?" Osbert said, scratching his head. "Of course not, since you just arrived today yourself. Master Matthias and *der Greif* returned only yesterday. Herr Ziesolf and the others are at the wharf, bringing the ship's cargo back for storage here."

Matthias, back?

A wave of relief spread over her body like a soothing balm.

She had tried to suppress her concern over the fate of *der Greif* while on her own journey to Flanders, rationalizing that fretting over the other vessel would only serve to distract her from what she needed to accomplish. She was not very successful, as her worry concerning the overdue ship was a vexing daily occurrence.

Thanking Osbert, Christina turned on her heel and rushed back in the direction of the river, this time having little thought for the anonymous individuals she passed along the way. Before long, the familiar silhouette of *der Greif* came into view in the distance, a bevy of still indistinct shapes moving purposefully about the adjacent wharf. She resisted the impulse to begin to run, but she could not restrain giving a hearty shout as soon as she came into earshot.

She was heartened to see several of the men lift their heads and look in her direction. They then turned from her and toward the unmistakable figure of Ziesolf, who was clearly providing them with instructions. While they returned to their tasks, he sped to meet Christina.

"God be with you, Herr Ziesolf!" she said in a happy voice before clasping the man's proffered hand.

"And to you, Master Frederick," he replied formally, not daring to risk the chance a curious ear might overhear him address her by her true name. "It seems a fair wind has blown both of your ships home at the same time."

"Aye, and praise be to Blessed Jesus for it. What was it that delayed Matthias' return for so long? I had expected to greet him before we departed for Flanders. Certainly, I never imagined it would take him nearly three months longer."

"The extremely cold weather we endured here in London this past winter was mild by comparison with that experienced in the eastern Baltic, the waters of which were frozen over well into spring. Novgorod's own river Volkhov was unpassable until nearly June. Matthias thought it best to delay his departure until the *Winterfahrer* made their return from Novgorod to Lübeck. Once the fur merchants arrived, the portions of the cargoes belonging to Herr Kohl, I mean to you, were quickly loaded on *der Greif* and

Matthias departed straightaway. They had an uneventful passage and returned yesterday afternoon."

"And the skins? Did Matthias say anything about the number and quality of the pelts?" Christina asked anxiously, besides herself with curiosity.

She knew that, despite the fact the ship's hold undoubtedly contained wax, honey, amber, and other treasured commodities, the true success of the venture would be determined by the value of the cargo of furs.

"The hold is fairly near to bursting, my friend," Ziesolf responded with a look of satisfaction on his face. "Matthias said the fur on the pelts is long and dense, prompted by the increased coldness of the season. They should fetch an excellent price. Eventually, that is," he corrected himself.

A goodly profit gained in Bruges and two ships fully laden with valuable goods safely wharf-side in London. It seems God's good grace has fallen upon me once again.

She began to walk once more toward the ship, then noticed Ziesolf hesitating. She halted and turned back.

"Is this not all good news? What is it you aren't telling me?"

He beckoned her closer to the river to ensure none could overhear them, save the fishes.

"These are troubling times, I'm afraid. The upper classes of the city are divided, as are those of the entire land. The King is outside London now, assembling his troops along with those of earls Gaveston, Warenne, and Gloucester for his campaign to Scotland. Despite the fact he has only been able to raise a little over four thousand soldiers, he cannot be dissuaded from his goal."

"Is it enough to succeed?" Christina asked, as always trusting Ziesolf's opinion in all things military.

"I don't know," he admitted. "It depends on how many men will answer the call to arms of the Bruce; then, whether he will offer a pitched battle or not. There are too many factors of which I have no knowledge to even support a wild guess. At least Edward's army is well provisioned, thanks in large part to you."

"You said the people are divided. You mentioned those who support the King, who are those numbered among his opponents?" she asked.

"The Lords Ordainers grow ever more powerful, led by the likes of Edward's cousin, Thomas of Lancaster and Guy Beauchamp, Earl of Warwick. They seek to limit much of the King's authority, residing it in themselves instead. They refused the King's demand for their levies as his liegemen, claiming their work to be too important to join the march north. There are rumors that claim, if the king himself does not depart soon, the Ordainers will seek to halt his campaign altogether."

"And the merchants and tradesmen?" Christina asked, "How do they fare?"

"Not so well, it seems."

Ziesolf shook his head from side to side for emphasis.

"As is common during times of war, the King has increased rates of taxation most thought were already too high. As a result, commerce has slowed significantly. Mercers appear very hesitant to speculate in the purchase of expensive goods like cloths and furs, especially when the nobility's attention is focused on their animosity toward each other rather than accumulating finery. Coupled with the unseasonably cold spring, it seems a wagonload of cabbages garners more interest than a bolt of silk."

Damn! It seems good fortune does not make a permanent home on my doorstep after all.

"There is other worrying news as well," continued Ziesolf.

Christina groaned inwardly, then exclaimed somewhat testily, "Well, what is it, man? Please, darken my mood even further, I beg of you."

"Revele has died. Volker has been elected the German's new chief alderman by the general assembly. I know you disliked Revele, and certainly for good reason. I am not certain you will love his successor any better."

Volker, the new chief alderman?

Christina's heart sickened as she recalled the sight of the man's decrepit form on his wedding night, his head lolling as spittle drooled unchecked from his mouth like that of an idiot.

No, he is not the chief alderman of London's Germans. It is in fact his wife, Katharine, who now holds sway. Pity us all, Lord Jesus!

Fear clenched her heart

"Volker has wasted little time in seeking to establish his authority," Ziesolf continued. "He has called for a meeting, eight days from now, in which he seeks to establish new compacts and statutes controlling Hanseatic trade throughout England, as well as the behavior and privileges of those whose business it is to conduct it."

Yes, I can imagine Katharine's sly hand is involved in this as well.

While Ziesolf was briefing Christina on the troubling affairs that had developed since her departure, the crew of *der Greif* and those employed in her household had diligently transferred the first barrels and casks of cargo from the ship to the wagons and carts that awaited them on the wharf-side. Now, loaded to capacity with a treasure of Novgorodian furs, they departed for their destination. Leaving Ziesolf to oversee the continued offloading of *der Greif's* hold, Christina followed behind the small convoy carrying her goods, her mind turning over the information she had learned from the old knight. The time she spent in reflection while following the slow wagons did nothing to ease her mind. If anything, she arrived home with greater concern for her future than when she had left the wharf.

The men set to swiftly unloading the goods, stacking them hastily about the yard so they could gather one more load from the ship before the light began to fail. Christina loitered about the space for a while before concluding the workmen fully understood what they needed to do and required no supervision from her.

She walked into the manor, suddenly eager to find Trudi.

I know I should be happy to learn of der Greif's safe return, especially with such a valuable cargo aboard. Yet, I cannot rid my thoughts of Ziesolf's troubling words. A merry reunion with Trudi will most certainly raise the veil of my dark mood.

Christina had not made her way completely through the great hall when she heard a loud feminine voice call to her from the portal into the kitchens.

"Master Frederick!" cried Sarah, "So glad to see you returned to us. I'll go fetch Mistress Trudi, she'll be so pleased, she will. Won't be a minute!"

Before Christina could speak, the scullery maid was off. True to her word, she returned in a matter of seconds with a beaming Trudi in tow.

"Oh, it's so good to have you home at last! We had all begun to worry about you!" Trudi said, although refraining from showering Christina with her customary hugs and kisses. "Sarah, fetch some ale and a savory platter, I am sure our master has not yet eaten. Bring it to the solar when you are finished. Off with you now, girl!"

As soon as the young woman had disappeared from sight, Trudi leapt forward, abandoning her previous display of reserved propriety. With tears of joy running down her face, she held Christina in a tight embrace. Buoyed by her friend's affection, droplets began to stream down Christina's cheeks as well. For the time being at least, the happiness of their reunion displaced the worrisome thoughts that had plagued her for the past few hours.

They walked to the solar together and were soon seated in their favorite places. In a short while, the maid arrived with a delectable platter of assorted meats and cheeses, rich yellow butter, and a thick pandemain loaf. Of her own accord, the maid had added a bit of honeycomb, which she knew to be one of Christina's favorites. A jug of ale completed the hastily assembled spread.

"Thank you, Sarah," Christina said, impressed by the weight of the girl's efforts. "I could not ask for a more appetizing selection of my favorite foodstuffs."

"You're most welcome, Master," she replied, demurely casting her eyes downward as she executed a clumsy curtesy, but not before Christina caught the look of pleasure that crossed her face upon receiving the compliment. She then turned rapidly and departed, leaving Trudi and Christina alone once more.

"Where have you found these girls?" Christina asked incredulously. "They are like little wrens, happily flitting about from task to task as they build their nests.

"They only seek to please you, My Lord," Trudi replied coyly, then broke into a series of giggles as she could maintain her mock composure no longer.

Christina joined in her friend's laughter.

How good it is to be with Trudi. When we are alone, we can be just two carefree girls again, with no more worries in the world then figuring out how to avoid our chores and flirt with the local boys. Sometimes I wish we had never left Lübeck.

After several unsuccessful attempts, Trudi was finally able to control her sniggering and her face grew unexpectedly serious.

"Um, I have something to tell you, Christina."

Oh, no!

Involuntarily, Christina's thoughts turned fearful once more.

What bad tidings await to fall on my ears now?

Christina said nothing, silently staring into Trudi's eyes imploringly instead.

"I wish to be married."

"What? What?" was Christina's flabbergasted reply, repeating herself before exclaiming, "Oh sweet Jesus! This is unexpected! Is it Peter?" she suddenly thought to ask, recalling Trudi's predilection for changing her affections at a moment's notice when they were growing up.

"Yes, of course," she responded. Almost shyly, she added, "Are you happy for me, Christina?"

"Oh, you silly little goose, I'm over the moon with happiness!" she cried, leaping up to throw her arms about her friend and kiss her face wildly. "How could I not be?"

"It's that, well, it has always just been the two of us. Things will not be the same if I am married," Trudi whispered hesitantly, a look of concern on her face.

"Wait. Will you not still live with us here at Bokerel House? You are not leaving, are you?" Christina's voice grew tense with concern, finding the idea of permanently losing Trudi's presence in her life intolerably heartrending.

"No, not at all. Have no fear, you will not be able to rid yourself of me that easily!" the young woman snorted, then said more seriously, "I could not bear to be apart from you, my sweet sister. It is bad enough when you voyage away, I could not bear to lose you forever."

They held each other closely for many minutes, the bond of their affection for each other causing neither to want to be the first to separate.

Parting from her confidant at last, Christina asked, "When is it you plan to be wed?"

"Perhaps in three or four weeks?"

Her response constituting more of a question than an answer.

Christina stared at her friend intently, suddenly suspecting Trudi had more news to tell.

In a hushed voice, she asked, "Trudi, are you with child?"

"Aye, or maybe. I don't know really. It's been two months since I last bled, but I told myself maybe it was because you were gone. Anyway, it's not through lack of trying," Trudi's impish grin prompting Christina to chuckle once more.

"You wicked girl! You'd once suggested we open a brothel; are you proceeding with those plans on your own now?"

"Well, from what Ziesolf says, they seem to be the only businesses turning a coin now, those and ale houses, of course." Trudi countered with a saucy grin on her face.

The mention of business profits immediately prompted Christina to cast a worrying thought toward her own woes; she immediately cast it from her mind to concentrate on Trudi's far more pleasant news. They spent the next hour in planning for Trudi's upcoming wedding. Christina excitedly described two bolts of Flemish cloth she had purchased she believed would be perfect for a new gown for the bride. Christina experienced a pang of regret she could not indulge herself with a feminine ensemble as well, but consoled herself with a vow to commission a new, French-cut surcoat for her own wear.

Ziesolf entered the solar and the topic of discussion changed to Christina's recollection of the details of her journey to Bruges. The telling of this was unusually brief. Astutely realizing he had interrupted a conversation between the two women to which they did not wish to make him privy, Ziesolf excused himself and withdrew to his own chambers. On their own once again, Christina and Trudi talked deep into the night, each realizing the intimacy of their relationship was soon to be indelibly changed.

The next days passed quickly for Christina, as plans for Trudi's upcoming nuptials vied for attention with her efforts to find buyers for her merchandise. Although the first was proceeding well, the second task was largely disappointing. The market for her inventory of fine goods was sorely depressed, as the mercers, drapers, tailors, and skinners of the city were very reluctant to make purchases on speculation, save at bargain prices. It seemed the merchants of London were collectively holding their breath, hoping the political turmoil that gripped the land would soon settle, returning business to its normal profitability.

Christina attempted to maintain an open mind as she made her way to the gathering of Hanseatic merchants called by their new chief alderman.

Perhaps we are to discuss as a group a plan to stimulate increased trade, Surely, Edward's war will end soon and the nobles of the land will cease their loathing for each other. Things will return to normal eventually, won't they?

Christina entered the yard of the house that had been Revele's, but which now was the home of his daughter and her husband. She was somewhat surprised to notice Roger, the servant who had always controlled the access to the alderman's compound, was nowhere in sight. In his place was a handsome young man wearing an intricately graven breast plate that rivalled those of the royal household guard. His demeanor, however, was no less arrogant than his predecessor.

"Who are you and what business have you here, lad?" he asked dismissively.

"I am Herr Frederick Kohl, master merchant of the Hansa here in London town," she replied with an answering tone of arrogance in her voice. "Who are you to question me so?"

A look of confusion appeared on the sentry's face; it was apparent he was unsure of what to say next. The sum of his experience and instructions did not extend to provide him with a course of action should he himself be challenged. He pursed his lips, desperately desiring to utter some cutting rejoinder; yet, nothing coming readily to mind.

"Will you stand there wasting my entire day, or will you let me pass?" Christina asked wearily.

It is bad enough to be here once again, must I give this rapscallion a thrashing so that I may enjoy the small pleasure of it?

Two other men now crowded behind Christina, apparently arriving for the same purpose. Realizing he had somehow lost the advantage to the young merchant who stood before him, the guard moved aside with a surly expression fixed on his face, but letting them all pass without further attempts to challenge.

They entered the great hall together, the others veering to sit on the benches toward the right front of the room, while Christina was content to have a seat at the left rear. Over the next half hour, several more men arrived, filling most of the available seating. By Christina's count, there were now eighty-two in the audience, waiting with mounting impatience for the arrival of the aldermen.

When Father attended these assemblies in Lübeck, he would always come home with a pain in his head, complaining most people spoke only to impress others with their wisdom, usually proving the exact opposite to be the fact. This left useful discussion and important decisions to occupy only a fraction of the time. I wonder if this will be much of the same?

Eventually, the door at the front of the hall opened and the aldermen stepped through, walked to the front table raised upon its dais, and seated themselves at five of the six high-backed oak chairs. Before Christina could even query herself as to why an extra chair remained, her question was answered as the door opened once more and the child-like figure of Katharine Volker, née Revele, entered and seated herself to the right of her husband.

One of the men in the front row, whom Christina knew to be Reinhold Hagen, stood and exclaimed, "Esteemed aldermen, this is most irregular. What reason does this woman have to be here, let alone to sit among you at the high table. This is a meeting of Hanseatic merchants, not a family outing."

Several others voiced their agreement until they were silenced by the act of Kathrine slowly rising to address them.

"So, why am I here? That question is most fairly asked, Herr Hagen, and I am happy you have done so. My husband, Herr Volker, and the other aldermen need no assistance in conducting the business of the Hansa in London, especially from a young inexperienced girl such as myself. So why do I sit among them? For my young ears, that is why! Some of you think you can sit there so smugly whispering treacherous comments amongst yourselves, simply because the aldermen cannot hear them? Take care what you now say, for I will hear everything!"

Hagen slowly sat back down, his shock at the undisguised venom in Katharine Volker's voice readily apparent. Others among those seated twisted uncomfortably in their seats. They said nothing, as they seemed cowed by the ferocity of the young woman's words. The aldermen sat speechless as well, except for Volker who turned his head toward his wife, who whispered something in his ear. He smiled and nodded, then she moved away, her narrowed eyes scanning the crowd sharply for signs of dissent.

As for Christina, she sat perfectly still, having no desire to draw attention to herself. Although the merchants gathered in the room had been caught unaware by Katharine's onslaught, Christina had known it was only a matter of time before the woman would seek to exert her influence.

After all, she told me as much, herself.

In a high-pitched, hoarse voice, Volker said, "My wife speaks truly. Too often, there are a few who seek only to breed discontent amongst us. This will no longer be tolerated as those who do will be identified and punished."

This is madness! Yes, it is common for there to be disagreement, but it is only by hearing differences of opinion that a best course of action can be identified. Does Volker wish to make himself a king now too?

The old man continued.

"We can only protect our privileges here by thinking as one, acting as one. It is time we strengthened our bonds as Hansards, not weaken them by irresponsibly acting alone."

Christina listened carefully, anticipating what Volker said next would somehow be directed toward her.

"We have maintained a good relationship with the guildsmen of London for many years; we sell and they buy, they sell and we buy. This is how it has been and this is how it should be. Recently, there have been instances where our merchants have broken this tradition, selling directly to certain unsavory individuals, bypassing the English guilds altogether. This practice must be outlawed before we are cast from London like noisome beggars!"

Volker's vitriolic ramblings were mercifully interrupted as he fell into a fit of hacking coughs, eventually expelling a large gob of phlegm onto the floor to the front of the table before him. He wiped his dripping mouth with the sleeve of his gown. The man steadied himself, placing both hands on the table, while he audibly gasped as he fought to replenish his lungs with air.

While he continued to struggle to breathe, his wife reached over and placed a hand on his shoulder, pulling it down so she could whisper something else into his ear. He listened and then drew fully erect once more, gesturing toward her with his hand he had understood. She looked out at the assembly once more with a haughty smile on her lips.

Christina couldn't help but feel the woman's arrogant gaze was directed toward her, as had been the previous words of her husband. She could do nothing, as immobilized in her seat as a fly entwined in the silk of a spider.

Finally, it seemed Volker had recovered enough to continue.

"Yes, we must strengthen our bonds as Hansards," the alderman repeated himself as he struggled to organize his thoughts. "We must have trust in each other for, without it, we are alone in this land. Yet again, there are those among you who put more faith in the honesty of others than your brethren. Why else would some of you choose to deposit your coin with the Italians, rather than with us?"

Again, his attack seems pointed directly toward me; can this just be because she has poisoned his mind?

"This practice of using foreign bankers must end. If you claim the Hanseatic privilege, your coin must also be deposited with us."

Volker paused, apparently unable to recall what it was he intended to say next. Again, Katharine put her mouth to his ear. Seconds later, he once more cleared his throat and continued.

"And what of those who greedily set out upon their own ventures, with no thought of the rest of us? Are we not brothers? Should not what profits one of us benefit all of us as well? Therefore, I recommend the owner of any ship departing from London must offer at least a one-third share, minus freight charges, to any other Hanseatic wishing to make an investment."

Volker gazed out upon the assembly, disappointed to see only a few nods of assent. Most, like Christina, sat in stony silence, now awaiting further attempts to narrow their independence. They did not need to wait long, as Volker spent nearly another hour enumerating his comprehensive list of reforms, claiming them to be of advantage to the entire Hanseatic community in London.

Yes, I do see how these rules will provide a benefit; a benefit to those who sit before us, that is. They are designed to enrich these old men off the toil and risk of those of us who still venture out into dangerous waters. Volker seeks to weaken our initiative by condemning any individual action that is not consistent with the rules he seeks to enforce. Surely, there are enough here who will never agree to such measures to block his self-serving plans, are there not?

After the chief alderman completed his astonishing call for reform, two other aldermen brought up minor orders of business. These evoked no discussion and the meeting descended into an uncomfortable silence. At last, Volker called an adjournment, scheduling a resumption in one week's time to vote on the suggested statute changes.

Father had said it was common for the men to gather amongst their friends to further discuss what had been proposed. That is certainly not the case here today. Everyone hastens for the doorway as if a cry of "fire" has been sounded.

Christina wasted no time in departing either, having no desire to be engaged by any of the aldermen or, more especially, Katharine Volker. Once free of the alderman's residence, she trod briskly through the streets, not caring in what direction her feet carried her. Her mind worked apace with her legs, feverishly trying to conceive a plan to block Katharine's schemes, as that it was Katharine who stood at the root of what had transpired at the meeting, she had little doubt.

It is no coincidence these changes are proposed now. Each of the aldermen has long served in his position; if they felt such statutes needed to be enacted, why had they not chosen to bring them before the assembly previously? No, the only new factor is Katharine, and her influence over Volker.

Christina decided she would visit as many of the other Hanseatics as possible prior to the next meeting and attempt to persuade them to oppose the chief alderman's proposals.

Perhaps enough already intend to resist. I cannot imagine any of the younger merchants would be in favor but, if so, they would number but a few. There are many others whose feelings are not so easy to plumb; they are the ones who now must be convinced.

Chapter 14

A Most Unexpected Turn of Events
London, September, 1310

Over the next four days, Christina met with several of the merchants who had attended the assembly. She was somewhat disappointed by their general reticence to discuss Volker's proposals, but well understood their reluctance to do so as well.

They are acquainted with me little, if at all. On the other hand, they have known Volker and the others for many years, some for as long as they have been in London. They have habitually trusted their aldermen to make decisions based upon what is best for the Kontor. Even though they may find these new statutes troubling, they do not dismiss them out of hand. If only they knew it was a new hand that now steered the ship, they would be more troubled by the treacherous rocks that lie ahead. But how can I convince them it is Katharine Volker who now controls the chief alderman? Who amongst them would believe a mere girl is capable of such gluttony for power?

Her efforts were not entirely without success, however. She found Reinhold Hagen aboard his cog, *Schwarzer Schwan*, supervising a few men engaged in mending the seams of a panel of the ship's great sail. She hailed him and his head swiveled in Christina's direction.

Recognizing her, he smiled and said, "Is it a passage you seek out of this feckin' city? Better to leave now then after those toothless bastards let that little trollop chew your ballocks off like she did theirs!"

Hagen leapt off the deck and joined her on the wharf.

"I was wondering when it would be you'd get to me," he said. "I'd heard you were making the rounds of the merchant captains, stirring up trouble, some might say," he remarked, viewing her with an inscrutable expression.

"Well, er, not really. I'm only trying to find out the opinions of others," Christina replied, not certain if she had been wrong to come to Hagen.

He kept a straight face for a moment longer, then broke into a toothy grin. Christina breathed a sigh of relief as she realized he had only been speaking in jest.

His face grew more serious and he said, "I'm afraid trouble is coming for us, whether we seek it or not. It's clear they look to enrich themselves at our expense; we take all the risks and they take a share of the profits. They must be out of their minds to think I'd agree to something like that!"

"Nor I," Christina echoed. "Do you think there are enough of like mind to stand with us against the aldermen and their cronies?"

He paused, considering her question well before replying.

"I do believe so, but it is a near thing. Much better if we pulled a few more to our way of thinking. I think I'll make a few visits of my own, Frederick."

"And Katharine Volker, do you really think she is at the heart of this?" Christina asked carefully.

"Aye," he said without hesitation. "Who else could it be? Volker has sat at the high table for nigh on twenty years and I don't believe an independent thought has ever wormed its way into his misshapen skull. The other aldermen are followers as well, leaving only Katharine new to the mix."

Christina felt vindicated by Hagen's assertion. She had been thinking perhaps she had been giving too much credit to the young woman's ability to disrupt things so severely.

"What's more," he continued, lowering his voice to where it sounded barely above a whisper," I have a suspicion her intrigues didn't begin only after she was wed. There is talk in dim places she was offered as a final bargaining chip in a transaction or two, a task she went about much too cheerfully. There is even a foul rumor her father may have sampled her wares as well."

Christina was aghast at the depravity alluded to in the merchant's accusations; yet, she could not help but believe their veracity. She decided it best to be silent about her own experiences with the woman.

"What has become of the brother, Albrecht?" she asked, changing the topic slightly.

"As soon as Herr Revele became ill, his son was shunted off to Lübeck, supposedly to serve an apprenticeship with one of the father's business acquaintances. Yet, does it not seem unusual an ailing father, especially one as shrewd as Revele, would rid himself of his primary heir at the exact same time he would need him most? I cannot but see the hand of Katharine at work here once more. God knows what means she used to convince her father to send her brother away, suffice it only to say she was successful."

Christina felt sick at heart.

How much more terrible could this saga become?

"Is it then too much of a stretch of the imagination to believe Revele's corpse reeks of his daughter's stench? Christ knows it would be far easier for her to influence Volker than her father; would she have any hesitation to clear him from her pathway to power? Whether through venom, poison or witchery, I believe she would use any means possible to achieve her ambitions."

"Does the mother have no awareness of what has transpired?" Christina asked, remembering faintly the handsome woman who had sat beside Revele when first she had visited the manor.

"Alas, I believe she is a simple soul who cannot perceive the inherent foulness of her daughter," Hagen replied.

With nothing else to say beyond affirming their intentions to meet with more of the other merchants prior to the next assembly, Christina and Hagen parted ways for the time being. He returned to his tasks on his ship and she back to the street. Her prior intention was to have visited at least two others of her fellow Hanseatics before the end of the day. After her conversation with Hagen, however, she was simply too despondent to carry on.

Is patricide such a normal occurrence in this land? First my uncle, and now most probably Herr Revele, each murdered by his own issue. Is wealth and influence such overwhelming obsessions?

Knowing the answer to her self-query would always be "yes" for some lost souls, she murmured to herself in a low voice, "That is the way of the world," and walked straight home.

She vowed to renew her efforts on the morrow.

A hearty meal and congenial company that evening helped raise Christina's spirits considerably. Although she had spoken with Ziesolf and Trudi previously concerning the surprising events that occurred at the merchants' meeting, she held back from adding to their worries by repeating the suspicions of Reinhold Hagen.

It's as much for me as for them. I can't really bear to spend any more of my time this day with Katharine Volker's name sullying my lips.

Instead, Christina listened as Trudi detailed the progress being made with the preparations for her marriage.

I've never really seen her so joyful.

Trudi ticked off on her fingers the delicacies to be served for the wedding feast.

Even though I ate my fill at dinner, I find myself growing hungry just at the mention of clay-baked pike and such. I'm so happy for her.

As the hour grew late, Christina bid her friend good night and went to her apartments. She had not been asleep for long when an insistent muffled rapping could be heard from outside her chamber door. Although still not fully awake, she had the presence of mind to grab her day cloak, place it about her shoulders, and pull it tightly shut. She opened the door to her bedroom then, finding the knocking continuing unabated, went to the door to the passageway. She opened it a crack and found the hulking shape of one of the watchmen well illuminated by the lanthorn he held in his grasp.

Before she had a chance to speak, he whispered, "Beggin' yur pardon, Master, but thers a man wants to speak to ya."

"Well, tell him to fuck off, Warin, you big lump! Tell him to come back when it's not the middle of the night, for Christ's sake!"

She was just about to shut the door irately in her man's face when he hurriedly added, "Thet's what I did surely, but he sed he needed to speaks to yas naw. Sed he wuz from Peers somethin'"

Christina's anger quelled instantly, as if it were a candlewick thrust suddenly into a tub of water.

"Piers? Did he say Piers Gaveston?" she asked with a sense of mounting dread.

What would be so imperative he would send a man out at this hour?

"Aye, thet wuz it, Gaveston it was," the watchman remarked.

"Good man, Warin, you've done well," she said, her head now clear and her thoughts decisive. "Go now and take him to the solar. Tell him I will be down in fifteen minutes.

Whatever it is he needs to tell me, I'd much sooner hear it privately. I wouldn't want to chance one of the fellows sleeping in the hall to awaken and overhear what it is Gaveston's man has to say. I'd like to think I can trust them all but, in these times, who can be certain?

After dressing, Christina trod quietly down the passageway to the solar. She opened the door and was relieved Warin had had the presence of mind to light a couple of the candles set about the room, as well as a bit of wood that crackled and gave off a faint glow from the fireplace.

At least I'll not be stumbling over whoever the hell this is in the dark,

Closing the door behind her, Christina turned about and scanned the room, locating the figure who must be her visitor sitting patiently in the chair normally favored by Ziesolf. The man stood and moved from the shadows into the light. Christina immediately recognized him as one of Gaveston's servants who had been in attendance at their first meeting.

"Yes, man, what is it that is so important you wake me from my sleep?" she asked.

"A thousand apologies, My Lord," he replied with a deference to Christina to which she was not accustomed. "What I have to tell you is a matter of grave urgency; else I would not have burdened you with this late visit."

She said nothing, instead motioning for him to continue with a wave of the hand.

"Four days ago, we of Earl Gaveston's remaining household were visited by a messenger, one who required one of us to venture to St Helen's Church at Bishopsgate at vigil the following night to receive information important to our lord. Although many in our midst were skeptical, it was finally decided I would be the one to attend. Appearing at the church at the appointed time, a man dressed in a monk's habit took me by the arm and led me down the stairs and into the crypt. You cannot imagine my great surprise when he brought a lanthorn forward and I saw before me none other than John of Brittany, Earl of Richmond."

The man, whose name she could finally recall, stopped momentarily while he gathered his thoughts.

"Please continue, friend Hugh," Christina said, urging him to return to the telling of his surprising encounter with one of the most renowned of the Lord Ordainers.

"Well, suffice it to say I was shocked beyond words for who could imagine a meeting with one of the great magnates of the land in a church crypt in the middle of the night, even in these perilous times. I had no reason to speak, only to listen. Earl John said most of the Ordainers had agreed it was necessary to remove the Earl of Cornwall from the presence of the king. Although Earl Piers had been banished repeatedly in the past, he had always returned to Edward's favor more strongly than ever. They believed steps must be taken to remove his influence over the king once and for all. Consequently, their plan is to arrest Earl Piers and bring him to trial for his alleged crimes against king and country. With these men presiding over the court, there is no doubt a hasty execution will logically follow. God have mercy on our souls, he said."

"Yes, God must please have mercy on us," Christina repeated, unconsciously crossing herself. "Were his words intended only as information, or did he suggest a course of action?"

"As we know, Earl Piers is currently in the north, awaiting the king's arrival. He is certainly surrounded by many hundreds of men loyal to his cause; yet, it also stands to reason there are some who are assuredly false. Although my master knows many of the Ordainers hold animosity against him, he is unaware their hatred has now spilled over into a serious plot against his life. Therefore, Earl John urges Earl Piers be told of the treachery planned against him, so he may be on his guard at all times. Any delay only improves the possibility their direful plot will be met with success."

"And has word already been dispatched?" Christina asked, although beginning to perceive the reason this man was sitting in her solar in the middle of the night.

"Yes," he replied, surprising her somewhat by his affirmative response. "As soon as I returned to my fellows, I saw to it a pair of riders was dispatched, heading north to alert my master of Earl John's warning. Getting only a few miles outside of London, they were set upon by several mounted men wearing the livery of Lancaster. Greatly outnumbered, they turned and fled back toward London. When our riders were within sight of the city walls, their pursuers veered off, apparently content they had stayed them from venturing northward."

"Now, you seek another means to convey your warning to Earl Piers, perhaps by sea?" Christina stated, clearly understanding where the man's reasoning was leading.

"Yes," Hugh answered once again. "Before departing, our master had told us, if we were ever in great need, Master Frederick Kohl was the one man who could be trusted to provide assistance more than anyone else. Earl Piers has never required your friendship more than he does right now. That is why I am here."

Christina exhaled slowly, having anticipated this as the reason for Hugh's visit the more the man talked. She rose to her feet and began to pace slowly about the room.

What am I to tell him?

She tried to sort out the conflicting options clouding her brain.

Should I simply agree to do as he asks? Obviously, this would require me to depart London immediately, leaving my business affairs in complete disarray. I have unsold goods in my storerooms and two ships lying idly anchored in the Thames; what am I to do about these? Not to mention the aldermen's assembly three days from now. If I am not present, I rob the opposition to Volker's propositions of what could be a critical vote. My freedom to trade in London as I see fit could be suppressed permanently if the chief alderman has his way. Do I risk all of this to help a man I have known for only a short period of time?

She focused her gaze momentarily on Gaveston's servant who, although he had stood at the same time as she, waited motionlessly for her response.

Yes, I have only met Gaveston a few times, but how long does it take to get the measure of a man? He knew me not when he faced down the gang of toughs who threatened my life at the Nag's Head. How easy it would have been for him to ignore the plight of an inconsequential youth and return to his cup while I was being callously slain in the mud. This he did not do and I am alive today because he chose to assist me.

Emotion began to cloud her face at this recollection.

When no one else in London would deal with me fairly, who was it that purchased my first cargo, and at an equitable price? Gaveston. Even being able to count the man as a friend has given pause to my enemies, as Herr Revele plainly said to me.

So, I owe him for my life as well as my livelihood. How have I repaid him? When he asked that I hold der Greif at the ready, should he need to escape from London, I sailed on, ignoring my promise. I have betrayed him once; I shan't do it again!

"I will go," Christina said simply.

"I thank you, Master Frederick, but not nearly as profoundly as my master, who will benefit greatly from the information you carry to him," said Hugh. "I will leave you now, so you may carry out your preparations unimpeded by my presence. May God protect and guide you on your journey, as he will continue to hold my master tightly to his bosom as well."

The servant then rendered Christina a slight bow. She opened the door and he descended the stairs, with her following closely behind. They walked quietly together through the dimly lit expanse of the great hall. At the exit door, Hugh bowed once more, then passed through into the courtyard. Before she eased the door closed once more, Christina heard the snick of the wrought iron gate opening, then closing, as the man disappeared into the night.

If I closed my eyes, and then opened them once more, could I convince myself my nocturnal visitor was no more than a fairy presence, sent to do me mischief?

Christina permitted herself to muse for a few brief seconds.

Then, knowing the tasks before her were only too real, she went to the buttery to fetch two flagons of ale. She suspected it was going to be a long night.

She was surprised to find Ziesolf already waiting at the head of the stairway fully dressed.

"Couldn't sleep?" she asked.

"No, but not for fear of trying. Too many strangers skulking about the house for my liking, "he replied with a grin. "It looks like you couldn't either; or were you just getting up for an early morning sozzle? If so, mind some company?"

"Aye, if ever I needed your counsel, I figure now is the time."

Sensing the seriousness of her mood, Ziesolf ceased his joking manner and followed her to the solar. Christina poured them each a cup of weak ale and they settled in comfortably. She then related the details of her conversation with Gaveston's servant, leaving nothing from her telling.

"And your answer to the man's request?" Ziesolf asked, his mouth once more forming into the semblance of a faint grin before saying, "Or should I ask when do we leave?"

Christina managed a tired smile of her own before replying, "You know me only too well, old friend, but it is once more when do I leave, not we. There are too many loose ends to attend to here for both of us to be gone for a month or longer. You are the only person I trust to see to it our business does not come to ruin."

Ziesolf's singular functioning eye stared at her for a few seconds before he said, "Yes, the business is very important and I do understand your concern for its wellbeing. What you must realize though is you are its most important facet. What successes you have attained have been directly through your own strength, intelligence, and audacity. Therefore, it stands to reason you must be kept safe, otherwise there will be no business. That is why I will accompany you on this journey."

Christina started to protest, but Ziesolf continued before she had the opportunity to voice her arguments.

"You have both courage and considerable ability as a fighter, but that may not be enough to protect you where you are going. When men are at war, the laws of the land and normal rules of behavior are followed laxly, if at all. What does become stronger are military bonds. A knight, even an old one such as I, commands unconditional respect and obedience from those of lower rank and consideration from those who are higher. Sadly, a young merchant, even such an extraordinary one as yourself, does not. You would probably be at best ignored and, at worst, robbed and killed before you had a chance to get very far on your mission."

Although her basic nature led her to want to argue, Christina held her tongue.

There is no disputing what Ziesolf has said, damn his good sense!

The night sky was already taking on a rosy hue in the east when Christina and Ziesolf finished concocting their plans. As Christina returned to her apartment for a few necessaries, Ziesolf notified those members of the household she needed to address. In less than two hours' time, they were all gathered in the solar, awaiting her return.

Taking a seat, Christina began speaking without preamble.

"Early this morning, a member of Piers Gaveston's household visited us, entrusting me with a vital message that must be delivered to the earl. I have agreed to do this and must now leave London immediately."

Christina scanned the room, noticing that, although everyone appeared to be listening with avid interest, Trudi's face betrayed a sense of shocked anger.

She realizes this means I will not be present for her wedding. Oh, Trudi, you must realize this breaks my heart almost as much as it does yours.

Christina ignored Trudi's reaction for the time being, knowing she must cover her points sequentially, otherwise risking that something important might be overlooked.

"Herr Ziesolf will accompany me as there is no man better suited to traveling through a countryside at war than he. I would also like to ask Malcolm to accompany us, as he is of the Scottish lands and has knowledge of the ways and language of its people.

The groom was startled at the mention of his name, rising a bit from his stool as if he were about to scamper away like a spooked deer in a forest glen. He slowly lowered himself back down onto his seat and flashed a reassuring grin toward Christina.

"Aye, uf curse. Wun wee Scotsmun in a scrap is worth tane feckin' Anglish!"

"Good man, Malcolm. Hopefully, we'll be doing more skulking than fighting, but I'm sure you'll be a great help in either case," Christina replied, trying hard not to answer his smirk with one of her own.

Christina continued, saying, "Since Herr Ziesolf will be away, we need someone to take charge of the work of the men in the yard. I was hoping I could rely on you, Peter, to take that on."

The smith appeared greatly surprised; he nervously ran his thick fingers through his thick, black mane.

"I . . . I thank you kindly, Master Frederick, but I don't know anything about telling other people what to do, other than the boy who works me bellows. Surely, there must be someone better suited than me."

Ziesolf interjected, "Peter, you may not realize it, but you tell the men what to do all the time and more importantly, they do what you say because they respect your knowledge and experience. If you have any problems, just ask that one to say a word. There's not a man amongst them who'd risk the lash of her tongue."

Ziesolf smiled, nodding toward Trudi. Normally, she'd be the first one to add her own comment to reinforce the knight's jest. Strangely, she remained silent this time.

Peter looked to Trudi and a worried look found its way onto his face. He then turned to face Christina.

"Aye, I'll do what you ask."

"I thank you, friend Peter, I know I leave our men in capable hands. As for my business, that will be your charge, Jost."

The young man looked at Christina through eyes grown wide with astonishment.

"But . . . but, Master Frederick . . ., Cousin, how can I do what you ask? I have only served you a few months. There is so much more I need to learn!"

"Yes, Jost, I am well aware of your shortcomings," Christina said with a wry smile, "but I am not asking you to conduct trading on your own. I will provide you with specific instructions as to what is to be dispatched and to whom, as well as the prices to pay for specific goods, should they become available."

The young apprentice seemed somewhat relieved by Christina's reassurances, but still appeared nervous and pale.

"Also, you will have Matthias to advise you, at least until he departs for Bruges."

At this revelation, Matthias asked sharply, "What? Will you not be traveling north on *der Greif*?"

"No, my friend," Christina said, "It is a luxury I cannot afford. Although I have confidence in no one at the helm more than I do you, you are also the only one besides myself I can entrust negotiating with foreign merchants. I cannot afford to let my business cease trading while I am away; I need you to continue it forth in my stead."

Christina clapped her hands together and said briskly, "So, you all have your parts to play in this little adventure. I only hope I may quickly provide Gaveston with the message I am duty bound to deliver; then, speed back home to you. May God protect you all, as each of you will be included in my prayers each night."

Those in the room stood, wishing the Lord's blessing on her as well. As the others began to disperse to attend to tasks now imminently important, Christina asked Jost to accompany her to the fabric store to set prices on what remained in her inventory. Noticing Trudi still tarrying in the solar, she told Jost to carry on and that she would be with him shortly. As he departed, Trudi's measured steps took her to the door, which she closed firmly. She turned to Christina, staring into her eyes with an uncommonly impassive expression on her face.

Christina said, "I am so sorry, Trudi, I will be missing your wedding! You know that I . . ."

Trudi sped forward and slapped Christina hard across her face. She then aimed her foot squarely into Christina's crotch and kicked. Christina was so surprised by the sudden attack that she did nothing to defend herself. She stood silent, massaging her injured cheek with her hand, and looking at her lifelong best friend with frank astonishment.

"The first was for my friend Christina being so stupid, the second for the idiot man she seems to be becoming more and more each day!"

Dumbfounded, Christina could only manage to ask, "What?"

"Yes, what indeed!" Trudi retorted, her eyes flashing with a fiery anger she had never seen in her friend. "I have gone along with your merry little charade because I believed you thought you had no choice, that unless you posed as Frederick you would lose everything your father had worked so hard to attain. You have done well for yourself, Christina, you have succeeded in a world in which women do not have, nor even been given, the opportunity to try.

I am proud of you, my sister, but pride does not remedy the sickness I feel in my heart every time you sail away, perhaps never to come back to me. When you return, you regale us with the tales of your exploits; who you fought, what storms you endured, what other unimaginable dangers you faced that threatened your life and limb. It's almost unendurable to know, not only have you confronted these perils in the past, but they loom ahead in the future as well."

Tears ran down Trudi's face unimpeded; she let them fall onto the bosom of her gown unnoticed.

"I try to set my fears for you aside, arguing with myself these are the risks that make up a merchant's life, the one you have chosen. But what you do now is something new. Frederick Kohl, would-be boy warrior! Would-be English nobleman! Would-be spy! Well, fuck you, Frederick Kohl! Or should I say, Christina Kohl for, try as you might to forget, you don't carry your brother's cock between your legs! Not only do you risk the dangers of going into a war, but you must face them as a woman in disguise. Do not do this, Christina! For the love of Sweet Mary, Mother of Our Lord, don't do this!"

Trudi said nothing more, she was simply overwhelmed by the emotion of her impassioned plea. Her breath came in deep gasps as she reached out to grasp the side of the table to prevent herself from falling.

Christina took a few seconds to gather her thoughts before saying, "Everything you say is true, my dear, sweet Trudi. I realize I have led you into a life not of your own making and for that I am sorry. Yet, you have been with me all my life and you know me better than I know myself, I think. In all that time, have you ever found me to go back on a promise; to not do something I had told someone I would do for them, even if it meant getting into trouble myself? This is me, Trudi, this is who I am. I can no more change this about myself than I can change my love for you. I promised Gaveston I would help him, should he need it, and he needs it now. That is why I am traveling north. Not because it is what I desire, but because I must.

Christina and Trudi looked into each other's eyes, their two worlds so close; yet, separated by a chasm neither could fully comprehend. Almost clumsily, they came together in an embrace that gradually became more desperate as their love for each other struggled to surmount the obstacles between them. After a few moments, they reluctantly parted, each realizing their time together might now be measured in the few meager hours before Christina's departure and perhaps no more.

Chapter 15

***

On to Berwick
At Sea, September, 1310

Christina strode slowly down the passageway, still emotionally wrought from her unexpected confrontation with her friend. She brushed her wounded feelings aside as best she could and, finding Jost awaiting her in the storeroom, flashed him a wan smile.

"Are you alright, Cousin?" he asked, his face clearly clouded with concern.

The young imp probably had his ear to the door the whole time.

She prayed he had not heard every word of her row with Trudi.

With rising anger, Christina's mouth began to form the words of a sharp rebuke of her apprentice but stopped short, realizing she would have done the same thing herself, were she in his place.

Suddenly, a new thought came into her mind.

Panic overtook her and she blurted, "What did you hear, Jost?"

Looking confused, he answered, "Hear?"

"Yes, hear!" she snapped.

She had to know if Trudi had inadvertently revealed her secret to Jost.

"Do you mean after I departed the room?" Jost asked, seemingly innocently.

Her cold glare was sufficient affirmation to prompt him to elaborate further.

"Nothing really. The door closed behind me and I came here like you told me. There was the sound of some talking at first, but I couldn't make nothing out. By the time I turned the corner, all I could hear were my own footsteps."

Jost expression was fearful now, obviously wondering what he had done to make his master so angry.

"It's. . . It's no matter. I apologize, Jost, for my ill humor. Mistress Trudi and I had some unpleasant words and I'm embarrassed, that's all," Christina said, relieved her cousin apparently remained ignorant of her true nature.

"Are you alright?" he repeated. "Your face looked so unhappy when you entered the room."

Yes, and now I feel even more miserable knowing I upset you so needlessly.

"I am fine, Jost, thank you for your concern."

The young man's face brightened slightly.

"Here, I have something for you."

Her hand delved into her leather traveling pouch. Finding what she was looking for, she presented Jost with a folded sheet of vellum, neatly embossed with her seal in reddish-yellow wax.

"Please give this to Mistress Trudi should I not . . . should I fail to return by Twelfth Night," she stated in a flat voice.

He solemnly nodded, cognizant of the unspoken meaning of his cousin's words.

She broke the ensuing awkward silence by busying herself with providing guidance to Jost concerning which lengths to send north with Matthias and those that should be retained for future sale in London. They had made a good start when Thorsten came through the door.

"Herr Ziesolf told me the news, that we'd be sailing as soon as possible," Thorsten said matter-of-factly.

"Aye, and how soon would that be?" Christina asked anxiously, hoping the sailing master would pose no good reason for a delay.

"Well, with the help of your yardmen and Mistress Trudi's larder, we should be able to provision *Seelöwe* by the end of the day. Most of the crew are still available, as they knew of your intention to make another voyage to Bruges soon anyway. They'd rather work for a master they know and an owner who has treated them well than take a chance on someone worse. So, two men missing, but we can make do without them if need be. Will we be carrying a cargo, Master Frederick?"

Thorsten's question took Christina by surprise. In her haste, she had forgotten to consider whether to carry a cargo north. With the necessity of making an immediate departure, the answer seemed obvious.

"No, it will be work enough to get the ship ready to sail by tomorrow. I just can't see finding an appropriate cargo, making the purchase, transporting it to the ship, and loading it aboard without creating an unacceptable delay. For this voyage, time is more important than profit."

Thorsten's bushy black eyebrows arose in surprise. This was a most unusual comment for a merchant to make, even one as singular as the young man who stood before him.

"Aye, then. I will see to it we take on additional ballast to make the journey safely. We sail on the morning tide then, if that suits you rightly?"

"Good man," Christina replied, appreciating the master as a man of few words, especially at a time like this. "Let Herr Ziesolf and Mistress Trudi know what you need and they'll see it is done."

With Thorsten confirming the morrow as the day to set sail, Christina was able to cross one worry off her list. She spent most of the morning finishing her inventory with Jost, then took time out to enjoy a hardy midday repast with Trudi. While they ate, they laughed and talked of times past; mostly when they were small, disobedient children. To the casual observer, their behavior seemed completely normal. To someone more perceptive, the fact any discussion of future events was conspicuously avoided would seem oddly puzzling.

Her belly now almost uncomfortably full, Christina decided to visit *Seelöwe*. She had no doubt in Thorsten's ability to ready the ship for its imminent departure; rather, she just needed some exercise to dispel the nervous energy that threatened to engulf her. As she approached the ship's moorage, she saw her confidence had been well placed. The sailors and yardmen seemed to be working well together to ready *Seelöwe*. As she was about to go aboard, a familiar voice sounded behind her.

"Well, ya wasn't thinkin' ya could scurry outa here and hog all the fuckin' fun fer yurself, did ya? Who's gonna git yur scrawny little ass outa trouble if Ah'm not around?" Reiniken words were spoken so loudly they could be heard across the wharf with ease.

"Wig!" Christina yelled, overjoyed to see the huge man standing before her with Ziesolf by his side.

"In the flesh, Yur Worship, in the flesh. Ah wuz sittin' on the shitter when Old One Eye here came up, asking me if Ah fancied a sea voyage. Well, Ah told 'im no, there wuz too many fancy women who wuz counting on me fur their daily exercise. Then he said there was a good chance we'd need to slit some Scottish gullets. They be right bastards, Yur Worship, how could Ah say no to that? So, Ah wiped my ass clean, and here Ah am! Want to see?"

"No, no, I'll take your word it's spotless!" Christina laughed.

Same old Wig, never has a more blasphemous man walked the face of God's earth. But if he is by my side, God help any ten Scotsmen who have the misfortune to cross our path!

"Well, Ah'd best be gettin' to work; Ah'm not bein' paid for mi chin-wagglin' now, am Ah? Besides, Ah hear the boss is a real fuckin' asshole!"

Reiniken snorted a laugh and winked at Christina. He sauntered to the wagon loaded with supplies and grabbed a cask that must have weighed two hundred pounds. He lifted it easily onto his shoulder and carried it onto the ship as if it weighed nothing.

"Thorsten had mentioned he was short a crewman or two, so I thought Reiniken might be persuaded to join us," the old knight remarked dryly.

"I can't think of anyone I'd rather have by our side should we need to defend ourselves," Christina added.

She made a cursory tour of the ship but, as she suspected, the provisioning of the ship was progressing well. A brief discussion with the ship's master confirmed the fact *Seelöwe* would be ready to begin its journey north at day's end. Satisfied all was in order, she headed back home. She vowed to go to bed early, knowing it would be her last night in her comfortable bed for weeks to come.

Slumber did not come easily, as the events of the past day vied with her concerns for the future to occupy her brain. What sleep she was able to get came in short snatches, troubled by nightmarish images born from her conscious mind's anxieties.

Shortly after she heard the bell for matins, Christina could endure it no longer. She arose, washed, and dressed, then made her way to the larder and made a large plate of food to break her fast. Sitting down in the kitchen, she found her appetite was surprisingly light. Feeling guilty to be wasting food, she put what was left over into her pouch for later. Christina walked quietly through the hall; the sound made by the snores, groans, and farts of the sleeping men more than drowning out her own faint footsteps. In the yard, she bid farewell to Warin as he let her through the gate.

Once in the street, she turned and placed her hand on the stone archway that defined the entrance to Bokerel House. She offered a brief prayer, asking God to protect those within whom she could no longer defend herself. Taking a deep breath, she turned and began walking away.

The leather soles of her heavy boots slapped along the cobblestones as she made her way through the dark and mostly empty streets. She did not need to consciously think about where she was going, her feet knew their own way. Wisps of fog swirled uneasily in slight gusts of wind that seemed as if they were the laborious breaths of London town itself. Several times, her eyes caught a glimpse of movement in the shadows of narrow alleyways; but whether it was a cat, a rat, or a human, she could not discern. She did nothing to satisfy her curiosity either knowing, whatever it was, would probably be up to no good. She walked on with a purposeful stride.

By the time Christina reached the river, the fog had grown so thick she could not discern the nebulous shape of *Seelöwe* until she was within thirty feet of the prow. She hesitated before boarding, taking one last look behind her. Although she could see nothing, her mind's eye pictured the expanse of the city she had grown to know so well.

I wonder when I will next be here?

She refused to concede the fact she may never return at all.

Realizing indulging in melancholic thoughts accomplished nothing, she pulled herself up one of the hawsers securing the ship to its mooring and stepped purposefully onto the deck. All was quiet, save for the rhythmic moaning of *Seelöwe's* sturdy hull rubbing against the fending ropes as it rose and fell with the movement of the Thames' murky water. Not wishing to wake any of the ship's company prematurely, she strode soundlessly to the forecastle cabin she had chosen to use when aboard and went inside. She made her way down the right side of the space and found the raised pallet that would serve as her bed. Making herself comfortable, she rummaged around inside her pouch. Identifying the shape of her leftover apple, she fetched it to her mouth and took a large bite. Relaxing as best she could, Christina settled down to wait for the day to arrive.

In a little more than an hour, she heard the first sounds of the men aboard beginning to stir. Repeated heavy footsteps beat a path from below deck to the starboard side of the ship, as the men emptied their bladders into the river. Little by little, the sounds of the ship coming to life began to include an increasing amount of casual conversation.

I guess it's time for me to make an appearance on deck; I certainly don't want our departure to be delayed because Thorsten believes I am not aboard.

She found the ship's master already calling out orders to the men readying their departure. He gave a small wave of his hand in acknowledgement of her arrival, but did not take his experienced eyes from the flurry of activity before him. She assumed a place to his side to view the unfolding scene below.

Two crewmen detached the forward hawser from its bollard on the wharf and cast the heavily braided rope over the lapstrake planking of the port side before scuttling aboard themselves. Now freed, the bow began to slowly drift away from the wharf. Another couple of men duplicated these movements with the line securing the aft of the ship. A few seconds later, Thorsten threw his weight against the rudder post and *Seelöwe* began to ponderously move further out into the river. Others of the crew hoisted the mainsail a few feet toward its massive spar and the shortened sail began to catch the wind, but only enough to provide it some headway. The ship moved faster as the powers of wind and current united. Soon, they had gained the central channel of the Thames.

"If it keeps up like this, we'll be back for dinner!" Thorsten laughed, happy to finally be returning to the element he loved best.

"I'll be well satisfied if we return by Saint Martin's Day," Christina responded, well pleased they had made such an auspicious start to their adventure.

Although the gloominess surrounding them was growing subtly brighter, she found she could still only discern a few brief glimpses of the buildings lining the riverbanks through the fog.

It is like a mystical fairyland.

She was awestruck by the otherworldly beauty filling her eyes.

I remember the tales my grandfather told Frederick and me as we sat on cold winter nights near the fire. The heroes of these stories set off to kill dragons and trolls, not to deliver messages to English noblemen. I do not think anyone will be reciting the tale of this adventures to their sons and daughters!

Suddenly, their way quickened and the huge expanse of the great bridge loomed before them. *Seelöwe* passed easily under the central arch, popping out on the other side like a bit of cork, rolling slightly from side to side. The ship quickly steadied and they resumed their journey downriver.

As they were passing Greenwich, the fog began to clear a bit. Christina left Thorsten and walked the length of the ship to join

Ziesolf at the forecastle. As was his habit, he peered into the watery expanse looming before the ship, though for what purpose at this time she had no idea.

Without taking his eye from the river, he said, "We make good progress. We shall easily gain the estuary before dark. I would think it would be wise to anchor for the night, before beginning our journey up the coastline on the morrow."

"Do you still believe it will take us only five days to reach Berwick-Upon-Tweed?" Christina asked, recalling the estimate Thorsten and Ziesolf had agreed upon previously.

"Aye, it is a goodly guess. The wind has a mind of its own though. We can only pray its decision agrees with our purpose."

Christina said nothing for a few minutes, then asked, "The River Tweed, is it navigable?"

"Well, I certainly wouldn't have confidence a cog ship could sail its length, if that's what you mean. Even with *Seelöwe's* shallow draft, I wouldn't trust us not to run aground. Besides, I wouldn't expect to find Gaveston greeting us from the shore. It doesn't seem too crafty to just wander about on foot in the wilds, shouting his name. Hopefully, we won't need to travel too far from Berwick, perhaps Gaveston will be right there, if you're lucky. Otherwise, its horseback for us," Ziesolf answered.

In a quiet voice, she asked, "Do you think this whole thing is a fool's errand?"

"Yes," Ziesolf answered simply without hesitation. "But if it is a choice between doing something unwise and besmirching your honor by breaking your word, it is better to be foolish, I think."

As they neared the broad mouth of the river, the breeze freshened, blowing fortuitously steadily from the southwest. By mid-afternoon, they had cleared the headland. Christina was surprised the sailing master gave no order to shorten sail, instead laying the rudder over to run almost directly downwind.

Christina found Thorsten at the rudder post and asked, "Will we not anchor for the night?"

"We should take advantage of this goodly wind while we have the chance if our goal is to make all speed northward. An extra knot or two an hour could shave a day off the voyage. That is, if you desire it so?" he asked, looking to her for confirmation.

"Aye, like a dolphin, right?" Christina grinned, throwing Thorsten's initial boast of *Seelöwe's* speed back at him.

"Well, maybe an elderly, fat one," he admitted with a twinkle in his eye.

They made good progress all that day, only anchoring when the light had grown so faint that they could hardly make out the English shoreline on their port beam. Subsequent days proved much more laborious. The geography of the English island turned away to the northwest, requiring a seemingly endless series of tacking back and forth before the wind to effect progress. Although the crewmen were nearly exhausted by the time they reached Berwick-Upon-Tweed, Christina was well satisfied they had completed their journey in just over six days.

The sun was well hidden behind gloomy storm clouds as they sailed *Seelöwe* into Berwick's well-protected harbor. Thorsten ordered the sail to be shortened as the moorages were crowded with ships and boats of every kind. He eventually spotted a suitably inconspicuous spot along a sagging wharf, to which *Seelöwe* was soon secured.

"Do you really believe this to be the best course of action?" Christina questioned the old knight yet again as they prepared themselves to disembark from the ship. "Would it not just be quicker to identify ourselves as who we truly are, rather than rely on a convoluted deception?"

"That sounds a bit strange coming from you," Ziesolf replied sarcastically, knowing Christina would understand his meaning without stating it openly. "Is there anyone here you would recognize as being a loyal supporter of Gaveston, other than Edward himself? Can we take the risk of stating your purpose openly, perhaps to a covert ally of those who seek to do him harm? In these worrisome times, two foreigners discovered dead in an alleyway with slit throats would hardly warrant comment, let alone an inquiry. Better to be cautious, Frederick."

Christina worried her lip in frustration, but knew Ziesolf to be right. Still, his plan seemed tenuous at best. Posing as the captain of a free company of German mercenaries and his squire, they would make enquiries of officers of the local garrisons as to Gaveston's whereabouts, claiming he has contracted for their services. The scheme hinged on obtaining the information they sought, without causing undue suspicion from those they asked.

All it will take is for someone with half a brain in his head to ask where the other sixty or so Germans in this so-called company are to completely scupper the plan. Hopefully, they'll not care enough to ask. Hopefully.

They left the ship and began walking through the muddy streets of the Berwick toward the imposing stone castle on the hill they could see in the distance.

"My God, have the Scots already attacked?" Christina asked, "The place looks like it's already been sacked! Has Edward been defeated so soon?"

"Both the English and the Scots have coveted possession of this town for as long as anyone can remember. About twenty years ago, the King's father, Longshanks, came to town to settle the

232

dispute over the Scottish throne. Five years later, with Scotland in rebellion once more, he came back; only this time it wasn't to conduct diplomacy. He sacked the town and put thousands of its inhabitants to the sword. Since that time, the English have kept their foothold here, right on Scotland's doorstep."

"If he planned on keeping the town, why in God's name would he destroy the bridge?" Christina asked, pointing to the ruined pilings hinting at where a substantial structure had once stood.

"I believe it was the Lord's work, rather than that of a worldly king, that caused it to fall. I have heard a great flood swept it away, as well as one or two others before it."

Christina asked no more questions, but opened her heart to pity the poor innocent souls who had suffered so badly through no fault of their own, other than choosing to live at such a spot coveted by both kingdoms.

Moving at a brisk pace, they soon had mounted the hillside pathway leading to the castle's gatehouse. Before they were too close, however, a sentry detached himself from a group of similarly attired soldiers to challenge them.

"Gute day," Ziesolf replied, "I be *Edler* Kurt von Ziesolf, Kapitän of the Lübecker Rot Company. I must speak with captain of your guard. "

Christina head began to turn involuntary to stare at Ziesolf, then she caught herself. She had been caught unaware he would see fit to disguise his speech as well as his identity.

It makes sense that, to address the soldier in perfect English, would have stood an excellent chance of arousing suspicion. Still, I wish he would have told me beforehand.

The guard eyed Ziesolf and Christina for a moment before saying, "Wait here. "

He then turned away and disappeared within the gatehouse. In a few minutes, a tall soldier with a weathered face appeared and walked their way.

"Aye, what kin I be doin' fur ya?" the man asked, eying them a bit suspiciously.

Once again, Ziesolf introduced himself, then said, "I have contract made with Earl Gaveston. Where he is? We go to fight for him. "

"What, the two of ya?" the Englishman laughed, then spoke loudly over his shoulder to the men lounging by the castle wall. "One old man and a boy? God, boys, we's won the war now!"

Before the soldier's cronies could join in the joke, Ziesolf stepped forward and slapped the sergeant soundly across his face. Totally surprised by the speed of Ziesolf's swift attack, his face clouded and he fumbled for the dagger he wore at his side. Before he could clear it from its scabbard, Ziesolf's long sword was out and pointed a few inches from the man's chin. Christina had drawn her blade as well, assuming a fighting posture to discourage any of the other soldiers from joining the potential fray.

"Is this how you English speak to a knight?" Ziesolf demanded, flicking the sword tip side to side for emphasis.

"No, I ask your pardon, Sir Knight, I . . ." the man began a profuse pardon before he was once more cut off by Ziesolf.

"Now, I ask again. Where be Earl of Cornwall? He already paid for sixty swords; do you wish to cheat him? Be quick or I send squire here to bring all company!"

"The Earl of Cornwall has taken winter quarters at Roxburgh Castle, you may find him there," the sergeant replied, having made the sound decision it was far better to provide this belligerent stranger with the information he sought than continue to defy him.

"How far? How long?"

"About thirty miles. There is a good pathway right along the riverbank, so it shouldn't take more than two or three days," the soldier muttered.

"Thank ye for that," Ziesolf said, stepping back and slowly sliding his sword back within its scabbard. "We leave now."

Ziesolf calmly turned his back to the incensed captain of the guard and began walking down the hill. Christina, on the other hand, kept her falchion at the ready as she kept watch on the soldiers as she backed away. Realizing the men had no stomach for a further encounter after a few hundred feet, she too sheathed her blade and turned to walk beside Ziesolf.

"Did you not think the manner in which you treated the guard captain was not too great a risk?" she asked.

"What? Taking umbrage at an insolent fool's impudence? Do not question me on this, Christina. No knight worthy of his spurs would suffer this to happen."

Christina did not pursue the matter further. She now realized what Ziesolf had said was true, this was a different environment, where the rules of conduct and behavior were set by warriors instead of normal society. Not for the first time was she happy Ziesolf stood beside her.

"Where to now?"

"For you, a return to the ship; for me, I will go to purchase horses for us. Do we still need four?

"Aye, unless you think Wig needs two for himself?" Christina responded with a bit of a smirk on her face.

She had been surprised when Reiniken had volunteered to accompany her and Ziesolf, should the need arise to ride to Gaveston's location.

"But, do you even know how to ride a horse, Wig?" she had asked concernedly.

"Are ya havin' a fuckin' joke? Did ya think mi ma spread her legs and shat mi out onto a ship's deck? Old One Eye and his like ain't the only ones to have had a horse betwixt their legs. The Archbishop of Cologne had hundreds of dumb bastards like mi in his horse. Taken from mi ma's tit when Ah wuz fourteen, stayed till Ah wuz twenty; when Ah thought Ah might as well choose who Ah wuz riskin' m' life fur, instead of some wrinkled old fucker in a pointy hat."

So, it was quickly settled Reiniken would join Malcolm as members of their small party.

As they neared the harbor, Ziesolf left Christina to procure suitable mounts. Back aboard *Seelöwe*, she spent the remaining hours of daylight impatiently awaiting his return. It was well into the night before his shadowy figure came back aboard.

She led him to her cabin before speaking, guarding against the outside chance someone with a keen ear might be lurking about the wharf.

Once inside, she asked, "How did it go? Did you find horses?"

In the dim light cast by the small lanthorn, she saw the old knight's lips form into a slight smile.

"Aye, but please don't ask at what cost."

"You realize I must know, don't you?" she replied.

"Well, you have to suspect the king's army is requisitioning everything from destriers, to coursers, to palfreys. Even the availability of cart nags is few and far between. But, like everything else, there are horses to be found, but at a premium. I was able to purchase the four we need, but at forty-two pounds sterling."

"What? Why that's robbery, unless they are coursers at least!"

"As any good merchant worth her salt knows, price is driven by the two principles of supply and demand. The need of Edward's army for horses is great, leaving very few left for anyone else. A decent rouncey, a young palfrey mare, and two serviceable nags were the best I could do, I'm afraid."

His smile now somewhat self-deprecating.

"Lord Jesus, now I see why some merchants say they pray for war! Such a profit to be made," Christina remarked. Then, changing the subject, she asked," How will we find our way to Roxburgh then?"

"Well, I learned its quite hard to miss. We'll travel the cart road southwest along the river until we reach the Tironesian monastery at Kelso, where we should be able to see the castle. From that point, we can cross the causeway and be at our destination minutes later. Plus, we will have Malcolm to guide us if we get lost. He claimed to be well familiar with this countryside, did he not?"

"Aye, but when does Malcolm not seem assured of himself?"

They both chuckled at the truth in Christina's statement.

Chapter 16

Treachery!
Scottish Marches, September, 1310

Christina was awake before the dawn. A short while later, she joined Malcolm and Reiniken on the wharf-side, though of Ziesolf there was not yet a trace. The mystery of his whereabouts became apparent when he appeared a few minutes later, leading their already saddled mounts.

"Did your seller add the horses' tack as a gesture of goodwill?" Christina asked sarcastically, already suspecting Ziesolf's reply.

"No, I'm afraid not," he answered before adding, "Please don't ask his price."

This time, Christina refrained from inquiring further as she knew his response would do nothing save exasperate her.

Ziesolf had already chosen the rouncey for himself, an alert bay gelding of about fourteen hands. Reiniken's choice of mounts seemed obvious, an older cart horse with a tinge of gray in its otherwise black tail and mane, but of an uncommon size that seemed to dwarf the other horses.

Whether by choice or through the process of elimination, Malcolm went to the remaining nag; liver-chestnut in color, and only about thirteen hands in height. He whispered something in its ear, then stroked its rough coat. He produced an apple from his pocket and, taking his eating knife from his belt, sliced it into small bits to be heartily consumed by his new-found friend.

Christina claimed the palfrey, a well-muscled sorrel mare with a slightly nervous disposition. She approached the horse deliberately, cooing to it in unintelligible, reassuring tones. The mare flinched slightly when she placed her hand on its warm and slightly perspiring neck. As she began to rub in a circular motion Christina could feel the horses tense muscles begin to relax. Having gained her mount's confidence, she vaulted onto its back, then turned to settle comfortably into the saddle. She took the reins into her hands and bent forward to stroke the animal's neck once again, drinking in the uniquely pungent smell of a horse.

How good it is to have friends.

Christina reminisced as they waited for Ziesolf to return from the ship with the provisions he had packed the previous morning.

Trudi and Anna's uncle Manfred maintained the largest stable in Lübeck. I remember him letting us exercise the gentler horses in the paddock from the time we were ten years old. Within a few years, there was not one I could not ride at breakneck speed, even doing acrobatics on their backs when no adult was looking. Its lucky I didn't kill myself!

Ziesolf returned and divvied up the provisions amongst the riders. He looked toward each of his companions in turn, confirming they were ready to set off. Observing no objections, he stirred his reins slightly and rode down the mud-covered cobblestones of the street with Christina, Malcolm, and Reiniken following closely behind.

The horses kept up an ambling gate until the buildings of Berwick disappeared to their rear. Believing they were about to quicken their pace, Christina was surprised when Ziesolf slowed them to an intermittent walk, pausing every few hundred yards or so to stop and observe the surrounding countryside.

"If we spend half our time enjoying the scenery, the war will be over before we get to Roxburgh!" Christina complained after their fourth or fifth such pause.

"Caution is warranted, Frederick," Ziesolf stated mildly. "Even though we are well-armed, we are still but few. That makes us a lucrative target for any band of brigands whose desire for our horseflesh outweighs their good sense. See that copse of trees overhanging the road up there ahead to the left? How easy it would be to have a couple of nimble jacks jump us from above while their mates swarmed us from the ground. Then where would we be? Bruised, angry, and walking on our own shanks, if we're lucky. Lying in the ditch with our throats cut, if we're not."

"And the Scots as well, I suppose?" she asked, somewhat chagrined the thought of being attacked by common villains had not occurred to her.

"Probably not, at least on a well-traveled road linking major concentrations of Edward's forces in broad daylight. In the dark, who knows?"

"Aye, is der a reiver alive who don't love a spreath, be it fur horse or cattle," Malcolm chimed in cheerfully.

"Shut yur gob hole, ya Judas-haired whoreson," Reiniken complained. "Who th' fuck knows whut yur sayin' anyways?"

Christina looked at her companions and grinned, hugely entertained by the friendly jibes between the two. As the sun was beginning to sink low, they left the pathway, traveling a few hundred feet through a grove of sparsely-spaced birch and alder and into a small meadow. They unsaddled the horses and tethered them to graze hungrily on the fescue, meadow grass, and patches of white clover that bloomed in small, dense patches about the pasture-like field.

They made their camp with their backs against a sheer granite escarpment, reducing the opportunity by one direction from which an enemy could catch them unawares. After partaking of their meager rations, each curled up in a heavy woolen blanket; save Christina, who stood the first watch. By the time Malcolm relieved her, she was shivering from the cold. She found a spot somewhat out of the whirling wind and pulled her blanket tightly around her, even covering her head. She wished they had been able to light a fire, but the risk of discovery was too great. Even if they could have managed to shield the flames from inquisitive eyes, the smell of wood smoke would have been apparent for a mile or more distant. Soon, even the thought of the decreasing temperature left her thoughts and she drifted off into a listless slumber.

Christina awoke well before dawn, feeling the strongly compelling necessity to steal well away from the camp to conduct her morning business. Moving her stiffly frozen blanket away from her face, she was surprised to find a thin dusting of snow had painted the world around her. She arose and quietly crept away, circling around a thicket of brush so that, should anyone be following her footsteps in the powdery snow, she would see them before they discovered her. Christina took one last look around before finally dropping her braies with a sigh of relief.

When she returned, the men were stirring. They ate a spartan breakfast from their provisions, each seemingly more comfortable with his or her own thoughts than idle conversation. After saddling the horses, they were once more on the way to their destination.

Christina was surprised that, in less than an hour into their ride, she spotted the imposing battlements of a vast castle complex in the distance ahead. Reigning in her horse, she dropped back to fall in alongside Malcolm.

"Is that Roxburgh castle already in the distance?"

He replied, "Nay, tis Wark, I think, on t'udder side a th' river."

As they rode further on, her eyes confirmed what the Scotsman had told her. It was early afternoon before they sighted another huge stone structure a mile or so ahead. This time, Christina had no reason to ask, as the buildings were clearly ecclesiastical in nature, rather than military.

"My God," she exclaimed to Ziesolf, "It's enormous!"

"Aye, it's a fortress onto itself. Give me fifty men and adequate provisions and I could keep the Scots at bay for a year!" he replied, appraising the abbey's architectural design with approval.

They reluctantly passed the village tavern, their empty stomachs yearning for a savory bowl of thick stew and a mug of ale. All thoughts of tarrying were forgotten, however, as the immense fortress of Roxburgh now loomed before them. The tall walls of the castle were elevated into the sky even further than those of the abbey as they were built upon a mound rising at least seventy feet above the surrounding countryside.

Christina and her companions crossed over the aqueduct and slowly rode uphill outside the entire three-hundred-and-fifty-foot length of the castle's exterior wall. She could feel wary eyes following their progress, imagining it would take very little alarm to trigger a flurry of arrows down upon their heads should they display any sign of belligerence. They reached the apex of the pathway, which then hooked back upon the approach to the castle's main entranceway. They crossed the bridge over a deep dry ditch, dismounted and walked the remaining small distance over the drawbridge and to the sentried castle foretower.

"Halt. What would your business be here, stranger?" one of the soldiers guarding the gateway asked of Ziesolf, assuming him to be the leader of their small party.

"I am Frederick Kohl, master merchant of London town, and a boon friend of the Earl of Cornwall. I bring private tidings for his Grace," Christina stated, stepping forward a few feet beyond the others.

The sentry eyed them carefully for a few moments before turning to one of the other soldiers on duty to say, "John, take these men to see the castellan."

Before Christina could begin a protest, the guard turned to her and said, "The earl and his men are off on a chevauchee, raiding deeply into the Scottish territory to the north. Sir Neville is the castellan here. He might have some idea as to when the earl plans to return."

Shit!

Christina could hardly contain her frustration.

Why is it nothing can ever be straight-forward? Who knows how long it will be before I can deliver my damned message to Gaveston and go home?

Having no viable alternative, Christina and her friends followed the soldier under the foretower's heavy iron portcullis and toward the gaping entrance to the castle proper. As they moved forward, Christina was suddenly gripped by an alarming wariness, feeling as if they were being led into the maw of a ravenous beast. She pushed the feeling aside as best she could, scolding herself for acting like a scared child. Regardless, her sense of unease remained.

At the steps leading to the great stone donjon, their guide separated himself from them to speak in muffled tones to the sentries posted at the entrance. One departed through the iron-reinforced door to the interior, ostensibly to announce their presence. The other remained at his post, making no movement to welcome their entry.

"Let me take your horses to the stable," John offered. "I'll see to it they're fed and attended to."

"Thank you," Christina spoke graciously, "My man Malcolm will give you a hand with that."

The two men took the reins of the horses, leading them in the direction of what must be the stables. Christina, Zieolf, and Reiniken waited in the courtyard for several minutes more before the soldier who had left returned.

"Follow me," he said simply.

They stepped inside the doorway, the walls of which were well-mortared and several feet thick. The clock-wise circular stairway led them to the second floor, where they once again were instructed to wait. After an interminable amount of time a servant entered and showed them through into the hall.

As they walked into the room, a well-stoked blaze was burning in the great fireplace at the head of the room. A few feet to its fore, a thick oaken table stood with several benches placed around it. Seated between the table and the fire was one whom Christina assumed was Sir Neville. Although his face was indiscernible in the faint light, it was easy to see they had caught him at his dinner, as he gnawed noisily upon a roasted chicken carcass. Setting it down on the plate before him, he stood and wiped his greasy hands on the sides of his tunic. Taking his tankard in hand, he took a long pull, then set it back down. Apparently now sufficiently fortified, he at last took notice of Christina and the others standing before him.

She had not anticipated the height of the man, exceeding hers by more than a head. His long dark hair hung about his shoulders in oily locks. Sir Neville smelled of days-old sweat and decaying food. His face was narrow and swarthy in complexion, coupling a large aquiline nose with thick, sensuous lips down its midpoint. A large, bulbous belly strained against the fabric of his tunic, incongruous with his thin shoulders and spindly legs. He reminded Christina of a large, unpleasant spider she had once found in her room when she was young before unceremoniously squashing it with the bottom of her shoe.

"Well met, Master Merchant," he greeted her mildly. "God be with you this day."

"And may he hold you in his favor as well, Sir Castellan," she answered, bowing slightly.

"So," he began, coming around the table to stand directly before Christina. "Have you traveled far this day?"

"It has been a two-day journey from Berwick, where we departed my ship."

"Well, has it now?" he exclaimed good-naturedly. "But where are my manners? You must be famished! You there," he pointed at one of the attendants in the room. "Take these other men to the kitchens and see they are well fed. Bring more food and drink here for the master merchant. He and I will speak more while he dines."

Christina would have preferred for their company to stay together, but didn't want to risk offending the knight by refusing his hospitality. She nodded her agreement in the direction of Ziesolf and Reiniken, who followed the servant out of the room. Sir Neville walked back to the other side of the table and sat back down, gesturing for Christina to take the seat across from him.

Before anything could be said, a different servant entered, pouring a tankard of ale for Christina as well as filling that of the knight. He held his drinking vessel slightly higher, in an apparent salute to Christina. She matched the gesture and they both drank. She gulped down a bit more than good manners allowed, as she had not realized before her throat was totally parched.

Sir Neville flashed a wan smile and said, "Now, what is this I hear about you being a friend of our good earl?"

Christina recounted a heavily-redacted account of her dealings with Gaveston, leaving out the more intimate details. Midway through her telling, another servant arrived, this time with a platter groaning from the weight of the food piled atop. Although she knew it would be exceptionally rude to interrupt her tale to eat, she had to fight hard to resist.

When she had finally finished her telling, she asked, "Is there more you wish to know, Sir Neville?"

"No, no, or not now at least. Please enjoy your food before we engage in more serious talk"

Although his last statement seemed oddly phrased, she took no time to ponder his words before she began to attack the splendid repast set before her. She ate herself full to bursting, taking time out every now and then to respond to an innocuous question or two from Sir Neville. She finally pushed the platter to the side, unable to even gaze upon any more food.

"Well, as you may already know, the earl presently harries our enemy to the north. Unfortunately, I know not when he may return," Sir Neville said.

"That is what I have already been told, my lord," Christina responded noncommittally.

"Which leaves us in a quandary, does it not, Master Merchant?"

Christina looked directly into the man's eyes, but said nothing.

"Well, you can't just stay here forever; now can you?" the knight said with a bit of sarcasm flavoring his words.

"No, but I hope Earl Piers returns sooner than that, God protect him well," she responded innocently, crossing herself for added effect.

"Yes, yes, not forever, I agree," he said in a clipped tone, seemingly hovering on the edge of his patience. "But it could be a long while, weeks even. I am his castellan, entrusted by the earl himself with guarding the king's mightiest fortress on the Borders. Tell me your message, Master Frederick. You may then voyage back to London, knowing your mission has been successfully completed. As soon as the Earl of Cornwall returns to Roxburgh, I will inform him of what you have told me and he may act accordingly. Does this plan not seem for the best?"

Christina hesitated, worrying her bottom lip between her teeth.

What he says does make sense; yet, it seems almost too conveniently so. If he can be trusted, there is no harm in doing what he proposes. Gaveston will be warned as quickly as I could do myself, and I will be on my way back home. Should Sir Neville prove false, however, the earl will remain unaware of the plot against him and the time and effort I have spent coming this far will have been for naught. What it comes down to is, do I trust this man?

"I am torn between my duty and the generosity of your offer. I will discuss this matter with my companions and provide you an answer on the morrow." Christina proposed.

"Boy! Who do you believe you are to come into my castle and attempt to dictate terms with me?" Sir Neville's speech was colored by the ferocity of his anger that had finally boiled over.

The servant in attendance dropped the plate of stewed apples he was carrying noisily on the floor, so shocked was he at the violence of the castellan's outburst.

"Get out, you clumsy oaf!" Sir Neville, shouted, sending the servant scurrying for the door.

In a calm, measured voice, Christina said, "Sir Neville, please realize I take my promises seriously, you as a knight must surely understand one's vow may not be broken lightly no matter how advantageous to one's self doing so might be. So, when I promised to deliver my message to the Earl of Cornwall personally, and to no other, that is what I feel I must do."

The castellan stared at her for a few long seconds. Gradually, his face lost its red flush as he took several deep breaths to compose himself. The corners of his mouth gradually lifted as he fixed her with a poor semblance of a smile.

"Please, pardon my outburst; perhaps too much ale? It is just I have so many worrisome tasks weighing heavily on my mind, to add yet another must have overwhelmed me with frustration. Of course, you may take as much time as you need to decide what to do. Until then, you will be my guest here at the castle. I will take it as my personal responsibility you are well looked after."

"And my men?" she asked, "Where may I find them?"

"They have already been fed, and will be bedded in the stables. I apologize for their rustic accommodations, but the castle is already overcrowded by the addition of the earl's troops to those of the garrison."

"Thank you, Sir Neville, for your kind hospitality and understanding. I will take your leave, if I may, to join my men"

"Oh, no!" he responded, rising to his feet once more. "I would not be able to face Earl Pier's wrath, should he learn I have relegated such a close friend of his to a bed of loose straw with the horses. I myself will show you now to more suitable quarters here in the tower."

This man's sensibilities run from hot to cold and then back again. I cannot risk offending him once more over such a trivial matter as to where I sleep. I will confer with Ziesolf in the morning to work out a suitable scheme to leave here and find Gaveston without the questionable assistance of Sir Neville.

"Again, I thank you, Sir Neville."

"Good," he said, "Now let us be off." He walked around the table and took one of the large tapers from its sconce on the wall. He led Christina out the door and up the stairway once more. He halted at the third floor and made his way to the second door, which he opened and stepped inside. In the candlelight she saw that, although the room was small, it was well furnished with a large rope bed and thick, colorful, wall hangings.

"I hope it meets with your satisfaction?"

"Yes, very much so. It is much more than I expected," she responded graciously.

"Excellent. I will have a servant bring hot water and toweling. Also, a bottle of wine. We will speak further tomorrow, young Frederick. Sleep well."

Christina thanked the castellan once again and he left. She sat on the bed and took off her boots, massaging her cold and aching toes through her woolen hose. Returning from a brief visit to avail herself of the privy, the shaft of which was conveniently inset into the outside wall, she heard a knock on the door. Thinking it had not taken very long to heat the water, she padded across the floor and opened the door for the servant to enter with his burden. She was shocked to see two grim-faced men standing before her, neither of which held a bucket nor a bottle of wine. One reached out unexpectantly and pulled her violently forward by the shoulder of her tunic. The other's arm flicked forward and she felt a sudden, sharp pain on the side of her head, then nothing more.

Christina opened her eyes to a slit to examine the room about her. It was large and airless, smelling of sweat, mold, and human excrement. Three rush torches were ensconced on the wall to her left, while a series of three heavily barred cells stood to the right. The room was quite long, perhaps more than twenty feet. At the other end was what she surmised was the solitary exit.

Four men were standing beside a small table, laughing and joking amongst themselves. Detecting Christina's small movements, two of them moved forward and picked her up bodily, sitting her firmly upon a small stool. It was then she noticed her hands were bound together by a length of cordage.

"Well, look who finally woke up, boys!" said the shorter of the two nearby men, the smell of his breath like that of an overripe scallion patch.

Christina raised her head but said nothing, the small motion making her stomach a bit queasy from the blow she had previously sustained.

"Don't say much, eh?" her questioner asked flippantly. "Oh, I think we're gonna have a good talk, you and me. You'll be singing like a feckin' lark in no time!"

The taller of the two stepped forward and slapped her cruelly across the face then grabbed her hair roughly, pulling her face to now look his way. There was no humor in his expression as he came straight to the point.

"Let me ask him, Tom. What message do you have for Gaveston and who is it from?"

Again, she chose not to speak.

"Good," the man muttered. "I had hoped you wouldn't give in that easily."

The two men pulled her to her feet and, unexpectedly, cut the cord that held her hands together.

Merciful Mary; they're not setting me free, are they?

250

Her answer came a second later as the shorter man punched her savagely in the stomach, causing her to double over from the sudden, intense pain.

The two men grabbed the sleeves of her tunic and pulled it over her arms and head. They threw it to the side and did the same for the linen shirt she wore beneath. She attempted to struggle, but was hit once again for her efforts. She managed to remain standing as they released her arms and stepped a few feet away from her.

"What the hell is that?" one of the other men asked as he picked an evil-looking scourge from the table. "Don't matter none. Got to come off before we start."

Although a bit dazed, Christina fully realized the seriousness of her plight. It was clear the men intended to torture her until she disclosed her message for Gaveston. What's worse, the man who spoke was referring to the cloth wrap that bound her chest to conceal her breasts. Without doubt, she was about to be revealed as a woman.

"No, stop! I'll tell you!" she pleaded, her intent to protect Gaveston now forgotten in her fear as to what was assuredly about to happen.

She struggled as best she could, but the men were simply too strong. They soon had the wrapping removed, leaving her chest bare to their astonished, leering stares. They then set about removing her braies, throwing her roughly onto her back as they pulled them down and off to expose her naked sex.

"I thought him no more than a gelding, but instead we've got ourselves a filly here," the man with the scourge said in a low, throaty voice. "No need to use the whip here. I'm sure she'll respond to a gentler persuasion. Should we all take a turn before we put the question to her again?"

He absentmindedly placed the scourge back on the table. He then began to fumble with the front of his own braies as the other men urged him on. Soon, he had his engorged member in his hand, slowly stroking it as he eyed Christina's now nude body.

An unexpected wave of calmness passed through her body.

You have one chance at this, Christina, otherwise you are lost.

Rather than trying to cover her nakedness, she now sought to display it. Christina moved to place her back against the stool, then held her head up to face her attackers. In what appeared to be obvious panic, she moved the upper half of her body away, inadvertently causing her to spread her legs and provide the men an unobstructed view of her cleft. The two who had disrobed her stepped back to ogle her now fully-exposed body.

"What a shameless slut!" the man who had held the scourge exclaimed; his purplish cock now fully aroused. "Do you think this is going to be pleasant, your ladyship? I'm gonna hurt ya, and you're gonna scream alright, but from pain, not pleasure. Hold her arms, boys, so she can't thrash about.

He began to walk slowly toward Christina, while the other two men obediently bent down to hold her arms.

With totally unexpected swiftness, she turned to her side and secured a firm hold on the hilt of the taller man's knife. She scuttled backwards, smoothly drawing the blade from its scabbard as she went.

All will now depend on their gullibility to my deception

She held the weapon clumsily forward in both hands before her, its tip wavering in apparent response to her fearful quivering.

Christina knew she had very little chance of defeating four armed soldiers in the small confines of the room. Even while she engaged one, the others would attack from her rear and sides, wounding her gravely, even if not killing her outright. She realized her only chance lay in convincing the men to drop their guards, not taking her seriously as a threat. If she was able to take the first two unaware, she just might have a small chance of escaping with her life.

"Stay . . . stay back, do you hear me? I'll stab you!" she said in a quavering voice, as she now sat with her legs beneath her.

The one called Tom and the taller man had cautiously backed away when Christina had first made her move. Now, they inched closer as they realized such a girl posed little danger to them, even with a sharpened blade in her hands.

"Hold on now, girly," Tom said in a condescendingly soothing voice. "Don't be scared, we were just having a bit of fun. We wouldn't think of hurting you, would we now?"

"Oh, for Christ's sake!" said the man with his braies around his ankles, "Just grab the fuckin' little cunt!"

The other two men made various noises in assent.

"Really?" she said, ignoring everyone else for the moment except Tom.

"Of course. Let's be friends now, shall we?" Tom replied.

The taller man had now stepped to exactly where Christina wanted him to be. She deftly moved the weapon, a long seax with about a sixteen-inch blade, to her right hand and sprang to her feet, thrusting the blade upwards through his chin and into his brain, killing him before he had the opportunity to fall to the floor. She pulled her right arm forcefully backwards to dislodge the blade while simultaneously using her right arm to clear her initial victim's body to the side.

Tom stood motionless, transfixed in horror as to what he had just seen befall his crony. He began to raise his right arm to ward off her anticipated blow. Christina stepped forward and shifted her weight, spinning in a full counter-clockwise circle to gain momentum. Confused by the unorthodox maneuver, he tried to turn his body away, but he was already too late. In a blur, the arc of the weapon cut through the air, passing through his throat with ease as it severed both carotid arteries. He fell backwards as his crimson blood showered upward spectacularly.

Christina now turned her attention to the man who had threatened her so cruelly. He was trying to raise his braies and draw his sword simultaneously, neither of which was being accomplished very successfully. She kicked out with her leg and her foot caught him squarely in his chest. He tumbled backwards and he hit his head hard on the floor. He sprawled there motionlessly, apparently unconscious.

The last man had finally managed to draw his weapon, but he had backed himself into the corner of the room. She noticed he was young, perhaps no older than herself.

"Please," he pleaded, staring in fright at the naked and bloodied avenging angel before him. "It was them, not me. I wanted naught to do with it!"

Christina looked at him, then bent her head and spit blood before saying, "Please? Please, you say? What did you say when what you thought was a helpless girl pleaded with you with the same word? You only laughed and waited in line impatiently for your turn to violate her."

"Please," he repeated once more. "I promise I'll never do anything like this again. As God is my witness, I promise!"

He let his sword drop clattering to the floor, then fell on his knees in supplication.

"I think I believe you," she said

He looked up at her hopefully.

"But not so much I'd risk the virtue of the next girl who falls into your filthy clutches," she muttered.

Christina thrust her crimson-stained blade deeply into his heart. She drew it out quickly and turned about, hearing faint groans and rustlings behind her.

It was apparent his eyes were still not properly focused as Christina appeared before him once more.

"Well, it seems that cock is not so mighty after all," she exclaimed, looking down dismissively at its now shrunken state.

"Fuck you, bitch!" he spat back at her.

"No, I don't think so, at least not with that you will," Christina said, flicking her blade deftly to almost sever his genitals completely from his body.

His injury elicited an almost immediate scream of pain, a sound that was cut short by the thrust of her blade deeply into his open mouth. Silence now permeated the room, save for the sound of her own ragged breathing. She sat back down on the stool heavily, her body trembled uncontrollably, threatening to shut down completely from shock. She lost control of her bladder, her effluent mixing with that of the dead men strewn about the floor. She sat in a stupor for an interminable number of minutes before finally gaining a modicum of control over herself.

"I have no time for this now," she spoke the words aloud.

Rising on still-quaking legs, she removed the hood from the first man she had killed and, together with the jar of ale the men had been consuming, conducted an impromptu scrub of the worst of the blood and other soil from her body. Christina then quickly dressed, fearing reinforcements to her assailants would arrive at any minute.

Although it was difficult to focus her thoughts, she attempted to piece together a plan for escape.

But from where? I have no idea where I am or what it is I face ahead of me. How can I proceed when I know nothing?

Christina took several deep breaths to still her panic.

Although I know nothing factual, I can make a few assumptions, which are better than outright guesses, I think.

She examined the door to find it was bolted from within.

The men did not want to be discovered, so they locked the door. Good. That could mean not everyone in the garrison follows Sir Neville blindly. If he has gone to bed and there are only a few happy to do his dirty work, I may be able to walk right past the sentries at the donjon's door. If not . . . if not, it probably doesn't matter.

She undid the tall man's sword belt and placed it about her own waist, sliding the seax within its intended sheath. She then slid the bolt aside and cautiously opened the heavy door. She strained her ears to hear if anyone stirred in response to the loud metallic groan of the door moving within its pivots. Hearing nothing, she stepped through the portal.

As she had suspected, she had been imprisoned within the lowest level of the tower, evidenced by the stairway only leading in an upward direction. Ascending silently up the steps to the first floor, she was ecstatic to confirm the structure was indeed the donjon and not some other tower to which she had been carried while unconscious.

The last thing I need is another complication.

She continued to the third floor, praying fervently she would find her room undisturbed. Entering, she found everything as she had left it when she went to answer the door. Christina quickly pulled on her boots, grabbed her pouch, and exchanged her own falchion for the seax.

She smiled with ironic consternation

I wish the servant had had time to bring the wine.

She left the chamber and closed the door quietly behind her before walking down the stairs and halting before the portal leading outside. She offered up a quick prayer, then stepped boldly through the darkened doorway. Glancing to the side, Christina saw two guardsmen warming their hands above a small cast iron brazier that glowed red in the darkness of the night. They looked in her direction with mild interest. Ignoring them, she descended the steps purposefully and headed in the direction in which the sentry and Malcolm had led their mounts the previous day.

Chapter 17

Escape and Capture
Scottish Marches, September, 1310

Christina kept waiting for one of the sentries behind her to issue a challenge, but no order to halt was forthcoming. Breathing a sigh of relief, she continued forward. The stable soon loomed ahead of her. It had been greatly expanded from what must have been the original structure by the addition of a series of ramshackle temporary buildings. Christina stood looking at the various openings in dismay.

Where do I even begin to look? It's much too dark to locate them by sight alone; yet, I can hardly wander about calling their names aloud either.

She refused to let the other alternative enter her consideration; that Sir Neville had already seen fit to have them murdered and that their bodies were growing colder at this very minute.

How can I find them? More importantly, how can I find them before the alarm is raised to seek out the killer of Sir Neville's henchmen?

Her heartbeat now uncontrollably quickening.

"Come to see how the fuckin' peasants live, Yur Worship?" an unmistakable voice asked softly from the shadows.

"Wig!" she exclaimed in relief, perhaps a little too loudly as well.

"What t' hell are ya doin' out in the middle of the night?" he asked, beginning to walk toward her.

"Sh!" she replied, motioning him to stay as she walked toward him; then, "Take me to Ziesolf."

He looked at her quizzically before beginning to walk deeper into the building. By the time they worked their way around the tethered horses, Ziesolf and Malcolm has already arisen. While they gathered their belongings, Christina provided an abbreviated version of her ordeals from earlier that evening.

"I suspected things here were not as they seemed," Ziesolf remarked acridly. "That is why I thought it best to set a sentry of our own."

"I'm certainly glad you did," Christina agreed. "I could have spent an hour or more searching through this maze for you. An hour we don't have, by the way. I'm certain the castellan will turn out the entire garrison to search for us by the morning. What time is it, by the way?"

"Still a few hours before sunrise, I figure," Ziesolf responded while appraising the color of the sky.

"Am I tuh saddle th' horses, then?" Malcolm interrupted.

"No, regrettably not," Ziesolf answered. "The clopping of their shod hooves would draw too much attention, not to mention the noise the lowering of the drawbridge would make. Do you remember the small sally port we passed as we approached the castle? Give me a few minutes head start, then approach it separately. Stay well in the shadows and do nothing to draw attention to yourselves, understand?"

They all nodded their heads while saying nothing. Even Reiniken refrained from joking about, realizing the grave situation in which they now found themselves.

Shortly afterwards, Christina began working her way around the inside loop of the castle wall. She attempted to maintain a leisurely pace, as if perhaps she had been unable to sleep and needed a bit of exercise before returning to her bed. Inwardly, her nerves were taunt as a bowstring and it seemed to take an eternity before she finally approached the squat, heavy door set firmly in the thick stone of the castle walls. A single guard stood to the side of the door, while two more sat reclining against the wall.

Has something gone wrong?

She feared the sound of the drum-like beating heart would certainly draw the attention of the sentries.

Where is Ziesolf?

She ambled a bit closer and was relieved to discover the standing sentry was Ziesolf himself, while the other two remained motionless despite her approach.

"Dead?"

"Yes. I couldn't take the risk they would cry out," he said. "Even if they were not aligned with Sir Neville's foul deeds, they would certainly not permit strangers to breach what they had been set to guard."

Christina and Ziesolf soon were joined by Reiniken and Malcolm. The group passed through the door and crept along as closely to the outside of the castle wall as possible. They were assisted in remaining unseen by the cloudiness of the night and the dampening effect of a subtle fall of snow. The gurgling of the waters of the Tweed and the Teviot muffled their incidental noises as they made their way to the corner of the massive structure. After a few moments to catch their breathes, they left the shelter of the towering walls and set off at a trot down the cart path leading back to the village of Kelso.

Without warning, a horn sounded within the castle behind them. It was soon joined by others, raising a mighty din into the frigid night air. Whether someone had discovered the dead sentries at the sally port or the remains of Christina's abductors within the bowels of the donjon was immaterial. What was important was the fact a pursuit would soon be mounted and, if they were captured, their deaths would be almost assured.

They quickened their pace. As they neared the approach to the causeway, Ziesolf suddenly stopped. He then turned about, retracing their steps until he veered down to the water's edge.

"If they have dogs, they'll soon loose them on our scent. We'll wade through the waters for a few hundred feet to throw them off, if we're lucky that is."

"No, we can't do that, Ziesolf," said Christina adamantly. "The water is too cold; we'll freeze to death if we can't dry ourselves afterward. If we couldn't risk a fire on our journey here, how the hell can we light one with an army in singular pursuit of us?"

Ziesolf stared at her for a few seconds, before finally nodding his head in agreement.

"Well, let's be off then. We need to be over the causeway and gone from the town before the villagers join in the hunt as well."

They soon found themselves outside of the village and traveling stealthily northward, hoping the possible threat of encountering a Scottish raiding party would be sufficient to at least slow their pursuers. As for themselves, they did not have the luxury of taking caution against a possible enemy, outweighed as it was by the danger posed by a real one. A few hours into their flight, the lightening of the eastern sky provided proof the day was dawning. Sir Neville's pursuit would now begin in earnest, if it had not already.

They climbed a small knoll and paused once more to catch their breathes, chancing a glance backward toward the castle. One look confirmed the castellan's men had already extended their search into the village of Kelso as several small figures moved purposefully among the thatched cottages, obviously seeking to uncover the fugitives. It would not be long until they would extend their search outward.

Christina and the others pressed on, knowing it was essential to keep moving to stay ahead of their pursuers. They waded across a small brook, stooping to drink from its pristine waters like feral forest creatures. The ground beneath them was gently undulating, providing little concealment other than a few granite boulders or a small copse of trees. Malcolm said they would need to escape the valley entirely before they could find adequate safety from the eyes of their pursuers in the deep forests of the border lands.

While they hurriedly consumed the remaining scraps of food they scrounged from their pouches, Christina took the opportunity to further study the surrounding terrain. Ahead to the left a small but solidly constructed church stood in the distance, perhaps a mile or less before them. A cluster of peasant cottages were scattered about one side while a stone manor house stood on the other. To the right, more open countryside. Neither direction seemed particularly fortuitous to their cause.

It was when she looked back the way they had come that Christina's worst fears were confirmed. About twenty mounted men were riding in their general direction from the abbey. It did not seem they had spotted the fugitives yet, as the horses moved at no more than a trot. She knew it would not be long, however, before they sighted the trail of their quarry and the chase would soon be over.

"This way!" Ziesolf shouted, beginning to run in the direction of the hamlet to their front. "We might get lucky and find there are Scots there. Even if not, it will be a damned easier place to defend ourselves than out here in the open."

They ran toward the village at the best speed they could muster. As Christina and Malcolm were clearly the fastest of the group, she chanced another glance behind. Obviously, the riders had seen them now as their horses ran at full gallop. It was now only a question as to whether Neville and his men would catch them before their quarry reached the questionable safety of the structures ahead.

"Come, run faster!" Christina pleaded with Ziesolf and Reiniken, both of whose endurance was seemingly flagging.

She looked again and her spirits sank. Sir Neville's horses were too fast. Clearly, the riders would be upon them before they reached the village.

Ziesolf stumbled, falling to one knee. He raised himself and drew his sword.

"I will make my stand here, I think. Save yourself, I will delay them as best I can."

"I'm with One Eye. Fuck this runnin' bullshit, I wanna kill somebody!" said Reiniken, as they both turned to face the rapidly approaching enemy.

Christina's cheeks flamed in frustration. Although she knew the two men would give a good account of themselves, there were simply too many foes to defeat. Even if she stayed to help, it only meant they would die together. She turned back toward the village, torn as to what choice to make.

Unexpectedly, she saw a large party of men from the village mounting their horses and riding in their direction.

Could they be Scots?

Her mouth gaped open in amazement.

If so, will they help us? Clearly, we're not English. Can we convince them the enemy of their enemies should be counted amongst their friends?

"Are they Scots?" she asked Malcolm.

He squinted for a second before saying, "Nay, Anglish, they are."

It seems our last hope is gone. Well, we can't fight them all. Better to concentrate on those we know wish us harm.

She drew her falchion and moved beside Ziesolf. He turned to her and gave a nod of approval then fixed his eyes back on the soldiers from the castle. She noted movement to her right. It was Malcolm, a long dagger in his right hand.

"Ah hates these wee basturds," he muttered, a savage smile fixed on his lips.

The castellan's horses thundered toward them; the rhythmic sound of their approach now matched by a similar one behind them. They were now near enough to see the spray of clotted earth kicked up behind their flying hooves. Christina estimated they were only a minute or two away. She shifted her stance to a more comfortable one and waited.

"Ignore the riders as best you can and concentrate on killing or wounding the horses. If you bring them down, the man comes too," Ziesolf advised.

Christina now saw the swarthy face of Sir Neville astride an ugly brute of a black destrier bearing down on them. The lips of both were pulled back, revealing their teeth clenched into a rictus of a murderous grin. Unexpectedly, he reined his horse in about twenty feet in front of the small band of defenders, signaling for his accompanying riders to do the same. He stared at Christina for a few seconds with a triumphant look upon his face before slowly dismounting and drawing his sword. His men did the same, fanning out into a broad semi-circle before they all began to warily inch closer.

"Hold!" demanded an authoritative voice from behind them.

Christina turned about in surprise. Her concentration on the imminent danger to their front had been so complete she had completely forgotten about the riders bearing down on them from behind. She saw there were perhaps twice as many men in their party as in that of Sir Neville. At their fore was an older man with a gray beard mounted on a magnificently caparisoned warhorse. On his head, he wore a silver coronet. She believed it was he who had spoken.

Although Neville immediately halted and took a knee, the look on his face was one of furious frustration.

"My Lord de Percy, thank you for your assistance in running these foreign dogs to earth. Only this past evening, I entertained these Germans as guests at Roxburgh. How did they respond to my gracious hospitality? With treachery and mayhem! They murdered four of my servants most foully, then attacked and killed two men of the watch. After escaping through a sally port, they left it unbolted. I believe they were hurrying now to tell the Scots, to bring them back to steal through the unguarded entrance, slitting our throats while we peacefully slumbered and taking the castle for themselves."

"This is a grave charge, Lord Castellan, one punishable by a traitor's death. First, they must be tried, however."

"Yes, Lord Baron, I agree wholeheartedly. I will now return them to the castle where they will be treated fairly, much more generously than they deserve."

Sir Neville motioned for his men to take Christina and the others into custody.

"Halt your men, Sir Neville. It is peculiar to say the least to find a band of Germans wandering about the Marches. This greatly concerns me, as it will those whom I serve. What if they represent a larger band of mercenaries who now ally themselves with The Bruce? I believe I will take them to Stichill to be tried, where they may be questioned more fully as to their intents and purposes."

"But, Lord de Percy!" Sir Neville interjected.

"Castellan, do you question my authority to do this?"

"No, but . . ." Sir Neville began before being cut off.

"Then it is settled. Bring them to the manor." The baron said, directing his comments to his followers to the left of his horse.

Several men dismounted and disarmed Christina and her companions. They were then escorted through the field toward the village. Baron de Percy and his followers rode ahead, while Sir Neville and his men trailed behind. Christina imagined the castellan's hateful eyes burning smoldering holes into her back.

In less than a half hour, they arrived in the yard of the manor house. The dwelling was small, especially by the standard of the great houses of London, but seemed to be solidly built. It was not the standard of construction that drew Christina's attention. Rather, it was the great number of horses and men gathered about the space.

One of the baron's men took her by the arm and led her through the doorway of the manor and into what must certainly be considered the structure's great hall. She was brought to a bench sat along the left side wall and she sat down, soon to be joined by Ziesolf, Reiniken, and Malcolm. There, they waited for the proceedings against them to begin.

Sir Neville walked into the room and stood before a long trestle table that had been moved hastily to the front of the room. After a few minutes, the door at the back of the room opened and Baron de Percy entered and sat himself down. Curiously, it was not the central, better, chair in which he settled himself, but the one to its right. This decision was made clear upon the entrance of the next figure, one who caused Christina's jaw to drop in amazement.

Gaveston walked to the central position and seated himself. He seemed to take no notice of Christina; his eyes instead focused directly ahead toward Sir Neville. He slouched back into the chair to make himself more comfortable.

In a solemn voice, he said, "From what Baron de Percy has told me, you accuse those four captives of murder, as well as conspiring to deliver Roxburgh Castle to the Scots. If you may, Sir Neville, provide me now the details of what has transpired."

The castellan proceeded to relate his false version of the previous night's happens, elaborating them further to stress his own innocence and Christina's guilt. When he had finished, Gaveston asked for Christina to be brought forward as well. He then asked her if she had any words of her own to add.

"Indeed I do, your Grace!" she cried, "We are innocent . . ."

The Earl of Cornwall cut her telling short with the wave of his hand before remarking mildly, "I have heard enough."

"But, your Grace . . ."

"Enough," he repeated, this time a bit more forcefully.

Bitter tears of frustration began to form in the corners of Christina's eyes.

You bastard; the only reason I am here is to help you! Now you will not even listen to my telling of the story, while you seem to readily accept the words of this varlet. Damn you, Gaveston, damn you to hell!

"I have need of no more words," Gaveston said as he slowly rose to his feet. "It is clear to me I have been betrayed most foully, by one in whom I placed great faith and trust. It sickens my heart as it is not only treachery against myself, but of our dear King Edward as well. Take him away, and may God have mercy on his soul, as I will have none on his person!"

Sir Neville leered at Christina, his visage all but consumed by his smug sense of satisfaction.

De Percy's men approached to take Christina into custody.

Gaveston's face betrayed a small smile as he said, "Forgive me, please. Was I not clear? I meant Sir Neville, not Master Frederick."

The soldiers paused; a bit confused. It was not until Gaveston made a small fluttering gesture toward the castellan with his fingers that the men moved to Sir Neville and grasped him by his arms.

Sir Neville's face grew apoplectic as he shouted, "What? You believe this boy over the word of one who wears the spurs of a knight? Are you a fool?"

Gaveston replied, "Aye, a fool it seems in that I have permitted you to retain your position this long. I have suspected you to be an ally of those arrayed against me, a suspicion now confirmed. Say no more, I may yet provide you with a good death."

The guards took the struggling castellan from the room. For his part, he had the good sense to refrain from speaking further.

"Master Frederick!" Gaveston shouted, running around the table and clasping his friend in a tight embrace.

He let it go and stepped backward. A look of concern spread across his face as he beheld the amazement on Christina's own.

"Surely you did not doubt my love for you?"

"No, never for an instant, your Grace." Christina lied, perceiving no compelling advantage to being truthful.

"You must know I am delighted to see you, my dear friend, but what causes you to be so far from home. Could it be you missed me so much as to brave such a journey?" he remarked facetiously.

"No, although London did seem dull without having you there," she paused before adding, "I have traveled here to relay a message to you, one of great import I think."

Gaveston's eyebrows raised in surprise. He led her through the doorway leading deeper into the house; to a small but comfortable solar. The earl closed the door behind them and seated himself on a bench, motioning for her to do the same.

"So, what are these tidings of which you speak, Christina?"

She recounted precisely what the servant Hugh had told her, leaving nothing out. As she spoke, Gaveston's face became increasingly troubled. When she had finished, he said nothing for a while, apparently mulling her words over carefully. Christina waited patiently for him to initiate further discussion.

Finally, he said, "Firstly, I am deeply indebted to you for your sense of duty to me. I know of no one else who would imperil themselves to such a degree to bring news of a threat to my notice. I am greatly confused, however. You see, I have long been aware of the schemes of Lancaster, Black Dog Warwick, and their cronies. It seems your efforts have delivered me old news at best."

All of the dangers we have faced have been for naught?

She stared at him incredulously, too stunned to speak.

"You say the servant's name was Hugh?" he asked.

"Yes," was all she was able to say.

"I have no such man in my employ as far as I know," he added, "Although I believe there was one of such name a year or so prior. He had been engaged in some sort of impropriety and was released from my service by my steward. It might be he held a grudge against me and my staff, but it would seem too subtle by half if he sought to remedy it through you."

The import of what Gaveston said resonated through Christina's brain like the great bells of St. Paul's in London. She shared the earl's confusion. It seemed nonsensical for the man to believe he had revenged himself in such a way.

There must be another answer.

She wracked her mind for a more plausible explanation, but could think of none.

The two friends exchanged stories of what had transpired since they had last been together. After hearing of his exploits, Christina began a recounting of her own experiences. She was not far along in her story before she stopped speaking abruptly, a pallor forming over her face. Alarmed, Gaveston stared at her, unsure of whether he should summon his own chirurgeon to attend to her apparent apoplexy. Before he could move, she began to speak with a tone of certainty upon her words.

"It was her."

Gaveston asked, "Are you well, Christina? You look as if you have encountered a dead spirit."

"Not a spirit, but a devil," she replied. "Katharine Revele."

"The German alderman's daughter?"

Aye, but no more. The father has died and she now is the wife of the new one, who sits totally bewitched by his scheming bride. She has inherited the smoldering coals of her father's dislike of Frederick Kohl, fanning them to where they glow white hot with hatred. Christina opposed new trade policies her husband sought to enact. But it was she who spoke through him, just as surely as it is the bowman who aims the arrow and not the bow. With Frederick out of the way, the scales will easily tip in her favor.

Gaveston looked at her with obvious concern her in his eyes.

"Friend Christina, if there is aught I can do to assist you, you have only to ask. Remember too, I have the king's ear and he is an ally of inestimable worth."

"I thank you, Your Grace, for the love you have shown me. Know you well, I will call on you should the necessity arise. For now, I only ask your leave to return to London with all possible haste," she replied.

"As you wish, but now let us leave this dreary place and return to Roxburgh which, I must admit, fares not much better. At least, I may set a goodly feast before you and then offer you a warm bed before you set off."

She readily accepted his offer. A rider was dispatched to alert the garrison of the army's imminent return and to notify the cooks of the earl's wishes. Within a few hours, the forces were assembled. Christina and her companions rode beside Gaveston as they wound their way back to the castle. In less than an hour they had passed through the forecastle and into the courtyard.

A wave of nausea passed over Christina as she saw the donjon looming before her. Although she had only been within its confines for less than one day, the images of what had transpired as well as thoughts of what might have been were indelibly printed on her memory. She considered asking Gaveston if they might not spend their time in another location within the castle, then thought better of it.

A place is only a place. No evil exists in the setting of a crime, only within the hearts of those who wish to see it done there.

While Ziesolf, Reiniken, and Malcolm enjoyed the company of the higher ranking among Gaveston's entourage, the earl and Christina supped privately in the keep's solar.

"Although you may believe your journey to me was for naught, know Christina you have nonetheless provided a valuable service."

"What is that, Piers?" she asked, taking another sip of full-bodied wine from her bowl.

Uncharacteristically, she exhibited sparse appetite, her emotions associated with the castle prohibiting her from enjoying Gaveston's table more fully. Imbibing the fruits of his cellar was another matter.

"Rooting out Sir Neville Allen's treachery. Although there was something off about the man I could not quite place, I had nothing tangible upon which to substantiate my doubts. It was fortunate for both of us he had not subverted the entire garrison to his cause. It seems his followers only numbered a dozen or so; otherwise, he would not have needed to be so circumspect in his attack on you and I might have returned to find the gates barred against me."

I would hardly refer to what happened to me as fortunate.

A shiver ran the length of her body; although, she did concede the point Gaveston was trying to make.

"Must you leave in the morning?" he asked hopefully. "Would it not be better to rest for a few days before beginning your travels once more?"

"Alas, I am sorry, but my mind is set on returning as soon as possible before Katharine Volker has the opportunity to cast even more mischief about her malevolent self."

"I suspected as much," Galveston said, then thought a few seconds before continuing. "A few days ago, I received a dispatch carried by a messenger from King Edward. This man, Sir Giles d'Argentan, is one in whom I place explicit trust. I traveled with him a few years back on the tournament circuit in France and found him to be a brave and faithful companion. Now, he must return to Edward with my response. It would ease my worry for you if you would allow him to travel with you and your men back to Berwick."

Christina considered Gaveston's offer for only a few seconds, before saying, "I would be honored to travel in the company of such a renowned knight. I am certain his presence will greatly ease our way, should we encounter any further difficulties."

Within the hour following, weariness overcame her and she begged the earl's leave to go to her chamber. Although it was on the same level as that she had occupied the night before, she was relieved to find it was the one to the other side of the hall. Soon, she was warmly snuggled beneath the heavy covers. Despite her comfort, sleep proved an elusive quarry.

Christina arose from the bed as her eyes slowly adjusted to the faint moonlight that filtered into the room. Wrapping the thick woolen blanket from the bed about her body she stood, absentmindedly peering at the door. She began to shake uncontrollably, to the point she feared she was about to lose control of her legs and fall to the floor. Making her way back to the bed, she sat down heavily. Christina held her hand out in front of her and saw it was also trembling. She could not rid herself of the horrifying knowledge she had nearly lost her life in the dungeon located just a few dozen feet below. Although she had faced death previously, it had not affected her so fundamentally.

Could it be the threat of the rape?

She asked the question frankly, knowing the answer instantly.

Even facing the long odds against Sir Neville earlier that day, she had felt she still maintained some degree of control over herself; even her death would have been at a time and place of her own choosing. But to be held helplessly, while the four men violated her repeatedly and without mercy. was more than she could bear to imagine.

I will never let that happen to me again; I will cut my own throat first.

She sat there for the remainder of the night with her knees pulled to her chin. She did not come close to sleeping. Her mind consumed by thoughts of such darkness she feared for the sanctity of her immortal soul.

Chapter 18

A Pause on the Way Home
Scottish Marches, September, 1310

The morning dawned late as dusky gray clouds crowded against each other in the steel-colored sky. The sun provided scant warmth and, what little it did, was swept away by a steady, frigid breeze emanating from the north. Christina felt as though the weather perfectly mirrored how she felt inside.

Gaveston introduced her to Sir Giles, who turned out to be a pleasant man of about thirty years old with broad shoulders, a quick wit, and a trim waist. Three others accompanied him, each an obvious fighting man; well-armed, alert, and suitably mounted. Christina admitted to herself having such companions for their ride to Berwick was quite reassuring.

Malcolm appeared from the stable, leading both his horse and hers. She smiled at the sight of her mare despite her melancholic mood. She had always dreamed of owning her own horse and this was her first opportunity to do so. She thanked Malcolm and took the reins from him into her hand. She stroked the palfrey's neck affectionately, then took the bits of apple she had saved from her breakfast earlier that morning and fed them to her one by one. The mare gobbled them greedily, then bumped Christina with her muzzle, demanding more. She laughed with delight and scratched her mount's ears. Her companions looked at her and smiled. It was the first time they had seen her mood lightened in days.

Galveston appeared and she bid him farewell. As they crossed the courtyard, she turned in her saddle and saw him still watching them from he had stood. Christina waved to him and he returned the gesture. Before long, they were through the gateway and she could see him no more.

He truly likes me; why, I do not know.

A slight smile ghosted across her lips at the thought.

How could a noble of such high standing have such affection for a merchant's daughter, and one who disguises herself as a man, no less? Although our relationship seems complicated, it may really be quite simple. Could we not just be two people who find pleasure in each other's company?

She smiled more broadly, happy for the second time that day.

A couple of hours after passing the abbey, it began to snow in earnest. What had been a few lovely white, drifting flakes wafting slowly to the ground, now had changed to a swirling maelstrom that seemed to separate them from their connection to the earth. In a matter of minutes, the mane of Christina's mare had already turned completely white.

Sir Giles appeared at her side and shouted over the now shrieking wind, "We must stop! The pathway will soon be lost to us. There is a fortified tower not too far from here. They will surely provide us shelter from such a storm as this!"

Christina nodded her head in agreement. They fought their way forward for another quarter mile, then veered off into the forest following a trail she could not perceive save for the straight break in the trees. Although they were heading more directly into the wind now, the thick timberland to their sides provided some degree of relief. They were almost upon the tower before they could make out its massive dark outline rising fifty feet or more through the storm. The riders dismounted and led their shivering mounts through the nearly knee-deep drifts that had accumulated before the entrance to the tower.

The door before them was constructed of thick wooden planks, with the heads of large nails protruding through providing proof of a matching, horizontal layer of boards on the other side. Sir Giles went forward and pounded on the door mightily. After a few seconds, he tried again. Christina heard a faint, female voice. She looked upward and was surprised to see a young woman with striking red hair leaning out of the second story window. She yelled once more, but her words were unintelligible over the storm's fury. She disappeared, closing the wooden shutters behind her.

The group of men waited, unsure whether the woman intended to offer them shelter or if she had merely shouted for them to leave her in peace. The answer came a few moments later when the door was thrown open and she stood before them, her hands on her narrow hips.

"Well, you'll not be bringing the beasties in with you now, will you? See to them first; there's room in the barn over there," she instructed, gesturing with her hand toward their left. "After that, I will welcome you into my home."

The men walked in the direction she had indicated and discovered a large barn only a few hundred yards away. They passed through the door and found the structure was divided into an area for horses in the front and a place to the rear where several large reddish-brown cattle loitered. They tethered their horses, removed their saddles, and dried them as best they could. Having done as instructed, Sir Giles led them back to the house.

As they walked through the three-foot wide entrance, Christina gauged the thickness of the stone walls to be at least three feet. Before continuing on to a second sturdy door, she looked up to see the dropped-Gothic arch above them was pierced with a murder hole.

A very good design to discourage unwanted visitors.

Going through, Christina found herself in a single large room with defensive loopholes regularly placed in the walls. Because of the storm, these were now covered by wooden shutters; these could be thrown open at a minute's notice for light or to fire arrows at a disadvantaged enemy. It was apparent that, although this was considered a family dwelling, it also served admirably as a formidable fortification.

"Rid yourself of your outer garments and come on up, if you will. You can warm yourselves by the fire while I and the girls fix you a bit of stew."

They took off their traveling cloaks and stamped their boots to rid them of at least the worst of the clinging snow. A short, straight flight of limestone steps led through a mural passage up to the stairs inside the southeast corner of the structure. Here, the flight of steps branched out from the central newel post in a clockwise fashion, built so to provide an advantage to the tower's right-handed defenders. These opened onto the next floor, which consisted of another large open room dominated by a large, roughly hewn trestle table with several benches along each side. There were large window embrasures at three of the sides, each with a matching loop window. An integral seat was built under the windows to take advantage of what limited light passed through. The western wall was dominated by a huge stone fireplace with an enormous lintel fashioned from a single slab of stone. Several logs burned merrily inside, over which a large iron pot dangled, giving off a most delicious smell.

"I am Lady Cecily Baldewyne, wife of Sir Edgar Baldewyne. I humbly welcome you to our home and to the hospitality of our modest hearth."

"I thank you kindly, most gracious lady, for the kindness you have shown both me and my fellow travelers. I am Sir Giles d'Argentan, knight of King Edward's household."

Lady Baldewyne bid the men to make themselves comfortable. Some took a seat on the benches while others stood warming themselves closely by the fire, trying hard to stay out of the way of the two young women who bustled about the cooking pot. Between the fire and the heat generated by the number of bodies in the confined space, the men's bodies were soon chilled no more.

Christina walked over to where Lady Baldewyne sat on a gayly embroidered cushion placed upon a window seat. She looked up from her embroidery and gazed upon Christina with a friendly smile of her full red lips bordering perfectly-spaced, white teeth.

Her face was the color of cream, with a faint scattering of tawny freckles sprinkled across her nose and the cheeks beneath her deep green eyes. She wore her fiery red hair loosely about the shoulders of her simple kirtle. The only thing marring the beauty of the woman was a large corona of a yellow bruise mottled with purplish highlights encircling her left eye.

Christina smiled back and said, "I wish to add my thanks to those of Sir Giles, Lady Baldewyne. I am, Master Frederick Kohl, merchant of the German Hansa in London town.

"I am pleased to make your acquaintance, Master Frederick. Please though, call me Lady Cecily. How is it you find yourself so far from your home?"

Christina provided her with a short, largely contrived tale of her travels before asking, "And you, your Ladyship? How long has this tower been your home?"

"All my life, actually. My father was Sir Geoffrey de Vere, a favorite of the old king, who accompanied him north when the Scots asked his majesty to adjudicate the Great Cause to decide the heir to the Scottish throne. While in these lands, my father fell in love with the woman who would eventually become my mother. He petitioned Longshanks to allow him to remain here in the Marches. The king granted him leave to stay, as well as title to this tower. My mother died giving me birth and I was raised by my father, until his death a year ago."

"And your husband?"

"A retainer of Baron de Percy. After Father's death, someone was needed to hold the keep against the Scots. He was the one selected for the task, which included marrying me, of course."

Christina sensed there was much left unsaid in the second part of Lady Cecily's story.

If she would have wanted to volunteer more, she would have.

Christina cautioned herself again pursing her natural curiosity.

Instead, she asked, "Where is your husband now?"

"A couple of days ago, a Scottish raiding party drove away a few of our cattle who were grazing in the far meadow. Sir Edgar and his men chased after them, leaving me and the two girls here to look after things until their return. I know not when that will be, I'm afraid," her smile now turning rather bleak.

One of the young women appeared at Christina's elbow and said to Cecily, "Food's ready, mistress."

Further conversation between Christina and Cecily was forestalled as everyone seated themselves at the table. Even

Reiniken bowed his head respectfully as Cecily said grace. Soon, they were all enjoying the savory stew, liberally ladled onto thick trenchers of rustic tourte bread.

While the men ate, they engaged in gentle conversation with their gracious hostess. After eating his fill, Malcolm entertained the gathering with a song. Christina had no idea as to the meaning of the lyrics he sang, but quite enjoyed the melody. On the other hand, the two girls laughed in delight before engaging in an impromptu dance as the song drew to an end.

Finally, Sir Giles said, "That was a wonderful repast, your Ladyship, and we thank you kindly."

The others at the table murmured their assent.

"But we have troubled you enough. Perhaps the snowfall has slackened but, regardless, we will gather our horses and be back on our way now."

"Nonsense," Cecily stated firmly. "It will soon be dark and I could not in good conscience ignore my Christian duty to provide you shelter from the night. There is plenty of room in the undercroft for you to stay. Mean as it is, it is at least shelter from the cold."

Before she could say more, a pounding sounded at the door below. Cecily went to the southern window and opened the shutters, looking down to identify who it was wanting entrance to the tower. She turned about suddenly; a look of distress etched upon her face. Without speaking, she hastened down the stairs.

Christina heard the doors open. Then a loud voice spoke; she could not discern the words but the anger of its tone was unmistakable. Within a few seconds, the young woman mounted the stairs, followed closely by a hulking brute of a man nearly the size of Reiniken.

"So, are you running a brothel now when I'm away?" he said harshly to Cecily who cowered in the corner fearfully. "Well, speak, damn you!"

"No," she replied in a small voice.

"Likely so," he grunted, "Who'd be paying good coin for the likes of you anyway?" He noticed the remnants of the meal that had been served. "What, giving away my food as well? There better be enough to feed me and my men or there'll be hell to pay! You'll have to butcher out that wee one over there," he said, gesturing toward the smaller of the two serving girls.

Cecily held her arm out toward the frightened girl; who ran to her mistress and nestled closely under her arm for protection.

"Yes, husband, we will set it to cooking directly."

"Good. Now, who might all of you be who enjoy the merry hospitality of a wife in her husband's absence?"

Sir Giles introduced his companions.

Sir Edgar did not seem much impressed, remarking, "I don't really care who you are, really. I guess I can't just throw you out into the cold or you'd be complaining to the king. You can sleep in the barn, if you like. Mind you, if you're feeding my hay to those nags of yours, I expect to be paid in good coin."

Christina heard the doors below open once again and soon about a dozen rough looking men dressed in motley attire crowded into the space.

"Well, what are you waiting for?" Sir Edgar sneered toward Sir Giles. "I told you where you can sleep. Or were you expecting to have my bed instead?"

"No," Giles answered, although the struggle to control his temper was evident. "I was not. Thank you once more, Lady, for your kindness. We will trouble you no more."

Christina had to bite her tongue to keep from upbraiding Cecily's loutish husband. His behavior toward Sir Giles had been reprehensible, unworthy of a man who had also been knighted. In the end, she thought better of it, believing such a man would only take out his anger on his wife or the other innocent women in his household once they had departed.

They went down the stairs and gathered their belongs. Clad once more in their heavy cloaks, they passed through the entrance portal to find the ferocity of the storm had somewhat abated. Although snow continued to fall, the light of the waxing moon breaking through the clouds provided sufficient light to reveal the barn in detail. It was further illuminated by the glow of a fire that burned steadily at the structure's rearmost point.

While the others stood momentarily stunned, Sir Giles burst back through the door, yelling for Sir Edgar, who half-tumbled down the steps with a look of ill-humor on his face. Giles ran back outside, beckoning for him to follow.

Sir Edgar's eyes followed the direction of the other man's gaze toward the barn.

Discerning the threat for himself, he shouted, "If I find one of you to be responsible for this, I'll gut you, king's men or no!" before calling back inside for his own comrades to follow.

They all ran across the field that separated the barn from the tower as best they could, their speed greatly hampered by random, white drifts. By now, the blaze had grown to engulf the entire back corner of the roof. The only saving grace was the fire was greatly slowed by the accumulation of snow upon the thick thatch.

Reaching the barn at last, some of the men went directly to the rear of the structure to free the terrified cattle while others did the same for the horses in the front. A few of the men climbed upward, crawling along the roofline to try to extinguish the flames by pushing forward great sheets of snow onto the blaze.

Christina ran to where her mare fought frantically to free herself from her tether. The palfrey attempted to rear onto her hindlegs, only to fall back down as she reached the limit of her restraint. The terrified horse's eyes seemed enormous as they rolled upwards to appear almost totally milky white. Christina murmured soothing words as she moved toward her, but was knocked aside as the horse flailed about. Finally, she was able to free the reins. She attempted to lead her mount out of the barn, but the mare was too strong. She found herself running alongside, trying in vain to slow the horse. Her efforts were futile, however, as she lost her grip on the leather strap. She fell into the snow as the horse galloped away into the darkness.

Sir Giles appeared at Christina's side and helped her back to her feet. Before she could thank him, she noticed Lady Cecily at a second-floor window, gesturing frantically.

She must have heard the yelling downstairs and opened the window to see what the commotion was about,

Christina waved her own hand in response.

Without warning, she heard a slight sizzling sound at her side, followed by a sharp cry of pain. She turned to see Sir Giles collapsed beside her, the fletching of an arrow protruding from his shoulder. She took an instant to look up and saw several indistinct dark figures roughly three hundred yards from where she stood moving cautiously her way. She now understood Cecily had been trying to warn them of their approach.

She grabbed Giles and helped him to his feet, shouting, "It's the Scots! We're being attacked!" before assisting him back into the relative safety of the barn.

Within a few seconds, both bands of men had joined them. All had drawn their swords which, luckily for them, they all still wore. Many looked anxious, others worried, but some displayed the calm assurance held only by those who were seasoned warriors.

Rising to his full height, Sir Edgar said, "There's too many of the bastards! They'll cut us down like sheaves of wheat. Our only chance of saving ourselves is to flee. Between the cattle, the horses, and the looting, they'll be too distracted to try to track us down! Let's go!"

Christina was dumbfounded.

"What of the women in the tower; what of your wife? Does your plan include them as well?"

Sir Edgar turned toward Christina, savagely retorting, "Who are you to question me, boy? I will not risk my sword's service to my liege lord on such a foolhardy task. Bother me no more, else I will cut off your ballocks!"

"At least you would then have a pair of your own!" she replied contemptuously. "You have taken a knight's solemn oath to protect the innocent; now you readily desert three such to save your own skin! Coward!"

He ignored her words this time, gathering his followers and peering out the doorway.

Christina thought about the gentle young woman now the lone defender of the tower as well as of the two girls who were little more than children. She knew with certainty what would befall them should the door be breached. She remembered her own near-rape and the terror she had felt afterwards.

I will not desert these women to such a fate.

Christina shouted at Edgar's back, "Go then, I would not want the battlefield sullied by the likes of you. I will not live in a world where the strong care not for those who are weak. Should I be killed, I will die a good death knowing I fought to do right. If I am alone, so be it. If others stand beside me, we may yet turn the day. Out of my way, base creature, for me I go to welcome the Scots!"

"See you in hell then, damn your soul!" Sir Edgar shouted as he ran out the door and toward the wooded copse to the right. Most of his men followed him in flight, although three seemed to have been shamed by Christina's words into remaining behind.

Christina heard a guttural sound beside her and turned to see Ziesolf had pushed the arrowhead the rest of the way through the shoulder of Sir Giles, He snapped the head off the shaft cleanly, then pulled it back through the wound, tossing it to the side. He then helped him back to his feet. Although Giles' face was very pale and he was sweating heavily despite the cold, he gave Christina a wan smile before unsheathing his sword.

"I stand beside you, Master Merchant," he said.

"So, are ya plannin' to fuckin' talk 'em to death, Yur Worship?" Reiniken snorted. "Let's go give 'em some steel instead!"

They rushed through the doorway of the barn out into the cold, deadly night.

"Slash and move!" Ziesolf shouted as he ran forward, "If they isolate and surround us, we're lost!"

The Scots halted their advance across the field as the forces erupted from the barn. They seemed surprised these men did not follow the first band who had disappeared into the woods. Seeing Christina and her companions turn to face them instead, many began to run in their direction to meet their challenge. Others were already at the door of the tower, attempting to force it open with hefty blows of their long-handled axes. A few still ran toward the treeline, intoxicated by the pursuit of the fleeing Sir Edgar. Savage war cries filled the air; their words incomprehensible, their meaning only too clear.

Christina ran in the direction of the tower. She could infer her companions were engaging the Scots to her rear from the clashing sound of metal on metal behind her. Looking slightly to her side, she saw two enemy warriors angling toward her at full speed. Just before their paths intersected, she suddenly swerved to face them, still advancing at full speed down the slight slope. Her sudden change of direction confused them. They stopped and raised their weapons, a broad-headed war axe and a massive two-handed great sword. That was their mistake.

Christina slid onto her back, her forward momentum carrying her effortlessly past the two men in the snow. She reached out with her falchion and hacked at the axe man, nearly severing his ankle from his right leg as she glided past. The injured man toppled to his side, entangling himself with the other Scotsman. Christina rose to her feet and thrust the tip of her blade upward through the side of the swordsman just above his kidney, pushing it forward until it entered his heart muscle. She swiftly retracted her blade and moved on, knowing her blow had finished the man.

A hairy, wild-eyed brute swung a massive war club at her skull. She ducked and felt the wind of its nail-encrusted head pass barely over her head. Without thinking, she slid her blade through his guts, twisting it to achieve maximum damage. Again, she disengaged, heeding Ziesolf's advice. She continued her advance in the general direction of the tower.

Christina's lungs were burning, both from the intensity of her exertions as well as the acrid smoke that wafted from the burning barn since the wind direction had changed. A new man walked to bar her path, seemingly more patient to greet death than her previous opponents had been. He moved forward cautiously, his arming sword at the high guard. He suddenly accelerated his advance, cleaving his weapon down toward her neck. She parried desperately, locking their swords momentarily together. Christina's head was so close to the man's face she could smell his rancid breath issuing past his black and broken incisors. She cocked her head backwards and brought her forehead crashing downward into the bulb of his nose. Blood began to gush from his nostrils almost immediately as he wobbled backwards slightly, stunned from her unexpected blow. That bit of hesitancy was all she needed. Her falchion danced forward and, with a flick of her wrist, cut into the side of her victim's neck, severing his right carotid artery.

She was only about a hundred feet from the tower now. She wanted to glance back, to see how her comrades were faring, but she did not have the luxury of time. She saw with horror the marauders had finally breached the outer door. The sound of fierce chopping emanated from inside, indication they would soon gain full entrance. Suddenly, she heard a man scream and one of the Scots stumbled from the doorway, clutching at his face as a cloud of thick steam rose from his head and shoulders.

The murder hole; well done!

She had no more time to waste congratulating the defenders of the tower as two more attackers bent on mayhem appeared to her front. She was fatigued now, largely negating the advantage of her speed. They came forward quickly as Christina's mind raced frantically to decide a strategy that might let her survive for a few more seconds.

She suddenly felt a gush of wind pass her by. One of the Scots to her fore looked at his chest in amazement, seeing the head of a war axe protruding from its center. He crumpled and fell without uttering a word. His companion's eyes involuntarily shifted from Christina for an instant and she snatched the opportunity to swing her sword in a broad slashing motion toward his unprotected thigh. Her falchion's blade fulfilled its design purpose admirably, cutting deeply through the flesh and shattering the bone beneath. He too toppled down with his warm blood staining the snow beneath him.

Another frightening high-pitched scream issued from the cavernous doorway of the tower. Yet another besieging Scot stumbled back out into the night. He turned toward Christina and she readied her sword. One look at his grotesquely scalded face and ruined eyes caused her to feel a momentary pang of pity as she dismissed him as a threat.

That leaves just one left at the door by my count; pray to God the cauldron heats once more before he hacks his way through.

As if in defiance of her appeal, the rhythmic sound of the last axe man's blows on the door became more frantic. Suddenly, they were no more.

As Christina mustered her last bit of energy to make a run for the tower, a huge figure bolted towards her from out of the darkness. She had little time to do more than throw herself to the side to avoid its furious onrush. She raised her sword in a futile attempt to ward the monster off. Then, just as suddenly as it had appeared, the maddened horse faded into the smoky haze from whence it had come.

Wearily, she regained her feet and broke into a stumbling run toward the now silent entrance to the tower. Christina ignored the sobs and groans of the injured Scots she passed, having decided they posed no immediate threat to her. She moved through the doorway with scant caution; her only thought to reach the final attacker before he had the opportunity to harm the women inside.

Christina mounted the narrow stairway a bit more carefully, fully anticipating an ambush from above at any time. She emerged into the room where she and her companions had supped only an hour earlier. A wave of heat fell upon her face, issuing forth from the well-stoked fireplace. The cauldron, which had once held savory stew, now lay on its side near the table. Otherwise, the room was unoccupied.

She glanced upward, fearing the worst. Christina cautiously climbed the next set of stairs, her blade before her at high guard. Her eyes crested the level of the floor and she beheld a sleeping chamber, which was also deserted. The thick stone walls held out all noise from the outside. From the interior of the tower not a sound could be heard.

In this eerie silence, she ascended once more. Passing around the right angle of the stairs, Christina noticed a small pool of blood on one of the stone risers. With a renewed sense of urgency, she rushed forward; suddenly emerging into yet another room. A spearpoint flashed toward her with lethal intent. She only had time to fall heavily against the stone wall, painfully hitting her hip and shoulder on the unyielding stone. Christina lifted her falchion in a feeble attempt to block what must be the finishing thrust to come.

Yet, come it did not. She glanced upward to see Lady Cecily holding the thick boar spear at the ready in both of her hands. Her flashing eyes fixed on those of Christina, changing from a look of ferocity to one of recognition.

"Master Frederick! I . . . I'm so sorry, I didn't know it was you; I thought it was one of them," she said, gesturing vaguely toward her side.

There is no time to tarry here; who knows what transpires outside?

Cecily withdrew the threat of her potent weapon and Christina ascended the remainder of the way to the final floor of the tower. This was clearly a storeroom as assorted chests, sacks, and boxes were arranged neatly about. Along one wall was hung a variety of weapons, including a mate for the spear Cecily still held in her hands. The two girls huddled in the corner, a feral look in their eyes and a long dagger brandished forward in each right hand. The remaining Scotsman lay lifeless on the floor.

"I pulled him up so's any that followed wouldn't know we were putting up a fight," Cecily volunteered in answer to Christina's unspoken question.

"Well done, Mi 'lady, but now we must escape. Should they attack enmasse, we few cannot hope to defend the tower, now the entrance has been breached. Our best hope lies in escaping into the woods and hiding until daylight. The Scots will not risk remaining here, with the powerful forces of Earl Gaveston and King Edward less than a day's ride distant. We can then continue on to Berwick on foot, if need be."

"I agree. Let us be off then."

Chapter 19

An Auspicious Surprise
Scottish Marches, September, 1310

They descended the stairs cautiously, fully anticipating to meet more attackers on the way. Luckily, none appeared and they were able to exit the tower unmolested. Cecily and the two girls huddled closely to the stone walls of what had been their home, while Christina walked a few steps forward to better assess whether any immediate threats were present. Seeing none, she turned about to beckon them forward, then stopped and looked about again to try to determine what she felt she had missed. It was the noise, or rather the lack of it. Other than the moaning of injured men and the crackle of the flames that were now fully consuming the barn, the cold night was silent.

The conflict was at an end.

Christina's eyes scanned the fields, straining to perceive any remaining figures through the haze, whether they be friend or foe.

Seeing no one still standing, she was gripped by sudden horror.

The Scots have fled the battle, nut what of those who fought on our side? Am I the only one to remain?

"Ain't this a fuckin' mess?" a familiar voice spoke behind her. "Uh, sorry, yur Ladyship, Ah didn't see yas standin' over there."

She turned to see Reiniken; his wan face barely discernable through the gore that was splattered upon his head and shoulders. He held his arming sword in his left hand, his right now hanging limply by his side.

Seeing the direction of her gaze, he said, "Big bastard with a goddam mace caught mi on the arm; broke the bones likes they wuz twigs. I spilled his fuckin' guts in payment though, I did. Sorry again, Yur Ladyship."

"Wig!" Christina finally was able to shout.

Tears of joy cascaded from her eyes as, overcome by unbridled emotion, she rushed forward to pound her hand on his good shoulder. He managed to fix her with a cross between a grin and a grimace before finally moving slightly away.

"Sorry, Yur Worship, but Ah bin beat about enuf fur one day. Have ya seen t'udders?"

"No," she replied hesitantly; fear again welling insider her.

They began a search of the battlefield for their comrades. It was not long before they came across Malcolm sprawled face first in the snow, his dagger scant inches from his outstretched hand. A terrible blow had cut deeply into his shoulder, leaving his blood to intermingle indiscriminately with his reddish locks.

"Oh, my God, no!" Christina moaned as she beheld his lifeless form. "Why did I have to bring you with us?"

"At least he died on the soil of his homeland," Reiniken said in an uncommonly gentle voice. "Besides, without him we might have lost. He fought lak a man twice his size. Killed at least two of 'em before they got 'im. Ya would have bin proud of 'im."

"I am, Wig, and of you all as well."

Before any more could be said between them, the voice of Sir Giles shouted, "Over here!"

They walked as rapidly as possible in the direction of the sound and soon discerned the English knight kneeling over a prone, motionless figure. With a sickening certainty welling in her heart she realized the man was Ziesolf.

"No, no, no," she repeated to herself before joining Sir Giles beside her fallen comrade. Her sorrow fought to engulf her as she looked into his face, seeing not the disfiguring scars that had frightened her as a child, but the visage of one whom she loved as a true friend.

Suddenly, his one functional eye flickered open, looking at her without comprehension.

"He is most grievously wounded, but I have at last staunched the flow of blood," Sir Giles stated, gesturing to the bloody cloth exposed beneath Ziesolf's torn tunic. "With luck, and God's merciful grace, he will live to fight again."

"Not if I have my way about it," Christina declared. "He has fought and suffered enough in his life. No more, I say, no more."

"We should move him into the tower where he may be warmed before the fire."

"Yes, of course," she replied before asking. "And your men?"

"Two are dead, may God bless their souls, but Geoffrey fought through the battle miraculously unscathed. We were able to catch one of the horses. He rides even now to Berwick for assistance."

Christina and Giles returned to the tower where they pried a broad plank from the ruined door. Returning, the three of them managed to gently move Ziesolf onto the makeshift litter. A few minutes later they set him down before the fireplace.

"We will take up positions at the foot of the tower, lest the enemy return," Sir Giles stated, nodding toward Reiniken before the two of them proceeded down the stairs.

Christina watched the wounded, tired, aching men descending the stairs. She shook her head in admiration.

God help the Scots if they do.

Lady Cecily sent the girls up the stairs to fetch blankets for Ziesolf, now shivering despite his nearness to the fire.

She turned to Christina and said in a measured voice, "When I saw my husband and his men run from the barn and turn, not to save me, but into the forest, my heart sank in despair. I considered climbing to the battlements above and throwing myself over the side, or simply opening the door below to the Scots and letting them do what they would to us and be done with it. Before I could decide, you emerged, leading a group of men of a far different ilk. They defended bravely while you fought your way toward the tower, toward us. If not for you, Frederick, we most certainly would have been lost."

With tears finding pathways down her pale cheeks, she leaned forward and kissed Christina chastely on the lips. After a second, she moved backwards a step to stare once again into her eyes.

"Lady . . .," began Christina, not knowing quite what to say.

"Shh," Cecily replied, pointing upward as the girls reappeared down the stairs carry two thick woolen covers.

Christina checked the dressing on Ziesolf's wound, confirming the bleeding had been staunched. Remained by his side, she later attempted to feed him a bit of thin, warm bone broth and a few mouthfuls of ale, but he took nothing before he lapsed back into a deep sleep, marred by several deep moans. Fortunately, his breathing seemed clear and his heartbeat steady.

Early in the afternoon, several armored horsemen galloped into the clearing, led by Geoffrey, the soldier originally dispatched by Sir Giles. A large cart appeared soon after. Ziesolf was carried down and placed gently in the bed of the wagon along with the two girls. They were soon joined by Reiniken who, with his broken arm, conceded it would be too difficult to ride,

Christina was moving to mount one of the additional horses the soldiers had brought when she heard Sir Giles' voice say, "Perhaps you would prefer a different mount, Master Frederick?"

She turned to see him leading her sorrel mare toward her, fully bridled and saddled.

"I found her wandering near the barn; It seemed a shame to leave such a loyal beast."

Christina laughed with delight and threw her arms about the horse's neck, hugging it fiercely. When she let go, the horse turned to bump her with its nose.

"I'm sorry, but I have no apple. I promise I'll give you a dozen when we get to Berwick!"

Sir Giles then said softly, "I had some of the men look after young Malcolm. The ground was too hard to dig a grave, but they made a cairn over his body from the stones in the fence over there. It's the best we could do."

She thanked him and climbed onto her mount; her buoyant mood now somber once more. As they began the long ride to Berwick, Christina looked back upon the carnage of the battlefield. All that remained were the bodies of the Scots, ten of which were clustered in a rough circle around where Ziesolf had fallen.

I wonder if they will return for them? I hope they do. No one deserves to have their flesh rot away unmourned, or be consumed by scavengers; not even such savages as these.

It was already dark when the small column of travelers arrived at Berwick castle. This time there was no belligerent warden to bar their way. Instead, a small crowd of people had gathered, lining the pathway leading to the gatehouse. The accounts of the victory of the intrepid few over the Scottish raiding party must have spread rapidly throughout the town, as the gathered masses broke into a mighty cheer as Christina and her companions passed by. Once inside the castle courtyard, the royal chamberlain greeted them on the king's behalf, then had them escorted into the castle; the wounded in one direction for their injuries to be tended, Lady Cecily and her servants in another.

The chamberlain then turned to Christina and said, "King Edward was immensely impressed by the news of your exploits over the past days. He is not presently at the castle but, if he were, he would have met you himself. On the morrow, he requests you attend him at court, so your valiant deeds may be properly celebrated. For now, he asks you to enjoy the comforts of his castle; hearth, kitchen, cellar, and chamber. He also invites you to make use of his private chapel, so you may properly thank God for the guidance and divine mercy he has shown unto you."

The chamberlain led her to a large room on the second floor of the castle that had apparently been hastily vacated for her use. A rectangular table stood along the wall covered with an ornately embroidered cloth. It almost sagged beneath the weight of a veritable treasure of culinary delicacies; eel pie, stuffed capon, a succulent joint of roast pork, and many others too numerous to note. She poured a bowl of dark red wine, savoring its sweetness as it cascaded down her dry throat.

I wonder if it originates from my own cargo from Bruges?

She smiled as she began to devour the feast set before her.

Before long, the combination of her immense fatigue and the weight of the food on her stomach caused her to have considerable difficulty in keeping her eyes from closing. Christina reluctantly rose from the table and walked to the huge bed that dominated the room. She was barely able to remove her boots before her great weariness finally overcame her efforts to hold it off.

I'll just lay back for a bit to rest my eyes.

Alas, this was a vow she was destined to break. Christina awakened to find bright sunlight streaming through the large windows of the room. She evidently had not been disturbed when servants had entered, leaving logs in the fireplace burning merrily, a large basin of water, and a complete set of clean clothing. They had also cleared the table from the night before, replacing it with a large selection of exotic fruits, cold meats and cheeses, and a large loaf of pandemain bread.

She peeled off the filthy garments she had worn since she had departed London and washed her body as thoroughly as she could manage. Although she tried to avoid the motions that would aggravate the pains of which she knew, there were still plenty yet to be discovered; these prompted grunts, grimaces, and even small yelps to escape from between her clenched teeth.

They seemed to have thought of everything else, but there was no way they could have anticipated this.

She reluctantly wrapping the soiled binding cloth back around her chest, vowing to find a clean replacement later that day.

Christina examined the curious garments that had been left for her. The plain, bleached linen shirt was of a purely white color and of a very fine weave, as were the corresponding off-white braies and black hose. Most extraordinary was the overtunic, which was also of brilliant white.

How impractical is this strange tunic! With my penchant for exploring unkept spaces, it will be filthy before the day is out. Perhaps, it is appropriate for courtly folk, but it certainly doesn't suit me.

Christina had no other choice, other than to again don the bloody garments from the stinking pile she had earlier remove; she had no desire to do that. After dressing, she partook of her breakfast, taking particular care to not allow anything to soil her pristine clothing. She then left the room, setting her direction to find the castle's sanctuary.

As she trod down the hallway, she took the opportunity to ask a servant as to the chapel's whereabouts. He provided her with the information she requested, although she felt his eyes furtively lingered on her strange clothing a bit too long for her liking.

Is someone having a jest at my expense?

She found the chapel to be a small circular room, set into one of the corner bastions of the castle. She entered the intimate space and, moving to in front of the altar, knelt, crossed herself, and lowered her head. She offered a prayer first for the soul of Malcolm, whose sweet voice she would never again have the pleasure of hearing this side of Glory. Then to the health of those who had been injured in her service, Reiniken, Sir Giles, and of course Ziesolf. She asked God to look kindly on Trudi and her betrothed, as well as all the others who lived and worked at her home in London, as well as her mother and those she knew in Lübeck. Lastly, she prayed for the safety of Lady Cecily and the hope of a better life for her. She asked for forgiveness for her own many transgressions and un-Christian thoughts before once more lifting her eyes. She crossed herself again, then departed the chapel.

Christina had not gone far before a liveried soldier rushed down the hallway to meet her.

"The king requires your presence in the great hall immediately! Come now!" he said breathlessly, before departing back the way he came at the same rapid pace.

Well, the king is undoubtedly busy, so I have no time to tarry.

She quickening her own pace to follow the man more closely.

Yet, he still wishes to take the time to thank us for the service we have provided against his enemies. If so, I think he is a good king.

They entered the great hall of the castle, which was already populated by a crowd of what were unmistakenly nobility of high station. She lingered in the rear until her escort turned and impatiently beckoned her forward. She walked toward the dais at the front of the room, which was dominated by a massive carved chair in the center. Upon this, she recognized the tall figure of King Edward, his long locks escaping from under the heavily bejeweled golden crown resting upon his head. To his distaff side sat his queen, Isabella, an impassive expression fixed upon her lovely young face. To his other, Sir Giles stood stiffly erect.

Christina stopped before reaching the edge of the raised platform and bowed deeply. Consequent to her motion, she was surprised to see Reiniken's grinning face in the front of the spectators. Her heart warmed to find that next to him stood Lady Cecily. Beside them was a thick pallet on which Ziesolf rested, his head turned forward and his good eye seemingly open and alert. Cecily flashed her an encouraging smile and tilted her head in an upward motion, prompting Christina to swing her gaze back forward to see Edward had ascended from his seat and was motioning with his own hand for Christina to rise. She did so slowly, uncertain as to what to do next. Unexpectedly, one of the nobles walked to her side and placed a scarlet cape about her shoulders. Then, the king began to speak.

"When my friend, the Earl of Cornwall, first told me of a young German merchant with a sense of honor and bravery far outweighing his years, I listened to his words in disbelief, believing

300

them to be greatly exaggerated. Upon making your acquaintance myself, I too was impressed, but more by your intelligence and your shrewdness than any martial qualities you may possess."

Christina felt her face reddening with embarrassment, unused to such lavish praise expressed publicly, let alone by the ruling monarch of the land.

"Now, you come before me once again, this time with a new advocate extolling your sterling qualities. Sir Giles, one of those whose word I trust implicitly, has rendered me a new tale concerning you, Frederick Kohl. He told me how you risked your life to alert Earl Piers of a scheme of treachery against his person. Then, that you led your stalwart companions against a band of ungodly Scottish warriors in a desperate battle fought against overwhelming odds. Did you do this to save your own life, or perhaps those of your dear friends? No. You saw it as your duty to rescue helpless innocents you had newly met who would otherwise have suffered the cruel ravages of the northerners arrayed against them."

I certainly wouldn't describe Lady Cecily as helpless,

Christina smiled to herself, remembering the fierce look on Cecily's face as she almost skewered her with the boar spear.

"It is customary that a squire must serve a knight for several years, learning to maintain his weapons and how to use them when called upon to do so. It seems you have certainly fulfilled this training. This man before me, a distinguished knight of the Teutonic Order, has demonstrated his own valor on the battlefield, as Sir Giles relates, slaying nearly a dozen of the Scottish foe before finally succumbing to his wounds. He has been your knight, and you have been his squire. I have spoken with him and he has deemed you worthy."

What in heaven's name transpires here?

Christina's confusion mounted as Edward paused for a second to take the massive great sword from the hands of Sir Giles.

"Now, kneel before me."

Christina obeyed, perceiving little choice but to do so.

"Frederick Kohl, in the sight of God Almighty, do you swear to never avoid a dangerous path for fear of losing your own life, and do you swear to be charitable and to always defend the weak and helpless, and do you swear to be loyal to your liege lord, whom I will be from this day forward?"

Finally, at last realizing the king's intent, Christina swallowed the large lump that had formed in her throat and said in a firm voice, "I do, Sire."

Edward stepped forward and brought the flat of the great sword down firmly on each of Christina's shoulders in turn. He then drew his gauntlets from his belt and slapped them lightly across each of her cheeks.

"Lest thou wouldst forget," he murmured. He then stepped back and said, "Arise, Sir Knight."

She did as she was told without conscious volition, so astonished was she by the extraordinary turn of event that had just occurred. Anonymous well-wishers clustered about her, offering their congratulations. Separating herself from those worthies, she made her way through the throng to the side of Ziesolf. The old knight peered up at her from his pallet. For the first time she could remember, tears appeared in the corners of his eye. She reached down to clasp his hand. He squeezed hers tightly, although not with his usual strength.

"Great Jesus!" Reiniken exclaimed, "Does this mean Ah now gotta show ya some respect?"

He clapped her heartily on the back with enough force to cause her to stumble forward.

Christina sensed a presence to her side and turned to see the smiling face of Lady Cecily scant inches from her own.

"I congratulate thee heartily, Sir Frederick. There is none I know who deserve the honor of being deemed a knight than you."

She put her hand upon Christina's, who could feel the warmth radiating from the woman's soft palm.

"I thank you, Lady Cecily," she replied, feeling very embarrassed once again, although she could not readily identify the reason.

"I am sorry to trouble you, especially after you have done so much for me already. I have learned you soon plan to sail your ship southward, back to London. Should you have the space, I would ask that you take me with you."

"Lady?" remarked Christina, stunned by Cecily's request.

"There is nothing left to hold me here. Life in a lonely tower with Sir Edgar has grown intolerable, you have borne witness to how lightly he regards me. My aunt is Eleanor de Clare, one of the ladies in waiting to Queen Isabella. I have petitioned the king that I may join her, to which he assented. If Queen Isabella and my aunt are also in accord, that would be my wish. If this not be the case, I will choose to enter a convent rather than endure the life that now stands behind me."

"Yes, of course," Christina replied. "And your two servants?"

"Luckily, their families live just outside Berwick. They will be happy there amongst those who love them. I myself will make a completely new life, although I will miss them dearly."

Christina looked at her and smiled encouragingly, hoping the future Cecily envisaged would be a happy one.

"Congratulations, Sir Knight. It seems you have made quite a favorable impression on my husband."

She turned around to find Queen Isabella standing behind her, her head inquisitively cocked to one side like a little bird.

Startled, Christina executed a hasty bow before finding her tongue to say, "I thank you, Your Majesty."

Queen Isabella fixed a peculiar tight smile on Christina before remarking, "You are just one of many gallant young men the King has graced with his favor; do not let his affection go to your head."

Before Christina could reply, the queen gave a slight nod of dismissal before turning her back to walk away. She was perplexed once more by the queen's obvious aversion to her. She knew not from what it stemmed, but realized it was prudent to stay well out of Isabella's sight, lest her animosity become more tangible.

Later that afternoon, Christina walked to the wharf where she found *Seelöwe* moored just as she had left her days before. She informed Thorsten, the ship's master, she would like to set sail on the next favorable wind and then provided him with a brief synopsis of the events that had occurred during her time away. She omitted the part about being knighted, as she still did not really know how she felt about the idea herself.

Thorsten seemed a bit embarrassed, shuffling his feet before saying, "You may not want to depart quite so soon. You see, we have had little to do since you left so one day I was gabbing with some men in a tavern near Crossgate. I happened to mention we would soon be returning to London and bemoaned the fact our hold would be empty. Well, one of the fellows of the name of John Shearer said he might know of a remedy for that. It seems several of the Flemish woolmongers have left the town with the arrival of the English army, creating a bit of a buyer's market, you know."

Christina did indeed. The chance to purchase a hold-full of bargain wool interested her mightily.

Perhaps I might even be able to turn a profit from this strange journey.

The next day, Thorsten introduced her to Shearer. They traveled to one of the man's barns to inspect the fleeces, the composition of which surprised Christina greatly.

"Aye," said Shearer, "They are fine fleeces of the Lincoln breed. See how the locks are twisted into spirals near the end? That's how you can tell. Fine luster too, don't you think?

The fleeces were massive, weighing probably as much as twenty pounds each. The staple was long as well, some over a foot in length. The wool was quite coarse; Christina questioned its suitability for fine fabrics, buy felt it would do fine for the coarser English cloth.

After a bit of haggling, they agreed on a price. Soon, a steady stream of wool carts was traveling the short distance to *Seelöwe's* moorage and their burden was being loaded aboard.

Not the finest of cargoes, but certainly better than returning to London with nothing to show for our troubles.

Early the next morning, Sir Giles meticulously supervised a group of soldiers who carefully carried Ziesolf's litter down the hill and to the ship. His condition was still serious, but he was at least able to speak more than a few words, although he remained very weak. They placed him in the cabin he had occupied on the northward journey. Christina had arranged a pallet for herself next to him so she could attend to his needs as they sailed for home.

Her own cabin has been set aside for Lady Cecily, who had arrived the previous day upon a cart carrying a large traveling chest. Christina was surprised, as the young woman had fled her home with only the clothes on her back. As two of the sailors carried the trunk aboard, Christina asked her if she had made a journey back to the tower house to fetch her belongings.

"No," she answered, "I feared that, if I returned, I would find my husband awaiting me. There is nothing I desire to remind me of my old life. The ladies of the local nobility were gracious enough to provide me with clothing and a few other essentials. That is all I require."

As the ship's crew made their final preparations for departure, Christina stood on the wharf with Sir Giles. They exchanged farewells and he began to walk away.

Before he had traveled more than a few steps, she had called out after him, saying, "I beg your indulgence, Sir Giles, but I have one further request of you."

He turned back and replied, "Yes?"

"I have left the horses we purchased at the small stable on Walkergate street. I . . . I was wondering . . .," Christina began hesitantly, "You see, I have grown rather fond of the sorrel mare I was riding. Would it be possible you would take her as your own to look after? I would hate to think of her being mistreated by a less amiable master."

"No," Sir Giles replied unexpectedly. "I will not."

Christina looked at him crestfallen before his broad face burst into a wide grin.

"I will do better than that, my friend. When the king returns southward, I will fetch your mount along with me, presenting her back into your good care at my first opportunity."

Christina flashed Giles an appreciative smile and thanked him for his kindheartedness.

"By what name is it that you call your mare?" he asked. "There are too many others that are merely called 'horse.'"

Christina thought for a minute, then said, "Pearl, I will call her Pearl. My dead sister was Marguerite, a name meaning pearl in some ancient tongue. I will call her this in remembrance of a sister I now rue having not taken the opportunity to know better."

"Pearl, a good name it is," Sir Giles agreed.

"I will wait eagerly for you to grace my doorstep in London," she told the man she had grown to like and respect over the past few days.

He walked away. Christina now realized there was now nothing more to delay their departure.

Chapter 20

Homeward Bound
At Sea to London, March, 1310

The crewmen worked the now heavily laden cog from the harbor and into the open sea. A mild wind blew in sporadic gusts almost directly from the east. Although the measure of their progress south was painfully slow, the gentleness of the waves more than compensated for their lack of speed. Despite this, Lady Cecily, who had never before made a sea voyage, spent the first few days in a test of wills with her distressed stomach, a contest in which she was repeatedly defeated. Christina would knock lightly on the cabin door, often to hear no comprehendible response. After a while, she took it upon herself to quietly enter, taking the befouled slops bucket to the side of the ship and throwing its nauseating contents overboard.

Although she greatly pitied the suffering young woman, having had occasion to suffer similar indignities herself more than once, she knew the effects of Cecily's illness were only temporary. On the other hand, her concern for Ziesolf grew graver with the passing of each day.

His periods of lucidity seemed to have become less and less frequent. He could only manage a few sentences before he would lapse back into silent unconsciousness, broken only be an occasional groan. She frequently cooled his feverish brow with a dampened cloth, an act that seemingly provided him with some small degree of relief. It was a struggle for her to manage to work a bit of ale or broth down his throat, but she knew she must not allow him to become dehydrated. Christina seldom slept in snatches of more than a few minutes, so worried was she he would pass away untended in the night as her father had done.

She remembered with horror how her father had suffered similarly after the attack on *der Greif* on her initial voyage to London. She felt just as helpless now, knowing the decision of whether Ziesolf would live or die rested not on her own ministrations, but on God's good race. Consequently, she prayed constantly, hoping to draw the Lord's attention to the plight of one of his most faithful servants.

The fickle winds continued to vex their progress. As the darkening skies portended the end of their third day at sea, Christina stood on the deck despairingly noting the same stretch of land off the starboard beam as what had greeted them that morning. She suddenly heard a familiar voice calling her name. She ran in growing terror to her cabin, fearful Ziesolf was finally given up his last hold on life. She burst into the cabin dreading the worst. Incredulously, she found him to not only be still living, but no longer burning with the ravages of fever.

He opened his eyes and whispered, "Well met, Sir Knight."

She clasped him in a gentle embrace and said, "I was so afraid you would leave me, just as Father did. I was so afraid . . .," further words were muffled by her sobs.

Christina fetched a cup of ale and held it to his lips. He managed three or four swallows before a coughing spasm caused her to take it away. It passed quickly and she was able to feed him several spoonfuls of broth before he indicated he had had enough. After a few more words passed between them, Christina noticed him growing once again weary. She left the cabin quietly, though her soul called for her to shout out in joy.

Ziesolf was not the only one of her patients to commence a recovery. Christina stood the next morning on the forecastle deck, attempting to gauge the breeze as Ziesolf always did. As she looked to landward, she was pleased to find the bit of sandy beach that had marked their lack of progress the day before had at last passed behind them.

"Would you mind some company?" said a pleasantly contralto voice from the deck below.

Christina looked back to the main deck to see Lady Cecily gazing upward toward her. She wore a thick madder-dyed woolen cloak about her shoulders, topped with a green hood rimmed in white hare fur.

Christina marveled at the woman's beauty.

With the paleness of her skin and the contrast of her crimson plaits, she resembles the blossom of an exquisite flower; I have not seen such beauty before.

"Well? Am I now invisible to your eye as well as deaf to your ear?" Cecily laughed.

"Of course not, please forgive me, Mi 'lady," Christina replied, her face growing warm with embarrassment.

Cecily mounted the steps and stood beside Christina before inquiring, "Do we now begin to make some sort of advance against the wind?"

"Well, we can never really advance toward the wind, but must rotate the sail to take it at least on our quarter. But, yes, we are now making headway south."

"And what of Sir Ziesolf?" Cecily asked next.

"He is through the worst of it, I believe. He is still very weak, but is now able to take down a bit of nourishment. In his entire life he has never conceded to a foe; he will not do so now," Christina said, making a concerted effort to believe her reassurances herself.

"And the other one? The large man with the broken arm?"

"Other than the nuisance of the splint that still immobilizes his arm while the bone heals, he is his same old self. Why just yesterday he challenged one of the other sailors to a contest as to who could hold a huge weight over his head the longest. Reiniken won the wager, even though he only used one arm," Christina replied cheerfully, basking in her affection for the man. "I must ask as to your own condition, Mi' lady. How do you fare?"

"I feel well enough for the time being, God be praised. I have never known such illness. I thank you, Sir Frederick, for the kindness you showed me, though I am mortified beyond words as to the degree of foulness you witnessed as having had escaped from my person."

Christina gave no response, as she could not but agree with the lady's assessment of the revolting nature of the slop bucket's contents as well as what had escaped its catchment upon the surrounding floor. Instead, she spoke of more pleasant matters; her household, her business, and the excitement of living in the city of London. For her part, Lady Cecily related the story of her isolated upbringing in the Marches, avoiding for the time being tales of her life since her marriage to Sir Edgar.

Over the coming days, their conversations gained confidence in both depth and detail. They mutually agreed to no longer use honorifics; no longer "sir" and "lady," but now just Frederick and

Cecily. By the time *Seelöwe* entered the Thames estuary, their friendship had grown heartfelt and abiding.

They soon stood once more on dry land. Despite his protests, she firmly refused to allow Ziesolf to walk the distance to their home. She hailed a wagoner who had just delivered a load of goods to a ship moored further up the wharf. In a few minutes, the crewmen of her ship were loading the passengers' meager baggage onto his sturdy cart. They then helped Ziesolf up to sit upright beside the driver, a concession against Christina's better judgement as she would have preferred to see him reclining in the cart's bed. They then departed.

As for Christina, she preferred to walk, taking a slightly circuitous route to excitedly share some of the most impressive sights of the city with Cecily. After viewing the Great Bridge, the battlements of Tower Castle, and Saint Paul's cathedral, they finally arrived at Christina's manor house; cold, hungry, and tired, but in high spirits.

Christina pulled on the bell rope and the gate portal was soon opened by Black Peter, the smith. He grinned widely and opened the gate fully to allow them access.

"Master Frederick! We are overjoyed by your safe return!"

"I thank you, Peter. You know not how glad I am to see your face once more; as well as to soon behold that of your bride."

"Alas, Master, I have none such," he said, turning his head away.

What?

Christina caught her breath in sudden alarm, instantly fearing some calamity had befallen her household in her absence.

Taking Lady Cecily by the hand, she hurried across the courtyard and through the doorway into the great hall. Inside, she found a smiling Trudi, flanked by the other members of the household. Ziesolf sat upright at one of the side benches. Clearly, they had been gathered there since the old knight's arrival had signaled the travelers' return.

"Trudi!" Christina shouted, relieved her best friend appeared both happy and healthy. "Is there something amiss? Have you decided against your marriage?"

"Yes," she said simply, her face becoming more serious. "I found I could not wed. That is, not without the presence of my gentle master in attendance. Now that you have returned to us, I ask we proceed with haste. It seems there is another who has chosen not to be so patient."

Trudi cast a curious gaze toward Lady Cecily, but said nothing. Her hands then moved to tug at the sides of her surcoat, revealing a gentle swell where once her belly had lain flat.

Cecily looked sharply at Christina.

Inferring the meaning of her gaze, Christina said hastily, "Lady Cecily, this woman is Mistress Trudi, my friend and the keeper of my household. She was to be married to Master Peter, whom we encountered at the gate outside. It seems they have delayed their wedding until my return."

"I wish you love and happiness in your nuptials, Mistress Trudi," Cecily said kindly. "I hope this will prove only the first of many healthy babes borne to you and your husband."

"I thank ye, Your Ladyship, for your most gracious blessing," responded Trudi, beaming warmly at the young woman whom she obviously found herself already liking.

"Trudi, might I ask you to please show her Ladyship to the solar? I will be along shortly, as soon as I greet the others who attend here."

The two women left Christina's side readily, walking through the hall already deeply in conversation. Cecily threw her head back and laughed, catching Trudi casually by the hand. They disappeared through the doorway leading deeper into the house as Christina turned to accept the welcome of the others in the room. Afterwards, two of the men helped the exhausted Ziesolf to his chamber, as the hall gradually cleared of well-wishers.

"Master Frederick, there are so many things of which I must appraise you!"

Christina turned to see the cheerful face of Jost; who was springing from foot to foot, barely able to contain his excitement.

"On the morrow, Cousin, please on the morrow! We will meet after midday meal and you will tell me of all your good works that you accomplished while I have been away. For now, I am bone weary beyond words."

A look of disappointment spread across his face as he began to walk away.

"Oh, Jost!" she said suddenly as he eagerly turned back toward her. "I almost forget to tell you *Seelöwe* has returned with over sixty sarplar of coarse Lincoln wool in its hold. Could you make plans for its transport here, if you please?"

"Certainly!" he replied, happiness returning to his face at having been entrusted with a new and challenging task. Then he hesitated a second before adding, "I do not wish to trouble you further, but I have a message of some import I was instructed to give you at my first opportunity."

She felt an all too familiar pang in her stomach.

"Yes?" she said with some trepidation

"It was from the head alderman, requiring your attendance immediately upon your return."

He now turned away once more, but this time with a merry spring in his step.

A fury mounted within her having nothing to do with the boy.

This is that damnable Katharine at it again! How much I would rather face a hundred Scots than peer into that smirking face once more! Why must she bedevil so? I wonder what hardship she has now devised for my discomfort. Can I not have even one night to enjoy before a new problem arises to vex me?

Christina took a deep breath, trying to banish all thought of Volker and his minx of a wife from her mind for the time being. Forcing a smile, she began her way to the solar. Having spent longer than expected in the hall, her weariness sought to engulf her before she reached the top of the stairway. At last, she opened the door into the solar, finding Trudi and Cecily conversing animatedly on two stools pulled closely together near the fire.

"By your leave, Your Ladyship, I will leave the two of you alone for now," Trudi declared. "I will have one of the maids bring refreshments while I attend to arranging a chamber for you. I hope I will have an opportunity to enjoy the pleasure of your conversation again some time near in the future."

She gave a slight curtsy, then broke into a fit of giggling as she turned and ran out of the room.

Cecily joined in the merriment, laughing heartily herself.

She turned to Christina and said, "She is the most enchanting person I have ever met, Frederick! How I envy you growing up with such a wonderful friend!"

Christina could do no more than voice her agreement.

How fortunate I have been to have such a friend as Trudi; both that of her old self as well as the new.

Cecily and Christina chatted for about half an hour before a scrumptious repast of both savory and sweet was placed before them. They took their time eating their fill, interspacing mouthfuls of delicious food with pleasant conversation.

When the maid came to clear the few remnants of their meal away, she was accompanied by Trudi, who announced, "I have taken the liberty to have your things brought to your room, Lady Cecily. A hot bath awaits you as well, should you so desire."

"Thank you ever so much, Trudi. I can think of nothing else more pleasing to me. Would it be possible for you to show me the way there? The combination of today's excitement and this wonderful meal have led me to where I can barely hold my eyes open. Had you delayed another five minutes, I fear you would have suffered the terrible sounds of my snoring!" she tittered with laughter at her own jest, joined immediately by Trudi's own giggles. Cecily wiped her eyes before saying to Christina, "I beg your leave, Frederick, but I must wish you a good night as well. I have never felt so merry, nor so welcomed into another's home. Thank you once more for such a pleasant time, I shall recall it with fondness for the rest of my days."

Christina rose as the two women of whom she felt such great affection departed. Suddenly, she felt strangely melancholic.

I will travel to the Tower on the morrow to arrange an appointment for Cecily with Lady de Clare. If she is agreeable, as one would certainly think she will be, Cecily will become part of her retinue. Am I happy about this? Of course; yet, it fills me with sadness I will no longer have the daily pleasure of her company.

Taking one final sip from her bowl of wine, she sat the vessel down deliberately and journeyed to her own chambers. Christina was pleasantly surprised to find her own large tub issuing vapors of flowery-scented steam from the watery surface within. Before she could fully undress, the door slowly began to open.

Trudi entered and ran to Christina, throwing her arms around her neck and hugging her fiercely. With eyes streaming tears, she kissed Christina's lips, then both her cheeks in quick succession.

"Oh, Christina, it is so good to have you back home at last!" she sobbed.

Sensing her mistress' extreme weariness, Trudi helped her from the remainder of her clothes and into the bath. After a thorough scrubbing removed the greater part of the accumulated filth accrued during Christina's three weeks of traveling, Trudi bid her to rise, then dried her body with a length of coarse toweling. She helped Christina into her bed and, with one final kiss, left her alone for the night. Within a matter of seconds, Christina was asleep.

She groggily awakened upon hearing the door to her outer chamber softly open then, a second or two later, close once more.

I wonder at the time?

She opened one eye to confirm the night was still jet black.

Surely, it cannot already be a maid come to spark the fireplace? Regardless, there is no need for me to rise yet.

Christina turned her back toward the window before beginning to drift off to sleep once more.

Curiously, she sensed a presence at the side of the bed behind her. She felt the coverlet shift as it was pulled back. A transfer of weight was made onto the goose-down mattress, as if someone had placed first one knee, then another, before turning to lay a few inches from her.

How very nice. I had almost asked Trudi to stay the night, so we could snuggle once more beneath the covers as we did when we were younger. Now, she returns of her own volition.

Hesitantly, the figure moved nearer. Christina could feel the warmth of full breasts through the linen shift that now pressed against her back. Lips nuzzled her bare shoulder and a softly skinned arm entwined her waist. Christina luxuriated under the gentle ministrations she was receiving, placing her own hand to lightly hold that which lay across her middle. Slowly, their mirrored hands moved down Christina's belly, before unexpectedly moving to the side to trace her hip. The other hand disengaged before slowly, inexorably, it moved upward and back toward Christina's center, its nimble fingers entwined themselves in the thatch betwixt her legs, lightly pulling and teasing the coarse dark tufts.

What is this? Trudi and I have not enjoyed each other's bodies in such a manner for many years; why does she seek to do so now?

Suddenly, the fingers moved further downward still, over the swell of her pubic bone, and closer to what was now the slickened moist wetness of her cleft. With a sense of urgency, the fingers thrust rapidly downward, causing Christina to emit a small yelp of pleasure. Then, they were unexpectedly withdrawn as the figure beside her bolted from the bed.

Christina turned over, only to behold Lady Cecily standing outlined by the merest hint of moonlight now creeping into the room from the window. The sanguine curls of her hair fell loosely around the shoulders of her white gown, surrounding the paleness of her facial features, which were now set with an expression of astonishment and confusion. Her mouth gaped open as she struggled to speak; yet, so great was her bewilderment that no sound issued forth.

Christina moved from the bed to stand in front of her. She took both of her hands in her own, offering no resistance when Cecily pulled them away.

"What is this that you play at, Frederick, or whatever your name may actually be!" she cried.

318

"Christina," she replied, "My name is Christina. It is a perilous game at which I play, but one that fate has decided to set before me. I have meant no harm by it, and certainly meant to cause no pain to you, in whom I hold the highest esteem."

"But I loved you, and have since we departed the tower!" she beat both of her fists on Christina's chest before turning away to sob uncontrollably before the window.

Christina went to her and wrapped her arms about her body. Cecily turned in her embrace, gaining a bit of distance, but staying within its confines.

"How could you use me so cruelly?" Cecily asked in a small voice. "Were my affections no more than a sport for you?"

"Please, never believe that to be true," Christina protested, reaching down to softly stroke Cecily's pale cheek. "I have grown to love you as well; yet, how could I even begin to dream of a life together with you; not only a woman, but a married one at that? I believed us destined to remain only friends, an idea I cherished dearly, as it seemed the best we could be."

"Oh, Christina, why did you not trust me?"

"I could not bear the thought you would be repulsed by me," she answered, her own voice now cracking with sobs.

Cecily lifted her chin to peer deeply into Christina's eyes before saying, "That is something I will never be. What I fell in love with is not what is on the outside, but in here." She moved her hand to fall lightly upon Christina's left breast. "Your compassion, your courageous fearlessness, your kind affection; these are qualities not defined by your sex, but by who you truly are."

Cecily hesitated before adding, "That is the person with whom I fell in love, and remain so still. I am yours, my dearest, if you will have me."

Christina moved forward slowly and kissed Cecily's lips gently. The other woman pulled her closer, melding their two bodies tightly together as one. After what seemed an eternity, they separated their embrace and Christina led her new love back into the bed where they nestled together, happily satisfied within the warm comfort of their shared embrace.

After a time, Christina felt her eyes once again become heavy. For once, she drifted off with no worrisome thoughts of cargoes, intrigues, or plots of vengeance; these she would face on the morrow. Instead, she slumbered peacefully, with placid dreams of the beautiful woman who shared her bed and of the happiness she felt filling her heart.

Alphabetical Listing of Characters

Albrecht Revele – son of the chief alderman

Anna – Mechtild Kohl's servant in Lübeck and Trudi's sister

Arnst –briefly a crewman on *der Greif*

Arthur Pendragon – mythical English king

Bardi Family – Florentine bankers in London

Baynard (Master) – London wine merchant

Beatrice – Mechtild Kohl's servant in Lübeck

Bess – the chief cook in Christina's household

Paul Butiler (Master) – a London wool merchant

Cecily Baldewyne (Lady) – a woman rescued by Christina

Christina Kohl – the young daughter of a Lübeck merchant

De Grood family – Bruges vintners

Dietmar – A crewman on *der Greif*

Edgar Baldewyne (Sir) – husband of Lady Cecily

Edmund – chamberlain of Edward II

Edward I (Longshanks) – king of England

Edward II – king of England after his father's death

Eleanor de Clare – Lady Cecily's aunt

Ernestus – A crewman on *der Greif*

Frederick Kohl – Christina's younger brother

Frescobaldi family – Italian bankers in London

Gerhardt Kohl – Christina's uncle in London

Gilbert – the clerk for the wool guild

Gilbert de Clare – the Earl of Gloucester

Godfrey – one of Sir Giles' men

Guy de Beauchamp – Earl of Warwick

Gherwen Strateken – Thomas Kohl's business partner

Sir Giles d'Argentan – household knight of Edward II

Heinrich – a childhood friend of Christina and Trudi

Henry II – English king from 1133-1189

Henry de Percy (Baron) – English magnate in the north

Hermann Claessoen – Thomas Kohl's business partner

Hugh – a manservant of Piers Gaveston

Isabella - queen of England and wife of Edward II

Johann Revele – chief alderman of the London Hansards

John – one of Roxburgh Castle's garrison men

John of Brittany – Earl of Richmond

John Shearer – a shepherd in Berwick

Jost – Christina's cousin and her apprentice

Katharine Volker – wife of chief alderman Herr Volker

Kurt Ziesolf (Herr) - Teutonic Knight and Christina's mentor

Lords Ordainers – powerful noblemen against King Edward II

Malcolm – stableboy at Bokerel House

Marguerite – Christina's older sister, now deceased

Mary - a servant girl in Christina's household

Matilda Kohl – Christina's aunt

Matthias – master of *der Greif*

Mechtild Kohl – mother of Christina

Neville (Sir) – castellan of Roxburgh Castle

Noel (Friar) – Jost's teacher in Luneburg

Olbrecht Bromse – previous owner of *Seelöwe*

Osbert – a watchman at Bokerel House

Otto – a childhood friend of Christina and Trudi

Pauwels (Master) – a cloth merchant in Bruges

Peruzzi Family – Florentine bankers in London

Pearl – Christina's sorrel palfrey mare

Peter Nirrnheim – Thomas Kohl's business partner

Petrus (Black Peter) – the smith in Christina's household

Piers Gaveston, Earl of Cornwall and Christina's friend

Reinhold Hagen – a Hanseatic merchant in London

Robert, the Bruce – Scottish warrior and future king

Richard – a journeyman Christina bested in a duel

Roger (Goodman) – Herr Revel's chamberlain

Sarah – kitchen servant in Christina's household

Sybille – a Flemish prostitute at the Nag's Head

Tammo – a bargeman in Bruges

Thomas Kohl – Christina's father

Thomas, Earl of Lancaster – one of the Lords Ordainers

Thorsten – *Seelöwe's* sailing master

Tom – one of Christina's abductors at Roxburgh Castle

Trudi – Christina's best friend and the keeper of her household

Adolphus Volker (Herr) – seceded Revele as chief alderman

Volkmar – Christina's uncle in Luneburg

Warin – a watchman at Bokerel House

Wig Reiniken – mercenary hired by Christina's father

Historical Notes

The first decade of the fourteenth century was a very troubled one for England. The thirty-four years reign of King Edward I ended with his death on July 7, 1307, leaving his twenty-three years old son to rule as King Edward II. The relationship between the two men had been tempestuous, with the father reportedly violently ripping out handfuls of his son's hair and calling him an "ill-borne son of a whore" shortly before his death. One of the primary causes of their quarrels was the younger Edward's infatuation with his favorite, Piers Gaveston.

Gaveston, the son of a Gascon nobleman, was not always in the ill-favor of Edward I, who had made him a member of his son's household in 1304 to serve as a role model and advisor. The king's opinion of the man rapidly deteriorated until, in early 1307, Gaveston was banished from England for the first of many times.

As soon as he heard of his father's death, one of the new king's first acts was to recall Gaveston to the royal court. Shortly afterward, Edward II raised Gaveston to become Earl of Cornwall, a title normally reserved for members of the royal family. This earldom gave Gaveston vast landholdings throughout England, as well as an annual income of £4,000 a year, suddenly making him one of the wealthiest men in the land.

The new king's overt favoritism for Gaveston over all others, combined with the earl's own arrogance and undue influence over Edward's decisions, enraged many other influential members of the high nobility. Whispered rumors also abounded that the relationship between the two men was "unnatural" as well. It was not only the lords of the land who had cause to dislike Gaveston, however. At the coronation feast of, Isabella, daughter of Philip

IV of France, as the queen of England, Edward largely ignored his new wife, choosing to lavish his attention on his friend instead. Supported by the deeply-offended king of France, Parliament, particularly the earls of Warenne, Hereford, Lincoln, and Pembroke, pressured Edward into exiling Gaveston once more. Edward did not turn his back on his friend, easing his separation from court by appointing him to be the King's Lieutenant of Ireland in May, 1308, with lands and an annual income in excess of £3,000 a year.

In July of 1309, Edward II was forced by Parliament to agree to several concessions limiting his rule. In return, Gaveston's English lands and titles were restored, allowing him to once more stand at Edward's side. One would think a man twice exiled would have learned to avoid the ire of his enemies, but not so the newly-reinstated Earl of Cornwall. By the time of the February 1310 Parliament, the political atmosphere had become so toxic that several other earls refused to attend if Gaveston was present. In March of that year, Edward was forced to appoint a group of earls, bishops, and barons to further reform the royal household. Edward did not fully perceive the danger these Lords Ordainers posed to his reign. Instead, his attention had turned northward.

Although his father, Edward I, had campaigned several times against the Kingdom of Scotland, earning the sobriquet "Hammer of the Scots," the country had never been fully and finally conquered. Edward II believed defeating Scotland would greatly enhance his popularity and diminish the power of his political enemies in Parliament. Edward's plans began to quickly unravel when most of the Ordainers declined to add their personal forces to those of the king, claiming their reform work was too important to the realm to divert their attention elsewhere. So, when Edward departed for Scotland in September 1310, he could barely muster 4,500 men, as well as only three of his earls: Gloucester, Warenne, and, of course, Gaveston. The campaign would prove frustrating and inconclusive, but much greater threats would await Edward and Gaveston on their return south.

"Her Perilous Game" is set largely against the events described above. Nearly all the locations and historical sites mentioned are real, many of which, such as Berwick-Upon-Tweed, Kelso, and even Stichill, may be visited today. Roxburgh Castle now lies in ruins, having been destroyed in 1460.

Edward II, his Queen Isabella, Piers Gaveston, and the earls mentioned by name were major figures in English history. Some of the others, including; Henry, Baron de Percy; Sir Giles d'Argentan; and Sir Geoffrey de Vere, were actual people as well. Although the daily actions of these men and women throughout the course of the novel are fictionally contrived, they are set against a background consistent with most historical perspectives. For others of our cast of characters; Ziesolf, Trudi, and of course Christina herself, they are completely fictional, although they would have had no trouble fitting in amongst the people and places of that long-ago time.

About the Author

Lee Swanson

Lee Swanson has enjoyed a lifelong interest in medieval history. He lived in Germany and England for over twenty-five years, first as a soldier and then as a teacher before returning to live in the United States.

Graduating summa cum laude from the University of North Florida with a master's degree in European History, Lee's thesis centered on the Hansa, a confederation of merchants from primarily northern German cities. Many of the colorful characters who populate his novels are drawn from the lives of these resolute wayfarers who traveled the waterways of Europe in search of profit and prestige.

Lee, his wife Karine, and their dog Banjo now split their time between coastal Maine and San Miguel de Allende, Mexico.

www.LeeSwansonAuthor.com